ENVY

ENVY

THE DEADLY SEVEN, BOOK 1

LANA PECHERCZYK

"Envy eats nothing but its own heart."

– PROVERB

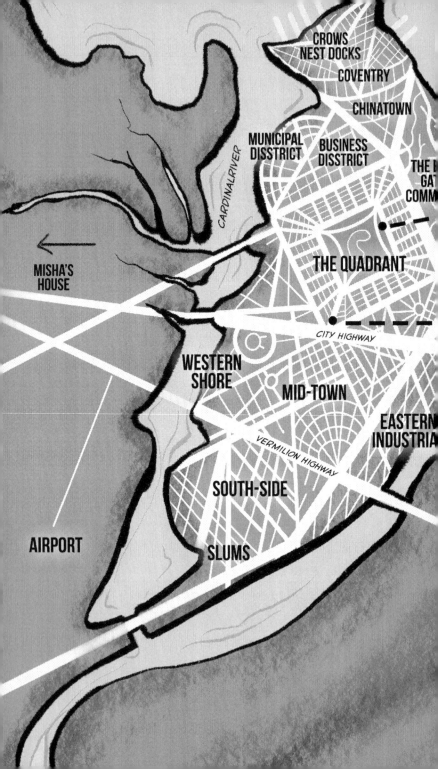

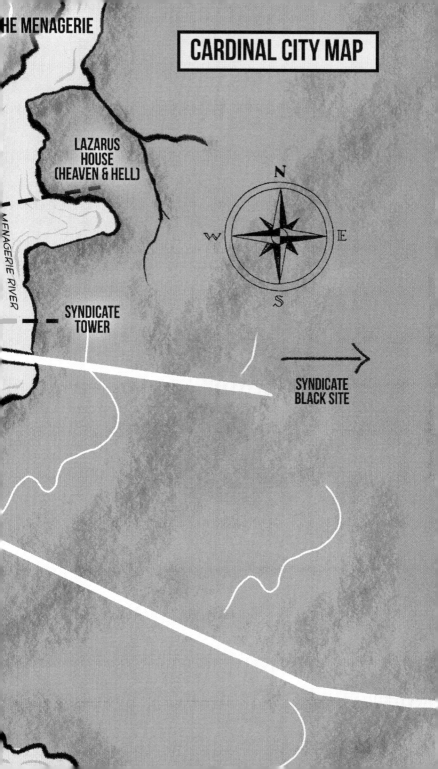

ONE

EVAN LAZARUS

He woke in a strange place.

Thick, pungent air dragged into his lungs from the darkness. His head pounded and his body ached to the point of pain. Soft and lumpy beneath him. Hard and cold at his sides. When he fumbled around, his movement stirred the rancid odor. He knew exactly where he was.

Dumpster.

And if he'd hidden in a Dumpster, he most likely wore his combat uniform—a quick pat down his leather pants and tug on his hood confirmed that. His hands came away sticky, and when he touched his thumb to his forefinger, the tackiness remained. He held it to his nose and sniffed. Sweet, metallic, thick: Blood.

But whose?

And, how did he get here?

Before panic set roots in his chest, he thought to himself: *Evan Lazarus. Your name is Evan Lazarus. You fight the deadly sin envy. You save people.*

Sometimes.

Maybe.

He must have done something terrible... something worth hiding from. And rather than call for help, he'd hidden, because, why would the Deadly Seven help him? They were only his family.

Evan moved to lift the lid on the Dumpster, but a pain pierced his torso. The sensation brought memories of the previous night flashing in a dizzying torrent. Multiple pairs of hands forced him down. Fists slammed into his eye sockets and cheekbones. Blinding pain. Swollen vision. Boots pounded into his abdomen. Air wheezed from his lungs. A crow bar to his ribs, jaw, knees. He'd bucked hard, but they'd ruthlessly pinned him down, driving his limbs wider until pain screamed in his joints, leaving his torso vulnerable to more violence... then he'd yielded and smiled and laughed. Because he'd deserved it.

Evan scrubbed his face with his hand to wipe the memory, but the words of his assailant came hurtling back: *"If you're looking for validation, kid, you're in the wrong place. You should have thrown the fight like we told you to."* Then the lights had gone out.

Evan laid in the dark Dumpster, eyes closed, acutely aware of every ache and stab of pain in his body. They'd left him for dead.

But he wasn't dead.

Well, he couldn't stay there forever.

Taking a chance he pushed the lid open and let it crash against the wall. Sweet, crisp air burned his lungs and he almost choked on the freshness. Dawn peeked over the tall grungey cityscape, casting the alley walls into stark chiaroscuro. Any other day he might have been awed enough to paint the atmospheric sight, but today his mood was murky and heavy like the sky.

It would rain soon and, dammit, his fighting leathers chafed when wet. At least he'd left his weapons at home before he'd allowed himself to be a boxing bag at the fight ring the night before.

He searched for a plastic bag in the Dumpster then crawled out and peeled his jacket and mouth scarf off, leaving him in a used-to-be-white T-shirt and blood-stained leather pants.

Suddenly, the air rippled to his right, lighting his senses on fire. His arm shot out in time for a projectile to hit his palm, fingers snapping shut over the object within. A baseball. From… he pushed his awareness out, searching for envy. There. To the right. The sense of deadly sin trickled toward him, wriggling in his gut like grimy feathered fingers, sparking an intense hunger to search and destroy. This supernatural sixth sense was something all his siblings had, except each sensed a different sin. If they didn't chase down the worst of sinners and eliminate or contain, then the sense would drive them insane.

Perhaps it already had.

There were a lot of sinners in Cardinal City.

A lot of envy.

He forced his urge to fight down. This particular sense of envy was small. Tiny. Not worth his time.

Children. Two of them.

Shit.

They might have seen him get out of his battle gear.

"Hey, nice catch, mister. Wish I was that good." A dirty little leaguer trotted over. Grime on his cheeks. Dirt on the cuffs of his jeans. Holes in his sneakers.

"Hey yourself, kid." Evan stuffed his jacket and scarf into the plastic bag, hiding evidence of his secret. "Go home. It's early."

So early. Or late. He couldn't decide. His dry throat begged for a drink. And an aspirin. Also a shower and then sleep and the sweet oblivion it brought. Josie would have to manage opening the tattoo shop on her own, his bed called to him.

Light flashed from the alley exit a few meters away as early morning commuters began their assault on the city. Evan turned in the opposite direction, intending to find a dark spot so he could hit the rooftops and trail the dying shadows home.

Fire-escape up ahead. Perfect.

As he walked, he blindly lobbed the ball over his shoulder. A cry of amazement proved he hit his mark as the kid caught it in his glove.

Envy from the children spiked three-fold, echoing in Evan's gut, and they ran after him, asking for an autograph.

Double shit.

"Why would you want an autograph?" he asked, testing the waters.

"Because you're one of *them!*"

Evan fisted his plastic bag. He paused. Turned.

The second boy was pale with wide blue eyes. Dark hair stuck up in the middle of his crown in a natural Mohawk or one hell of a cow-lick. Freckles hid behind his grubby cheeks. The first boy swam in an oversized Yankees jersey. Taller and similar facial structure to the second. Must be brothers. Yankee boy clutched the ball in his hand.

"One of who?" Evan asked.

"You know, the Deadly Seven." The smallest boy jumped around him like an eager grasshopper, spiky hair bouncing.

"You got the wrong idea, kid."

The eldest shot him a withering stare. "We're not stupid. Or blind—"

"Yeah, blind," chimed in the youngest.

"We saw you take your jacket off. *The* jacket." He wiggled his brows and eyed the plastic bag in Evan's hands.

Evan groaned and then took a deep breath while he decided how to handle them. Fuck it. They were only kids. Who would believe them? "Probably not a good idea. I'm not very popular at the moment."

"That's okay, Mr. Deadly sir, I like you."

Those three little words stabbed Evan in the heart.

"Well, that makes one of us." He continued to stroll toward the fire escape.

"C'mon, please?" The children jogged backwards in front of him, holding out the ball. "It will only take a minute. Wow. Is that blood? Did you catch some baddies?"

Only himself.

Evan stopped under the escape ladder and sighed. He shouldn't be talking with them, but it was nice to have anyone—even a couple of runts—have faith.

"Can you sign my baseball? *Please*."

The Yankees kid smiled and threw his ball high above,

intending to catch it in his glove to show off, but the round projectile hit the fire-escape instead. A loud clang sounded and the rusty retractable ladder dropped.

"Look out!" Evan shouted.

He shoved the boy out of the way only to have the broken ladder impale his own shoulder. He landed heavily on his knees and tried to breathe through the crippling agony, except the ladder pushed down and he was already drained and sore from the night before.

He heaved.

Pain splintered in his shoulder and black dots danced before his eyes. He almost lost sight.

He could do this. Especially in front of the kids. Fuck the night before. Screw the injuries he still recovered from. *C'mon, Evan. Do this.*

Squeezing his eyes shut, he gathered focus, and breathed through the fog until ready. Gripping tight, he lifted the lance from his flesh. A wet, tearing sound made him cringe, but he heaved out of harm's way. Pain splintered the back of his head as he hit the brick wall, crumbling mortar and rock. A fresh wave of nausea rolled through him.

Perfect. He couldn't even save himself.

The sound of a small boy's voice broke through his agony. "Mason, he don't look so good."

"Yeah. Mr. Deadly, sir, are you okay?"

That was debatable. He tried to laugh, but a strangled sound came out.

You wouldn't see his siblings in this situation.

Evan flared his eyes to focus through the blur. He bit his lip and held his wrist in front of his face to view the Yin-

Yang tattoo. The bio-indicated ink itched like a motherfucker and was almost black. Fuck balance. It was all a lie.

"Mr. Deadly, sir?"

"Stop calling me sir." Evan ground his teeth. "Leave. I'll take care of myself."

"But, you guys saved my friend once," the older kid said. "After the bombing. She… she was stuck under a wall and you… you got her out. She can help you. She's a doctor. She helps everyone. C'mon, Mr. Deadly, sir. You need to get up." The boy's little hands grasped onto Evan's big arms and yanked but to no avail. "Mason, call an ambulance."

"No," Evan tried to say, but it came out a grunt. He didn't need the hospital, just few minutes and his special body would take care of the rest. If only he could tell them that, but the boy already sounded further away. Evan was slipping, head swimming, walls fading. Tiny footsteps echoed. A siren wailed. The alley blurred, becoming as black as his temper, and everything faded.

TWO

DR. GRACE GO

"Extra! Extra! Two years since Cardinal Bombing! New leads could find perpetrators."

Grace Go stopped in her tracks as the newspaper boy's powerful voice carried across the busy sidewalk and bustling morning crowd. Someone bumped into her from behind and cursed at her. She cast a hasty apology over her shoulder and forced her feet to move out of the crushing horde's way. Being an emergency physician gave her exceptional acting skills and emotional control. The trick was to detach yourself from the world. Disconnect from the emotion of the trauma. Spend your life busy and avoid focusing on your own miseries. Like the letter she crumpled into her bag and its headline, written in bold: *Notice of Case Closure.*

She had fourteen days to come up with the goods on the bombing that killed her parents, and forty-nine other innocent souls. It was the only way she'd get justice for the people left homeless and destitute and maybe, just maybe, she'd be able to put her parents to rest.

A twisted feeling churned in her stomach as the words *new leads* bounced around her head. She closed her eyes to center herself and shivered. A brisk rub of her scarred forearms barely warmed her, because the coldness in the pit of her stomach wasn't elemental, it was guilt. She'd survived. Her parents had died. It should never have happened.

Another bump on the shoulder as someone rushed past.

"Sorry," she said without looking up, and clutched her bag tight.

Street sounds amplified. Tires roared on the wet street, and the heavy footsteps of human traffic became a stampede. The repetitive clinking of loose change in a homeless man's cup rattled her spine. Her head felt light. Dizzy. Must be low blood pressure. She'd had only four hours sleep last night, too busy scouring the internet for the identity of the mystery woman she'd seen at the bombing, but she did that every night. Why would it matter today?

Because it's been two years, dummy. Two years since her parents got sick of coming second to her crazy work hours. Two years since they decided to buy an apartment close to her own. Two years since she'd heard her father's guffaw of a laugh, and her mother's sweet, soft voice. Grace squeezed the tears from her eyes and resolved to deal with the pain like every other time. Squash it deep down and keep busy.

An arctic breeze wafted the paperboy's voice back across the street again. "*… New leads bring us…*"

Her heart stopped—new leads—and started beating

again. Remembering what it was that halted her the first time, her foot left the sidewalk to cross, but a horn blared a warning and she jumped backwards with a gasp, narrowly missing the fender of a pickup truck as it tore down the street. Water sprayed onto the path, bathing her black jeans in cold.

A man cursed out the window and flipped her the bird, his voice quickly swallowed by the cacophony of city life once again.

Grace tried again. This time, she checked carefully both ways, then rushed to the other side where the grubby newsboy smiled back at her as she drew near. He stood next to a stack of folded papers and an upturned baseball cap for money.

"Hey Taco." Grace smiled and held up a coin.

Taco grinned and handed her a folded newspaper. "Hey Miss. Grace. Boy am I glad to see you."

"I always love seeing you, Taco." The cold pit in her stomach returned when she remembered the letter in her bag. It would affect Taco and his younger brother. She scanned the front page of the newspaper. "New leads, huh?"

He shrugged, unconcerned as only a child would be. "Wasn't them."

Then Taco gave her shifty eyes and checked over his shoulder. His mouth opened like he wanted to say something, but there were too many people around and he shut it again.

Odd, Grace thought. She hoped he was okay. She'd had a soft spot for Taco and his younger brother since the bombing. Most of their family perished in the explosion except for a single aunt who was pulled from the wreckage, much like

Grace. Grace had found them an apartment in her own building, but even being rent controlled, it was hard for the woman to manage. Better to stay a minute and see if Taco was okay.

"I agree. It can't be them. I don't think they've been sighted around town for months. Probably given up or gone missing," Grace elaborated.

"Nah… just waiting."

"For what?"

"Someone to believe in them."

"Yeah, I know, buddy," she said with a sigh, and resisted the urge to ruffle his hair. It was flattened on the top, most likely from the cap he'd removed to collect payment. "It would be nice to have something to believe in, wouldn't it?"

"I mean it, Grace. They didn't do it."

"You're preaching to the choir." She'd been touting the same words since the bombing. During the first month the police had humored her and listened to her wild stories. She'd told anyone and everyone about the strange people she saw dressed in white robes and masks. Except, the CCTV footage showed only the Deadly Seven lurking suspiciously before the bomb went off. Looking back now, no wonder they thought she suffered post-traumatic stress. The things she saw sounded crazy. She still had trouble organizing the events in her head. Better to avoid the subject in public, and tackle it at home because either someone doctored the video footage, or she really was insane.

"You watch the game last night, Taco?"

"Sure did. We won!"

"Didn't Cardinal City lose?"

"Nah, nobody goes for Cardinal these days. They're at the bottom of the ladder. Miss. Grace…" Taco hushed his tone and ushered her closer. "I *really* need to tell you something."

The poor boy was busting to tell her something. It looked like he needed to pee.

Grace dipped her head, close enough to hear the wheeze in Taco's lungs as he took a breath. Sounded congested. Way too much fluid in there.

"We found someone in the alley this morning," Taco said. "Took him to the hospital for you. And get this, he was… well. You need to talk to him."

Grace's brows lifted. Another homeless person for her to rescue? While her heart warmed at the altruistic innocence of those boys, they flirted with danger. "Have you been out before sunrise again? You know the neighborhood's not safe, Taco."

"It wasn't too early."

"Taco!" Grace shook him gently by the shoulders. "It's dangerous. Do you hear me? Never go out at night again. *Promise me.*" The desperation made her voice tight. The things she'd seen in Emergency on night shift still gave her nightmares. The streets were filled with stupid and violent people, they were certainly no place for children.

"Okay, okay."

"Say it."

"Fine. We won't go out at dark again."

"Even for a few minutes before the sun comes up."

"Yeah, okay." Taco coughed.

"Good. And that wheeze doesn't sound good. How long have you had that?"

"Yeah but—"

A shadow smashed past the two of them at an alarming speed, scooping up Grace's bag, tugging it roughly from her shoulder. She almost lost her arm as the bag tore free. The cry of surprise barely left her lips before the crowd swallowed the thief again.

"Damn it!" Grace desperately tracked the path the thief had gone.

"You want me to chase him Miss. Grace?" Taco's words caught on some phlegm and he coughed into his fingerless gloved hands.

She shook off the irritation of having her bag stolen. No use chasing him down. He was too fast, and she was already late. Muggings were a dime a dozen in Cardinal City, hence why she never carried valuables. "No, that's okay. There wasn't much in the bag, anyway. You've got work to do and, besides, like I said, that cough doesn't sound good. Come and see me at the clinic tomorrow, okay? Promise? I'd better go."

Grace gave a hasty wave and then plunged back into the horde, barely hearing Taco's protest. She had to stop encouraging his self-proclaimed mission to clean up the streets. Cardinal City was a lost cause.

Big rain drops started to fall, and she flicked out her newspaper to shield herself, rushing until she arrived at the hospital a few blocks away.

By the time she walked through the emergency entrance, she'd mentally catalogued the items she'd lost in her bag.

She rarely brought her wallet to work because she had an account at the cafeteria. Only her phone was in the bag and it was a cheap burner she'd picked up recently when her old cell had died.

That left the letter.

Grace pushed through the emergency entrance and into the waiting room with her game face on. Her heart wrenched at the sound of babies crying, people coughing and groaning. As heartbreaking as it sounded in there, the free clinic was worse, and the reason she worked there two days a week. Those poor people needed medical assistance, and the busy environment was music to her empty soul. When she went through the triage bay door, she paused to gather herself. Hospital smells assaulted her nose: disinfectant; plastic; bleach. It all infused her lungs with an odd sense of rightness. This was where she belonged.

This was who she was.

And she was good at her job.

Grace moved into the secure area and passed the exam bays. All beds were full, and all curtains were drawn. A man laid on a gurney in the hallway, sleeping on his side. He looked stable, so Grace assumed he was where he was meant to be for the moment.

A curtain to Grace's right opened and closed, and Doctor Raseem Patel stepped out. Grace and Raseem interned together years ago but lost contact when she deferred from surgery after the bombing. He wore scrubs, a beaded necklace, and his long dark hair was tied back into a bun at his nape. Despite being a modern, young and hip doctor (his

words, not Grace's), Raseem took his job at the hospital seriously, and followed the rules to a T.

"What on earth are you doing here, Grace?" Raseem's
thick dark brows rose. "Don't get me wrong, I'm glad you're
here but… aren't you a few hours early? I just checked the
roster."

Grace bit her lip. Out of everyone, he'd probably send
her home. "I know. Thought I could be some help."

"We'll always need help, especially in the ER, but… walk
with me." His tone sounded ominous.

Grace followed him to the rotation board where he stood
staring, hands on hips.

A yellow square with an affirmation in Grace's handwriting was stuck next to each of the surgeon's names. She
had a habit of randomly placing them around the place.
Someone had to lift morale, and it may as well be her. The
nurses were tired, and the surgeons were exhausted. She
should know, she was one once.

Envy ate nothing but its own heart, and she knew that
better than anyone. It was all she thought of when she recovered from the bombing that had taken her parents' lives. Her
anxiety reared its head too much, and she was fearful of
having an attack in the operating theater, so opted to stay
out. It was either give in to the guilt and self-loathing, or put
it to use. So rather than pine over who she used to be, she
put her efforts towards making others feel better.

The Post-it notes were an idea she'd taken from her
mother, the high school teacher. *A moment of kindness from
you could mean the world to someone else.*

"Is everything okay, Raseem?" Did he hate the notes? Were they too intrusive?

"Well, it's like this." He shot her a sidelong glance. "You remember how we did that emergency appendectomy together in our first year on rotation?"

"How could I forget? The guy had a pericardial tamponade. Completely out of left field considering what he was in for. I still can't believe we saved him."

"Right. But you get what I mean."

"Ugh." Was there a question?

Grace paused and inspected the man. Often people spoke without words, and sometimes you had to look harder because the truth was crippling. His lips were pinched around the sides, and his pupils were dilated. She caught the twitch of his fingers at the side. He was definitely agitated about something. She cast her mind back to the appendectomy surgery. It had been hours long, and almost a disaster on many fronts. Not only did the patient almost bleed out on the table, but in closing, an exhausted Raseem had fumbled with the stitches, and Grace took over before anyone could notice.

Grace squeezed the man's arm. "Don't worry, Raseem. Your technique is second to none. Even the interns gossip about how great it is. You got this, buddy."

He gave her a soft smile and rubbed the back of his neck. "I'm being stupid."

"Nope. You're not." She was the one afraid to get back into an operating theater. "Sometimes the unexpected happens. Getting anxious before an unfamiliar case is normal."

"You never did."

She swallowed and looked away.

"Sorry," he added. "I know you haven't operated in a while."

"And you're in there every day. You're going to ace it. Do what I used to do. Say something funny to break the ice."

"Yeah, that's a good idea," he mumbled absently. "A joke."

"Do you know what else is a good idea? Letting me clock on early."

"Don't you have anything better to do?"

Grace pretended she didn't hear the tone of pity in Raseem's voice and shook her head.

"Okay then. If you really want to, I guess they do need the extra hand in there. I'll see if someone can handover. It's been a wild night. Meet me here in five."

Yes. She mentally fist pumped. For a minute she thought he would tell her to go home or tell the Chief of Staff. Grace went to the staff locker room and pulled on a fresh pair of green scrubs. When she returned, Raseem waited for her with the ER schedule open on his iPad.

"They're all a bit busy, so I said I'd show you," he said.

"So, busy night, huh?" Graced asked.

"Busy and mad. You know how it is. I know the city has gone downhill since those vigilante cowboys disappeared but, honestly, sometimes I wonder if they feed people crack in the tap water for this amount of crazy to turn up in one night. We've had a few gangland stabbings, bullet wounds, another stuck a cucumber up his anus, and then there's the special one," he said.

"The cucumber wasn't special enough?" Grace laughed.

Raseem handed her the iPad and brought up a patient file. "I consulted briefly on this one. Puncture wound is cleaned and stitched by a nurse. You might want to check the suture work. We suspected internal bleeding, maybe some broken ribs. Bruises over his body. Diagnostic scan reports are just in. I haven't seen them yet."

"Why is he so special?"

Raseem gave her a wry look. "Probably high. Didn't want to relinquish his bag of clothes, fought with the attendants when he was brought in, bit of an A-hole... take your pick."

"Is he dangerous?"

"If we hadn't dosed him, maybe. He's a big man. Just check the scans then bump him out unless he needs surgery for the internal bleeding, then call me. He's in the observation unit."

Raseem handed her the iPad, gave her a lip twitch of gratitude, then walked away.

She checked the scan report and her jaw nearly dropped to the floor. Wow. Just wow. Raseem would be sorry he handed this one over.

THREE

EVAN LAZARUS

From the corner of his eye, Evan watched his mother pace beside his hospital bed. Preferring to fixate on the scrap paper in front of him, he ignored her muttered obscenities and traced the lines of the portrait he scribbled with the HB pencil he'd found on the floor.

"I mean, it's not like I didn't prepare you for this," Mary Lazarus said, stopping to glare at him in the way only a parent could. "It's not like you didn't spend your entire life training to avoid this very thing." She punctuated her last words by hitting her palm on the bed.

"Exactly. I'm big and ugly enough to take care of myself. How did you know I was here, anyway?"

She ignored his question and continued with her lecture. "A mother will always be worried about her children, no matter how big and strong they've grown. I gave you the tools to be what this city needs, what this world needs, but ultimately it has to be up to you. Your sin doesn't control you. You control it. Evan. Are you listening?"

"Yes."

"I encouraged you when you chose to slip out into the night and fight crime. I supported you when you chose to pack it all in. But, Evan"—she made a pointed look at his faded bruised face and arms—"I won't stand by idly while you punish yourself for something that's not your fault."

Evan stopped the sweeping line of his pencil stroke and lifted his gaze to focus on her.

The woman stood at five-five but had a deceptively powerful body you wouldn't expect to see on a fifty-year-old woman. Sheathed in black workout attire, she looked fresh and fit. Her dark, silver-streaked long hair had been pulled into a convenient bun at the base of her neck. There were tiny worry lines around her eyes and in between her brows, but if he saw her on the street and had to guess her age, he'd say early forties. You'd hardly know beneath her slick surface laid an ex-assassin of the Hildegard Sisterhood and a sleeping dragon capable of killing the instant it woke. And she'd taught him everything she knew.

"My visions don't predict everything, Evan. I'd much rather you return home where you belong. What's this?" Mary's eyes snagged on something. She caught Evan's wrist in her strong vice-like grip and turned the inner flesh toward her eyes, displaying his Yin-Yang tattoo. Each of his siblings had one, but Evan had embellished his with black geometric and organic patterns that traveled up the natural lines and veins of his body, turning his arm into a work of art reminiscent of his paintings. His eldest brother, Parker, had infused the tattoo ink with an acid based indicator that reacted to each of their individual sins. The more envy registered in Evan's body, the darker his tattoo. It was almost black.

Mary sighed and dropped her forehead to his wrist. She inhaled a shuddering breath, gathering herself. The sight broke Evan's heart. She was disappointed, he knew, but he couldn't help himself. The urges were too strong. Envy had driven him to fight in the underground ring. When they wanted him to fail, it urged him to win. Now he sensed envy in the hospital. In *every* bed. In *every* room. Sick people wanted to be someone else. Staff wanted to be somewhere else. Everyone wanted something they didn't have. Including him.

He tugged his wrist from his mother and scribbled madly on the portrait.

"We should just go," Evan stated, shifting to get out of the bed. "The longer we stay, the more likely they'll discover things they shouldn't about me."

She pushed him back down. "Absolutely not. Your sudden absence will raise more red flags than not. Besides, I've seen the outcome. It's best we stay."

Mary's supernatural visions were what led her to rescue him and his siblings from the lab that created them. Those visions kept them safe from the Sisterhood she betrayed, and the mysterious Syndicate who bank rolled their experiment.

Evan resisted, and she responded with more force. "You may be ten times bigger than me, Evan, but I can drop you like a fly."

He eased off. She was right.

Large brown eyes looked down at him over a straight, no-nonsense nose. Evan supposed he and his siblings didn't look so different from her. It was easy to mistake them as relatives. Evan's biological mother was Caucasian—pale and dark-haired. Mary had been born in Mexico, had olive skin and dark eyes. Her husband Flint, their father figure, was Caucasian too, rounding out the perfect appearances for their family brood.

"I brought spare clothes for you to dress in. Lord knows you can't wear the battle gear home."

"I wore it last night. Nobody seemed to care. In fact, they cheered louder when I took a hit."

"La Hostia." Mary pulled out the gold crucifix from her top and kissed it.

"Since when did you find religion? You didn't even pray when you were a fake nun back in the day."

"I'm not praying now. I'm cursing. And maybe it's because none of you children listen to me."

"Okay, okay. Sorry. What else did you see?" Evan asked, scratching the tattoo on his wrist. "What's got that gleam in your eye?"

Mary toyed with the zip on her jacket. The smile dancing on her lips was almost undetectable before she squashed it down, letting the hardness take back her features.

"I'm relieved to see you're alive, that's all." She tapped on his drawing. "You need to stop this business about Sara. Focus on finding your own woman. Evan. Look at me."

He did.

"It's not healthy to pine after your brother's dead fiancée."

The pencil snapped in Evan's fingers.

"You know there's another reason for this..." he waved at the paper, unable to come up with the right word.

"Obsession?"

"Investigation! I thought you of all people would understand the dreams. I don't pick them, they pick me."

Mary opened her mouth to say something, then shut it. There was nothing else to say. Hadn't been for two years. He couldn't prove it. *They* couldn't prove it. As far as everyone else knew, Sara had died a martyr in the explosion that ended life as he knew it. But Evan knew. He'd always known.

Sara had been filled to the brim with deadly levels of envy. She wasn't as innocent as she seemed, and when he'd told his family after the fact, they blamed him. Some said he lied, others accused him of making a mistake or taking too long to tell them, and then there was the kicker from Wyatt —*You're just jealous I had someone who loved me.*

They were supposed to support each other as a family, but the truth was, since Sara had entered their lives years ago, they'd never been the same.

"Whatever," Evan said and scrunched up the drawing. "Maybe you're right. She's dead. It's over. You would have seen a vision otherwise. My dreams aren't the same thing as yours. I'll never be as good."

Mary sighed and searched his eyes with hers. "Look, I'm not saying you're wrong, Evan. I'm not all-seeing. Far from it, in fact. The older I get, the less my gift seems to work, and yours... it's something new. It's bio-engineered. Mutating animal DNA mixed with human. It's one of a kind and we're learning as we go. But, what I am saying is, you need to focus on yourself, on finding the one who will be your perfect balance. From what Gloria said about your condition, I don't believe your dreams are the ability she spoke of. It might be a side-effect, but not the one that should manifest when you meet your perfect balance."

Evan rolled his eyes. "Not this again."

"Yes, this again. I've always believed you would be the first, Evan. You will show them all the way. You're the youngest, you've been exposed to your sin the least. Despite what they all think, Sara wasn't the *one* for Wyatt. He would've felt a noticeable biological response. Gloria programed your DNA that way. Wyatt didn't develop any special abilities, so Sara couldn't have been his match. Simple as that. Everyone needs to forget her and move on."

Mary's faith in him kept Evan from an early grave. But he shook his head, staring down at the crumpled paper in his hand. The idea of there being one person out there for him was too hard to comprehend. "It's all bullshit. My birth mother told you bullshit."

"Watch your language."

"Sorry. But it's true. She was a genius geneticist but she was grade-A crazy. Mad scientist doesn't even begin to describe her drivel."

"Have a little respect for the woman who gave her life for your freedom."

"I shouldn't have brought it up." Evan resisted the urge to say she was the one who'd enslaved them in the first place. Instead, he finished scrunching the portrait into a tight ball and threw it at the curtain surrounding his bed just as it parted on the rails with a fast, metallic whoosh.

The ball bounced off the head of a young brunette woman dressed in green scrubs.

"Oh, good aim," she said, patting her head.

All at once, every hair on Evan's body stood to attention.

Three words, and she held him captive. He could do little else but stare.

Babe. Hot. One word impressions flashed through his mind.

Fascinating. A sprinkle of freckles covered the tip of her button nose. A fine white scar feathered up her chin to her rosy pink lips.

Lick. He had the irrational urge to lick his way up it.

Want.

What the?

He blinked madly as his body reacted uncontrollably. Heat flared up his neck, hitting his cheeks. Pin pricks of sweat tickled his skin as it flamed. He was a long way from being a school boy, so when the telltale tightness grew in his groin, he rushed to cover himself with the sheet.

Shit. What the fuck was wrong with him?

Biological reaction.

The woman bent to pick up the crumpled paper and straightened. When her whiskey brown eyes met his, there was an inexplicable moment of intimacy, of human connection. The world around him fell away, and he felt nothing, no envy, no self-disparagement. It was him and her and the strange notion that she saw through it all. The moment lasted long enough to make his heart thud once... twice in his chest, and then it was gone.

She lifted the paper ball in her hands. "Is this important?"

He shook his head like a dumb-ass.

"He's an artist," Mary said with a pointed look at the paper. "He's very talented."

Evan cleared his throat and glared at his mother, but she didn't seem to mind.

"He has an exhibition in a few nights—"

"Mamà," Evan warned.

"He's also a tattooist. Has his own studio."

Christ. He scrubbed his face, letting his hand drag down over his stubble. He caught a whiff of his body odor and flinched. God, he must look awful. He wanted to crawl under a rock or, better yet, sink beneath the floor and never come out.

Mary kept talking about him. Stop. Please, God, stop embarrassing him. He ground his teeth. "*Mary.*"

"Right." Understanding entered Mary's eyes as she ping-ponged between him and the doctor, then she gathered her things, including the plastic bag holding his Envy fighting leathers. "Right. I'll get out of here and let you do your job, doctor. You'll be wanting some privacy. I'll go and get a coffee. I'll wait for you outside, Evan."

With a secretive smirk, Mary opened the curtain to exit, and then closed it behind her, tugging the width tight to the edge, ensuring maximum privacy.

The last sense of envy in the tiny space vacated. Evan turned his gaze back to the doctor in surprise, realizing only then why he hadn't sensed her approach. She held no envy. None.

FOUR

DR. GRACE GO

After the patient's mother left, Grace deftly discarded the balled up paper on the bed, and then assessed him. At first glance she noticed his perfect bone structure. High cheek bones, razor cut jaw, intense green eyes. Good looking in a rugged sort of way except his overgrown brown hair and facial scruff meant he didn't look after himself. Big, muscular, powerful… dangerous. Raseem said he had been a handful to constrain when admitted—she believed it. The hospital gown barely contained his broad shoulders and revealed a full sleeve tattoo on one arm and possibly more from the dark shadows underneath the gown. The artwork both intrigued and puzzled her with its simultaneous violent and harmonious subject matter. Skulls with flowers. A snake around a heart. Death with life. Her eyes tracked down the inked arms to where his fists clenched in his lap. Knuckles were grazed.

She had the impression he'd brutally earned that carved

physique with every punch thrown. Possibly psychopathic from the way he watched her, tracking every movement.

But she'd seen the way his mother adored him.

She smiled. "Good morning Mr. Lazarus. I'm Doctor Grace Go. You were admitted earlier this morning with a"—she squinted at her iPad—"shoulder laceration and suspected internal bleeding. You've had some scans and have been administered something for the pain. How are you feeling?"

"Go?" His voice came out a low rumble. He scrubbed his scruff, inspecting her face. "You're Japanese?"

"Ah." Grace blinked, mentally thrown off key. Most people joked about her last name, but he'd identified its origin. "Sort of, not really, half I guess. My father was."

He answered with a dismissive grunt.

Boy, this guy needed a Post-it note.

She cleared her throat and lifted her iPad. Right. Scans.

"Mr. Lazarus—"

"Evan." He growled the word as though she'd done something wrong.

"Evan. Your scans are back and, good news, there are no signs of internal bleeding. However, there's something interesting the radiologist picked up on that I'd like to discuss before checking your sutures."

The man grew quiet, deathly still, until the wall of silence between them electrified. He had presence, she gave him that.

She turned the iPad to face him and pulled up the scan, zooming in on the area she needed. "Were you aware that you have three extra organs?"

He said nothing and, after a beat of awkward silence, she felt his eyes on her face. That charged energy prickled her skin until she turned to meet his gaze, inches from hers. Try as she might, no other words came to mind. In a sudden off-putting moment, she realized he held her captive and not the other way around. There was something about him. He drank in the details of her face, caught on the tiny scar at the base of her lip, and instead of glossing over her imperfection, he appeared intrigued with it. Then he seemed to catch himself staring, and his brow furrowed.

"I'm sorry, what?"

"You have three extra organs. See here, here and here?" She pointed to the dark masses on the scan behind his ribcage and stomach. "It's incredible, really. They don't appear to be the same shape as any other organ. And preliminary scans can't pinpoint a common function. Something new entirely."

Evan took the iPad and squinted at it, peering closely. "Huh."

"So this is new information to you?" Grace asked.

"Yes. First time I've been scanned."

"First time?" He piqued her interest more with each passing minute. "Right, well it's called supernumerary. It's more common than you think. Usually it's an extra kidney or spleen… or the occasional tooth and the like. We'd have to run more diagnostics to identify their purpose."

A loud pop and spark burst from the iPad, lighting the area as though a camera flash went off. Evan dropped the sizzling device into his lap. "What the hell was that?"

"Oh no. I'm so sorry. It must have shorted out." Grace

went to pick it up, but he stopped her with a hand to her wrist. Another spark ignited at his fingers. Grace yelped and he let go, eyes widening to meet hers, just as shocked as she was.

"You must have a residual static charge or something. Are you okay? Are you hurt?" she asked.

"Me?"

"Yes, you. Are you burned?"

"I'm fine. You?"

"Just a small… static shock." Was that all it was? She sighed at the smoldering device. "Your scan; I can get another iPad and download it from the cloud."

He pushed the tablet away. "No need. Can I go?"

"You don't want to investigate the organs further?"

"No."

"Oh. Okay, then. I'll check your sutures and if everything is good, you can go." She placed a palm on his good shoulder and applied pressure. He didn't budge. She had a sense he wouldn't budge unless he wanted… for anyone. "Please sit back. I need you to pull down the top half of your gown to expose the wound."

He glanced at her hand as if it burned him.

She put the charred iPad down on a side table and when she turned back, he still hadn't moved. "Mr. Lazarus, you haven't removed your gown."

He grunted. "Shoulder wound."

A man of many grunts. "Right. Of course. How silly of me. Sit forward and I'll help."

Evan leaned forward. He was so large that she lifted to her toes to peer over his shoulder and pluck the rear snaps apart. He went to catch the falling fabric and their hands clashed. Another jolt zapped between them.

Grace squeaked and let go.

He also let go.

The gown swished down, leaving the expanse of his chest exposed, and then some. From her vantage point, Grace saw indecently down the chiseled ridges of his front. Enough to confirm the tattoos covered half his body and didn't go all the way down. They stopped where the light sprinkle of hair began under his stomach. She glimpsed the top of his shaft, where it joined his torso. Was he—? She squeezed her eyes shut, but that made it worse. The after-image had burned into her retinas. She opened her eyes again to find him slowly covering himself, as if not to draw attention, but when he tilted his head to her side, there was a moment of shared awareness.

She'd seen. He knew she'd seen. She knew he knew she'd seen.

"Let's check your wound," Grace said, silently thanking her relentless training. She could do this. Ignore it. Oh no, she called his erection an *it*. This was officially the worst examination she'd ever had to do, and that included the geriatric who once sat on the handle of a back scratcher in the shower.

She faced his shoulder, trying desperately not to breathe in. At first, it was his dirty appearance that put her off, but then under all that there was a delicious pine and musk scent that came out to envelope her, infusing warmth into her bones. He shouldn't smell that good. No man should.

Grace peeled the white tape from his neck to expose the wound.

He sat stiff as a board, gaze focused on a central point in front of him, hands gripping the sheet at his side, muscles taut. Perhaps he felt as awkward as she did. Good. He deserved to lose that gruff attitude. Grace went back to the sutures, assessing the nurse's skill. They looked fine. No swelling in the wound. Healing rather well, in fact. But she pretended to take longer than she needed. The bruises on his torso concerned her, and she needed a moment to think on how to approach the topic. They reached all over his body, front and back, like a macabre purple and yellow painting. She decided he'd appreciate the direct approach.

"Do you want to tell me how you obtained the puncture?" she asked, and pressed the wound dressing down, smoothing the tape with her finger. "The notes say they found rust and metal filings in there."

"A broken fire escape ladder fell on me."

She sighed and pulled away. "And the bruising? Was that a ladder too?"

He said nothing.

Grace stepped back for a better look at his injuries. She clenched her hand into a fist and hovered it over a bruise under his ribs. Perfect match for knuckles.

"I've seen this kind of bruising before, Evan." With his physique, it wasn't hard to leap to conclusions.

"You done?" Without waiting for her response, he swung his legs over the other side of the bed, showing his naked back.

More tattoos. A quote of some kind weaved with a pattern. More skin. More bruises. More suffering.

"I'd like to talk some more about your other injuries," Grace said. "The bruises."

"You don't give up, do you?"

"No."

He shook his head and stood, heedless of his nudity, to pick up a pair of jeans. She caught a flash of a taut, tanned ass and turned hastily away with the absurd thought to wonder why his butt was the same color as the rest of his skin. Usually there was a tan line. He either fake tanned, or sunbathed in the nude. Or maybe that was his natural skin tone. For a moment, Grace's mind got stuck on imagining his naked body in its entirety, and then remembered where she was.

She picked up the iPad, intending to go back to the patient notes, but it was well and truly fried. Just like her wits. Normally, she'd be fine with his level of body confidence. She saw naked people every day. Nothing to it. In fact, it had become such a common sight that she thought she'd become numb to it.

You'd have to be blind and stupid not to be affected by his body, even in its current state of disrepute.

He slipped on a T-shirt.

Those bruises.

She cleared her throat.

"Um, so the stitches can come out in about a week. If you make an appointment to see your general practitioner, they can be removed there. And about the bruising. You were lucky enough to escape internal bleeding this time, but I can't say you'll be so lucky the next. Please look after your body. It's the only one you've got."

"Can't you do it?" This brought his intense gaze back to her.

Grace's eyes widened. Look after his body?

"The stitches," he elaborated.

Did she detect a sparkle of amusement in his eyes?

"No," she said. "I'm sorry but this is the emergency department."

He walked around the bed until he faced her, invading her space. Now in a white T-shirt and jeans, he was no less imposing. She bet the other guy lost the fight. A step backward and her butt hit the gurney. He crowded her, caging her in by placing a palm on the bed either side of her.

"But I want to see you again"—his gaze dropped to the identification badge at her breast—"Doctor Grace Go."

"Mr. Lazarus—"

"Evan."

"—Evan. This is highly improper." Grace glanced at his arms in the way of her escape and, for a minute, the closeness was too much. His smell. His heat. Overpowering. Confining. Intoxicating.

Was that water dripping over the roaring sound in her ears?

Was that the smell of concrete and fumes?

"I like improper." He spoke into her ear.

He was too close, and she was unfamiliar with him. She hugged the broken iPad to her chest and shut her eyes to stop the past ruling her judgment, but the walls crumbled around her and she was back in the tight space underneath the building debris. The smell of asphalt. Her screams. The thick air running out of oxygen. She'd choked and coughed. Water dripped somewhere nearby. The telltale sign of heat flushing through her nervous system warned of an anxiety attack about to hit in full force.

Grace forced her eyes open. Her next words were slow and deliberate. "Move out of my way. Now."

He cocked his head, studying—always studying—and then something strange happened. A spark and a sizzle came from where he rested on the mattress. His eyes widened, and he hid his hands behind his back.

"I have to go," he said roughly. "See you in a week."

And then he was gone, curtain swaying gently in his wake.

Grace exhaled in a burst. What had just happened? She patted her clammy forehead with the back of her hand. In a desperate attempt to get her thoughts into order, she set about the space to tidy up.

What kind of gall did he have to treat his doctor that way? Was he just an asshole alpha male who liked to fight? Or perhaps he truly was psychotic after all. Or maybe those bruises were part of a bigger picture. Would he actually come back and ask for her? Oh God. Her stomach twisted into knots. Maybe she should have directed him to the clinic to avoid a scene in Emergency.

Grace tugged the sheet from the bed for the orderly, and a burned plastic smell hit her nose. She shifted the sheet out of the way to expose the mattress. What the hell? Scorched handprints marked the mattress. She dipped to inspect the charring and her mind raced back to the sudden noise that made him hide his hands. He made those marks. With his hands. How? Maybe it was he who burned the iPad, not the other way around. Confounded, she pulled the sheets off further and the paper ball that he'd thrown at her head fell to the ground.

She unraveled it and flattened its length on the gurney.

Cold seeped into Grace and she had to sit down. The portrait was her. The bomber.

FIVE

EVAN LAZARUS

With the sound of AC/DC's *Highway to Hell* blaring through his earphones, Evan stepped up to the entrance of Cardinal City's finest art gallery at the heart of the Quadrant's culture district. He stopped to stare.

Like many buildings in the city center, a modern version of gothic architecture had covered the old, and it was impressive. Instead of flowing decorative patterns casing the lancet windows, the curves had been fashioned into sharp edges giving the carved wings on spires a shiny futuristic vibe. Recently wet from the rain, platinum hood molds winked in the moonlight. He pulled out his earphones, and the city sounds replaced the hard rock. Some homeless people clinked bottles around the side of the building. Distant sirens wailed. Beyond the windows, through the stained silver glass, the muffled sounds of revelers pushed at him, telling him the party was in full swing. Late for his own exhibition.

His body tingled with unnatural energy and had for the

past few days since he'd met the doctor. The memory of her proud face, light sprinkle of freckles, and warm smile hit him. Every time he thought of her, his gut drew tight and his stomach flipped. The way his bones had hummed in her presence made him constantly think of touching her soft skin again, and again. He'd dreamed of her nightly. Couldn't get her out of his mind. It got to the point where he actually considered going back to see her about his stitches, despite the fact he'd healed. Maybe he could injure himself again. Put his own stitches in there.

The way her deft fingers moved when she'd checked his wound dressing; so confident and steady. He liked her surety, somehow it gave him peace.

The tingle in his body erupted into a burning zing.

He glanced down to see his Yin-Yang tattoo almost equal parts black and white, and the electricity gathering at his fingertips.

Part of him wanted to believe what it meant.

That she was it for him. The one. His balance. His salvation.

That this was some new power developing, and he was the first of his siblings to get it.

That unicorns existed and leprechauns shit rainbows.

Yeah, right. He scoffed and clenched his hands into fists, dispelling the sensation. When that didn't work, he blew heat onto his palms. Maybe it was nerves. All those people inside were here to see him. Envy grated from each patron and pierced through his skin, like a thousand hungry teeth gnawing the surface of his stomach, reminding him of his true purpose, and his reason for this exhibition.

Sara.

She'd torn his family apart, and he wanted to expose her true nature. Was it vindictive? Yes. Was it revenge? Maybe. He wanted to show them all that he'd been right. To shove their ignorance up their asses.

The destructive thoughts shamed him to his core. If his teachers knew how far he'd fallen, they'd be horrified. Especially Master Yang Lun. The small old monk would likely send him to strip the nails from the community board with his bare fingers for a few hours. Then he'd make him put them back in with his fist.

Studying under Shaolin Monks had been Evan's second stop on his journey to learning the art of war. The minute he'd turned fifteen, Mary had shipped him off, just like his six elder siblings had, to spend one year studying under a Master of War before moving onto the next. Their education lasted seven years. Being able to sense a deadly sin was no walk in the park.

With Grace, it might be.

He inspected his fingertips, still worn and scarred from the aftereffects of that training. In some places his prints had disappeared altogether from the constant shredding and blistering of skin. He flexed his fists and grimaced at the rubberiness of the action. Still stiff from the fighting ring, and worse from the beating afterward. It had taken longer than usual to heal. He was in no condition to keep someone like Grace safe and out of harm's way.

He opened the gallery door, taking a moment to acclimatize to the heat, the assault of sound, and barrage of sin.

Eye-watering envy.

At a glance, the crowd consisted of mid-to-upper-class narcissistically dressed bodies. Fit, fabulous and under fifty. Each and every person seemed to be fully aware of their tightly dressed appearance. Evan knew that proud look well because his elder brother, Parker, wore it every day. Cringing, he turned his back on the people to brush dampness from his shoulders, relishing the distraction at his fingertips. When he turned back, everyone had stopped and stared. At him.

He took a deep breath and adopted the Hollywood persona his brother Tony had told him about. Start off cool on the approach, ignore the looks and act like you've got somewhere better to be. Vacantly scan the room, then, when you're sure you can lock eyes with a beautiful woman, act like you've just arrived. *Big smile, let it hit your eyes… now show your teeth.* They don't need to know what's going on under the hood. Just smile.

"What the hell was that? You look like you've eaten a bad burrito." Speaking of the devil, Tony broke away from the feminine wall of desperation holding him up. He swiped two glasses of champagne from a timid waitress and stood in front of Evan holding one out. The man was ripped as you would expect an action movie star to be. His suit seams stretched at the biceps and shoulders. Evan was sure the thing would rip in two if Tony bent forward.

It was impossible not to see they were related. Same dark hair and wide lipped smile. Tony's face managed to put it all together in a face worthy of the screen, while Evan thought his own was a bit more forgettable. Slick versus messy.

"I did exactly what you told me to do," Evan growled as he accepted the glass.

"Nah, bro, that wasn't it. It's like this." Tony lazily lowered his lids, scanned the room like a predator, then grinned, flashing his Hollywood teeth, all the while saying, "You gotta show your teeth like this. Not Jim Carey in *The Mask* style. But all, I'm sexy and I know it style. And—you should've shaved, bro. I get the broken pencil over your ear, but holy shit, are you wearing flip-flops?"

The pencil was from the hospital. The one the doc worked at.

"Hey, I brushed my hair. I showered. That's good enough. Besides, nobody will think that a guy looking like me will be Envy. It's why you do the whole substance-abuse-cliché, right?"

Tony's features slackened, and he looked away. "Right."

Jeez. Fucking sore spot—noted.

The awkward silence extended too long and people stared. A movie star next to the night's star. He hated it.

Evan tried to bring the topic back to something more colloquial.

"So, smile, like how you do it. How Parker does it."

He conjured an image of his eldest brother at his recent press conference but failed to remember the exact expression Parker gave when he walked up to the podium last week. His long auburn hair had been pinned back like some Viking motherfucker from the History Channel as he spoke about his latest futuristic sustainable invention that minimized waste. Total riot. It'd been two years since they'd all hung up their capes, so to speak, and Parker was still saving the world. That son-of-a-bitch wasn't even trying. He deserved to be cocky.

"Yeah, sorta. But don't come on too sleazy, sometimes a half smile is good too, and when you know the paparazzi are watching, play it cool. Smirk like this."

"Right. Cos the paps are here for me." Evan snorted sarcastically. "Well there's only one actor in this group and it ain't me. So how about I do this." Evan emptied the contents of the champagne flute down his throat in one burning gulp.

"That works too." Tony laughed and clinked his already empty glass against Evan's. Then he glanced back at the giggling women waiting for him. A redhead finger waved at Tony who then leaned into Evan. "You want me to save you a piece of that action?"

"Uh. No thanks."

"What, you had them already?" Tony squinted at the women. "I haven't, have I?"

Evan shook his head. "How the hell should I know?"

"Do your thing. See if they go for you instead of me. Then I'll know."

Tony referred to their good cop, bad cop play. Evan would go in all broody artist, and then Tony would swoop in and rescue them all with some charismatic charm. He wanted broody, he got it. "*You* do *your* thing."

"What the hell is wrong with you?"

"Nothing. Just not up for it. Is Parker still coming?"

His brother exhaled in disbelief, one eye still on the girls. "Fine. Your choice. More for me."

"So… Parker?" He could be boycotting the night like the rest of the family. Well, that wasn't exactly true. Mary and

Flint would be here somewhere in a show of support. They always were. Liza was undercover in Vice busting a prostitution ring, and Sloan couldn't be bothered taking five minutes from her Fortnite game. Griff? He might turn up with Parks if he deemed it a suitably neutral affair. He was obsessed about following his tattoo to balance and systematically approached the sin of Greed with mathematical accuracy.

But Wyatt... there was no way in hell he'd come. Once, they'd been the best of friends and Wyatt was the brother Evan had looked up to the most. He'd held the same devil-may-care attitude Evan loved. But now, they'd barely spoken since the day Sara died and Evan accused her of causing the tragedy. Well, Fuck Wyatt. And the motorcycle he rode in on. If he needed someone to blame, then whatever. Blame away. Evan could handle it.

"Parks was supposed to be here five minutes ago," Tony replied. "But you know how he is. He likes to make a grand entrance. Even though they're your paintings, it's always about him after all." Tony's mouth twisted slightly as he took in the artwork closest to him.

Like most of the paintings, this one consisted of stark black and white lines, similar to a tattoo. But every so often, abstract slashes of color lit up the painting in meaningful ways. He'd titled it: *Twisted*. If it were up to Evan, he'd never title any artwork, but his agent insisted he do so for the event, so he went for morally ambiguous to fuck with people's brains. Art critics loved it.

"If anyone recognizes her, I'll just bullshit. It's what artists do," Evan said, preempting Tony's protest about the subject matter. "I'll say it's a political statement. She's the symbol of everything wrong with the Deadly Seven and showing her in every day poses highlights that her loss was a tragedy that affects the everyman, or some shit. They already blame us for the bombing why not amplify it? What do we care? We gave up."

"You're so full of it. Did you practice that in front of the mirror? And did you have to include her in every single one —and what's that, a butt tattoo? Wyatt won't like that. What do think he's going to do when he sees you've shared it with the whole world?"

"It wasn't me who inked it. I haven't even seen it in real life, I swear. I dreamed it. Could be made up for all I know."

Tony grunted and took another drink from the fresh glass that had somehow manifested in his hand. They both stood in stoic silence as they surveyed the paintings and sketches. Each canvas showed a different scene, black and white and detailed in its subject, from the tiny cockroach scurrying across the café floor to the label on the Gin bottle on the table. Although each painting showed a different scenario, there was one unifying factor: Sara.

Evan wanted to take the pencil from his ear and scribble a mustache on the woman. Maybe some devil horns. Knowing these people, they'd probably pay more for it.

"Fuck Wyatt," Evan eventually said. "For the last time, I can't help it. I need to paint the dreams to get them out of my head. I may as well make money from them."

"We don't need money." Tony shot him a dubious glance.

"Fine. I did it because if someone turns up with a piece of information about her, then all the better."

"She's dead, bro, and has been for two years. When are you going to give up the ghost?"

"Evan. *Darling*. Where have you been?" An anorexic woman dressed in what appeared to be sausage skin was at Evan's side, fraught with desperation. Her dark hair had been scraped high into a tight-as-tight ponytail, giving her a fake facelift, causing her eyes to tilt up at the corners. Around her neck was the most enormous collection of plastic gems he'd ever seen. Her smile was forced. "The exhibition started fifteen minutes ago."

"I'll get us another drink." Tony swept the loose hair from his eyes and made his exit. Evan noticed him dump the empty glasses on a waitress's tray, take the last full flute, and then strolled away, hand in Gucci jacket pocket. Bastard.

"Sorry," Evan said to Azaria, his art dealer and agent, and then shoved his hands in his pockets, unable to meet her gaze. She clearly wished he'd taken more effort with his appearance. Despite this, envy emanated from her in waves, forcing him to close his eyes at the onslaught. The hazard with these shindigs was each guest desperately wanted his talent. People admired art because they felt the beauty resonate within them or some shit. He found it ironic it all came from his messed up mind. All he knew was that almost all of them wanted to recreate his talent for themselves, and they couldn't. He forced his eyes to meet her apprehensive stare.

"Well, lucky for you," she said, "we've sold all but five paintings—and one of those is the finalé up for auction. The use of color and substance in that one when all the others are devoid of value is genius. So five left is an incredible result for a debut considering you've only just arrived. Okay, so we can get around this late business. Work the room, answer some questions. The more you engage, the easier it will be to sell the last four and help us fetch the best price for *The Painting Within*. And don't forget the artist Q&A session in fifteen. Everyone is dying to know who the woman with the doll face is."

"Yeah, well, I'm not telling. It adds to the mystery." Plus he wanted someone else to point her out, to reveal something he didn't know.

She sighed but didn't push it. She'd tried to weasel that information out of him many times before and he wouldn't budge.

Their secret lives had always been very private, but every news network in the country had the rare, blurry footage of Wyatt dressed as Wrath, in full hooded and masked battle gear, clutching Sara's broken and blood-streaked body amongst the rubble. If they discovered Evan knew Sara, then it was entirely possible they'd figure out who he and his six siblings were. It was a dangerous game he played, but he was beyond caring.

"C'mon, let's work the room." Azaria playfully bumped him with her bony hip and then dragged him to the first cluster of people with an excessive amount of disposable income.

The group consisted of one female—a bronze skinned beauty that reminded him of Pocahontas with her slick, long hair—and two suited men, professional looking. Professional assholes.

"Gentlemen and lady, may I introduce the star of the show, Evan Lazarus."

The envy in the room manifested three fold as the trio gave him their full attention.

Evan forced a smile through his teeth.

"Evan Lazarus," said the tall, middle-aged man as he shook hands. The man had a mole over his lip, and he tried to hide it with a mustache. But Evan caught everything. He always did. Noticing the finer details was the curse of being an artist. Like his siblings, he went to college after combat training. He still remembered his art professor's words that first day: *Look around you. You're among the smartest people in the world. You see the world as no one else sees it. You appreciate the world in a way no one else does.* Like every other student there, Evan believed him. Then he grew up.

The man in front of him kept talking. "Pleasure to meet you. Your work is absolutely amazing. I particularly like how the strokes…"

Evan zoned out as the man said something wanky about his artistic style in relation to some other wanky artist from history. Banksy was thrown in there, which was even more wanky because you don't touch Banksy. He was a street artist legend of epic proportions. This guy was just trying to impress the people around him with his superior knowledge of the genre. Unlucky for him, Evan mostly had no idea what he spoke about. He'd spent most of his college days sleeping after fighting crime at night, but it had been a good alibi for his secret identity. So he smirked and nodded, wondering if Tony would ever come back with that second drink.

"Yes, I have to agree," said the dark beauty, bringing Evan's attention back to her. "I've already insisted James buy the one where your mystery woman is bathing."

She kept talking, but he was lost in the way her hair glistened down her bare back, reminding him of Grace's long lush hair. Her halter dress gathered behind her neck in white strips, then hung low down her chest in a V shape that almost reached her navel. Okay, that was definitely not something he imagined Grace wearing. She was too sweet. Too matter-of-fact for a skanky outfit that had been artfully attacked with a switch-blade. How were the straps staying in place over those mountainous breasts?

He made himself stare and attempted to feel something, anything, like he had earlier when he was with Grace, but... he glanced down at his dick—nothing. Fuck. That never happened before. Usually, it at least stirred at the sight of a pretty lady. He narrowed his eyes at her breasts. Shit. Again, nothing.

A spike in envy surged in the air and Evan glanced up to see the second man, dark skinned and solidly built, protectively drape an arm over Pocahontas's bare shoulders. Must be James.

The unspoken challenge undeniably pulled at Evan's core. He wanted a piece of him? Oh, bring it on. The night just got more exciting.

"The one where the woman is bathing is called *Wet Nightmares*." Evan asked. "Why did you pick that one?" Of course he'd guessed, but he wanted to hear her say it in front of her man.

"It's the way she gazes into the mirror as she dries

herself, totally unaware of us. It makes the viewer feel like a voyeur, but at the same time"—she blushed—"you feel excited, aroused."

Evan caught her gaze and held it. Right. Aroused. So the opposite of what he felt right now.

"Yes, well, it's a talent how you capture the moment," said the companion. "Don't know why you called it a nightmare though."

Sensing the bad for business discomfort, Azaria made their excuses and pulled Evan away to visit the next group.

"There—just over by *The Painting Within*," Azaria said, leading him onwards, one arm stretched forward with her champagne flute, the other gripping his forearm. "We'll speak with the Mayor next."

As they approached the auction item, Evan halted, surprised. The scene grabbed hold of him. The crowd admiring the painting were completely unaware that they were the people *within* the painting. He recognized them immediately from his dreams. He'd known each one intimately. Each curve of their face, each dimple, each freckle, every fiber. Sin wafted from the familiar strangers as they admired the artwork. Not only five days earlier had he been in his studio watching his brush reveal the beings in painstakingly slow strokes. His heart raced. He hadn't thought it possible. He thought he was insane to imagine it. To hope.

The only thing missing was...

A sharp rush of air escaped his lips. There she was—the apparition that completed the picture—in a caterer's uniform, walking away with her tray of empty glasses. He knew her face better than his own. He'd seen it more often than his own reflection. Sara. Wyatt's dead fiancé.

Alive and breathing.

He shook his head as if to clear the haze. Maybe he'd drunk too much, but no, that wasn't right. He'd only had one glass. It had to be her. She was here.

They all thought he'd had some secret, dirty crush on his brother's fiancé. But all along he knew, deep down inside, that the twist in his gut had been envy. Hers. She'd envied his family to the point of evil. She alerted the Deadly Seven to the disturbance at the front of the mid-town apartment complex. Strange, well trained, white-robed warriors had randomly damaged the cars in the street and when his family turned up, they picked a fight. They fought like professionals and when it looked like his family were turning the tide of the battle, Evan felt Sara's unique brand of sin flare from inside the building. Suddenly, as though called by the Pied Piper, the masked warriors retreated to her, and then the bomb went off, destroying all evidence of their existence. Even the camera footage only showed Evan and his family. He didn't say anything about Sara until it was too late and Wyatt was dragging her lifeless body out of the rubble.

And now she was here, somehow alive.

He stepped forward in a daze, the noise from the crowd dimmed, and time moved drunkenly.

She looked different. Her blond hair was now brown. Instead of bright green eyes, they were red-rimmed with large inky irises as dark as her soul. She turned her head, caught his eye, and smiled.

The spell broke.

Anger rose in his blood. She knew.

She knew.

Years of combat training rushed to the surface, and he instinctively reached for his Katana. It wasn't there. Of course. Tonight he was Evan, the tortured artist, not Envy, the youngest member of the Deadly Seven. He searched the crowded room for his brother and found him. Tony leaned against the wall with a bored expression. He'd be assessing the women next to him, gauging which one he'd take home tonight. Maybe all. He'd been known to glut himself wherever he could.

Evan scanned for his parents, Mary and Flint, but they were nowhere to be found.

He was on his own.

And she was getting away.

Shit.

He squared his shoulders, centered his mind like Master Yang Lun had taught him. Filtered out the sounds and all sin except hers. Calm. Tranquility. Focus. There she was, at the end of the large room. He made to move, but two large brown eyes suddenly appeared in front of him, blinking.

Fuck. *Shit!* He jumped back to avoid bumping into her. "Doc? What the hell are you doing here?"

"Mr. Lazarus?" Grace asked innocently, ignoring his quip. "Could you spare a moment to answer a few questions about the woman in the paintings?"

She casually touched him on the arm, and that energy zapped between them, ensnaring him. But there was something more, an absence of sensation. Nothing but her fingers on his arm. It was as though he'd stepped into a vacuum. All the envy in the room had dissipated. His wrist tattoo tingled. He glanced down at the black and white Yin-Yang symbol. It shimmered before his eyes, color scrambling like ants to reflect the new equilibrium Grace brought to his psyche. She let go, and the envy in the room whooshed back.

Balance. The word whispered in his mind and his eyes widened.

It was true. She was the one.

It was all true.

The air rushed from his lungs as he took her in. It had only been a few days, but she was more beautiful than he remembered. Out of the ponytail, her dark glossy hair draped freely over her shoulders. Her lips, a rosy pink. Her neck, slender and pale, and when he followed the line of her proud jaw to her décolletage, down to her—

"Mr. Lazarus?"

Look at her face. Look at her face. Holy shit, his heart pounded. "Um, Doc, I'm sorry but this isn't the right time."

He had to go. Sara. He had paused too long and now she had completely vanished. Somewhere in the crowd, toward that corner of the room.

"Are you okay Mr. Lazarus?"

"Evan," he said absently.

"You look like you've seen a ghost."

"I have. Where did she go?"

"Who?" Grace scanned the room with impeccable accuracy. She didn't miss a thing, yet, she missed the most important thing of all. When she turned back to him, she'd pulled out a pocket notebook and pen, all business like.

"Who is the girl in the paintings?" Her voice cut into his thoughts. "Are you aware she resembles the woman one of the Deadly Seven was allegedly engaged to?"

"You know her?" He took hold of her upper arm, solidifying their connection.

Another warm sensation zipped up his spine and hit him in the face, causing him to break into a light sweat. Oh, no. It's that thing again. *Biological response.* It's happening. One thing to be in a private room at the hospital, but here, in front of so many people. Evan bit down on his tongue to suppress the flush overcoming his body, but his internal biology went into hyper-drive. Mary had warned him their DNA had been programed to respond to a person who embodied their balancing virtue. To send pheromones into the air to attract their mate. In this case, Grace. Suddenly, he wished he'd dressed more appropriately than a pair of tight jeans and a paper thin T-shirt.

Grace didn't seem to notice the turmoil rolling inside him, but watched him with concerned eyes. "Look, you left so suddenly the other morning and when I found the picture you drew, I just knew I had to chase you down. I've been after information on that woman for a long time and it's imperative I speak with you."

"Doc, I have to go. I'm sorry. You can't be involved in this."

As he began to move away, the envy in the room crushed him like a wall of water. He went in the direction he last saw Sara. He couldn't sense her unique brand of envy anywhere. There was too much in the air and after momentarily having his senses refreshed by Grace, it all smelled like soured perfume. It would take him a while to be able to distinguish each individual again.

Grace followed him. He turned to tell her to go, but was interrupted by Azaria.

"Darling. It's time for the Q&A. Could you please?" Azaria appeared at his side and waved her arm toward the front of the room. She gave Grace an irritated look, as though she occupied valuable space and needed to either fork up the rent, or leave.

Evan frowned. Nobody glared at Grace like that.

"Azaria," he snapped. "Make sure the doc here gets the best seat in the house. And some champagne."

Azaria gaped at him, but then let her expression go lax. "Whatever you want, darling. This way please, Miss. Evan, if you'd be so kind as to take the stage."

Evan cast one last glance around for Sara, but she was gone. He was beginning to believe it had all been in his head. One way or another, he'd flush her out, or go mad.

SIX

SARA MADDEN

Sara stood near the exit behind the crowd, and watched the artist take the stand to greet the emcee opposite him. She was supposed to be out of here by now, but there was one more thing she had to do. And if she was caught, the Deadly Seven were the least of her worries. She was on borrowed time.

While the hosts made their pleasantries, Sara separated a napkin from the stack she held and wrapped it around the used and empty champagne glass she'd retrieved from another waitress. When she finished, she gently tucked it into her apron pocket next to the other sample and then stopped at the sight of a stain on the disheveled hem of her white shirt. A single drop of blood had fallen right there on the seam. It bled along the stitching, morphing into a red maggot, wriggling and squirming, getting faster like the pounding of her heart.

She stared. It was just a blood stain. Red on white. Nothing more, nothing less. She tucked the shirt back into her apron and cast a hasty glance around the room. No one noticed. Good.

Then, taking a deep breath, she willed the panic down and stuffed it deep inside a locked box, the same place she kept all her earthly emotions, no longer needed, the nonsense of humans. And human she was no more.

SEVEN

DR. GRACE GO

When Evan's art dealer indicated for her to follow, Grace lifted her chin, set her shoulders and made her simple thrift-shop outfit behave like a Valentino. The red silk halter top lifted her bust higher, her hips swelled sexily in her jeans, and her legs lengthened beneath her. She was instantly taller, more confident and more secure. Nobody would belittle her with a glance. No. She was Grace Go. A doctor at Cardinal City General Hospital. She was great at her job.

She followed the woman to a place near the front of the stage and accepted a glass of champagne before the agent left to conduct the interview. Grace took a moment to gather herself and go over the past few minutes in her head.

She'd come into the room, fully intending to rail-road the artist and get some answers. She had less than two weeks to come up with the goods on the woman in the paintings. If she could find out more about her, the investigation would stay open. All the victims would receive compensation. Taco, Mason and their aunt. Herself. So many others she'd come to know well. She wasn't giving up now. She was close. She could feel it.

Evan's behavior had been erratic. While her medical experience pointed toward a psychotic prognosis after all, her heart didn't believe it. Something was wrong. Unable to tear herself away from the stage, she settled in to watch.

"Hello Dr. Go. You made it."

A blush crept up Grace's cheeks as she remembered the way the woman had shamelessly advertised her son's exhibition. "Yes, I did. But I'm here on business."

"Oh? She's here on business, Flint." The woman elbowed a tall handsome man beside her. Also middle-aged, he had a thick, trimmed beard, and stripes of distinguished gray marked his temples. He had an athletic physique that suggested he kept himself fit and busy. Grace's gaze snagged on his fingers clutched around a champagne flute. The tiny grease marks underneath his nails betrayed his trade. Possibly a mechanic.

"So I heard, Mary." Flint's eyes crinkled at the edges as he looked down at his wife, then he shifted his amused eyes to Grace. "Nice to meet you, Dr. Go."

"Oh, it's Grace. Please."

He nodded. Mary beamed. Once again, Grace felt like Mary knew something she didn't.

Evan sat down on a small stool situated in front of the colossal *Painting Within.* He gave it a cryptic glance then focused back on the crowd, eyes scanning before settling on her where they stayed a moment, unreadable.

"So, Evan," came the whiny voice of the art dealer, "tell

us about the collection. What inspired you to paint these particular scenes?"

Definitely a question Grace wanted answered.

"I don't think too hard. I just paint."

Great. His bare as bones answers weren't just for her at the hospital, the entire world enjoyed his curtness.

Azaria pulled a face at the crowd, riling them up. "You don't expect us to believe that's all there is, do you?"

The crowd, bolstered by alcohol, agreed with her. They cheered her on.

"What do you think, guys, should we get more information?" Azaria angled her microphone towards the crowd. Various voices rose above the others but nothing was clear. So she stood and asked again, microphone hovering. "Who wants to ask the question. You know, the one everyone is dying to have answered?"

Many hands rose above heads, like children in a classroom, eager to have their voices heard. One dainty hand was singled out, and Azaria made a security guard help the woman forward.

Before a word could be said, an incredibly loud clanging sound came from the entrance of the gallery. The front glass doors burst open, blasting arctic air in on a gust.

A tall man waltzed in with a model on each arm. He wasn't just large, he was *built*. Towering, imposing. His long, tarnished hair brushed the shoulders of his camel cashmere trench coat. His stylish scruff was trimmed to perfection. Confidence exuded from his golden pores. Dazzling eyes winked at someone he knew, and he nodded with a wicked grin to another.

"How you doing?" he asked someone. He shrugged off the models, and then his coat, handing it to some random stranger. Grace almost laughed, thinking, *That's not the cloak person*, but no one cared. They stared at him reverently like some sort of dark Norse god. His suit was expensive, tailor made to fit over his scary muscles, but he defied her original assessment and took the time for a selfie with a guest who had her camera out. He pulled a duck-face at the lens then retreated to his girls. "Drink?" he mouthed to them. They agreed, and he grinned, waiting expectantly for them to serve him.

He had no idea he'd just interrupted the main event, or maybe he did, and didn't care.

"You'd think the actual movie star in the family would be acting like the diva," grumbled a voice not far from Evan's parents.

Grace craned her neck to see who'd spoken and became momentarily star struck. It was Tony Lazarus, the movie star. Tall and sculpted under his Polo shirt, designer jacket and jeans. Short hair swept off his forehead as though he'd run his fingers through it. Perfectly tanned and manicured. He caught Grace staring and winked, then lifted his champagne flute to his lips, eyes back to the stage.

Flint grumbled something to Mary, and she shook her head disparagingly.

Grace turned back to the stage just in time to see Evan roll his eyes at the newcomer.

"Ladies and gentlemen," Evan said into his microphone. "I present my brother, Parker Lazarus."

The city's golden boy. Billionaire entrepreneur.

After a moment of surprised silence, a reverent murmur shimmered over the crowd.

Grace couldn't believe she hadn't pieced it together before. Lazarus. It wasn't a common name. If memory served correct, there was also a Michelin starred chef in one of the city's best restaurants, Heaven. His surname was Lazarus. Evan had an impressive family tree.

Azaria cleared her throat loudly. When she had no response from the still murmuring crowd, she carried on with her interview.

"So, where were we, darlings? Oh yes, the question everyone's been dying to ask."

From the corner of Grace's eye, she noted Evan's family grow still and watchful. Suspicion hardened in her like a stone. They all knew something, she was sure of it. Murmurs faded to silent quivers and soon disappeared altogether.

"Who wants to ask?" Azaria scanned the crowd at the front, then handed the microphone to an awaiting dark-skinned woman wearing a tight dress made from shredded white fabric.

She licked her glossy lips and leaned forward until they teased the mesh on the microphone. "Who is the woman in the painting?"

Evan lifted his mic to his mouth and spoke. "Why don't you ask her yourself?"

The crowd collectively gasped and checked the person next to them, to the left, and then the right again. Evan's family were equally shocked.

He continued: "I saw her not five minutes ago in this very

room, dressed in the uniform you see in the painting behind me. I'll freely give that painting to anyone who finds her and brings her up here. That's over seven thousand dollars' worth of fine art. Free. Even if you can only take a photo, I'd consider it."

Pandemonium washed over the room. Previously snooty, upperclass faces of stone collapsed into obscene, panicked motion. Even Evan's parents went on high alert. Bodies moved about, people pushed past their companions, camera-phones whipped out. Parker pushed his way through the crowd to where his family stood, glaring at his brother on stage.

Evan's lips curved in sardonic amusement.

If there was one thing guaranteed to get a crowd moving, it was money.

"I found her," a man shouted. The crowd parted and a frightened waitress jostled forward on a shove.

"That's not her," Evan grumbled.

"There she goes!" cried a woman somewhere. "Into the storeroom."

All heads turned to the storeroom door where they caught it swinging on its hinges.

Good God, it was like an Easter egg hunt.

A blood-curdling scream broke through the din of the crowd, shattering the excitement.

Then silence.

Where had that come from?

The woman screamed again. It came from the far end of the immense gallery, the end that had been blackened out for the night, so that no other paintings would steal the thunder from Evan's art. Evan jumped from his perch and launched himself into the thick of the crowd.

Suddenly, everyone around Grace herded in that direction too, but she wanted none of it. This game Evan played with the crowd was too much. The heat in the room swelled, and she found it difficult to breathe. The heat transferred to her body in a prickly wave that had her heart racing. Jostling bodies bumped into her, drawing panic to the surface. She could handle this level of confusion in the open street, but inside under a roof and four walls... too much. *Drip. Drip.* The building collapse burned behind her eyes. The scent of chalky dust filled air as though it were around her now. She coughed at the imaginary pollution and felt the heavy rock pushing against her skin, crushing her. Her heart beat faster and she couldn't help what happened next.

The walls closed in. She had to get out of there, so she ran.

EIGHT

DR. GRACE GO

Grace pushed to the exit, shoved the door open, and ran halfway across the darkened street before the subzero temperature registered. She'd left her coat. Her hot breath exhaled in a puff of white cloud. She wouldn't last five minutes outside in this weather at night. The bus would be another thirty minutes, and a walk home was just as long.

Only one thing for it. Shivering, she pivoted to retrieve her jacket, but slammed into a woman running in the opposite direction. The collision knocked the wind out of Grace and the distinct sound of shattering glass filled the air. They both fell hard to the asphalt, still wet from the recent rain. Grace's purse fled her fingers and skittered across the street, spinning in circles.

She blinked, staring up at the full moon glaring down at her. Next to her, steam rose from a sewer grate. And then she remembered her collision had broken something. Scrambling to get up, Grace apologized profusely to the woman lying opposite her.

"You stupid cow!" The woman rolled frantically to her side, flipping to her feet with unnatural speed. She didn't seem to care about her bleeding palms and checked the front pocket of her black waiter's apron, mortified. "Just look what you've done!"

Her face.

"Oh my God. It's you." Grace gasped and covered her mouth. "The girl in the paintings."

The girl from the bombing.

Only, she looked slightly different—off.

The last time Grace had seen the woman, she'd been standing in the lobby of the apartment complex her parents were inspecting. Grace had stayed downstairs to take a phone call from the hospital while her parents went up to look at rooms for sale on the top floor. Both Grace and the woman—then blond—were in the lobby when the fight erupted on the street. Through the glass windows, the Deadly Seven battled a group of white-robed and plastic Halloween masked warriors. Being the first and only time Grace had ever seen the heroes in action, it had been both terrifying and magnificent at the same time. Flashes of black leather and muted color burst around the air as each member expertly moved their bodies. Shadowed by hoods, their bright eyes flashed menacingly over the scarves hiding their mouths and noses. Each black hood was trimmed with a different color, representing a particular sin. Green for Envy, yellow for Sloth. Purple, red, blue, orange and one completely black. The strange costumes and expert skills, looked straight out of a martial arts movie. Grace almost believed it was a performance of some kind, until the first splash of blood arced against the window, making things real.

In the lobby, the blond woman turned to Grace. "Run," she'd yelled, then blew on a whistle, walking backward, deeper into the foyer and into the open elevator. The shrill piercing sound coaxed the white-robed warriors inside the building to her and then she set the bomb off, bringing the building down around them. Just before the door to the elevator had closed, Grace caught a glimpse of the face of a robed fighter as he took the mask off. She'd been unable to stop herself recoiling from the shock. Their faces were skin pulled tight over bones in shiny, slick masks. As though the flesh wasn't big enough to fit. Their lips were just a slash below the nostrils, and eyes were slits without lashes or eyebrows. She'd been so afraid, that she hadn't run like the woman told her to, she'd backed away frightened.

The woman's face was the last Grace had seen, and when she'd been fighting for her life under tons of rubble, Grace had committed it to memory.

In the moonlight now, her face was one and the same. Except her eyes… dark and bloodshot. Her hair was different. The facial skin appeared so smooth it was almost plastic as though brand new. Like the white-robed warriors, but not so extreme. Like the scars on Grace's arms.

The other woman crouched into an offensive pose, hands fashioned into claws aimed at Grace.

"Are you feeling okay?" Grace asked.

"Die!"

"What?" Grace barely had time to shield herself as the woman launched into the air, coming straight for her.

"No!" a deep voice bellowed. Something heavy hit the woman's side and bombarded them to the ground, skidding their bodies across the damp street.

It was Evan. She recognized flashes of his tattoos as his powerful arms struggled to pin the woman down.

"What are you doing, Sara?" he growled, shoving her. "What's the matter with you?"

Sara. That was the woman's name.

Sara snarled back at him, then slashed at Evan with something unseen. He hissed and blood oozed down his forearm to stain the cold ground in red hot, steamy blobs.

Instantly, Grace's medical training kicked in. She needed to get that wound stabilized.

Because she wasn't thinking about the imminent danger, only of his wound, she had to roll to the side, narrowly avoiding the wrestling pair as they came her way. The woman threw a punch at Evan. He took it in the stomach, doubling over, glancing worriedly in Grace's direction as he took another hit.

Why was he hesitating?

"Watch out!" Grace shrieked, pointing at the glint in Sara's hand now moving toward Evan's head.

Evan threw up an arm to protect his face, then dropped in a twisting maneuver that had his foot lashing out, knocking Sara over. Fresh blood arced across the pavement from Evan's arm, another new wound, and Grace instantly thought about his shoulder. Perhaps he'd burst his stitches too.

"Run, Doc," Evan said through clenched teeth, keeping

his gaze pinned on the wild woman beneath him. When Grace didn't move, his gaze whipped her way.

His distraction was the opportunity Sara needed to throw something at Grace, almost like a child throwing a tantrum, lashing out at the thing that took the attention away. It glinted and sliced Grace's bare shoulder. Glass clattered to the ground beside her.

Her hand clapped over stinging skin.

Sara elbowed Evan in the face, brutally knocking him to the side.

"For God's sake, run!" Evan shouted as he commando rolled back to his feet.

Grace took off, racing across the street to somewhere dark, somewhere she could hide. Her breath came hard and fast and loud in the quiet night. Next to the car? No, too open. There, in the alley. Behind the stacked crates. She ran. Heels wobbling, clicking too loudly. She kicked them off to muffle her steps. Behind her—she dared not look back— grunts and howls came from the two fighting in the street. Oh God, oh God. What if Sara won? Sara was so strong. So unnaturally strong!

Running down the alley, Grace ducked behind the crates, and pressed her body against the cold brick wall. Through the slats of the wood, she glimpsed the couple fighting.

Evan had her pinned on the ground, but Sara craned her neck upward and said something venomous to him.

An unearthly growl ripped from Evan's throat, his face contorted in fury and he put his hands around Sara's neck. But he didn't strangle her. The growl turned into a frustrated wail as though he unleashed something pent up inside. Some deep seated urge he'd held onto for too long.

Grace had no sane explanation for what she saw next. Blue lightning surged from Evan's hands into Sara with a crackling, sizzling sound that lit up the street. Sara's eyes shocked wide, and she convulsed under Evan's touch, choking and chest bowing high.

Oh God, oh God.

Grace leaned back into the safety of the shadows and squeezed her eyes shut. He's killing her. Murdering her. Breathe in. Breathe out. What the hell? Was she going mad? Was everyone going mad? Her doctor brain rationally catalogued information while her wild, beating heart kept her frozen to the wall. The woman's unnatural face. Almost as inhuman as those white-robed warriors from the bombing. Her eyes. That feral growl coming from deep in her throat, and a matching growl in Evan's. His hands. The iPad malfunction at the hospital. Scorch marks on the mattress. Sparks. It came from him. Somehow it was—

A warm, solid force clamped over Grace's lips. Her eyes snapped open, a scream bubbling on her tongue. A hard body trapped her against the wall.

"Shh. It's me. Evan."

She thrashed and bucked, but he held her firm with his body. His hair hung in stringy, wet lines down his forehead, but the shadows of the alley masked whether it was sweat, water, or blood. Then she remembered the sparks, the electricity coming from his hands. Did he kill that woman? Those hands were now on her face. They were hot. She tried to scream.

"Quiet, Grace," he hissed. "She's still out there."

She whimpered and forced the panic down, eyes wide over his fingers, unsure who was the lesser of two evils—him or Sara.

A frown flickered between his brows and he raked his gaze up and down her body.

"I'm not going to hurt you. I could never do that," he whispered. "But she shouldn't be awake, and she is. She's dangerous. Unpredictable. You need to stay quiet. Just a minute longer. Can you do that?"

Grace forced her mind to calm and practically assess the situation. His firm body pressed into hers, but it was a light pressure. He yielded slightly every time she moved or twitched, as though he were afraid to hurt her, and just held her in place. She sensed that if she really wanted, he'd let her go. He wasn't the danger. That woman out there was the murderer. In fact, he was injured. And he'd saved her.

She nodded.

Evan's hand slipped from her mouth, fingers bumping over her lips and down her chin. The light drag of his touch slid along her jaw to cup her nape with a firm grip. That touch meant everything. Control. Comfort. Protection. She relaxed further and kept her eyes locked on him. He cocked his head, ear angled back to the street, listening.

Grace could only look at him in the shadowed moonlight. It was an odd moment of closeness. His body pressed along hers. His hand warming her neck. Unafraid, he kept watch through the gaps in the crate. Determination kept his focus sharp, and his posture alert. It led Grace to believe he'd been in this sort of situation before, and he excelled in it.

There was definitely more to the tattooed, brooding man than he led people to believe.

Grace followed his gaze, straining to hear what he did.

Sara, still alive, canvased the area. Her footsteps echoed in the empty street. Her shadow moved toward their hiding place and Grace's throat constricted. Then a siren rent the silent night. Sara's silhouette dipped to collect something from the ground and then she ran, disappearing into the dark haven of the city.

They waited until the bright blue and red flashing lights heralded a series of police cars pulling up to the gallery.

Evan stepped back, eyes still focused in the direction Sara ran, then he turned to Grace. "Are you hurt?"

He tested parts of her body, checking for himself with swift, light motions.

His concern illuminated something inside of Grace, something she'd erected a long time ago; a dark wall of protection so high and thick that had surrounded her since her parents' deaths. Only now with Evan's gentle touch, was she able to see what she'd been missing out on.

"Your arm," he said, shifting it into the light.

"It's okay," Grace breathed, inspecting her wound. "Superficial. Probably why it stings so much. What about you? I saw blood. Your stitches." Her fingers lifted to his torn collar, intending to inspect his shoulder, but he flinched back.

"I'm fine."

Once again, Grace felt as though this entire situation was

her fault. But she knew wounds. She knew doctoring. Nobody would tell her otherwise. "You're cut all over, Evan. It needs to be checked out."

"Superficial."

Frustration bit at her insides.

"Sara shouldn't have recovered," he said, more to himself.

But the words reminded Grace of what he'd done. Of his hands around Sara's throat, squeezing. That electricity arcing through the air. His intention had been clear. "You tried to kill her," Grace whispered.

He frowned. "She tried to kill you first."

"But… I saw you. Your hands were around her neck." She didn't know what to think. She hated the woman. She wanted her dead. Didn't she?

"Grace. She's a bad woman. The things she's done. The lives she's ruined. She's killed so many people."

"You mean the bombing downtown two years ago."

A flicker of doubt crossed his face. "How did you know?"

"That's what I've been trying to talk to you about. I was there." Grace held up her scarred arms. "She's the one who set the bomb off two years ago. It wasn't the Deadly Seven like the media portrayed. Nobody believed me after it happened, but I've been trying to prove it for the past two years. Families of the victims are living on the streets, or struggling to feed themselves. They need compensation and the insurance company won't pay out as long as they think an act of vigilantism was to blame. So I'm trying to prove it wasn't. It was clearly some sort of arson or terrorist attack."

Wonder entered his eyes, and he looked at her as though she were a life raft and he'd been drowning. He stepped toward her, hands lifting to cup her face.

"You… saw her set off a bomb?"

"Yes, I—"

"And you're trying to prove it to help the families who lived there?"

"Yes, and—"

"Then you know how evil she is. Death would be too kind." He frowned and dropped his hands.

"Will you just let me finish?" Grace shook her head. "It's not up to us to decide who lives or dies. I… God I hate her, and I've never said that about anyone before, but she needs to be alive. Not only because it's wrong to kill, but we need her alive to confess, so that the people—those lives she ruined—can be compensated. It's worth more than some private vendetta you might have. Promise me you won't do that, don't kill her."

Evan's eyes narrowed until menace shone through. "She's pure evil."

"So will you lower yourself to her level? Look, I know I've only just met you, Evan, but I don't think you're a murderer." Not like her.

He thought about it, but said nothing, instead flicking a glance the way Sara fled.

"Evan. Promise me. Don't go after her with the intention of killing her."

"Fine. For a price."

"What?"

"A kiss." Hot lips met her mouth.

The kiss lasted an eternal, breathless second, and then he pulled away.

Too dazed to say anything, Grace nodded, belatedly giving her permission.

Still feeling the pressure of his mouth on hers, she couldn't think straight. His lips were softer than she'd thought, velvety and smooth. Salty. Wet. That tiny taste of him was divine. She wanted more.

His gaze turned dark, as though just noticing his hands on her cheeks, and his body pressed against hers. Grace felt his every muscle contract and tense.

"I'm sorry," he whispered, hands slipping away. "I shouldn't have done that."

Before she knew what she was doing, she pulled his hands back to her face. "Yes, you should have. Kiss me again."

Shock hit his eyes. Then a carnal gleam that made Grace squirm.

EVAN LAZARUS

GRACE'S WORDS echoed in Evan's ears: *Kiss me again.*

In their dark hideaway, away from the street, Evan stood dumb with his hands on the face of the beautiful woman. All he had to do was lean forward and put his lips on hers, but he was frozen to the spot, cataloguing her details in case it was all a dream and he was about to wake. If it was, he needed those details—needed them like he needed air—so he could sketch her and pin the portrait to his wall.

Her lashes were long and cast crescent shadows like wings on her cheekbones. Her freckled small nose was pink from the cold. Her square jaw made her eternally proud and confident. Her face had been dappled by the mist falling from the night sky, leaving little diamonds sparkling over her skin. But best of all, she looked up at him with eyes filled with want.

She'd just seen the real him. No layers of his alter-ego, but the pure, violent, impulsive and now, electrical him. He'd wanted to end Sara, and she'd seen the murder in his eyes, but she hadn't shied away. Instead, she saw his potential. Not a murderer, but... maybe a savior.

Kiss me again.

He pressed his lips to hers, this time slowly and with reverence.

She had no idea yet, but he wasn't going to let her go, and it had nothing to do with his body's strange biological response pushing them together, but everything to do with the way she looked at him.

His tongue darted past her lips, testing, until hers dueled with his. Sighing on a breath, her soft body sank into him, and his blood sang in response. Nerve receptors electrified. Waves of hot desire rolled through him, setting off his biological alarm that screamed. *This is your mate. Catch her, keep her.* Sweat broke out and his pores leaked pheromones. He knew it was wrong to influence her so, but for a short moment, he didn't care. He kissed harder, fingers smoothing around her face to take hold of her silky ponytail.

She responded to his passion with her own, lips, teeth and tongue fighting back. She tugged him closer by the belt, grinding into his painfully hard erection. Sparks in his body increased, building a sensation that wasn't entirely natural. He recognized the reaction barely in time to thrust away and punch the wall beside her head, grunting in agony as pent up electricity crackled through his body. Power surged from his hands and thundered into the wall, showering them in sparks and debris.

He sheltered her with his body.

Grace yelped.

Fuck!

Evan held his position over her until the last of the debris cleared, then he pulled back, agape, testing her once again for injury. He'd almost hurt her but, even though his mind knew he had to rein in the power rolling inside him, he couldn't. It was too new. His muscles contracted and released in waves, like an ocean in turmoil. *Shit*. What if he couldn't control himself around her? What if he never could?

"Grace," he grit out. It was one word, but it meant so much more. An apology. A prayer.

"Evan!" a deep voice boomed from the gallery. Parker.

Evan shoved away.

The sense of envy in the neighborhood slammed into him with staggering force.

She hugged herself with trembling arms.

Dark, envious thoughts whispered through his mind.

She's afraid of you. She'll never love you, a frightful freak of nature. Not like she could love someone else. Someone normal.

Don't go there.

Not when Sara was out there, in that dark place where nightmares became reality. He had to be strong. No matter what Grace thought of him, he had to be strong for her. For his family.

The family relied on him. Mary had been right; he was the only one left fighting for the truth to come to light. The only one fighting to restore their name. Mary said he had to choose this life, and he never wanted Grace to look at him like that again. The next time they saw each other, he wanted pride, not fear in her eyes.

Wishing to be someone else would never help him. *He* had to be better.

His hands flexed at his side, biceps pumping. A deep breath later, and he calmed himself. She hadn't run. She'd remained. A tiny kernel of hope flared in his chest.

"We need to talk," he said.

"I agree." She watched him warily.

"Not now"—he glanced at the gallery, at Parker looking for him—"Later. Tomorrow. Let's exchange numbers."

With her expectant eyes on him, he fished in his pockets and pulled out gum, a permanent marker, a folded program from the exhibition, and a rubber band. Dammit, he'd lost the broken pencil he'd kept on his ear. Out of everything that disappointed him the most. He fumbled with the items.

"Uh… I don't have a card," he said. "And my phone is inside. Here."

With a trembling grip, he unplugged the lid from the marker and poised the tip over his tattoo free wrist. He forced his words to come out steady. "What's your number?"

"I have a card." Grace stepped out from their hiding place and back into the street, in full view of the spilled gallery crowd and police. Evan followed her cautiously. For a moment, he thought he'd scared her off, but then she spoke. "My purse is around here somewhere. My phone got stolen the other day, but I have a card in there for the hospital and the clinic. Wait. I can't see it. Have you got my purse? It was right here."

Both their heads swiveled as they searched the street.

Grace slapped her forehead. "Great. Just great. She stole my purse. Not again, I've already been mugged this week."

Mugged? He would dissect the thief. Wait… "She has your purse. Was your ID in there?"

"Yes."

"*Shit.*"

Grace flinched at his anger.

"It's no big deal," she said. "Really, I'll just cancel my cards when I get home. Are you sure you're okay?"

"She has your ID, Grace. She knows where you live."

They stared at each other, letting the fact sink in.

"I'll walk you home," Evan stated.

This made her eyes widen further. "No, I'm fine. I'll manage on my own. I have my keys in my jeans pocket. Even if she did come to my place for some strange reason, she can't get in. I'm four floors up."

"Evan," Parker boomed from the gallery entrance. "Get your ass here."

Evan ignored him and opened his mouth to insist Grace let him take her home.

"Don't ignore me little brother." Parker's deep voice

oozed authority as he walked over, ensnaring Evan's attention.

Evan had no choice but to acknowledge his eldest brother.

"Parker."

"Where have you been? There's a naked dead body in the storeroom."

"I know. Sara did it."

Parker's shrewd gaze tracked somewhere behind Evan. "Who was your lady friend?"

Evan's gaze whipped back around. Grace was gone.

NINE

MARY LAZARUS

Mary stood idly by *The Painting Within*, grumbling to her husband Flint every few minutes about the incompetence of the forensic team sweeping the site. Truthfully, what annoyed her most was her lack of foresight to predict the drama. Not once in the past week had she had a new vision. She was drying up like a *vieja bruja*. Her worst nightmare becoming a reality. She always knew one day that her body would fail her, that her gift would wither and become defective. She'd only hoped to have the children prepared before it got to this point but, as it stood, the family was in turmoil.

"Tony, get your lips off that glass and go help find your brother," she growled.

He shook his head. "Nope. I'm here as Tony Lazarus. Movie stars don't give a shit."

She wanted to throttle him.

"He'll turn up," Flint said, always the voice of reason.

Stools and chairs were strewn over the room, evidence of the mass hysteria that had played out earlier. Mary was more concerned that not only was a woman dead, but Evan had disappeared suddenly. She flicked a glance to where the police interviewed the beaming Azaria. Notoriety could do wonders for the art world, she probably imagined all the publicity her gallery would receive.

Two men entered the gallery at that moment. Evan surveyed the scene, and Parker spotted them and indicated for Evan to follow him.

"It's Evan." Mary nudged Flint who'd almost fallen asleep standing up. It was getting late and he'd been in the workshop all day working with Parker on some new tech designs for suit improvements. It was all hush-hush at the moment, but they'd reveal their plans soon enough. First, there had to be a team to use the suits, but one of Mary's last visions showed the family united… all because of the doctor Evan had seen. She had hope.

"Right. Evan." Flint blinked. "Dead body in the store-room. Got it."

"What do you boys think?" Mary asked.

Evan strode up to them, eyes intense as he surveyed his family. "Obviously Sara did it. Did any of you see her?"

"Christ, Evan," Parker said as he joined his brother. "Give it up. We're trying to have a proper adult conversation here, and you're making shit up as you go."

"You call this make believe?" Evan gestured at his tattered shirt. "She attacked me in the street. Grace was there. She saw it all. In fact, she recognized Sara. Said she witnessed her at the bombing. Blowing. The. Place. Up." Evan jabbed his finger in his brother's chest, a hard jab for each word.

"Bullshit," Parker said.

"She has the scarred arms to prove it. I believe her. She was there."

Parker poked Evan back. "You're balancing on a razor's edge, brother. One more push and you're gone. I won't protect you when Wyatt gets word of this. Not again."

Evan narrowed his eyes.

The last time Evan brought this up, the fight that ensued split the family into pieces. They all used to live together in a privately owned luxury apartment complex above a restaurant Parker owned. Now Evan lived somewhere else, Tony was rarely home. Parker vacayed at his office. Sloan never left the entertainment quarters. Since that fight, it was all a mess. Mary remembered that night with a shiver. Wyatt had tried to beat the living shit out of Evan, and Parker had stood between them, negotiating peace. The result had Evan moving out, despite Mary's protests to keep the family together.

Stubborn, stubborn children. They need her visions. She couldn't be drying up now. She wasn't ready.

"What's it going to take for you to see the truth?" Evan asked Parker. "Are you so full of pride you can't admit when you've been wrong?"

"I'm never wrong." The words came out confident, but Parker hid his wrist behind his back.

"Sara cut up my arm, my chest, sliced up my girl."

Parker's eyebrow arched. "Your girl? Since when do you have a girl."

"Don't fuck with me tonight, Parks. I'm warning you. Don't push me."

"Or what?" Parker shoved him.

It was all Evan needed to explode. He released the storm brewing in his veins. Lightning, thunder and heat sparked from his hands and jolted Parker's chest. Parker flew backward, into the painting, knocking it from the wall. Tiny tendrils of smoke curled from two scorched handprints on his shirt, and his shoulder-length hair lifted with unshed static.

"Evan!" Mary cried. What the hell was that?

Everything Gloria had said from her deathbed in the lab years ago came crashing back. She'd just given birth to Evan, the last of her children. They were waiting for Flint to give the signal so Mary could spirit them all away before the guards outside noticed. Gloria had been weak, pale, and glazed eyed as she spoke to Mary.

When they meet a mate who embodies their exact opposite, their special ability will manifest.

Mary remembered being so worried about Gloria. How would she survive the escape so soon after giving birth? Looking back, she should have known her intentions to sacrifice herself. Her last words were filled with anguish and hidden meaning.

You promise me you stick with Flint and you show these children what they're looking for. You show them with every ounce of your being. They need to see what true love looks like so when they find their mate, they latch on with two hands. They save themselves. Promise me. Promise me you'll take care of them.

It was clear now that Gloria knew she wouldn't survive the escape.

It's all about balance, Mary. They will grow to be saviors, but unstable and in the wrong hands, they will bring destruction.

"He started it." Evan's voice broke through Mary's thoughts. His fists clenched and crackled at his side.

"Evan," Flint warned. "People are watching."

"I don't care. He deserved it."

"But none of you deserve to be exposed," Mary hissed with a pointed look at the people watching them. "Don't think I didn't notice, Evan. You've been keeping secrets, and we'll discuss that later."

He may tower over her, but he'd always be her youngest child. She'd raised him from birth and she expected honesty from all of them. She'd overseen his training. At some time in her youth, she had completed the training herself with all the instructors, and the ones she hadn't, she'd vetted thoroughly. Most of their savings had gone to pay for the training. The instructors were well compensated, so each had kept her in the loop. It pained Mary to see the children fighting and keeping secrets. She'd mentored them, loved them.

"Both of you stop it. Remember where you are, *who* you are."

Parker stayed on the ground, refusing to get up, eyes pointedly on Evan's crackling fists. Stubborn, stubborn boys.

Evan's guilty eyes shot to Mary and then he shoved his hands in his pockets.

Before she could continue with the stern rebuking, the insidious art dealer came running over, glaring at Evan. "What have you done? The painting is ruined."

The police officer who'd interviewed her ambled along in

her wake, taking the new commotion in his stride. He had his big jacket on and chewed on gum. It made his mustache bounce around his mouth. He kept a wary eye on Evan, but turned to Parker. "Everything all right Mr. Lazarus?"

Evan rolled his eyes, no doubt annoyed at the first attention going to his brother, not him.

Parker, still recovering from the electric shock, accepted a hand up from Tony. "Yes. Apologies for the family dispute. We've got it sorted."

"He destroyed a very expensive painting!" Azaria whined, chopping her hand in the direction of the fallen piece of artwork. Her tightly stretched face looked even more comical with the rise in eyebrows almost hitting her hairline.

"I'll pay for it," Parker said, and whipped out his credit card.

Azaria took it, glared at Evan, then huffed away.

The cop flicked his gaze up and down Evan. "I'm talking to you next. Don't go anywhere."

Evan saluted him with two fingers to his forehead. The cop's mustache twitched, then he moved away to where his partner finished interviewing some waitstaff.

"What the fuck was that?" Parker hissed under his breath.

"You know exactly what it was." Evan folded his arms, in a silent challenge. *Think you're so good, so smart? Figure it out,* his body language said.

Mary shot Parker a warning glare. *Don't rise to the bait.*

Parker's jaw worked as he ran a hand through his hair. His gaze flicked to the door. "It was the woman."

"Damn straight," Evan said. "The very woman you accused of lying, of not existing—making things up as I go, my ass. You just don't like to admit you were wrong. That someone else got there before you."

"I'm not the envious one, Evan."

"But you are blinded by pride." Evan shoved his wrist out, displaying the Yin-Yang, still equal parts black and white. "You saw what that looked like yesterday, Mary."

She didn't look at his arm, she looked into his eyes and studied. Yes, despite the turmoil in his outward appearance, there was something else inside. A confidence she'd been waiting to see for a long time. She smiled, palms lifting to either side of his face. Finally, she'd kept her promise to Gloria. Now she just had to make sure Evan didn't mess things up. "I'm so glad, Evan. You deserve a bit of happiness."

Evan's eyes narrowed on her. "You knew, didn't you? It's why you turned up at the hospital without having been called. You'd had a vision."

Mary dropped her palms with a crooked smile and an off handed shrug. He was right. The vision had come months ago. She'd seen a newspaper headline, the hospital, the woman and the lightning. "Maybe."

"Well, did you see Sara?"

Her smile disappeared.

"Don't use that tone on your mother," Flint said.

"The only Sara I saw was in your paintings. It doesn't mean she wasn't there. I'm just not the same as I used to be."

"I'm sorry," Tony said, slurring his words, a little intoxicated from all the champagne. "I'm still trying to wrap my head around this. Can we go back a few steps? Are you telling us what I think you're telling us?"

"That my second sight is failing." Mary slumped into Flint's awaiting arms.

"No, well, that sucks too, but I meant that Sara is actually alive. That we didn't kill all those people in the building collapse like the world thinks. She did," Tony added.

Silence descended.

"Wow," Tony said. "Just wow. I come out tonight hoping for a couple of nice drinks, blow off some steam before the big shoot tomorrow, and then end up with a dead body and a conspiracy theory. We'll never be rid of this life will we?"

Mary's jaw clenched. "You think those poor innocent people who died in the bombing wanted that life? Do you think that poor woman who got murdered while we were sipping on champagne and looking at paintings wanted her life to end?"

Tony paled. "No."

"Do you think I wanted visions showing me a world torn in two if you all got into the wrong hands? I'm not sure hiding is enough anymore. You all need to get off your asses and back into uniform."

Flint placed a steady hand on Mary's shoulders and she squeezed her eyes shut. She hadn't told her children about the worst of the visions. Over the past few years, she'd seen the same frightening future getting worse and worse and the reality of it terrified her. The sacrifices they'd all made to get here could be for nothing. Flint's grip squeezed gently, and she sank into him. It was the calming reassurance she needed to force her heart rate down to an acceptable level. What had she done wrong to have them running from their responsibilities? She took a deep breath and looked her children in the eyes. "I've said it once, and I'll say it again. I'll never force you to be the protectors this city needs. It has to be your decision. But you've been born with incredible gifts. You didn't choose this life, but you have it. Maybe, just maybe if you'd all listened to your calling, perhaps that woman didn't have to die."

Evan's palm rested on his mother's arm. "Whatever Sara is up to, we'll figure it out. We'll clear our names and get back to the business of saving the city. I will, anyway."

The unspoken challenge lining his words weren't missed by his brothers. Pity the rest of the family weren't there to hear it.

"Hold your horses," Parker said, lifting a hand. "If what you're saying is true—and that's a big *if*—Wyatt was going to marry an evil psycho bitch who likes murdering people. There has to be a reason behind that. Before we go telling everyone, we have to be sure. We need proof."

"My girl's word is proof enough."

"No offense, but she's not your girl yet," Tony said.

"You're right," Evan said. "We're not together. Yet. But that's beside the point. She's not a liar. So, here's what I propose. We have a family meeting so everyone is on the same page. In the mean time, I'll work on collecting evidence. Sara took Grace's purse. If she dumped it after she got what she needed, it could be around the area. All we need are her fingerprints, and that will be enough to prove to you all she's alive. Flint, can you please work with Sloan to see if there are any cameras in the area? Some might have caught Sara as she fled."

His father nodded grimly. "I'll get Sloan to help. God knows she needs time away from her console. She's been morose ever since she missed the first meet up with her online friend."

A little ache flared in Mary's chest as she remembered the best friend her daughter had never met. They'd planned to meet in real life, then they'd received the call out about the white-robed menaces damaging property downtown. Of course, it ended in the building collapse, Sara's death and the team being devastated. When the papers came out the next day, and the public blamed the Deadly Seven. Sloan never made that meeting with her friend, and he'd stopped engaging online.

Evan's fists clenched.

Mary couldn't be prouder of him. Parker looked her way, and knew it, too.

"I'm going out patrolling tonight," Evan said and met the eyes of his brothers. "Are you two coming?"

Parker lifted a brow. "After what you just did to me? I'll investigate this on my own."

He kissed Mary on the cheek, and patted Flint on the shoulder, then left.

Evan turned to Tony.

"I have to be on set at five tomorrow. Sorry, bro." Then Tony left too.

Evan looked at his parents. "I'm doing this on my own, aren't I?"

"Parker said he'd investigate," Flint said. "You know he will. We'll help anyway we can."

"I'll see you tomorrow for training," Mary added. "Those new skills need honing. We should really get you into the lab for testing. We'll work on your brothers and sisters. Don't worry. And Evan—"

"Yes?"

"—your work is perfection. Always so many layers to the art. Every time I look at them, I see something new."

"Well done, son." Flint patted Evan on the shoulder.

Mary took her husband's warm, large hand and left the gallery, casting a last glance over her shoulder as she left, trying to ignore the scowl in Evan's eyes as he glared at the ruined painting.

TEN

SARA MADDEN

Cardinal City was basically an island shaped like a bird, with only the tip of its tail connecting to the mainland. At its crown, you found the docks and markets. Its beak, Chinatown. The business and municipal districts were at the neck, and along the east coast, up high on the bird's back, lived the city's rich and elite on the rocky mountain cliffs overlooking Menagerie River. At the center of the bird's body you found the city's heart—four districts where people went to be entertained, fed, clothed and housed. Known as The Quadrant, the area pumped life into the waning city, but below its border was where the city's scum went to live and die, the cesspit of criminal activity, and the epicenter of sin.

None of it really mattered to Sara. She was but a blip of breath in the city's current life-cycle. She'd died in a blink, and after a few articles in the paper, she was a distant memory. You were born alone, and you died alone. Everything else in between was just trying not to be alone.

That's why she'd been surprised to see the exhibition

flyer with her face painted all over it. She had to go and see, no matter the risk. At least she'd made her trip worth it, and the boss would be proud.

The Quadrant was where Sara stumbled after her altercation. He'd fried her brain, and short-circuited her wires, but her new biology worked furiously to save her, and it had. For now.

At the lower end of the Quadrant, bordering on the highway that separated the haves from the have-nots, was the tallest southern building which appeared to be filled with office space. The offices could be real, and housed by authentic workers going about their day-to-day life, or they could be fake—each floor made of dummy corporations and actors hired to drink their double decaf soy lattes and laugh at their friend's jokes by the water coolers. She wouldn't put it past the Syndicate. Their influence reached far, and their resources came from bottomless pockets.

Most workers were gone by the time she slipped through the glass rotating doors into the lobby. The security guard at the front desk barely lifted his heavy gaze from his mini television as she went past, careful to hide the blood still covering her shirt. There was no doubt in her mind the guard's nonchalant demeanor was simply a cover to hide a lethal expertize. It was all part of the ruse. Make the building appear harmless, no one important in here at all, but if they somehow got to the top, past the biometric scanner in the elevator, then they wouldn't like what they found. No one in this building was who they seemed.

When the elevator doors opened, she stepped quietly into the maroon carpeted hallway.

"You're late."

She jolted as the monotone voice slid through her mind, almost sexless in its timbre. Whirling around, she faced the source—a nightmare dressed in white. Ribbed leather pants and steel capped boots made for kicking. A unisex reinforced jacket no doubt filled with concealed weapons. A white mask in the shape of a falcon covered the top half of a face. Platinum silver hair draped down shoulders to mid back. The only flesh exposed was a pale dainty chin, pink lips and a tiny nose hidden under the bird's hooked beak. Two deep violet eyes framed with thick lashes blinked back at her. The soft features in the nightmare's stature caused Sara to believe she was female. She couldn't be certain, though, because the brutal and emotionless way Falcon dealt with insurgents, made her something else all together.

And Sara loathed to discover the truth.

"Where have you been?" Falcon said. It was a name Sara had invented, but a name most other Faithful had come to adopt behind the woman's back. As far as Sara knew, the woman had no name, and was simply addressed as "my darling" by the boss.

"Out," Sara replied vaguely.

"You have not been cleared for extracurricular activities, replicate."

Sara jut out her chin. "I am a Faithful of the inner circle. I have information the boss will find invaluable. If you can't trust me to my own volition, then I don't know why you gave me access to this level."

Those unnerving eyes blinked at her, and then she lifted

a white gloved hand and crooked a creaky finger. "He's waiting."

Down the hall they went, and through another guarded door to enter into an enormous open space with windows overlooking the entire city—north to the Quadrant, and south to… well, the shit end of the bird.

The boss liked to see out, but for no one to see in, so the room was kept dark, with most light coming from dim lamps near the center couches, and the city's neon lights refracting from beyond the double paned glass. Nothing else was in the room but an enormous mahogany desk facing the south-side, couches in the middle, and empty space facing north.

There he was, staring at the Quadrant's central park, thirty levels below. A dark, tall silhouette, with his hands behind his back, he could almost be a statue.

Sara hesitated and looked at Falcon, but she had already taken a position near the stainless steel elevator doors and stared ahead with no emotion. When not even a twitch of the lip was given, Sara continued toward the boss and stood next to him, silent, just like he.

They stared at the city until Sara's jack-rabbiting heart steadied to a rhythmic thud-thud. During this time, Sara's thoughts derailed from panic to confidence and then back again. Why wasn't he speaking? He obviously knew about her extracurricular activity. He must know. Falcon knew. Why wasn't he talking?

Probably because he was okay with it.

Was he?

She stared down, down, into the dark night and zoned in

on the darkest rectangle at ground level—the tips of trees and a black lake spread out in a warped kidney shape. Only a soft twinkle of light from the park lamps glowed there. It looked peaceful.

"What do you call this new style of architecture they've brought to the buildings here, Sara?" The boss's voice was deep, thick and smooth. The kind of voice that cut through with a sense of efficient purpose. He never wasted or minced words. He was the kind of man who people listened to, because he only spoke when there was something important to say.

Sara looked up at him. The harsh city lights turned his usual soft, handsome features into sharp, villainous angles. When she met him, she'd supposed he was in his forties, but that was years ago. He'd told her a story about the Lazarus children once, and it sounded as though he was a grown man at the time of their birth. If that was true, he should look older than he did. Perhaps the same technology used to bring her back to life kept him young. Whatever the case, he was older than he appeared.

Remembering his question, Sara glanced back at the city and took in the buildings. A few towers and sky-scrapers surrounded the Quadrant, but not many. Most high-rises were in the financial district toward the head of the Cardinal City bird. Here, most were lower level buildings ranging from Victorian era architecture to something older, but most had received new facades that gleamed with aluminum, copper, and neon blue lights.

She shrugged. "I don't know. Neo-Gothic? New Gothic?" She wasn't an architect, what the hell did she know?

"I call it a sham."

She held her tongue. There was a story coming, and she knew better than to interrupt.

"Beneath that shiny exterior," he continued, voice as smooth as butter. "The old decayed building is still there. They've done nought but slap on a flimsy mask to cover a broken, decrepit truth. It's like using cosmetic surgery to fix bone cancer. No matter how nice the exterior looks, its structure is dying." He walked away from the Quadrant side, and toward his desk facing the south-side. "You see, this is why I face my desk south. At least here they are honest about their demise. Hiding behind a lie is not a long term solution. If you can't cut the cancer out, it's better we put them out of their misery."

Sara followed him, but stopped to stand beside his desk as he caressed the top of the single photo-frame facing him. A picture of a brown-skinned woman and a little girl smiled back at him. The young girl had brown hair and big brown eyes that made Sara think of a sad puppy dog.

"That view is a reminder of what will happen if we fail," he added softly. Although his eyes never left the frame, Sara knew the view he spoke of was out the window. When he met Sara's eyes, something hard and unforgiving stared back. "It's why you live down there, and not in the lap of luxury."

A flush came over Sara. "I know. To be closer to the sinners. To execute them whenever an opportunity presents itself."

"So why did you go to the exhibition"—he waved his hand slowly to the north—"all the way over there."

A lump formed in her throat.

"Because…" Because she wanted to see that family one last time. Because when her face was the center of the exhibition, a little voice inside her was curious about being a memory.

"Don't tell me you're missing them?" he chided. "Ruining their reputation was the only way to split the Lazarus family. To pit them against each other and ensure they gave up their crusade to save the city. We want them desperate, full of despair and ready to become their sin incarnate. They escaped us once, and I had a lot of explaining to do to our investors. This is our chance to get them back and on our side."

"I don't miss them. I was curious that's all. I thought with the situation regarding the replicates that gathering more samples would benefit us. If you gave me more time, I can get more."

"Time is what we do not have. Our replicates are expiring. *You're* expiring. There is nothing else we can glean from the Lazarus family and without that missing piece of the genetic puzzle, your cells will reproduce until you age rapidly and die at the tender age of three months. I've told you, we're working on it. In the mean time, you were supposed to be using your new life to maximize the sinners eradicated from the city. If you cannot follow orders and fulfill your end of the bargain, I will find another who will."

Sara lifted her chin. "I gave my life to the Syndicate, literally. I let myself get blown up. Don't tell me I haven't fulfilled my end of the bargain."

A shiver racked her body at the memory of her death.

She wasn't supposed to remember. They said she'd be reborn without the pain of knowing, without the deadly poison that withered her old heart thrumming through her veins, but it had been all saccharine, empty promises. The toxic accident that caused her past life's slow death was still fighting to re-emerge, and she remembered it all. Every detail of the bomb fragments ripping into her flesh, embedding in her skin, tearing her apart. The walls crushing her leftover body. She remembered the moment her heart stopped beating, and she remembered the regret.

A good man had loved her once.

Despite the elation of being Wyatt's bride-to-be, she knew she'd never truly be welcomed as their own, and that knowledge had eaten her up inside. Driven her to do the unthinkable—collect biological samples of her loved one behind his back, and hand them to the enemy. All so they could turn her into one of them. A copy. A clone. But better. An improved replicate.

The Deadly Seven were created to rid the world of sin, but when Mary Lazarus stole them from the lab and softened their minds, they didn't kill. They prevented. They didn't have the guts to eliminate. But Sara did, and that was the end goal for her and all the other replicates. To turn them into deadly warriors who could sense sinners just by being near them. Warriors who could kill without discovery. The silent death the world needed to bring it back into balance. She would be a goddess among men… immortal, powerful, omnipotent. If only the new scientists could get the process right.

They *needed* the blood of the seven to work out the

missing parts of the deadly genome sequence the original scientist had hidden under layers of false DNA. She was right to go to the exhibition, despite what he said. The answer had to be in their blood. It had to be, else she was doomed to live and die, over and over again, never fully getting rid of the toxins still disintegrating her heart.

"Do you have anything else to say for yourself?" the boss said.

"You mentioned once that the original scientist lied to you about the seven being imbued with special mutated abilities. It wasn't a lie. The youngest has developed powers," she said. "He's evolved."

"No," the boss whispered, incredulous. "It can't be."

"He electrocuted me with his hands. I was lucky to escape with my life."

The boss's gaze swung to Falcon's, and they shared an unspoken revelation. She stepped off her perch near the elevator and stalked toward Sara.

Sara's mouth went dry. Was this it? The end of her life?

Would they be satisfied with the tiny nugget of information she'd garnered during her battle with Evan?

Sara flinched when Falcon placed claws on her white, bloody waitress shirt. The enforcer ripped it open to expose Sara's chest. Buttons scattered across the floor. Red scorch marks in the shape of hands were imprinted down her neck and body. Evidence she'd spoken the truth. The lady looked to her master, waiting for instruction.

He stepped forward. "Explain."

"I-I…"

"Speak up, woman."

"I think it has something to do with the girl he protected. The doctor."

"Go on."

"She—" Sara licked her lips, took a deep breath and then stopped herself. If she was wrong about this, it would be her end. But if she was right—her shriveled heart clenched—if she was right, it would be their end. Sara remembered hearing tales around the Lazarus family dinner table, always after one of Wyatt's magnificent feasts. Mary told of a fabled mythical mate who would save them from their sin. They'd all laughed and scoffed, but secretly, they'd wanted it. Who wouldn't? But maybe it really was a lie. If Sara got it wrong, the boss would skin her alive.

"Sara. You were saying?"

"She's a doctor who treated him at the hospital. Perhaps she did something to him there that triggered his ability."

"So… Gloria lied to me. All those years ago she said their special abilities failed to manifest. I believed her."

Silence expanded in the room. Sara dared not draw her gaping shirt closed. Falcon stood beside Sara, a soldier waiting for the signal.

Then the boss whirled to face them and grinned, flashing his perfect white teeth. To anyone else, he could have been a charming aristocrat. A charismatic politician who wanted the best for humanity—to eradicate crime and to save the innocent. But to Sara that grin belonged to the devil.

And she'd sold her soul to him.

He started to laugh. A sly chuckle at first that grew to a loud boom shaking his entire body.

"He's developed powers," he kept repeating, shaking his

head, tears running down his cheeks. He took Falcon's shoulders and shook her. "He's got powers!"

Sara dared a glance at the enforcer. She too had a small smile lifting her lips which was unheard of. Falcon never smiled. Was this a good thing? Did she do good? Sara allowed herself a moment of elation.

"You know what this means, my darling," the boss said.

"Yes," Falcon replied. "His DNA is unlocked."

"We need him here, where we can study him."

"The doctor will be a problem."

The boss stalked toward Sara. He forced her face up with a finger under the chin. "You want this life, Sara?"

"Yes." The word trembled from her mouth. With every ounce of her being. She wanted to live. To be remembered.

His eyes dropped to Sara's mouth. "I don't think you do."

"I do."

"Then show me. Show me how bad you want it."

His finger trailed down her chin to her neck and collarbone. He flicked one side of her draped shirt to the side to view her exposed bra and scorched neck where he stared. It was all Sara could do to hold back the cringe.

His gaze lingered, but she kept hers straight on, locked on the shadows ahead.

What did he mean? Show him. Panic began to well. It was one thing to seduce Wyatt for information. Who wouldn't love bedding a sexy, lethal and loyal man who could actually cook. This man standing before her was something else entirely. Sara wasn't even sure if he was human.

Plastic, cold, calculated and dark inside. The boss let her shirt go, and the flap covered her chest.

He went toward his desk, speaking over his shoulder. "How will you bring him to us, Sara?"

Sara exhaled. "I would get rid of the doctor. She's seen my face and her death would destroy him. Failing that, I go back to the divide-and-conquer strategy. Then when he's weak, we take him."

"But you won't fail, will you Sara."

She shook her head.

"Good," the boss said, sitting in his chair and steepling his fingers. "Perhaps we try this another way. Perhaps it's time to take you out of the squalor, but first, my darling, show Sara what happens to replicates who disobey me."

He swiveled his chair to stare out at the south-side, ignoring Falcon's reflection in the window as she came up behind Sara, hand brandishing a glinting dagger. Sara closed her eyes and prayed the lesson would be quick.

ELEVEN

EVAN LAZARUS

The Lazarus House building had been designed to facilitate their secret mission to protect the innocent. Secret basement sub-levels dedicated to a workout area, research lab, medical, and tech workshop including tactical communications support and reconnaissance. Flint built tech in the workshop, and being an ex-assassin for the Hildegard Sisterhood, Mary spent her time honing and shaping the battle skills of any Lazarus stupid enough to enter the workout room.

The street level was split into two public establishments separated by a lobby. As you waited for an elevator, you'd see patrons eating at the restaurant called Heaven on one side. In the evening, you'd see on the other side, a nightclub called Hell. Currently being refurbished, the club was due to open in a matter of months. When designing the central city building, Parker had the idea to hide them in plain sight. So when the Lazarus family arrived and departed at strange hours of the night, it was easy to get lost in the crowd. It also explained why they had an excessive security system—surveillance cameras were everywhere.

But Evan wasn't headed down, he was headed up, toward the living quarters, namely the communal apartment reserved for family entertainment and eating. Sloan never left the gaming room. It was the room he waltzed into now, almost gagging at the stale smell. Empty soda cans and packets of chips littered the floor in a trail leading to a room where the flicker of a soft light glowed, and the *tick, tick, tick* sound of controller buttons being savaged were heard. Evan kicked trash out of the way and went to stand at the open doorway.

His sister sat on a sectional sofa with her back to him watching the big screen in front of her. The cat's ears on her gamer headset glowed blue. Her long, dark pig-tails looked ratty and unwashed. No doubt if he walked around the couch, he'd find her dressed in only underwear and socks. The socks kept her warm, apparently.

"Camping. He's a fuckin' bush camper!" she shouted at the screen. "Die, motherfucker."

Sloan paused, and glanced at him, covered the headset mic and said, "Envy." Then she went back to her game, dodging bullets and winning her Battle Royale.

When seeing each other in combat gear, it was a rule to address them as their alter-ego. Envy instead of Evan. She'd covered the mic, but still… if she was live streaming.

Oh shit, she wasn't live streaming, was she?

Better safe than sorry. Live streaming video went world-wide on the internet. He activated the voice modifier attached to his molar.

Parker may be a proud son-of-a-bitch, but he was a genius with the tech, just like Flint. Between the two of them and Sloan, when she deigned to help, they'd created a multitude of life saving inventions available to use, including the inbuilt molar voice modifier cap.

"I need you to find someone," he said, voice low and gravelly, careful to remain out of the view of the screen in case Sloan's TV cam was on.

"Sloan," Evan said again, but it was like talking to a brick wall. "Please."

When she ignored him again, he strode around the couch and hit the off button on her console, shutting the game and screen down. Then he glared at her and tugged his hood and scarf down.

She slammed down her remote. "I was in the middle of a battle. Do you have any idea what you cost me?"

"I need your help." He let electricity spark between his naked fingers, bringing a new kind of glow to the room. He hovered his hand over her gaming console in warning and raised an eyebrow.

Sloan stood, game suddenly forgotten, eyes glued to his sparking fingers. Evan was right about her attire, but hadn't been prepared for the change in her appearance. Pink and white cosplay socks with a yellow crescent moon tugged up her legs to mid-thigh. Her black singlet—sans bra, and something a brother really shouldn't see—rode up her soft belly, revealing she hadn't worked out in months. She'd put on weight since he'd last seen her. Hard muscle had turned to soft flesh, and he knew she'd spent most of her time on the couch. Slowly, she pulled her kitten headset off.

"What the hell is that?" she said, awe filtering into her voice.

"I've leveled up," he answered in a language she'd understand.

"No way." She stumbled in her haste to get to him, got tangled in the cord of her controller and fell to the floor. Cursing, she rolled, and began plucking the cord from her legs.

Evan let the sparks dissipate and offered her a hand.

She took it and he lifted her to her feet.

"Oh-em-gee, bo-*oy*. When did that happen? Is that from the mating bond? Have you met someone? Like a lady someone?"

"Didn't Flint speak with you?"

"Um." Her blue eyes locked to the side as she remembered. "Something about Sara?"

"I need an address for the woman I bumped into outside my exhibition."

"Oh, shit. That was tonight? What time is it?"

"It's eleven o'clock. And, yes, that was tonight."

"Sorry, little bras, guess I got distracted." She scratched her head.

"Sara stole her purse, including her ID. Considering Sara also murdered someone at the exhibition, I need to make sure Grace got home safe. Grace Go. She's a doctor at Cardinal City General. Also works in the free clinic."

"Hold up. Sara. As in *Sara*, Sara?"

It took Evan every ounce of restraint to stop from reaching over and smacking his sister in the head. She wasn't dumb, by any shot. She knew how to hack into any computer system or website on the planet. But she funneled that energy into the idiot box instead.

"Can you please just find her address?"

"Okay okay. Don't have a conniption. I get it." She gave him a knowing look. "Chicks dig a guy in costume."

She pulled her laptop out from between two cushions, opened it and rested it on her legs. She typed away at some horrible black screen with incomprehensible green gibberish, chuckling to herself under her breath. "I'll bet you've already hit that, right? Is that why you got new skills now, bras? Like electrical skills. I wonder what I'll get. I hope I don't have to screw a noob because I really can't be bothered with that. He'd better like playing Fortnite. Ooh, but maybe I'll get something dope like flying, or maybe some—"

"You need to get off your ass and meet someone first, Sloan. You won't find them in a computer game."

She grimaced and Evan knew she thought of the one who got away. The one who'd been ignoring her for the past few years. About the same time her ass had been stuck to that couch.

"Sorry," he said. "That was uncalled for."

Sloan shrugged. "It's okay. You're right. My pity party has gone on long enough."

Silence expanded as she continued her digital onslaught.

"So, can you find her address?" he asked, impatient.

She snorted through her nose and shook her head in mock disbelief. "Can I find her address. For your information: I can find her home; I can find her family tree; I can find out what she ate for breakfast."

"Home address will be fine."

She clicked a few more directives into the computer and a photographic database popped up. After a few more frantic commands, she stopped at the face of a woman who made Evan's heart stop. Grace.

Sloan wolf-whistled. "Boom! Dr. Grace Go, at your service. Sounds like a porn star name, and wow. You sure can pick 'em, bras. She's a babe with alpha level smarts." She clicked a few more keys and peered at the screen. "Graduated top of her class. Was up for a fellowship, but turned it down recently after... oh shit, bras. She was in the building collapse. Look." Sloan pointed to the screen. "See. Here is more about her career. After she recovered, she turned down the cardiothoracic fellowship so she could work at the local clinic. Who does that?"

Warmth flared in Evan's chest. "She wants to look after the people who need her the most. That her address?"

"Yep. But I'll do you one better." A few more clicks, then, "Voila. The building blueprints."

"Thanks Sloanie. I owe you one."

"Blueberry Protein Shake."

"What?"

"What she had for breakfast." Sloan winked at him. "You know, in case you ever need to make it for her. In the morning. Get it?"

Evan ditched a pillow at her head.

TWELVE

EVAN LAZARUS

The rain stayed away, so Evan traveled the city via rooftop. Sometimes he utilized the grappling hook and retractable tensile rope kept at his belt, but most of the time the buildings were so close together, all he needed to do was run, jump and leap.

Nearing midnight, he landed on the top of the rundown five-level-apartment complex that Grace called home. Not exactly where he imagined a doctor would live. Hell, not somewhere he imagined anyone would live.

He slipped off the roof soundlessly to land on the fire escape's metal platform and then skirted down the rails to Grace's level. According to the blueprints it had been level three, apartment second from the right. When he got to his target, his gut clenched at the sight of her window open a crack. The icy breeze gently billowed the white curtains inside. It was cold enough to freeze his nuts off. Why would her window be open? Against all his urges to rush inside, he forced himself to wait and gather more intel, starting with envy. He cast his awareness inside to search for intruders. Nothing. No sounds. No lights. No sense of envy. Could be a good sign. Could be bad.

He wasn't in the habit of breaking and entering on a whim, but he had to know. Had to be sure. If the window was open, Sara could have already been inside. He'd never forgive himself if he was too late. He placed his palm under the window frame and lifted. Immediately his tattoo itched like a motherfucker and he paused, holding his breath, heart skipping. That itch meant she was here. He was in the right place.

From inside, a soft sigh drew his attention.

Still perched on the fire-escape, he pulled the drapes to the side. Five feet away, Grace lay on a bed, pale skin gleaming in the moonlight, one naked leg artfully tangled in her sheet. Long lithe arms hugged a pillow lengthwise. A gust of cold air blew past Evan and ruffled her hair. She rolled into her bedding, hugging it tighter, exposing the soft curve of her round ass. Lace underwear. Hell.

His mouth felt like sandpaper.

Something primal stirred deep within him and, unable to stop himself, he stepped into her room, quiet like a breath.

Sparsely decorated, the room consisted of a bed, a dresser with family photos, and clothes strewn on the floor. His lips curved in a grin. His girl was messy. He liked. It meant that despite her no-nonsense doctor's demeanor; she wasn't immune to fits of passion. What wouldn't he give to explore that right now.

Another sigh had him glancing back to the bed. Grace gripped her pillow tight, a small crease now between her brow, gooseflesh across her arms. God, he wanted to be that pillow, to be pressed up to her breasts, to be embraced as though her life depended on it.

One step. That was all it took for him to be enthralled. His body reacted with a sudden fierceness that consumed him. Heat suffused his pores in a chemical reaction. Wanting more, he closed his eyes and tugged his face-mask down until it pooled around his neck. The scent of her freshly washed skin became his world. Lavender and soap and future wet dreams.

She breathed again, this time in a huff, sounding upset as she slept. He opened his eyes to see she'd rolled onto her back, taut nipples stretching to reach him through the white cotton of her lace trimmed singlet. All of it created a growing hunger that gave way to raw lust. He needed to be with her, to touch her, taste her. It was all he could think of. His body ached for her, fingers twitching at the thought of meeting her silky skin, as though an addict within reach of his vice.

Just one kiss. One touch. He stepped closer—

What are you doing?

—then stepped back, suddenly hyper aware of his situation. Uninvited, in a woman's room at night... dressed as Envy. The last time they were together, she'd run from him. Feared him. Kissed him...

Still, it was wrong, so wrong of him to be there, but being near her did things to his body and mind.

Slowly, embarrassed, he stepped back. He shouldn't be there.

Jesus Christ.

He rapped his forehead with the heel of his palm and

tried to force the heat inside to cool. He couldn't trust himself like this. His body was on fire, his thoughts weren't his own. He wanted to rip her clothes off and to take her like some sort of heathen animal.

Quivering hands lifted in front of his face. They didn't deserve to touch the woman in front of him. They'd sinned too much already, taken too much.

Maybe this was it, the end. His undoing. It was falling under the influence of his sin because he was envious of the nightgown Grace wore. Envious of the air she breathed, and of the room she was in.

It was better he kept an eye on her from a distance. Like across the road sort of distance.

Evan lifted the scarf back over his mouth and nose, then left the room to check the rest of the house. First, he had to make sure the doors were locked, after all, she'd left the window open.

The rest of the apartment was similar to her room: messy. Not dirty, just untidy. In the kitchen, Post-it notes covered the fridge. Each had a different affirmation on. He plucked one and read it. *Be kind, for everyone is fighting a hard battle.* He put the note back then, on a whim, found the blank pad and wrote a note of his own. *Keep smiling, beautiful.* He doodled around the words, then stuck the note in the middle of her bench, slot the pen behind his ear, and continued searching the small apartment.

He found more photo frames in the living room and picked up one to find Grace with two older people. An Asian man and a white woman, most likely her parents. He put the frame down and moved to the dining table, strewn with newspapers and article clippings and Post-it notes.

He shifted one out of the way and a headline caught his attention.

Victims of the Cardinal Bombing. The article listed the names and photos of people who'd died in the building collapse. Scanning down the list, his gaze snagged on a surname and his heart stopped. It was the same couple he'd seen in the photo with her. Her parents.

Resolve hardened in his bones, solidifying the wrongness of him being there. Time to go. And then, he'd make Sara pay. Make her rue the day she messed with Grace's family.

Evan put the paper down and checked the locks on the front door. Double bolted, but no good if she kept sleeping with her window open. He went back to her room, took one last look at her, and then slipped through the open window. His boot barely hit the metal landing when a gasp sounded behind him. He whirled to find Grace scrambling out of her bed, coming toward him.

Shit. Fuck.

He backed up, eyes wide, hands fumbling for purchase, ready to launch off the platform. He leaped onto the railing, balanced and poised.

"Wait!" she shouted, and he froze.

Her presence burned along his back.

Don't do it, Evan. Don't turn around. Go. Go now.

Instead, he turned his head a fraction until he caught the blurred shape of her body at the window. Try as he might, he couldn't leave. Not when every cell in his body cried out to join her.

"Just making sure you got home safe," he said, without facing her. It was a stupid thing to say because despite his voice modifier, she'd know it was him. Who else would say that? Maybe he wanted that anyway, otherwise why else would he leave her a note. His muscles locked rigid, knuckles white on the railing, waiting.

She didn't answer. Not a sound.

Finally he couldn't stand it any longer. He twisted and their eyes locked. Damned if he didn't want to pull his hood down, cast his gear off and push her back inside to her bed because she smiled at him and it was the most beautiful sight he'd ever seen. The neon street lights mixed with the moonlight to give her skin a soft glow. If he could capture the moment on canvas, he'd title it: *Sunshine of My Life* because that's what it felt like—a ray of sun pointed his way, shining just for him.

"Thank you," she said.

"You should keep your window closed. It's not safe."

Those words earned Evan a laugh, turning the sunshine into a fireworks finale, and then she shut the window, letting the drapes fall to hide his view.

She'd smiled.

At *him*.

He wanted to float off the railing, but instead, he almost fell from the platform. At least one thing was for sure, if this was his undoing, she'd be right there with him.

LATER THAT NIGHT, eager to relinquish the adrenaline and pent up frustration pumping in his veins, Evan roof-hopped, searching for deadly levels of envy. The sense clawed his gut the longer he exposed himself to its substance. The more he searched, the closer he got. A spike in envy coming from the south had Evan running and jumping over parapets and beams, desperate to hone in on the source.

He leaped over a building's edge, sailed through the air and hit the flat rooftop on the other side with the force of a Mac truck, shaking the concrete underneath. Micro fissures spider-webbed from the points of impact and shock vibrated up his legs, wrangling his sensors into a stupor until adrenaline kicked in and he was off again, racing. The heat of his breath pushed at the cloth covering his mouth. He pumped his arms at his side, hurtling his body over gutters and drainpipes, awnings and annexes, letting his senses guide him to the strongest of sin. The unmistakable direction tugged unpleasantly in his gut and he was just about ready to do anything to get rid of it. It didn't take long until he found himself in the mid-town area, below the freeway line that split the Quadrant from the lower class.

There.

Down there.

Footsteps slapped in the dark night below him. The buildings were smaller here, flatter, and easier to travel across. The sinner was quick, but not as fast as Evan. For the next five minutes, he stuck to the anonymous shape like glue, as though an afterthought, never far behind. Every time the shadow jumped, so did he. Every time he splashed down another Cardinal City street, Evan leaped to another rooftop, parkour style. Watching, waiting for the sinner to be alone, to take a wrong turn.

And now he had.

Slowly, like a shadow, Evan shimmied down a drainpipe and dropped silently to the street below, right behind the criminal. The minute his boots touched the asphalt, he felt the sensation of envy spike. There was more sin down here, so much the hunger rolled inside him to the point of pain. The sinner he chased was only the beginning.

His target turned down another dark alley diverting from the main street. Evan sidled up to the corner building, flattened himself, and peeked around. He caught a glimpse of a few gang members warming their hands around a drum filled with fire. A stiff gust of wind blew down the alley, lifting newspapers and cardboard discarded from a Dumpster. When Evan's eyes tracked the trajectory of the trash, he discovered two boots poking out from the mess on the floor. When the wind hit Evan, he caught the scent of decaying flesh. Dead body.

A spool of anxiety unfurled in his stomach. If the team were together, they'd have someone on comms in his ear, ready for news of this kind, and ready to notify authorities. The body would have to stay there until Evan got back to his apartment, and he could call in an anonymous tip.

He cast his awareness beyond the drum of fire to where envy was strongest. There was something off about that sense of sin, so he crept forward, careful to stay to the slick shadows and remain unseen.

Over the murmurs of gang members, a small voice raised in protest. "I saw it first. It's mine."

"Kid, everything is mine here," a gruff, older voice replied.

The gang members laughed and went back to their barrel of fire.

Then scuffles. And a muffled thud.

The sense of envy peaked so high that Evan knew this man would do anything—even kill an innocent kid—for whatever he had in his hands.

Anger surged in Evan's veins and he slid his twin Katanas free, counting the gang members as he went. One, two, three, four. Potentially all with weapons. Best to draw them away from the child. He whistled and then ducked behind an alcove wall, waiting as the sin-signatures came closer with the men.

This could get bloody.

The instant he thought it, he knew it didn't have to. He had a new weapon—electricity.

He sheathed the swords and amped up his voltage, building the pressure until it crackled and sparked at his fingers. One of the gang members cried out as they spotted the sparks lighting up his hiding spot. The second a head popped around his alcove, Evan struck out with his fist, letting loose a current of electricity at the same time. The smell of ozone filled the air with a sizzle and pop, and then the man dropped, crispy and fried, but still alive.

Evan tested him with his boot. He rolled to his side, moaning, but incapacitated.

Excellent.

Next.

Evan launched forward to meet the next guy coming at

him, and the next. By the time he got to the fourth man… he took one look at the crackling power in Evan's fists and fled. Evan could still see a snapshot of the man's surprised face in the blue light of Evan's power.

He did all of this without being noticed by the two on the other side of the flaming drum, but he didn't waste time in running over.

I know that kid, was Evan's first thought, swiftly followed by, *I recognize that purse.*

"I found it. It's mine," a small boy cried, wide eyes darting to the sides, looking for escape. He had the same oversized Yankees shirt, same dirty jeans, and the same holes in his sneakers.

The big thug raised his fingerless gloved fist. "I'm warning you. Hand it over."

The brazen boy shook his beanie-covered head and was rewarded with a box to the ears.

"Hey, kid," Evan said, voice modified and deep. "This thug causing you grief?"

The meathead's fist paused mid-air for another strike. The kid flinched. Both looked at Evan.

He sauntered forward, casting his own body into the light.

"What the fuck are you supposed to be?" growled the thug, never loosening his grip on the purse.

"Serious?" Evan cocked his head. Hell, if the public had forgotten what the Deadly Seven looked like, it wasn't good. No wonder an idiot like this threatened a child. He growled. "You left yourself wide open with that one, bud. I'm your worst nightmare."

Before the thug's jaw twitched in response, Evan closed the gap and connected his fist to the man's throat. Hard. The thug's head snapped back and he let go of the purse, choking and falling to the floor. Evan didn't use electricity. Somehow, he wanted to make this last. The man tried to get up, and Evan popped him again. This time he stayed down. Disappointing.

The kid bolted.

Evan released a throwing star his way. It pierced the purse straps and shot forward to embed in the alley wall, pinning the purse to the brown brick. The kid gasped, and then turned with his hands up, squeezing his eyes shut. "I'm sorry Mr. Deadly sir. I'm sorry."

"I'm not going to hurt you, kid. You remember me?"

He nodded, but had shrewd eyes. "Your voice is different."

"It's a disguise. Consider yourself lucky to have heard and seen the real me."

This made the kid beam.

"Okay," he continued. "So we never got a chance to introduce ourselves properly the other morning. I'm Envy. What's your name?"

"Taco," he said, bottom lip trembling, dropping his hands.

"Why are you out so late, and why are you stealing purses?"

"I didn't steal it. I found it, and … it belongs to someone I know."

Evan tugged the purse free from the throwing star and

inspected the contents. It was as he'd expected. Grace's ID had been removed.

"Where did you find this, Taco?"

"Just a little north of the line." The boy pointed in the direction of the Quadrant, and the gallery where his exhibition was held.

The line was the freeway that split the Quadrant and the South-Side. Some called it the poverty line because, as the further you got from it, the worse the state of living. The mid-town apartments, where they currently were, morphed into rickety buildings and slums further south of the line.

"How do you know who it belongs to? There's no ID." Evan turned the purse over in his hands.

"I seen her use it before."

"I'll take it back to her," Evan offered.

"But…" The boy sniffed and wiped his nose with the back of his fingerless gloves.

While the fire crackled behind them, warming his back, Evan focused on Taco. His face was gaunt with dark hollows under his eyes. The kid was clearly run down, sick, or suffering from malnutrition. Without another word, Evan fished into the purse and retrieved the cash. He handed it to the boy.

"Take it," he said.

"But… it's stealing."

"No it's not. I'll pay her back, so if you really think about it, the money is from me. Consider it a thank you for helping me out the other day." If it weren't for him, Evan would never have met Grace.

"Really?" The boy took the rolled up cash. "Does that mean I can get an autograph, too?"

"Don't push it, kid. Now scram before I change my mind about catching you out this late. The streets are no place for kids at night."

Taco took the money and ran, leaving Evan to wonder about the purse and Sara's trajectory from the gallery in the Quadrant, to where he stood in mid-town. Where was she headed?

THIRTEEN

DR. GRACE GO

Grace couldn't sleep well on the best of nights, but after her midnight visitor, her dreams became fitful. She tossed and turned, caught in a daze between irritation from the scratch on her arm, and thoughts colliding about the dark, heroic stranger at her window, and Evan. One minute, she remembered her fear in the alley when Sara attacked. The next, she remembered the kiss shared with Evan. The touch of his warm lips, the press of his firm body… but then she saw him strangle Sara, somehow electrify her—and then he turned up at Grace's window to make sure she got home safe.

It was obviously him. Must be him. Who else would turn up?

Just making sure you got home safe.

Evan being Envy would explain so much. She couldn't stop thinking about him. Curiosity had her picking apart his ability. Was it real electricity? Or had he somehow used a super Taser gun? Maybe it had something to do with his supernumerary.

She didn't quite know what to make of him or his involvement with Sara, or Sara being engaged to Wrath. Wrath would be one of Evan's brother's then, the one left clutching Sara's dead body over the rubble of the building. Maybe even one of the brothers she'd met at the gallery. Somehow she couldn't place a movie star or billionaire playboy clutching a dead body over the rubble.

One after another, her thoughts skipped from topic to topic, then cycled back again.

She was so close to uncovering the truth. So close to getting compensation for the lives lost by that tragedy. She could almost taste it.

It was all too much.

With her mind running a million miles an hour, Grace gave up on sleep and got out of bed at a cold four-thirty, well before dawn. Already formulating a day plan in her mind, she wrapped a blanket around her shivering arms and went to her kitchen, mentally going through recent evidence to see if any old clues were cast into a new light. By the time she put the kettle on, she'd mentally cycled through enough to realize she had nothing of value. Sure, she'd learned plenty that day, but in the end she'd gathered no proof of Sara's involvement in the crime, let alone her existence.

Stirring the milk and sugar into her coffee, she watched the liquid swirl.

Sara's body had been crushed in the explosion yet there she was last night looking fresh and new, not a scar in sight. Grace hadn't been a first responder, nor had she worked during the weeks after the incident when she recovered from her own injuries, but she'd seen the grainy video footage of

Wrath clutching Sara's limp and lifeless body. She was dead. Dead in the ground dead.

So how was she walking around?

The name Sara hadn't been listed on the bombing victim manifest, and it had been pointless to speak to the medical examiner about the Jane Does. Although, maybe now Grace knew Sara's first name, she could go back to speak to the ME on duty the day of the bombing. Maybe he remembered something odd about one of the bodies. She was willing to follow any lead to uncover Sara's full identity.

By six o'clock, Grace had showered and dressed in warm clothes, eager to get to work. It was a clinic day, so she'd be busy. Too busy to make lunch with her girlfriend Lilo at Heaven. Lilo would be disappointed, and Grace wouldn't hear the end of her thoughts about canceling yet another lunch date, but it was unavoidable. Grace's short break would be filled with the visit to the ME. Hopefully by the end of the day, she would have good news to tell Taco when he came into the clinic for a visit.

As she got to her front door, she gave her apartment a sweeping glance. As usual, the silence and emptiness was worst in the mornings and the ghosts of her past were the loudest. She could almost hear her mother humming as she tidied up Grace's mess and watered her indoor plants, and then there was her father grumbling as he investigated the crack in the wall above the kitchen sink. A pang of regret deepened in her soul. They'd been so proud of her achievements. Her father had given up everything in Japan when he fell in love with her mother. They'd come to Cardinal City both broke, but in love, happy to start a life together. The fact that their only daughter was a surgeon had meant the world to them.

Why the hell did you want to move closer to this dump, mom and dad?

The question echoed in her mind, and as usual, no one answered. No one answered because she already knew. They wanted to be closer to her. To keep an eye on her because she was too busy to look after herself, saying that one day, she would care for them when they were old and gray and repay the favor.

Grace quickly unbolted the locks on her door and hastened into the hall, almost tripping over a full smoothie cup in her pathway.

Damned kids down the hall must have left trash lying around again.

The disposable cup was cold as though freshly blended inside.

Odd.

She glanced down the hall but saw nothing that would indicate a stranger had gotten into the complex and left the gift. It crossed her mind that Evan had somehow returned, but that didn't quite compute. He'd originally arrived via her fire escape. That left the only sane explanation: must be trash.

She picked it up, and a note fell from the bottom.

Sorry about last night. E.

So it *was* Evan. Was it? Something about the entire thing felt wrong. From the little she knew of Evan, he didn't seem like a surprise smoothie in the morning kind of guy. He was a night owl. She took the cup into the kitchen, cursing as the liquid leaked over her fingers.

"Damn it." Grace cradled the cup until she got to the sink where it promptly spilled in a torrent of vanilla and milk. "Gross." She flinched. It smelled off.

She quickly wiped up her mess on the bench, eyes catching on another Post-it note that must have fallen, but on closer inspection, the handwriting was different, yet again.

Keep smiling, beautiful.

She smiled. This was more like Evan. It even had a little scribble drawing of a doctor on it.

Two random notes in one morning? Whatever the reason, she had no time to worry about it now. She left the apartment, locking it securely behind.

By the time Grace made it to the hospital, her nerves were on edge. Not only had the spilled smoothie rattled her but when she'd stopped by the newspaper stand, Taco wasn't there. Worry tickled the edge of her thoughts. If the boy was too stubborn to come to her at the clinic later, then she'd go to him. She made a mental note to return on the way home and visit his aunt's apartment with her medical kit. They lived in her building, so it wasn't far.

When entering the hospital, she discretely slipped past the triage nurse and into the back end where she found the administration office that housed the computers and iPads. Usually, this time of day it was empty, but today, the Chief of Staff sat in front of a computer, typing away.

Jeff Granger was a thin man with the personality of a rake. Balding on top, tufts of gray hair over his ears matched the hair growing out of them. Round spectacles slid half down his nose. Worn down by years of saying no to staff vacation requests and roster changes, the man barely said boo anymore, but he was excellent at his job. The hospital ran like clockwork, and Grace liked him because he was a case of, *What you see is what you get*.

"Morning Jeff." Grace walked in and surreptitiously eyed one of the iPads. "You're studious to be in so early. Guess this is why the hospital runs so efficiently."

"Flattery will get you nowhere." He clicked his tongue in disapproval. "Grace. I've been trying to contact you."

"You have?" She forced her grin to not waver and removed her coat.

"Yes, is there something wrong with your phone?"

"I was mugged yesterday and haven't had a chance to get a new one."

"Not good enough. You're a doctor at a busy hospital. You may not be on the surgical rotation anymore, but you are required to be on call at all times. Please rectify that immediately."

"I'll grab one today. Thank you for the reminder."

Jeff faced Grace with assessing eyes that snagged on the bandage around her upper arm. "You were injured?"

"Oh." Grace covered her wound gently with her hand. "It's nothing major. Flesh wound from later in the night."

"Perhaps that's why we've been given the order to let you go."

"What?" Her eyes bugged out of her head. "Let me go?"

"Oh. Pardon me. I didn't mean permanently."

Grace exhaled in a rush. She didn't know what she'd do without the hospital. She had money in the bank to last a few months, and she knew she'd easily get another job—she had great references—she just needed something to do. Always.

Jeff pushed the glasses down the bridge of his nose to see her better. "You're not required today at the clinic. You can have the day off. In fact, you must have the rest of the week off."

But it was only Wednesday. "I don't understand."

"This morning we received word from management that staff who have accrued unpaid overtime must take time in lieu. Since you're the doctor on staff with the most logged time outside rostered hours, you will be the first to take forced leave."

"But…"

"No buts. Let me do my job. I have a week's worth of rostered time to fill in."

"I don't mind working."

"Not possible."

"Is there anyone else taking forced leave?"

"At this stage, it's just you."

No. Grace couldn't accept that. She had work to do. People to help. Especially at the clinic. "Jeff, have I done something wrong?"

"Au contraire, you've been doing everything right for too long. It's a health and safety issue. Now—" Jeff stood and straightened his suit and tie. "I need to go and adjust the clinic schedule before it opens. Good day Doctor Go."

And then he left.

Grace's head whirled with possible explanations. Could it really be as simple as being an administration directive?

She shook her head, overwhelmed with the possibility of having days with no work. What would she do?

She didn't want to go home to that empty apartment. Especially after the smoothie incident. It still felt wrong.

She'd devote herself to the insurance case. That's what she'd do.

Perhaps this was fortuitous after all. First Evan turning up as a patient, then seeing Sara alive, and now this. It was as though the fates were working for her. A light feeling of triumph swam in her mind and made her brave… or foolish.

She had intended to swipe the iPad and check the patient records, but with the computer on and open to the Chief of Staff's user account, she sat down to take advantage of the opportunity. She didn't get far with only Sara's first name. There were hundreds listed in the hospital record system. It was a long shot, but worth a try. The next step was to speak with the ME. She checked the history for the Jane Doe brought in on the day of the bombing.

"Dead on Arrival. Brought in Dead," Grace murmured quietly to herself as she typed in the search parameters and squinted at the screen. "Gotch-ya. Declined for post-mortem due to the nature of factors leading to death." That wasn't unusual for a victim of a building collapse. It was clear the cause of death. "Medical Examiner on duty: Dr. Bryan Callahan."

After checking the roster, she discovered Dr. Callahan still worked at Cardinal City General and his shift began in the mortuary at ten. Now the trick was to find something to do until then. She cracked her knuckles in front of her, pondering her backlog of to-do items. Number one: get a new phone. Number two: leave Jeff a little Post-it note of appreciation. He looked a little frazzled today, and she knew covering her roster wouldn't be fun. Number three: chase down Evan and find out Sara's full name. Maybe ask him about the smoothie. No other reason she needed to speak with him. Just leave last night as what it was because her list went on and on. She could now make lunch with Lilo and then check on Taco... See? Nothing to worry about. She had plenty to occupy herself with. No need to concern herself with her empty apartment at home.

FOURTEEN

MARY LAZARUS

Mary Lazarus walked around the corner of the basement unit at Lazarus House, bypassing the electrical workshop where Flint was. She gave him a quick wave as he soldered some sort of gadget together and kept walking until she reached the gym. The voices flowing into the hallway had her chest clenching in hopeful glee. The boys. Sparring together for the first time in months… perhaps years.

"You think you're so hot? Come on. Come at me." Parker's deep voice was a rumble of epic proportions.

"You know what they say, don't you?" Evan taunted. "The bigger they are, the harder they fall."

Then it was fists thudding and grunts as bodies clashed and grappled. It was the sound of yelps and occasional pained hisses. It was the sound of Mary's hopes and dreams.

They'd actually turned up like she'd asked. Well, some of them.

"Score one to me." Evan sniffed.

Mary kept her breath shallow, so as not to be noticed.

"Guys, focus on the parameters of the experiment, please." Griffin's curt tone bled through his words.

If Griffin was there, it was a good sign. His analytical mind found the puzzle of Evan's new physiology too hard to resist. He'd be marking up each point of the fight with statistical enthusiasm befitting a data analyst of his caliber. Probably timing it on his watch, too.

Mary was supposed to have been at the mat half an hour ago, but she'd purposefully been late, and was glad. The three of them worked together just like old times. Sure there was a bit of trash talk, but that was normal between brothers. It was everything she'd hoped them to be. Everything she trained them to be. She only wished the rest of the family would pick up the mantle and join in. It gave her hope that the destitute future she'd foretold at the Sisterhood was far away.

Thinking of the Sisterhood brought back memories. The secret society had rescued her from a childhood where her own parents extorted her powers for their own use, starving her if she didn't do as she was told. The sisters blamed this lack of nutrition for her inability to have children of her own, but Mary had her suspicions. The rigorous training at the Sisterhood was also harmful to her physical condition. All she knew was, by the time she met Flint, she was infertile.

Perhaps it was a good thing because now she had seven highly capable and demanding adopted children to look after and Flint had never minded. In fact, after suffering his own troubled past, he embraced the parenting duties of the seven as if they were his own.

If Sara was indeed back… If Evan had been right, and

she'd been full of deadly envy on the night of the bombing, then a nefarious motive brought her to their family. It could be the Syndicate—the people who'd financed the lab that created the seven. It could also be the Sisterhood retaliating because Mary should have delivered them, signed and sealed, like the good little assassin she was. Mary's heart ached every day for the two that she couldn't save—Gloria, and another child.

It was inevitable that either the Syndicate, or Sisterhood, or both, would come looking for her children once they revealed themselves to the world. Mary only hoped she'd prepared them enough. So far no one had come looking for the children, and she hadn't *foreseen* any trouble, so had assumed everything was fine.

But Sara's reemergence was worrisome.

It raised too many questions.

"I know you're out there," came Parker's gruff voice from inside. "I can sense your pride, Mary."

She smirked and rolled out of her hiding spot to enter the room.

Parker and Evan were in the middle of the large workout space, shirtless and sweaty, wearing track pants. Wireless electrodes over Evan's tattooed body fed a signal to a computer system on the side where Griffin sat inspecting a computer screen.

Mary took in her third youngest. It had been two weeks since she'd seen him, and he looked the same as ever. White shirt buttoned up to the collar, sans tie. Thick black-framed glasses on his nose, not that he needed them, they were part of his alter-ego and more often than not, he enjoyed wearing them. His hair cut was millimeter perfect in a style that could have come from the twenties; crisp fade for the short back and sides, slick top combed immaculately, all kept in place by styling cream. Everything about Griffin oozed control.

"*Mijos*," Mary stated, lifting her eyebrow. "How goes the experiment?"

"Excellent." Evan grinned, pulling his larger bulkier brother into a headlock.

Parker's face reddened as he deftly slipped out of the hold, twisted and did the same to Evan, cutting off the circulation at his neck, grinning in a feral sort of way. "Now it's excellent."

Evan tapped his brother on the forearm, but was given no quarter. Then the air in the room electrified and the hairs on Mary's arms lifted. A crackling sound snapped. Parker yelped and fell back on the mat, rubbing his forearm.

"Cheat," he growled, then sniffed his arm. "You singed my hair off."

Evan laughed and then turned to Griffin. "Did you catch that?"

Griffin scowled at the screens. "Yes. Eighty volts. High enough to be harmful if contact was sustained for long enough. Ten more than last time, but less than you said you used the other night. It appears your output is erratic. With practice, you'll get stronger and more consistent."

Evan flexed his bicep. "Like strengthening a muscle that hasn't been used in a while."

"Precisely," Griffin said. "We just don't know what muscles."

"Not muscles, organs." Parker moved off the mat to stand at Griffin's shoulder. "Evan said he had scans at the hospital."

"Shit, that's right. Three unidentified organs." Evan joined his brothers.

Parker rubbed his chin. "*Three* organs."

"They studied many animals in the labs you were created in," Mary added. "Is it possible they took something from one of those creatures that resulted in the extra organs?"

"Like an Electric Eel," Parker said. "It makes perfect sense."

"No. An electric eel doesn't give off enough electricity to create lightning." This was Griffin.

"Could it be possible he's mutating?" Mary didn't like the sound of unexpected biological changes, but she had to ask.

They all turned to Parker, the only one with the kind of knowledge to answer.

"It's possible," he replied. "I've studied the notes on Gloria's laptop. A lot of what she did was only tested on rats. We don't know long-term effects of her human experiments."

"You mean us, right?" Evan asked, grimly.

"Whatever happens, we're in this together," Mary answered.

While Griffin and Parker talked genetics, equations and anomalies, Mary indicated for Evan to face her on the mat. "Speaking of practice, let's see how much control you have."

"You want me to zap you?" Evan backed off. "But you're not enhanced, like us. You could have a heart attack."

That earned him a swift kick in the chest. "Call me old again and the next one will be lower."

"I'm serious, Mary. Flint will kill me if I—*oof!*"

She lowered her kick.

"But…" Real worry blazed in her son's eyes as he covered his groin for protection. "I can't always control it."

"This is precisely why we're doing this. So you can learn to." She darted in and jabbed at his face. This time, he blocked with a well-practiced swipe. She jabbed again. And again. He blocked, darted back, blocked again. Soon, he grinned, and bounced around the mat, circling her. He used the advantage of longer arms to reach out and tap the top of her head, toying with her.

It warmed Mary's heart.

Once, Evan had been the jokester of the family. Being the youngest, he'd taken it upon himself to always lighten the mood and to keep them all from being so serious. When he'd come back from his training, he was hardened, but enthusiastic. After Sara died… he'd lost it all, becoming as dark as the sin he fought.

Okay. If he was toying with her, she'd bring her A-Game.

Mary's mind cleared and decades of martial arts training lifted to the surface, like bubbles rising in a pond. She was water. She was air. She entered her state of flow. The world around her fell away. White noise in her brain dimmed, and she cut out the distraction of the two talking. This time, she came at him with a rain of precise relentless attacks.

Evan was the first out of the seven to develop augmented skills. She had to be sure he was ready to be out on his own. The kids were all pilot test subjects, and if their mother

Gloria was alive today, she'd be pushing them to their limits, testing them, ensuring they were in peak physical condition. Who knew what genetics she spliced to give him powers. Electric Eels were only the beginning. There were things in that lab Mary couldn't explain. Frogs with bones extending and retracting through their digits, bees, platypuses, and rare insects in test tubes.

She kept drilling her youngest, giving him all of her years of assassin training. She was not to be trifled with.

"Come on, Evan. Use your skill to your advantage." She kicked his legs out from underneath him, and he fell heavily to the mat. "When I make contact, you should be able to electrocute me. Keep your body charged, and I should receive a zap."

"But I don't want to hurt you."

Mary ground her teeth. She wasn't a frail old lady. She'd spent weeks once, simply hanging from her neck to strengthen it. "Then I'll hurt you. Up. Go."

"Wait." Parker held up his finger, still reading the screen. "I have an idea."

Evan turned to his brothers.

Mary struck his temple. Fool for turning his attention from her. She did it again. This time, he dodged, giving her a chagrinned glance.

Good boy. She bounced on her toes, fists in the air, ready to strike.

"Electric Eels have the ability to create an electro-magnetic field around them and sense movement in that field. It borders on precognition," Parker said, reading the screen before lifting his gaze to meet Evan's. "If you truly dreamed the future and those finger prints from the purse come back as Sara's, then it's safe to say perhaps you have this skill. All this time you could have been innately amplifying your dream-state brainwaves and locking onto Sara's."

Evan's eyes went all dopey and he smiled. "I dreamed of Grace this morning."

Parker snorted. "And?"

"You don't need to know the rest."

"I meant, was there any indication you were seeing reality?"

"Well, for part of it, I saw her walking down the street."

"So…" Griffin added, tapping his pencil on his chin. "If you can project your brainwaves asleep, then you can do something similar awake. Load up on electricity and let it out a little and hold it. You'd be able to sense Mary's movements when she hits the field. You'd know the minute she twitches and be able to deduce her intentions."

"Interesting," Mary said. "Let's test the theory."

Evan's eyes narrowed on her. "So now you believe me about Sara."

"We'll believe you when those prints come back a match," Parker said.

"What prints?" Mary asked without taking her eyes from her opponent.

"I went patrolling last night," Evan elaborated as his eyes glazed with inward thoughts. "I'm trying to project the field now…"

"Patrolling… for envy?" She lowered her fists, shocked. He hadn't done that in months.

Parker arched a brow, no doubt sensing her pride. He

was the only out of the seven who never gave up fighting crime, he just did it on his own and in secret. He was too good to give up. Too smart, and too stubborn. He'd accepted his destiny long before Evan was even born, but it had done something to him. Something cold and dark slithered under the surface of Parker's bravado. A responsibility, or perhaps a duty with a heavy toll.

"I went patrolling," Evan murmured, still half focused on his magnetic field creation, "and found Grace's purse. Sara had her paws all over it. The prints will prove it."

Mary felt something in the air—a tangible change in atmosphere. He was almost ready for her to attack. But first, she had to ask: "If that's true, then we've raised more questions than answers. Why would Sara lie? Why would she do the things you said she did? What's her motive? And how is she alive?"

Evan shrugged, rolling his shoulders. "Don't know. Don't care. I just want her to pay." Then he extended his arm and gestured for her to *Bring it*.

Mary's resolve hardened. That attitude was not healthy. The minute they felt they had the right to choose who lived or died, was the moment they failed at being human. It became even more apparent that she needed to prepare him for battle. She feinted right, then left, then swung out with her foot.

He blocked her, almost lazily, as though he'd been waiting for her to move.

She went at him with a barrage of attack moves.

He blocked each and every one.

She kept at it. Charging him relentlessly, switching up

her style to catch him unaware. Within minutes, they were both sweating with exertion.

She hadn't landed a hit.

A slow clap came from the prideful spectator, a few feet away.

"You're an eel," Parker smirked. "Always knew you were a slippery sucker."

Evan whirled and closed the gap. He slammed an electrified palm into Parker's chest. Blue light flashed and a sizzling sound crackled. Power lifted hair on Mary's arms and tingled her tongue.

"Five-fifty volts," Griffin exclaimed as Parker hit the floor.

Mary laughed. "You look like you can control just fine, Evan."

When she turned back to him, a pink stain had colored his cheeks and ears.

"It's not with you guys I lose it," he mumbled.

"Grace?" she asked quietly.

He nodded, avoiding her gaze. Mary took a deep breath knowing none of her children liked to discuss their romantic relationships with her, and this was the big one. So she sighed. "All I can say is, practice makes perfect."

A ringtone cut through the air. Parker groaned on the floor and sat up, rubbing his chest. Strands of long, wild auburn hair lifted in the epitome of an electric shock victim.

"That's my phone," he grumbled and rolled to his feet. He stumbled to a side bench where their shirts and belongings had been discarded. "Yeah," he said into the handset.

While Parker spoke, Mary moved to Griffin's side. "Is there anything we should be worried about?"

Griffin turned his practical gaze her way. "Medically speaking? I'm not a doctor."

"I know that, Griff. Give me your best educated guess."

"I don't guess. I take statistics and assess the risk factors to calculate a probable outcome."

"Okay. All that." Mary knew better than to argue with him. He was so much like his birth mother Gloria that deep down she worried he wouldn't assimilate into society well, but he'd proven her wrong. He survived his seven year combat training, albeit barely and with some trauma he refused to speak about. He'd made a few friends, he'd excelled at his job as a data analyst, and kept himself extremely fit and well presented. There was one thing that niggled at her though. He was the only child to maintain equilibrium with his sin of greed. It should be a positive, but this balance came at the sacrifice of a normal, healthy life. It controlled every decision from his waking moment, to his sleep. It even controlled his sleep patterns. Last week, she saw him activating the timer on his watch before he went to dinner with his family, then check his bio-indicator as though he were mentally recording the effect spending time with his family had on his equilibrium.

"Well." Griffin shifted his glasses up the bridge of his nose. "From these figures, it is as you say. Practice makes perfect. The more he uses his power, the stronger it becomes. He hasn't had any problems calling the current to the surface which indicates his other control issue is perhaps mental, or sexual."

"Screw you," Evan said from his spot on the mat, unwinding the protective tape on his knuckles. "When you're around your mate, you'll know exactly how it feels. Mr. Control will be in hell."

Griffin frowned, shaking his head. "No. I'm not like you. I can keep my baser instincts in check."

Evan snorted and stalked over to Griffin, pointing in his face. "Your dick gets hard just like mine, brother."

"*La madre que me!* Language!" Mary blocked her ears. "From the looks of you, Evan, you've finished training. You don't need me here anymore."

"Sorry." He had the decency to look apologetic and pulled her hands from her ears. "But it's true. What do you think is going to happen when he meets his match?"

Griffin shrugged. "Maybe I don't need to meet her. I've got my condition in check."

"I'm telling you now, brother. You won't have a choice if you do. Your body will heat up like it's on fire. She'll be all you can think of, morning, noon and night. It's been days since I met Grace and every time I close my eyes, she's there."

"That was the lab." Parker came over, interrupting. "The results are back."

Mary held her breath, unsure which result would make her feel better.

"It's a match. The fingerprints are Sara's."

"I knew it!" Evan grinned and then saw the various shades of horror reflected back at him. "Sorry," he said quietly. "It's just… I was right."

"For Chris'sake, Evan," Parker growled, cutting him off. "Grow up."

But Evan couldn't stifle the smile stretched across his face, or the light glittering in his eyes.

"I'm going to find my girl. She needs to know," he said, then strode from the room, but Parker halted him by the shoulder. Their eyes met and Evan's smile completely dissipated.

"Shit," he said, finally understanding the warning in his brother's eyes. "Wyatt."

Parker glared. "We have to break it to him together. Family meeting at Heaven, two o'clock this afternoon. After the lunch rush and before he does the dinner prep."

Evan nodded grimly.

Parker turned to Mary. "If you and Flint can be there as well, that would be appreciated. Wyatt's going to need all the support he can get."

"Of course."

He was right. Because, even though this news made Evan's world come together, it would tear Wyatt's apart.

FIFTEEN

DR. GRACE GO

By ten in the morning Grace had purchased her new phone and was ready to confront Evan about Sara and the smoothie. If only she could find him. She walked into her third tattoo parlor of the day—a converted barbershop studio—hoping it would be her last stop. *Deadly Ink*, the sign read. Promising.

A bell dinged her arrival and a dark-haired woman behind the counter lifted her head. An array of tattoos marked her light brown skin. Famous faces and tribal lines peeked from behind her leather bustier and led up her skin, hitting the edge of her razor sharp bob at her neck. Short bangs finished an inch from her arched eyebrows, and thick black eyeliner lifted at the corners like bat's wings. Wow. Very gothic chic.

Grace gave the woman her best smile. "Hello."

"I think you're in the wrong place," she replied in a smoky voice. "We don't do temporary here. Maybe visit the grocery store, get a cereal box and take a look inside for a sticker, or something."

Shocked, Grace involuntarily checked her appearance and smoothed her hair, still in a practical ponytail. She wore jeans and a simple blouse under her navy blue coat. Nothing flash, but still, nicely presented. After getting over the affront, Grace pushed her shoulders back and lifted her chin.

"Maybe I want something permanent."

"You want a tattoo." Her eyes lowered over Grace. "Have you had one before? Do you know how much it hurts?"

What was that supposed to mean? "Do I look like a woman who doesn't know pain?"

"You look like a Disney princess in a winter coat."

"Well then, no to all the above. I've never had a tattoo. No, I don't know how much it hurts because I've never had one, and no… I'm not a Disney princess. I'm a doctor. But that's irrelevant. Is this how you treat all your new clients? Surely you started with a first tattoo once upon a time, didn't you? I mean, you weren't born with them, right? They're magnificent by the way. Truly great artistry. Did you design them yourself?"

When faced with a naysayer, Grace always found it better to be overly kind.

"I can't tell if you're joking, or being genuine."

"Why would I lie? I've just met you."

The woman's gaze softened. "Sorry. I've had a bad start to the morning. The boss is late and I have to cover for him. Did you want to come through and pick some art?" She lifted the hatch on the counter, making room for Grace to step through to the studio. "We're understaffed today, but we can book you in for another day."

When she did, she had a better chance to inspect the artwork on the walls and recognized a familiar style. Simple black lines with a splash of color. She narrowed in on the signature and grinned, whirling back to face the woman triumphant. "Actually, you were right the first time. I'm not here for a tattoo, but looking for someone who might work here. His name is Evan Lazarus."

The woman leaned on the leather client chair and folded her arms. "What's he done now?"

Grace breathed a sigh of relief. "So I'm in the right place?"

"Yeah, but like I said, he's not in, and I can't give his number out."

Grace turned and walked the room, idly picking up items to inspect. Bottles of ink. Needles. Antiseptic wipes. Metal trays and tables. It wasn't too different from a surgery.

"So…" the woman said, waiting. "Do you want ink done, or what."

"I…"

The bell dinged behind Grace.

"Josie, you didn't put the sign out—Doc. What are you doing… I mean, hi?"

Grace's heart skipped a beat. "Evan."

It was cold outside, yet he wore a thin, long-sleeved shirt and well-worn jeans with threaded knees. They were old clothes, but they clung to his muscles like an embrace. His unkempt hair curled over his ears in a boyish way that, when added to his shy smile, made him devastatingly handsome. Bright green eyes widened as he caught her staring, and his broad chest lifted as though he held his breath.

She didn't know why she ever thought him psychopathic.

They continued to stare at each other until Josie snorted.

"Oh," she laughed. "I see what's going on here. I'm heading out back."

Josie disappeared through a back door, closing it behind her, leaving Evan and Grace alone.

"I'm sorry for turning up unannounced," Grace started the same time as Evan blurted, "I'm sorry about turning up at your place last night."

Heat flushed Grace's cheeks, and his ears turned pink.

So it *was* him last night. Somehow, the thought made her pulse race, instead of being satisfied she'd solved the puzzle, and she wasn't sure why. Danger. Excitement. Wariness. A little bit of fear. And maybe he left the smoothie, too.

"I was just about to come looking for you," he said.

"Oh?"

"I found your purse." He held up her stolen purse.

Grace hadn't even noticed it in his hands that's how much she'd been taken with his clothes. Or more accurately, what was under said clothes. Wow. Yep. Those arms, those thick thighs… the way his golden skin pulled tight over each dip and groove was like an anatomy book she had at home. It was all making her lose her train of thought, but she managed to mumble, "Thank you."

"The ID is missing, but the money's all there."

Grace checked, and he was right. Fifty-five dollars, all there.

Evan ran his hand up and over his head, combing through his hair as though suddenly aware it hadn't been brushed. "Grace. I…"

He was going to speak about being Envy, she knew it, and the minute he did, alarm flashed in her mind. She couldn't. Couldn't deal with that part of him just yet. Images of his scan opened in her memory. There was so much more than what appeared on the surface of this man, and maybe she wanted to know everything, but she had to work out how she felt about it first. He was a crime-fighter, and a violent one at that. One thing on her list at a time.

"I'd like to know Sara's last name please," she raised her voice, made it forceful.

Evan glanced over Grace's shoulder to the back door. "Um. Sure. Let's take a walk."

"A walk?"

"Yes. You know"—an incorrigible grin—"like… putting one foot in front of the other.

"I know what a walk is, Evan. I meant, where to?"

"Wherever our feet take us."

"You mean, like no plan?"

He cocked his head, assessing her. "Don't you ever just head out and see where you end up?"

"No. That's ridiculous. My father always used to say, 'A wise man does not lose his way.' I think we should plan, simply because I have things to do and can't spend the day frolicking around." When she set her mind to something, nothing stood in her way; not the housework, not her favorite TV program, and certainly not a cocky handsome man.

"Frolicking?"

"Yes. Frolicking."

"Doc." His eyes darkened, and he stepped closer, voice deepening. "When I decide to frolic with you, you'll know it."

Her stomach tripped. She liked it when he called her Doc. She liked the thought of him frolicking with her. Under the sheets. In a hidden alcove. Cozying up in front of a fire... She didn't know whose fire, but it sounded nice.

"Do you know the second part of that proverb?" he asked.

"No. I didn't know it was a proverb."

"The second part is, *A brave man does not fear.*"

"Oh."

"Good. So, nothing to be afraid of. Not when you're with me. We can get lost together, enjoy ourselves and still make it home in time for dinner. Let's go."

Call her crazy, but that sounded like a really good idea. Maybe other plans could wait.

He poked his head through the back door to let Josie know he was leaving. An exasperated sigh filtered back, but Evan ignored it.

When the door to the street opened, Grace pulled her coat in tight. "You don't want to bring a coat?"

"Nah. I run hotter than most people, plus the sun's coming out soon. Come on. This way."

They were on the outskirts of the Quadrant, and walked a minute or two toward the center, passing other stores on the way. Most were run by small business owners, like Evan, until they got to the fashion district where expensive designer businesses reigned supreme. They continued in silence and kept walking.

Nervous anticipation coated the air. Grace supposed he would speak first, considering he asked her to walk, but he didn't. Instead, he shoved his hands in his pockets and chewed his bottom lip, darting a glance her way every so often.

"Grace. I want to talk about—"

"Sara."

He paused. "Okay. Fine. We can talk about her first. Let's go down this way." He gestured to the right when they hit the end of the street. Some buildings were taller there and shadowed the sun, keeping any heat from hitting Grace.

She turned with him. "I tried to look up her name in the hospital system, but there were too many Saras."

"She won't be in there."

"Why not?"

"My sister made sure traces of her identity were wiped."

Grace frowned. Pieces of the puzzle she didn't want to acknowledge pushed at the edges of her mind. His sister must be super talented with computers. "Why?"

"She knew our secret."

His secret. Just like that, the elephant in the room came crashing her way. He did more than crash, he sang and danced a jig. She took a deep breath and focused on his revelation.

"Your secret."

He shoved his hands in his pockets, watching. "Yes."

"Who you are after dark?"

"Yes."

"Okay. Okay. Wait." Something horrifying occurred to her. "Does that mean…" She couldn't finish her sentence because the last person who knew their secret had their identity wiped from the face of the planet. Would she be wiped too?

"No, Doc. I'd never let that happen," he said, as if reading her mind. "No one's going to touch a hair on your head."

"Okay, but…" Would it be that easy? And what about Sara's missing data? "But, surely someone would have noticed Sara's missing files."

"She probably replaced her name with something generic."

"Like a Jane Doe?"

He shrugged. "Maybe."

They were almost at the entrance of the Quadrant's central parkland. Evan was right. The clouds had split apart, and the sun shone through to the trees, giving every leaf and flower gilt edges. It was beautiful.

Evan walked toward the gates, but Grace stayed, so he turned back. "Are you hungry? A street vendor in there makes the best pierogi."

"Evan. I have to go."

Disappointment flashed in his eyes. "Is it because of… turning up at your place?"

She took a deep breath. "Look. Can I be frank with you?"

"You can. But I'd much rather you be Doc, or Grace. I like both." He smirked. "A lot."

That did weird things in Grace's belly. "Making sure I got

home was nice. Considerate. I get it. It's your job to keep people safe. But then breaking into the building to leave a smoothie at my door the next day is a little stalkerish. Maybe over the top."

His eyebrows snapped together. "What?"

"I kinda like you too, Evan, but I just don't have time for"—she waved between them—"whatever this is."

"You *kinda* like me?" He stepped toward her. "Kinda wasn't the message I got last night when you told me to kiss you. Be honest. It was me turning up as... well, you know who. I've scared you off, haven't I?"

"I don't know what to think about that, yet. I'm not scared... I, um…" How could she put this delicately. "I know you save people. I know it's hard. I saw the bruises all over your body, Evan. I know it's a lifestyle choice that puts you in the line of fire. You jump in front of danger willingly."

"Those bruises weren't from my night job." He looked down at his feet with a self-deprecating sigh. "It won't happen again."

"Well, whatever it was, I see the effects of violence every day at the hospital. I know how real it is. I'm not scared. It's just the opposite of everything I stand for. You hurt people to get them to do the right thing. I heal people. Plus, not respecting my personal space—the smoothie at my doorstep. I… Look, if you won't share any more details about Sara, I should go."

"Wait. I didn't leave a smoothie." He shook his head. "I can't change the rest of me, but that I didn't do."

"You didn't?"

If he didn't leave it, and the kids down the hall didn't leave it… then who did?

His frown deepened. "Tell me exactly what happened."

"I found a smoothie at the foot of my door when I opened it this morning."

"And?"

"And there was a note that said, *Sorry about last night. E.* I brought it into the kitchen where it spilled all over my hands, and so I poured it down the sink. It's just a smoothie, Evan. It didn't even smell that nice."

"It definitely wasn't me. Keep talking." He gently touched the small of her back and guided her back toward the park. "We need dumplings to talk this out and I'm hungry."

She had a bad feeling churning, but being led by his steady, strong hand felt good. A tingle burned into her spine, sending pleasant shivers through her body as they strolled into the park, under the dappled shade. Warm sun rays hit her face every few moments.

"What did it smell like?" he asked. "You said it smelled funny. Did you taste it?"

"No, it completely spilled. It was just… off-smelling. Why?" It was an odd question.

"It could've been poisoned."

"The milk probably went off." Although, it was cold and freshly made, but who would want to poison her?

"Don't take this lightly. Sara's alive. It's been confirmed."

She gasped. "How did you prove it?"

"After I left you. I went out patrolling and that's when I

found your purse. Got the prints lifted and tested." His expression twisted into something ugly. "It was her."

"This is … wow. I can't believe it. Where has she been all this time? Maybe she's been hiding because she's feeling bad for her part in all those deaths. With the right prompting, she might confess. We have to talk to her and find out what happened that day."

"Aren't you listening to me? She knows where you live. She's bad news, Doc. Evil. Rotten to the core. The only thing she feels bad about is being caught by us last night. The last time she messed with my family, she manipulated them into believing she was Wyatt's perfect bride, but it was all lies. I saw it, but no one believed me and it tore my family apart. Don't underestimate her. My bet is that the smoothie was poisoned. You can identify her from the bombing, she'll want you dead."

A cold feeling settled in the pit of Grace's stomach. "She did say something like that before she attacked me."

In fact, her exact word was, *Die!*

Grace rubbed her hands up and down her arms, wishing the coat was thicker.

"I'm not leaving you alone." Evan's fury laced voice shattered the peaceful outdoor atmosphere. Grace was sure even the birds stopped chirping. "I'm sorry. You can call me stalker Joe, or whatever you want, but you're not leaving my sight until we catch her."

"And get her to confess."

"To make her pay."

There was something dark lurking beneath his eyes.

"Evan."

He lifted his burning gaze to hers.

"We'll get her to confess," she prompted. "I don't know how you do what you do, but you don't get a nickname like *Deadly* for nothing. I know what you're capable of. I saw you strangle her in the street and... don't. Please don't. You can't kill her. You can't. We'll find her, then report her to the police. That will be punishment enough. That will be justice."

She said the words out loud to convince herself even though her heart wanted to follow Evan's path. Sara killed her parents. What justice was there in the world if murderers were allowed to go free, yet was Sara truly free? There was more to the story, and Grace knew never to jump to conclusions when sometimes, conclusions ended in death.

From the way Evan considered her, Grace knew he churned her words over in his mind. She hoped she'd put enough nerve in them to sound authentic.

"Just because we can kill," he said, "doesn't mean we do. I admit I got carried away with Sara, but you don't know what she's done to our family. The pain she's caused. Putting her down would do the world a favor."

"I can't believe you said that! You don't know what she's done? She murdered both my parents. They're gone. Never coming back."

Tears burned her eyes, and she looked away, using every reserve in her body to keep the words "Just kill her" from tumbling out of her mouth. But, it wouldn't honor her parents' death. They wanted her to be a doctor, and to save lives. They were proud of that. So was she.

She was better than this.

"I'm also a doctor, Evan. I have an oath to uphold. No matter who she is or what she's done, I can't willingly condone her death."

"Your oath is to treat people if hurt. Not to stop a murderer from receiving justice. She's a murderer, Grace. Like you said, you of all people know that."

"Justice is to turn her over to the police. We need her testimony."

"Sometimes the system doesn't work."

Maybe, just maybe though, a dark thought whispered, maybe you don't have to know about it. Maybe he can end Sara, end your suffering, and you can pretend you won't have a stain on your heart. You can pretend that saving the lives of other people make up for the fact that you allowed another to die. But as the thoughts formed, she rejected them. Sloth was a sin, too. For too long she'd been healing people, she couldn't turn her back now, else she may as well have died in that explosion because what kind of world would she be living in if she became the thing she despised?

"So you'll turn yourself into the very thing you're fighting against. You'll sacrifice your soul for revenge? Murder isn't justice, and I of all people know that."

Her loud words cut through the sudden silence. They echoed in her mind, whirling on repeat. Maybe she went too far. He looked at her, all calm and dangerous, hair moving in the new breeze. The tendons in his jaw ticked. The vein in his forehead popped. Then he stepped closer until they were flush against each other. So close. Eye-to-blazing-eye.

"You have no idea what I've sacrificed," he ground out.

Grace was done. There had to be another way.

"I'm sorry, Evan. This is where we part." She stepped away.

"I'm not leaving you alone."

She kept walking down the street, back toward the hospital, boots thudding in the silence. His own echoed softly behind her, almost indistinguishable. She bet he'd had plenty of practice sneaking up on people with those light feet.

He was determined, she had to give him that.

And he had shown up at her house to make sure she got home safe.

And he'd gone out looking for her purse.

And he'd saved her life.

Damn it.

He was trying to do the right thing, albeit misguided.

She didn't want to die.

"Fine. Follow me all day, if that's what you want, but I'm not changing my plans."

"Fine with me."

"Fine."

"Good."

"Let's go then."

Grace turned in a huff and strode away.

SIXTEEN

EVAN LAZARUS

Evan bristled from Grace's words about Sara.

Grace wanted to turn her over to the police, to get a confession, but his every instinct wanted to end Sara and her astronomical levels of envy. All these years, and wherever she'd been, her sin hadn't dissipated. He'd ignored her once, for the sake of his brother. He wouldn't do it again. He wasn't giving up but, for now, his priority was to keep Grace safe. She was innocent, his responsibility, and she buried herself deeper and deeper into this hot mess he created.

Evan followed Grace as she walked down the busy city street, all stubborn strides. They continued for long minutes, his fury slowly melting away until he became completely besotted by the floral scent of her perfume trailing in her tail-wind. The scent sparked all sorts of devious thoughts in his mind. He wanted to grab that swishing ponytail, yank it back, and pull her lips to his. Make her see reason. Make her forgive his harsh words.

Instead, he checked their surroundings and tried to stay

vigilant. Tall buildings and cathedrals blocked the sun, and cast moving shadows that creeped him out. He felt eyes and ears everywhere as though they were being watched. But when he checked, it was only the stone statues sitting proudly on top of parapets, guarding their buildings. An angel on one, a modern stylized gargoyle on another.

The smoothie incident concerned him. Leaving something like that at her front door meant Sara had somehow gotten into the building. Even if it wasn't poisoned, it was a message. She could get to Grace anywhere. A sharp pang of guilt speared through him. He should have watched her place until dawn, should have used her as bait to catch Sara, and proved he was the jack-ass she believed him to be.

They passed a narrow side street and Grace did a double take. He almost bumped into her and that swishing ponytail as she spun to peek surreptitiously at the teenagers tagging up a wall with graffiti.

The kids didn't appear threatening. Three skinny males in baggy clothes sprayed a pattern, or picture around the head of a sleeping homeless guy slouched against the wall, and his mountain of hoarded belongings. They hadn't noticed Grace or Evan.

A hand tugged Evan to the side, and out of view of the teenagers. Grace stared at him with a pained look on her face.

"Are you okay?" he asked.

"I'm supposed to be angry at you, but"—she shot a sideways glance back to the street—"I haven't seen Adam for months."

A dark, insidious feeling tried to punch through Evan. Adam? Who the fuck was Adam?

"I need your help," Grace confessed.

"Anything. Name it."

Her smile reminded him of the sun, and it warmed his skin. "The boy back there with the blue parka on, he's Adam."

"Okay."

"And, he came into the clinic once a few months ago." She took a deep breath and looked to the sky, as though trying to deal with a painful thought. "He told me about his foster family, and how he was treated." She shook her head. "I don't think he expected to live very long, or ever be back. It sounded like he was going to either kill himself, or... I don't know. He left before I could get any more details about him."

"Grace." Evan squeezed her shoulder. "Whatever you need."

"I need for him to trust me." She covered his hand with hers. "Can you follow my lead?"

He nodded and moved his hand to the base of her neck. The sense of envy in the neighborhood promptly dissipated. She sighed and pressed into his touch. The act sent the butterflies in his stomach flurrying. Whether she realized what she did or not, Evan knew he had a chance with her.

"Okay. Follow me." She walked into the side street and straight up to the boys.

The teenagers caught their arrival but dismissed them and went back to their graffiti.

"Hello Adam." Grace stood to the side, one worried eye on the homeless man, still snoozing.

Probably drunk.

The dark-haired boy in the blue parka snapped his head towards Grace. Adam had a twitch in his eye that betrayed his wariness, and looked a little feral, something like when Wyatt was about to lose his temper. Evan steeled himself by arming his reservoirs to the brink with power.

Let's test this magnetic field business out.

If the boy was about to make a move on Grace, he wanted to know about it.

"Who da fuck is this?" One of Adam's pierced friends asked. "You know this chick, Adam?"

Adam sniffed. "What do you want?"

Grace wasn't cowed. "I saw your artwork as I walked by and just had to stop. I think you're incredibly talented." She twisted to Evan. "Isn't he amazing, Evan? As good as you."

Well, Evan wouldn't go that far.

Adam eyed Evan, taking special interest with the tattoos peeking out of his collar and sleeve.

Evan made a show of checking the artwork out. The kid was pretty good.

"You did this?" Evan asked. "All of it?"

"Adam did most of it." The third boy stood back as if to give Adam center stage.

Adam gave a shrug that said he didn't care. "You ain't a cop, is you?"

"No, I own the tattoo shop on First."

"Deadly Ink?" the pierced kid asked, eyes widening. His

envy reached out with claws, making Evan cringe. All three teenagers suddenly focused on him.

"Yeah." Slowly, Evan let go of his power. He didn't think the boys would cause trouble. "I asked because I like your style."

"He had his first solo exhibition last night," Grace added. "It basically sold out within minutes. His name is Evan Lazarus."

Evan shot her a silencing glance. He hated bolstering himself like that, but then he caught onto what Grace was trying for. Adam needed to trust them, and to have some goals—something to look forward to, especially if his home life was tempting him to a life of crime.

"You should drop some sketches around sometime," Evan said to Adam. "Maybe show me your portfolio."

"Really?" Adam looked surprised.

"I'll pay you of course, but I'm serious. We need new shit for our customers all the time."

Evan looked to Grace for more guidance, and she smiled gently back at him.

Adam's eyes lit up, but then dimmed. "I don't have a portfolio."

"But he'll work on one, right, bro?" said the pierced dude.

"Yeah. Yeah of course."

"Well, bring in whatever you got. Even go around and take photos of your street pieces. Go in and ask for Josie if you need some ideas. Tell her Evan Lazarus sent you, and if she gives you any grief, go and see the Doc here at the clinic. She knows how to get into contact with me."

They left the teenagers, walking side by side.

Evan felt like he almost floated for two reasons. He'd possibly changed a delinquent's life for the better, and Grace was proud of his artistic achievements. He was still thinking on this when they turned into the entrance of Cardinal City General Hospital and walked through the sliding doors of the emergency department. They didn't stop there, but continued down a long corridor to a set of elevators where Grace hit the basement level button and stood back, waiting.

"Are you working today?" he asked.

"No."

"So, what are we doing here?"

She was silent for a moment, but her eyes challenged him.

His eyebrows winged up. He thought they were past this friction.

"Fine. We're seeing the Medical Examiner," she conceded.

The elevator doors opened, and they stepped inside. A few minutes later and they walked into the morgue. Methanol and other pungent scents hit Evan's nose, making him flinch. A series of metal autopsy tables sat in the center of the cold room, each carrying an exposed cadaver in an open bodybag. One wall was lined with sinks, taps and chemicals. Cupboards full of supplies lined the opposite wall. A potbellied man stood at an examination table, writing something on the foot tag of the closest cadaver. He wore green scrubs and a surgical cap.

When they entered, the ME looked up. His eyes were too close together, and stubble coated his round jaw. Envy spiked in the room when his gaze darted between Evan and Grace.

Hell, the man had eyes for her.

Evan glared at the man who in turn frowned back.

"You shouldn't be in here," the man said.

"Dr. Bryan Callahan?" Grace asked pleasantly, ignoring his statement.

"Who's asking?" Bryan glared at Evan then shifted to the cadaver and began zipping up the bodybag.

"I'm Dr. Grace Go. I have a few questions about a Jane Doe brought in a few years ago. Do you remember the one from the Cardinal Bombing?"

"Doctor?" Callahan asked.

"Yes. I work in Emergency."

"Where's your ID."

Grace fished around in her pockets and pulled a card out. Callahan read the details then glanced at Evan, letting his judgmental gaze wash over him. "Who's your bodyguard?"

Fucktard.

Between the giant douche attitude and the envy scraping his gut, Evan wanted to rip the man a new one. But he resisted. His training made him better than that. Despite Grace commenting about him being deadly like his name-sake, they'd all trained to prevent sin—not just end it. Death was a last resort. A very last resort. Like Sara.

"He's—" Grace started.

"None of your concern," Evan finished. "I believe the doctor asked you a question."

Callahan narrowed his eyes at Evan. "Despite what you

think, just because they're dead, doesn't mean we give out patient information to any meat head off the street."

Meat head? Evan folded his arms across his chest. The tingle of electricity in his palms grew with his escalating irritation.

Grace stepped in front of Evan, trying to block his line of sight to Callahan, but he saw over her head. "Please, is there anything you can tell us about the Jane Doe that wasn't in the records?" she said.

"There's nothing to tell. I write meticulous records." The ME dropped his gaze and continued zipping the bodybag. "Now, if you don't mind, I have work to do."

The hairs on Evan's arms prickled and they stood on end. Intuition. Precognition. Whatever you wanted to call it. This electricity field he could project picked up something his body didn't like. The ME was keeping secrets.

"Please, there has to be something," Grace tried again, the desperation tightening her voice.

"Like what?" Callahan snapped and moved to the body on the next table. "I don't understand what you're looking for. It was two years ago. Hundreds of bodies come through here every year and you expect me to remember something special about a random Jane Doe."

"Was there anything odd about the body? What happened to it after it left here? Did you actually see her cremated?"

"Look, lady. As you can see, I'm pretty busy. A patient transport vehicle got jacked this morning, can you believe it? Scum booted the driver and ambulance officer out of the moving van, then did the same to the patient on the bed. So,

I'm not going to say this again. I have work to do. You need to leave."

Grace's expression drooped, and it was the first time Evan saw her so defeated. His kind, stubborn ray of sunshine faded under the potbellied jerk's attitude.

Evan rolled his shoulders and cracked his neck. No one spoke to Grace like that. He zoned in on the man with predatory focus. Callahan had turned his back to attend the next bodybag lying on the table further along. He didn't see the way Evan stalked toward him. He couldn't feel the electricity thrumming in Evan's veins and how it projected from his body in a magnetic field. And when Evan's fingers curled around his fat throat, he had no clue.

That's why he jolted at the skin contact, not because Evan let loose the current building inside him, but because he was surprised at the sneak attack.

"Answer the doctor," Evan grit out as he turned Callahan to face him.

The man's eyes widened and darted to Grace, then back to Evan. Clearly he knew he was out-manned. Evan stood a full head taller than him, and could snap his fragile neck on a sneeze, yet Callahan groped around the table, desperately trying to find protection, but only came upon the dead body. His panic filled eyes darted back to Grace.

"Evan," Grace breathed a warning.

"Don't worry, Doc." Evan kept his hand on Callahan's throat. "Like I said before, I'm only deadly as a last resort. No harm will come to this man as long as he's telling the truth, and you're going to tell the truth, aren't you, buddy?"

To amplify his point, Evan squeezed a fraction. The man's pulse rabbited under his touch.

Callahan tried to speak, but his vocal cords were squashed. The sound came out a wheeze.

"What's that?" Evan tilted his head. "I can't hear you. Speak up." This time Evan loosened his grip, but his large hand stayed circled around the throat. "You want to try answering the Doc's question again?"

Callahan nodded. "What... ah... what was the question?"

"Jane Doe. Cardinal Bombing. Two years ago," Grace said, looking every bit as flustered as the examiner. "Was there anything unusual about her body?"

"I...uh, yes. It's coming back to me now."

"Of course it is." Evan arched an eyebrow.

"The explosion went off somewhere else in the building because her injuries were consistent with being crushed by heavy objects, not being blown to smithereens."

From the corner of Evan's eyes, he noticed Grace rub her arms as though cold. The action reminded him of her scars. She was a victim of the same building collapse. A survivor. These wouldn't be good memories for her. He had to make the man talk faster.

"Was she dead?" Evan applied pressure.

"What?" He choked. "Of course she was."

"Did you cremate the body? Did you see it yourself?"

"Yes! Yes I saw the body burn. I don't know what you want from me." Bryan's eyes glistened with unshed tears.

"It doesn't make sense," Grace murmured, looking around the room. "I don't understand."

"That makes two of—" Bryan coughed as Evan squeezed.

"So, you're telling me, there's nothing odd about the Jane Doe. Nothing at all?"

Callahan went silent, and his lips flattened.

Evan's senses screamed. Whatever Callahan thought at that moment was the truth they were seeking. Evan narrowed his eyes and growled. "Do you really want me to force it out of you?"

"I remember now," Bryan wheezed, cheeks red.

"Evan." Grace's cool palm on his forearm brought him back to reality.

He didn't want her to think he was a brute who couldn't control himself. She'd already seen him turn up in bruises, just like she'd seen him lose his temper with Sara. They were all low points for him. Not the real him. He wanted to be better. He didn't want her afraid, so he backed off.

Bryan choked, and breathed deeply, a hand fluttering to his throat. "She was sick. Had problems with her heart. The cause wasn't clear, but the rest of her insides were withering too. She would have died within weeks if the bomb didn't do it for her."

"What?" Evan asked. Sara was dying? A telltale prickling washed over his skin, and he speared the examiner with a look. "There's more, isn't there?"

Callahan's shoulders slumped. "Yes. A directive came from the top that I send a bio-sample package to the GODC."

"And who is that?" he asked.

"The Global Organization for Disease Control."

"I've not heard of them," Grace added.

Callahan shrugged. "Neither had I, but when you get an order from the top, you follow it."

"Why wasn't it in your report?" Grace asked.

"I was told to keep it off the books."

"We'll need the address."

"Like I can remember from two years ago!"

"Your memory had a remarkable recovery just now in relation to the Jane Doe. Do I need to facilitate another miracle of the mind?" Evan stepped menacingly toward him, and Callahan lifted his palms in surrender.

"Fine. Fine. It's 524 Shepparton Road, Western Shore."

Suspicion coated Evan's instincts. "You recalled that mighty fast for an address you wrote down two years ago. Have you sent any more bio-samples there recently?"

Callahan said nothing, but flared his nostrils. It didn't matter. Evan's sixth sense went haywire, like a compass losing its true north. Evan went for his throat again. The man was a dirty, rotten liar. He'd been sending bio-samples of dead people for years. But what for?

"What about the white-robed men after the bombing?" Evan snapped.

"What?" Callahan paled.

"You heard me." Evan's face heated, his fingers tingled. His hold on his ability slipped and a tiny spark zipped into the man's throat. He convulsed, eyes rolling back in his head. Okay, maybe it was more than a spark.

"Evan!" Grace cried.

"Just let me finish this, Grace." He focused back on Callahan, now shuddering as though he'd been stunned by a

Taser. "What about the white-robed people, Callahan? What happened to their corpses?"

"I... I... there were none. I don't know what you mean. Everything else was in the report."

Evan squeezed. Callahan choked. Evan released a little. "Last chance."

The tendons in Callahan's neck relaxed. "I cremated them all. Same order as the one to send the bio-samples."

"Evan." A cold palm to his forearm shocked him back to reality. "We have what we came for. That's enough. Let's go."

His arms trembled with restraint, and he leaned in close to Callahan. "Breathe a word about this to anyone, and I'll make it my personal mission to end you."

He let go, and ushered Grace out, mind whirling with the possibilities of their discovery.

SEVENTEEN

DR. GRACE GO

Grace stormed down the hospital corridor, feeling a complicated twist of emotions in her belly. Evan's sturdy palm at her back didn't make things better. In the park, the touch had felt reassuring and confident. Now, it felt... infuriating.

"Did you have to threaten him?" she muttered as a doctor walked past. Quickly, she swapped her grim frown for an easy smile and waved at the passerby. "Hello, Doctor—oh. Hello Raseem. How was the surgery?"

"A success, Grace, thank you." Raseem dipped his head, looked suspiciously at the large and deadly man by her side, then continued down the hall leaving Evan and Grace alone once more.

"Did you?" she asked again, bitterness lacing her tongue. When he didn't answer, she made a frustrated sound and clenched her fists. "God, you can be so—*God!*"

"Thanks," he grunted.

"It wasn't a compliment."

Evan stopped her with a palm to the shoulder. Face to face in the stark corridor, there was nowhere to look but his blazing green eyes. Yeah, well, buddy… she was the one with the right to be angry here. Physical violence was *never* the answer.

Unless of course you were a member of the Deadly Seven.

Then, she supposed, sometimes it was. Oh God, she was in trouble because one look from him lowered her resolve. He'd been so nice to Adam in the street that she let him control the meeting with Callahan however he wanted. What on earth would happen if he tried to kiss her again?

Trouble.

He looked ready to reply, then a nurse in pink scrubs turned the corner. It was Catherine from the ED. Catherine was a busybody. She knew everything about everyone, and then some. She bounced down the hallway, her usual chipper self, brown hair swaying in her wake. Her steps faulted when she noticed Grace. Catherine's eyes darted appreciatively over the intense man with his hand on Grace's shoulder, brooding. A smirk twitched at the corner of Catherine's mouth and she gave Grace a two-fingered salute.

"Doctor Grace," she said and kept walking.

"Nurse Catherine." Grace kept her face pleasant until Catherine had walked away, then shook her head, letting her anger rise.

"No. We're not getting into this here." Evan pulled her to the side, opened a door and then slipped in.

The door shut heavily behind them. The only light

streamed from a strip of frosted glass at the door, but it was enough to illuminate the supply closet they were in. At least there was nobody here to gossip.

"Go on. Say what you really think," Evan said and folded his arms. "I know there's more coming, so out with it."

"Out with it?" She blinked. Did he really want her honest opinion? Oh, yeah. Oh, boy he was gonna get it. She prodded his chest. "Fine. You know what I think? I think you don't know how to deal with the real world anymore. Sara messed with your head two years ago and no one in your family believed you. It tore you apart and you've been punishing yourself ever since. You came into my hospital covered in bruises and, somehow, I don't think they're from saving the world. You said so yourself, and nobody has seen a sign of you or your family protecting the streets in years. Well, I got news for you, big stuff. You were right all along. She was bad news. Still is. All this time, you've been fighting to save your family. You should be proud that you're the only one left trying to uncover the truth. You should have a little faith in yourself. Open your eyes, Lazarus!"

"Wow." His eyes widened as he processed her barrage. "Okay, Drill Sergeant."

Maybe she should have put a tap on her mouth, but he had a way of bringing everything to the surface.

"You know, Doc, just because you don't see us, doesn't mean we aren't out there at night. It didn't mean we all gave up."

"Is this true?"

He shrugged. "For some of us. Some of the time."

"Good."

"Good?"

"Yes, I don't want you to give up. I think what you and your family are doing is incredible. This city has gone to the dogs. I got mugged twice in two days! And… well, while I also like to believe in the system, I'm not blind. I can see that it's a little broken, but with Dr. Callahan, you went from zero to threat level deadly in three seconds."

"He admitted to working under the books!"

"You also strangled Sara, and… and… whatever electric power you have must be frying your brain circuits because violence isn't the answer. Hurting people isn't the answer."

"I didn't see you stopping me."

He had her there. "I didn't want to…" Why didn't she? Maybe because he looked so terrifying. Like he did now. Even in the muted light she could see his biceps bulging through his shirt, veins threaded in his exposed forearms as he clenched his fists. Heat emanated from his presence. With all that raw, restrained power, he twitched. The wrong sound, the wrong move, could set him off.

Grace's breath heaved in and out her shaky lungs.

"You were afraid of me," he said.

She looked up at him, alarmed. "No. I wasn't."

A step closer. "Yes. You were."

Her heart thudded loudly in her chest.

His finger lifted to her cheek, and she flinched. His resulting frown changed his expression from defiance to contrition.

"Doc," he whispered and pulled his hand back to clench at his side. "I never meant to scare you. I would *never* hurt you. Him, yes. I have no problems hurting a liar like him, but not you."

Hurt flashed in his shadowed eyes and she softened. Could she really blame him for his behavior? He was what they made him. Whoever *they* were. She had no idea, but it was clear there was more to his life than what she saw today. He had electricity coming out of his fingertips, for heaven's sake.

"I believe you," she whispered. "I don't know why, but I believe you won't hurt me."

To prove her point, she placed her palm on the solid wall of muscle at his chest. His hot skin burned through the fabric and her fingers flexed in response. A low sound of awareness came from the base of his throat as though her touch pained him. Or the opposite. Oh, yes. She could be happy with the opposite.

"How is your shoulder wound?" she blurted, to stop her derailing thoughts.

Silence. Heavy breathing. When she lifted her gaze, she wished she hadn't. Shadowed fire burned back at her from two dark eyes, intense and full of emotion.

He licked his lips.

"Evan?"

"It's fine," he said, voice rough and thick. "All healed."

"Can I—?" She couldn't finish the sentence from the lump forming in her throat. She shifted her hand to the collar of his Henley T-shirt and popped the top button, then the next, and the next until it gaped open, exposing the dip of his collarbone and smooth velvety skin sketched in ink. She'd seen a sample of that ink when she treated him for the shoulder wound, but it had happened so fast, she never got a good look. And she wanted to. She wanted to look her fill. Her finger traced a black line from the gaping collar to the right and peeled the shirt open to expose his shoulder.

He swallowed, Adam's apple bobbing.

Check the sutures. That's all.

But he smelled so good.

He was stubborn, and probably wouldn't go back to his GP. That was the only reason she was doing what she was doing, taking the liberty of… The stitches, or lack thereof, came into view and her mind stuttered to a halt. They were gone. A puckered scar was all that was left—purple and solid. It looked a few weeks old, not a few days. Her wide eyes met his.

"How?"

He shrugged. "Made in a lab. I'm a freak."

"No," she whispered, shocked, horrified that he would think that about himself. "You're magnificent. A marvel."

"Even if you don't like… my job?"

"I never said that. You're taking everything wrong. I believe you can make a difference, Evan, just not down the path you've been traveling." She looked away. "I've been down that road. I spent weeks in the hospital bed stewing in my sorrows and dancing with my demons, but I realized that if I gave in to those dark feelings, that I would lose part of myself. Don't get stuck on vengeance and pain." Her words sounded steady and strong, but deep in her heart, she remembered how close she'd come to crossing that line in the hospital. She wanted to give up her work as a doctor, and to chase down the bomber and make her pay—to use her knowledge as a surgeon to kill that person without a trace. She did actually focus fully on that for a while, but when she came across Taco and the other people displaced from the bombing, she realized it wasn't about her need for revenge.

"It's a blurred line, Grace."

"I know that but, to be honest, your people skills could use a little work." She was thinking of the ME, probably with bruises on his throat.

He snorted.

She smiled.

It broke the tension.

But her fingers still touched his hot skin, and she couldn't tear them away. He smelled divine. Manly, sweaty and spicy. She flexed her fingers again. His scent sang to her baser instincts, making her nipples bead under her blouse and push at her heavy coat. Suddenly, the heat in the small space was too much. She had a moment of panic knowing she was locked in that tiny confined room with him... panic that her claustrophobia would set in... then he breathed, and her palms shifted up his front, and she didn't mind. So much power rolled beneath her hands, she knew she'd be safe with him.

"I want to work on it," he rasped, frowning. "For you."

"Why? Why me?" What she wanted to say was, why trust her with his secret? Why try to impress her?

He enveloped her hands with his. "Every day I wake with the sense of envy clawing my gut. It starts slow, but builds to a sickening hunger I can't get rid of, not unless I stop the sin. That feeling wears me down. It wears us all down until eventually... we're doomed to become the sin we fight. I didn't realize how numb I'd become, that I had to let myself get beat up to feel anything."

She gasped. He let himself get beat up?

"Then I met you and the pain disappeared."

He showed her a tattoo on the inside of his wrist. A circle was separated into equal parts black and white by a curvy line—the Yin-Yang symbol.

"This ink has been modified to respond to the level of envy in my bloodstream. The blacker it is, the more sin in me, and the bigger risk of losing myself. Before I met you, it was almost black."

"It's perfectly balanced now," Grace said.

"Exactly."

Her heart stopped. "You think I had something to do with that?"

"I know you do." Evan's fingers dipped inside her coat collar and traced her neck, sending her senses into hyper-drive. He slowly popped the first button on her coat. "You have no envy, Grace. None at all. I've never met anyone in my entire life without at least an ounce. It's more than that. You're kind hearted, too. Exactly what I need in my life. You make me feel all the right things again."

Her fists clutched his shirt. She had no envy? Her mind raced, trying to come to terms with what he said. Was she never envious of anyone? No. Probably not since her parents died, and she survived. She remembered waking in the hospital recovery room, limbs bandaged, sutures and skin grafts over her body... and then the doctor came in with that look on his face. She knew exactly what he was going to say.

She'd worn that cold, distant look many times before. *We're sorry, Grace. Your parents didn't make it.*

She'd spent weeks, maybe months hating life after that, but then as she packed up their belongings, and moved them to her apartment, she realized there were many things in those boxes that pointed to their pride for her. From framed certificates, to science ribbons in grade school, to notices in the university paper, and receipts for her tuition and bank statements. They'd spent their life savings on her. For Grace to throw it all away in the name of revenge was wrong.

That was the moment she vowed to live for them. To be happy with the life she had, with the person she was, and that she'd spend it making other people less fortunate than herself live a strong, happy and healthy life. That's why she'd declined the cardiothoracic fellowship. She was a great surgeon, but the hospital had no shortage of doctors wanting to be the next CT-Superstar. They did, however, have a shortage of doctors willing to work for next to nothing at the free clinic. She missed the operating theater so much she ached, but with her anxiety problems, she was just grateful she could help people. One day she would have the guts to face her theater fears, just not today.

Grace looked at the man staring intently at her. He put himself on the line every day only to be ridiculed and blamed in the paper. The Cardinal Copy hadn't been kind to them over the years, often inflaming the truth with claims of property damage, and God complexes. She wondered if anyone had ever said thank you to him for saving their lives. Had she said thank you?

Grace tugged him down by the shirt and lifted on her toes until her lips hovered near his.

"Thank you," she whispered. "For saving my life. For helping Adam. For everything."

She kissed him. It was a simple, press of the lips, but it was a connection that shot through her, and sent every nerve synapse firing.

He froze. Didn't move. For a minute, Grace thought she'd overstepped, and when she pulled back, he looked tortured.

"Grace, I'm not expecting payment… or gratitude, or whatever you think this is. I…"

"I know. That's why I kissed you."

"It is?"

She bit her lip and nodded, conflicted. Because now that she had the taste of him, she wanted more—much more—but would he think it was only her gratitude?

As if reading her mind, he popped another button on her coat, and another, and kept going until it opened wide, exposing her burgundy silk blouse and blue jeans. His eyes lowered from her face, darted down her features and then went lower. His gaze felt like a caress. He locked on her breasts, and his lids drifted lazily down the rest of her body. "You're so beautiful, Grace."

"Evan…" she whispered, not sure what to say. He was a powerfully built man, a perfect male specimen. The kind she learned about in medical school and was literally created in a lab. The kind of special you usually read about in story books. Strong, gifted, fighting to save the world… and from the heat in his dark eyes, he wanted her. He needed her. Maybe they could be good for each other.

"Kiss me again," she whispered.

He dipped his head, but didn't go for her mouth. Instead, his lips found her neck and breathed in deep, nudging her with his nose.

"You smell delicious."

Then he tasted her sensitive skin, sending shivers down her spine. Both of them made an incomprehensible sound of pleasure. He licked and nipped and slid his hands to her back, pulling her body against his.

Grace went liquid. This embrace, it meant so much that her heart swelled achingly. Having arms to hold her again. If she just closed her eyes for a minute, she could imagine the pain of the world ebb away and enjoy having someone who needed her.

Not her skills as a doctor, but *her*.

"Oh, God," she mumbled in delight as he licked up a vein on her neck to nibble at her ear.

She felt him smile against her skin. "Thanks."

EIGHTEEN

EVAN LAZARUS

Evan couldn't believe he was here, tasting Grace's soft sunshine skin. Since the moment he'd met her at the hospital, she'd been living in his thoughts, a constant presence. And now, he had her pliant and eager in his arms. It wasn't like outside the gallery where they'd launched at each other in a desperate fit of passion, high on adrenaline. This was intended. She made the first move. She knew every dark detail about him, and she still wanted him.

He ran the tip of his tongue along her full bottom lip before pushing inside her mouth. Around and around he swirled, delving until she pushed back with a trembling moan into his mouth. The desperate sound connected with his groin, tingling and tightening and pulling him taut and heavy with need. Her sound hit the button on his restraint and unleashed his desire. Heat suffused his skin, burning his cheeks, scorching his neck. Biological response—it was happening. A moment of panic hit him, but he squashed it down under his new strange power sparking in little bursts, skipping down his spine to curl his toes. There was nowhere to go, nowhere to hide. It would always happen with her. And right now when he had her responsive in his arms… he liked it.

He took a risk and brazenly pressed his hips into hers, showing how he really felt.

She nudged back.

Hells, yeah.

He kissed her deeper, reveling in every sense she awakened in him.

Touch—so soft. Taste—salty and sweet. Smell—like sun-kissed linen washed in lavender. Sight—flashes of hot, steamy woman, eyes fluttering closed beneath him. And then there were her sounds—little whimpers of pleasure every time she took a breath.

It had never been like this with any other woman. Sex had always been tainted with envy… always niggling at him, never allowing him to fully let go. But now, nothing. Nothing but her in every sense, begging for more. He was consumed by her. Before he knew what he was doing, he gripped her ass. Damned coat was in the way.

So he moved his attention to the front, wanting her skin. Flesh against flesh. He tugged at the hem of her silk blouse and pulled it free from her jeans.

"Yes," she whispered against his lips. "More, Evan."

She plunged her cool hands under his shirt and splayed her fingers against his torso.

He gasped at the temperature shock and then did the same to her. Hot hands against cool skin. She arched into him.

Trailing his rough, battered fingertips up her body, he didn't feel they had the right to touch her. Silky. Smooth. Satin.

Bra. Nipple.

Shit.

He found both firm buds through her thin fabric and rolled between his thumb and forefinger.

"Evan," she begged.

"Grace." He loved the way her name hissed from his tongue on a breath when he pronounced the c. He slid a hand down her stomach, fingers first, to dip beneath the barrier of her waistband. "Say yes again."

She made a feeble sound and scraped her nails up his back. The stark contrast of her soft body at his front, and sudden pain at his rear had him panting, needy.

Fuck, he was a big guy and this little woman reduced him to one word thoughts and baser instincts. He would do anything for her at that moment, and somewhere deep in the scary part of his brain taking a back seat, he knew he always would.

He needed her to want him. To *say* she wanted him, and no one else. It was an irrational cave man urge. He pushed his hand under her panty-line, until they passed her curls to slide along her slick center. "Jesus," he moaned, gently stroking her, teasing her, relishing in her moans of pleasure. When his finger entered, she gasped, trembling beneath him. Hot. Tight. Wet. For him.

"Grace," he said. "You want me." Please. Say yes again.

"Yes." She pushed against his hand, wantonly driving herself against him. "God, Evan. More."

He pulled on her ponytail, just like he'd fantasied and lifted her lips to his, while the other hand focused on her core. Plunging, sliding, testing and playing. He probed her mouth with his tongue, like his fingers moved below. The pressure of electricity built inside him, and for a moment, he thought he'd not be able to suppress the power. But he didn't want to hurt her, just please her, and make her putty in his arms. It wasn't him letting go, it was her.

"Let go, Grace. I've got you."

Soon, she tensed in his arms, fingers flexing and scraping down his back. "Oh, God. Evan… I—"

A tiny pitched mewl cut off and she bit sharply into his pec to muffle her voice as she shattered, trembling and shuddering around him. When she went limp in his arms, he smiled, satisfied. His messy girl knew how to let go, to feel, and throw caution to the wind—in a hospital supply closet.

Then the hairs on the back of his neck stood on end.

Someone was coming.

"Doc," he warned, hand still down her pants and slick with her desire.

She made a muffled protest on his chest.

That feeling of urgency grew. All that energy he had inside had projected out of his body and into the hallway in a field, sensing any passer by in his web. He buttoned her fly back up and straightened her coat. "Someone's coming."

"What?" Haze cleared from her eyes. "Now?"

He cleared his throat and nodded.

"Oh, no." She dug into her coat pocket, pulled out her hospital staff ID and clipped it on her breast pocket, as if that created order from her disheveled appearance.

The person approaching was too close for them to escape unnoticed, so Evan flicked on the light to further illuminate the room full of shelves and supplies.

The door opened.

"And we'll need ten packets of gauze." Grace snagged a handful of plastic covered packages and indicated for him to do the same. Then she strode confidently out the door, past the gawking orderly, and into the hallway.

Evan bit his lip to hide the smirk dancing there.

"Doc needs her gauze," he said to the orderly, made an awkward face, and then rushed after his woman already halfway down the corridor.

He jogged to catch up. "Wait."

She was doing her stubborn stride thing again.

"I can't believe I did that," she said.

"You mean, I did that. To you."

"Oh my God, Evan."

"You said that a lot." He barely dodged the gauze she swatted at him. He laughed.

"What are you laughing at?"

"I'm happy."

A chagrinned glance shot his way.

"Plus, your hair." He pointed to the crooked ponytail.

"Damn it." She eyed a bathroom nearby and pushed her gauze package into his arms. "Give me a second. I'll be back."

Five minutes later, she returned from the bathroom in less disarray. Her still-flushed cheeks, and too bright eyes, made him want to push her back in there and finish what they started.

She pulled out a phone from her pocket to check the time. "It's getting late. I have to go."

"New phone?"

"Yes."

He took it and entered his number. Then dialed his phone so he'd have hers. His pocket vibrated to confirm the call, and he handed it back to her.

"Where are we going?" he asked as they left the hospital.

"You can't come with me, Evan." She turned to him on the street. "I'm having lunch with a girlfriend."

"I told you, I'm not leaving you alone. Not until we deal with Sara."

She frowned. "We can investigate the address after lunch. Then we can sit down and talk properly about what just happened."

"Where is lunch?"

"You can't come with me. Don't you have something else to do? It's just for an hour or so."

He checked the time. It was getting close to when he'd said the family would meet to break the news to Wyatt. He didn't like leaving her alone. Not one bit, but he couldn't miss the family meeting.

"I'll drop you off at the restaurant. Which one is it?"

"Heaven. Just a few blocks from here."

"Heaven? You're kidding me."

"No. Is there something wrong with the place—oh." Her eyes widened. "The head chef is your brother."

"Yes. I'm going there too." The anticipation must have bled onto his face because her eyes softened on him.

"Is he the one who was engaged to Sara?"

Evan nodded.

"You're going to tell him about her?"

"Yeah."

She patted him gently on the shoulder. "Don't worry, you'll be fine. You love him."

"Thanks, Doc."

"C'mon. Let's split a cab."

NINETEEN

EVAN LAZARUS

Evan helped Grace out of the cab and then followed quietly until they entered Heaven.

Heaven was a five-star restaurant decked out in luxury retro decor. Sometimes he felt like he stepped out of a Rat-Pack movie in the sixties. Sinatra crooned over the internal speakers, and on the weekends and nights, a performer played from a piano at the center stage.

The maître d, a bald man wearing a vest over a white shirt, greeted Grace. When he spied Evan over her shoulder, his eyes widened in recognition. He lifted a finger as if to say he'd be with him in a minute and then showed Grace to her seat.

Evan's eyes followed her like a hawk. After spending the entire morning together, he wasn't comfortable with the sudden distance. Her soothing presence receded in an ebbing wave, but he knew it was for the best. Shit was about to get real. At least he knew she wouldn't be in danger in here.

"Mr. Lazarus," The maître d said, returning. "I wasn't expecting you today. I haven't booked the private dining room."

He retrieved a menu from the cashier's podium.

"That's cool, Colin. Today we need a booth. We're all going to be here."

"All seven?"

"Nine. Mary and Flint, too."

Colin scanned the list of reservations with a frown on his face. "We're almost booked out. If I had known..." He glanced up and caught Evan's eyes. "You said all, so Parker will be here?"

"That's what I said."

"Um..." As he glanced at the bookings, his face went red, and little beads of perspiration appeared on his bald head.

Maybe he should have called or maybe they should've sent Liza here to get a table, she was better at organizing these things. Evan took a deep breath, closed his eyes and focused. It had been only minutes since Grace left his side, and already envy battered his defenses. He stole a glance her way to find her settled into a booth across the main stage at the center of the room. Instantly he felt better.

She was safe. She was there.

"Okay. I think I can do something with this booking," Colin said under his breath, marking notes on his ledger. Two-seconds later, he ushered Evan to a u-shaped booth. Trimmed in beige leather; it matched the rest of the soft, luxury decor in one of the most upmarket eating establishments in the Quadrant. A swell of pride hit Evan in the chest. Parker was the owner, but Wyatt had built the reputation of this place all on his own, despite losing what he thought was the love of his life.

That pride diminished when he heard an enormous crash from the kitchen. Wyatt ruled his kitchen with an iron fist, and it was well known around town that you needed balls of steel to work there. Being a Michelin starred chef hadn't come easy. But if you made it at Heaven, then you earned your bones, as they said in the mafia—you'd become a made man in the industry. The field was as cutthroat as the mafia, so he got the association. No wonder Wyatt's nickname here was the Godfather.

Evan's attention wandered across the glossy stage, past the piano and to the booths opposite, to where Grace sat. Even across the divide, he felt her magnetic pull. There was nothing he enjoyed more than watching her smile at the waitress serving her.

"Don't say it," he said over his shoulder without moving his eyes from Grace.

The immediate response was the clatter of a black leather handbag as it slid across the empty table top, skidding to a halt just before it slipped off the edge.

"You're a fucking party pooper, little brother." Liza had arrived, and she brought her potty mouth. "I wasn't going to say anything, *Jesus Christ*."

"Sure you weren't." Evan smiled at his eldest sister and drew her in for a hug. "I hope you've been looking after yourself, sis."

Tall, brunette, and blue eyed, Liza was the living embodiment of a Brazilian Barbie doll. But don't tell her that, she'd slice your carotid with a tainted knife before the words left your mouth.

A grim expression crossed her face as she took a seat. "As opposed to how you're looking after you?"

"Fuck off."

"Every day."

"Uh, TMI, sis."

Evan grinned and joined her in the booth.

"Speaking of. You tap that yet?" She nodded in Grace's direction, making an obvious movement with her eyes. "Your lust is making my eyes bleed."

"No couth. Seriously, sis, you've got no couth." He sheltered his eyes with his hand, embarrassed, hoping Grace hadn't heard. Thankfully, with the music playing through the stereo, he doubted it.

"Holy shitballs. You actually like her." Liza laughed and then flagged down Colin to order a couple of beers. In one minute flat, they had two ice cold brewskis sitting on their table, perspiring with condensation. Considering their location, they probably should have stuck with wine or some wanky champagne, but Colin was well used to their average tastes by now. The only two that gorged themselves on luxury were Parker and Wyatt. Sometimes Tony, but he wasn't fussy. He'd overindulge on anything given the opportunity.

"Sort of," he said.

She choked on her beer. "Sort of? You got a sort-of-dick-issue? *Jeez*, if you don't want her, I'd hit that. Does she have a brother?"

"No!" Hell, how did this sister always make him feel like a bumbling idiot. Maybe because he assumed she knew all there was to know about lust. But the truth was, she was as tight-lipped as a nun about her exploits. Sure, she teased them a lot, and they knew she went on dates, but she never spoke about them afterward. He had no idea if she was into women, or men, or both... or all of them. Unlike Tony, whose sexual accomplishments were often plastered over the entertainment news reels, Liza was a mystery, and that's the way she liked it.

"So how was the exhibition?" she asked. "Apart from the death and destruction?"

Evan glanced again at Grace. Finding his mate was a huge revelation, but it might not go over so well with Liza. She didn't think she'd ever be happy with someone who embodied the opposite of lust, so set herself up to never be disappointed by pretending the bonding story was a myth. He placed his arm lengthwise on the top of the booth, contemplating where to begin. Liza did the same and thrummed her fingers on the leather. He snorted. Tomboy.

She kept staring at him and then back towards Grace.

"So what's so special about this girl? What's got you hot under the collar?"

"You haven't spoken with Parker, or Griff? Mary?"

Liza shook her head. "Been busy, bro."

"You really want to know?"

Liza wiggled her eyebrows in excitement and then held up her hand. "Wait. There's Sloan. Tell me when she gets here. Can't believe she's not late."

"Well, she only has to come from upstairs."

Liza grunted in agreement.

Evan stood when he caught the sight of his other sister crossing the crowded restaurant and waved her over. He'd been so used to her in her socks and underwear that he almost didn't recognize Sloan fully dressed in jeans and a long sleeve flannelette shirt. She adjusted her fake black-rimmed glasses on her nose and then tugged on her hair. She widened her eyes in greeting.

"Bras," was all she said and slid in the booth after Evan.

"Ugh. You sound like a moron." Liza sipped as she appraised her younger sister. "You dress like one too."

"Whatever," Sloan said to Liza, then turned to Evan. "So when's this thing going down, I gotta get back."

Evan checked his phone. "Wyatt clocks off in twenty."

Sloan pulled her sleeve over her fingers and chewed on the hem at the wrist.

"You want a brewski?" Evan asked.

"Nah. We won't be long, right?"

The daggers Liza sent her sister would've pierced if she'd noticed. Liza opened her mouth to chastise when Evan chimed in.

"It's no trouble, Colin will get it." Evan ordered another beer by holding his finger in the air at the waiter across the room. The good man knew exactly what he wanted and brought it over.

"Thanks." Sloan gave Colin a small smile before he returned to his duties.

"So, sis, Evan here was about to tell me why his dick is so bottled up with frustration that he's about to blow."

Sloan's dark eyebrow lifted on one side. "You know there're pills for that, bras."

Evan snorted, cheeks reddening. "That shit doesn't happen to me."

"So, this sexy woman. Spill, little bro."

"You think I'm going to tell you now?"

"Okay, okay." Across the table, Liza threw up her palms. "I'm done with the smack talking. Serious."

Since neither of the girls were at his exhibition, and Sloan had only received the cliffs notes version last night, he explained what happened, from the bits about Sara turning up, and the bits about Grace—minus the nookie details in the alley. He displayed his tattoo. "If you recall, that was heavily weighted to the dark a few days ago. I spent the morning with Grace and simply being in her presence evened it out. It's starting to itch like a mother-fucker, which means it's going to regress soon, but I don't give a shit. For a few hours, it's been bliss."

They reacted with silence. Eyes reflecting thoughts turned inwards. If they understood him, they didn't reveal any emotion.

"There's more." He went on to explain the physiological reactions his body had when around her and what Mary had hypothesized about its purpose—pheromones for attracting a mate. She was the polar opposite to his sin, and his body recognized that intrinsically. Neither of them had believed Wyatt went through the same reaction, making his relationship with Sara a false start. When he finished his explanation, he pushed his sleeve back down. "I know we all gave up on finding a mate, and believed Mary's stories were a joke, but it's true. I'll prove it."

He touched Liza's hand and let a volt slip free. She yelped in surprise and then rubbed her hand with a scowl befitting a queen. Sloan laughed.

Movement in Evan's periphery across the stage caught his attention. Grace glanced at them and he gave a tentative smile back.

"So, let me get this straight," Liza said, eyeing him and Grace. "You step into the vicinity of this chick, your dick-dar goes haywire, fireworks go off, angels sing and all of a sudden she's your soul-mate and you unlock some freaky powers."

"Basically," he said.

"I don't think it matters." Sloan absently scratched her tattoo through her shirt. "None of us are going to live long, anyway. No point getting into a relationship when we're all ticking time-bombs."

Liza thwacked her over the head. "You're not listening. He's saying we don't have to be. If anyone gets to be morose about this, it's me. I mean, who the fuck isn't going to feel lust? Do I have to find a saint? I mean, I like sex. I don't want to give it up."

Both Evan and Sloan shot Liza a sympathetic glance. Liza was right. Her sin was the worst.

"I know it sounds far-fetched," Evan added. "But when I'm around her, the sin fades. I feel… normal. It's real, man. I don't know, there has to be some way you can find a partner without them being sexual vegans."

His sisters snorted.

"No meat. Good one," Liza said.

"Well, I try."

Another crash from the kitchen drew their attention across the room, and when Wyatt's shouting followed, Liza mumbled, "I hope his mate turns up soon."

TWENTY

DR. GRACE GO

Across the room, closer to the kitchen, Grace sat in her booth, picking at the stitched seams on the menu and re-reading the meals. She kept having to start again. There was too much going on in her mind right now, and the thought of Evan sitting across the stage with two stunning women made her heart spin. First, the Victoria's Secret model had sat down looking all I'm-so-hot-I-don't-need-to-wear-girly-clothes, and then there was sexy librarian girl with the black pigtails. Grace wasn't jealous. It was obviously his family. But, there were looks cast her way. She wasn't stupid. She knew they spoke about her. And after spending that glorious moment with him in the supply closet…

She blushed. Was that what she was calling it now? A moment? Did she want more?

Before she could finish her train of thought, a voice snapped her out of her daze.

"Oh, my God. Did you see who just walked in?" Her friend Lilo Likeke had arrived. A journalist at the Cardinal

Copy, Lilo was almost as busy as Grace, yet she always managed to find time to make baked goods, just like the ones in the Tupperware container she absently pushed across the table as she slid onto the bench.

Lilo's hair was cut in a short, wavy brown bob that set off her bronzed skin and brown eyes, now crinkled in a smile as she gazed across the room. Part Hawaiian, part Italian and everything friendly, Lilo had known Grace since the bombing.

Grace smiled in greeting at her friend, then went back to her menu, and tried to focus.

"Tony Lazarus," Lilo elaborated when Grace didn't respond. "The actor. He's here. Must be here to see his brother in the kitchen. Gracie, did you hear me?"

"Huh?" Grace looked up from her menu.

Her friend frowned at her. "Is everything okay? You're even more distracted than normal."

"Yeah, I'm fine. I'm sorry, what did you say?"

"Look over there. Holy shit, now look who's with him: Parker Lazarus. And that last one, with the glasses—he's gotta be someone important. Talk about sexy nerd. Wow. He's a bonafide babe. Look how he carries himself, with complete confidence. Serious, too. I wouldn't be surprised if the air parts way simply because it knows he's coming." She sighed wistfully.

Grace laughed and followed Lilo's line of sight to the three imposing men following the maître d down the opposite side of the room. She wasn't the only one looking. Every set of eyes in the establishment followed suit. The men were gorgeous, fit, tall and extremely well built. It was more like they stalked or prowled than walked. She narrowed her eyes as they all took a seat in the booth with Evan and recognized the facial similarities. Sharp jaws, wide lips, thick lashes.

"I wonder what kind of high-powered business deals they're making, and who are those women? Probably girl-friends. If only I was a fly on the wall of that booth. There's got to be something news worthy there."

"I think they're all family."

Lilo's shrewd gaze snapped back to Grace. "How would you know? Come to think of it, you're not in your usual hospital getup. I thought you worked today, and that's why we're lunching so late."

"I haven't filled you in on the past twenty-four hours."

"I know. You haven't texted me for days. What gives?"

"I got mugged and lost my phone."

Lilo gasped. "I told you to come to Krav Maga classes with me! Do you need a phone? I might have a spare."

Lilo rifled through her enormous leather satchel.

Grace stopped Lilo with her hand. "It's okay. I wasn't hurt and bought a new phone this morning." She glanced over at Evan. "The tattooed one with the messy brown hair, stuck between the two girls, is Evan Lazarus."

Recognition flooded Lilo's large brown eyes. "The artist? From the exhibition. Where the murder happened?" With each sentence, her tone lowered a fraction more, adding more drama.

"Yes. He didn't do it, of course. I spent the morning with him."

Lilo blinked a few times, taking in Grace's words. "Like,

spent the morning with him? *Or spent the morning with him.* Lucky you."

"Not that kind of morning. Well. Maybe I suppose. But... oh gosh, now you have me flustered. To be honest, I have no idea what's going on between us, if I want something, or..." She left the words hanging.

Lilo reached across the table and squeezed Grace's hand. "Never mind. My love life's not exactly going according to plan either. But enough talk about men. What looks good on the menu?"

"All of it. Is your yoga friend still coming? What was her name?"

"Misha. And, no. Her father had some dramas at his little Polish restaurant across the bridge. He also owns the food truck in the Quadrant park and apparently there's been some gang activity in the area. She had to go and help him out."

"Is everything okay?" Grace asked.

"Yes, she's fine. It's all good. For now anyway."

Somehow Grace knew that wasn't what kept the pinch in Lilo's eyes, or the twitch in her fingers as she plucked at the menu. "Lilo, I can tell when you're troubled. What's up?"

"It's just Donnie. I'm not sure it's working out, but I don't know how to tell him. Even though nobody at work knows we're dating, it could still cause trouble."

Donald Doppinger (a.k.a. Donnie Darko) was Lilo's secret boyfriend at the Cardinal Copy. Both investigative reporters, Lilo was at the start of her stellar career, while Donnie had been in the game for at least twenty years. A Pulitzer Prize contender many times over, he didn't like the way it looked to date a newbie reporter—especially one as young and talented and beautiful as Lilo. He claimed people would think she slept her way to the top, but Grace believed the truth was, he didn't like being overshadowed by her brilliance. He wanted all the attention for himself. Lilo was up to date with all the new tech. She blogged, she YouTubed, and she Instagrammed. Digital immigrants like Donnie couldn't keep up, so they sabotaged the bright young things by any means necessary.

"Lilo." Grace reached across to steady her friend's hands. "You're incredibly talented. Not because of him but because you're the hardest, most tenacious worker I've ever had the fortune of meeting, let alone be friends with. Don't let anyone else tell you otherwise."

The small, shy smile Lilo returned warmed Grace's heart.

Lilo tapped her Tupperware box. "I made you brownies. I know they're your favorite and you probably had no time to eat, as usual."

"Aww, thank you. I'm sorry I was distracted when you arrived."

Grace lifted the lid to take a peek inside, but shouting and clanging brought Grace's attention to the open kitchen a few feet away. A chef dressed in grubby white blasted a terrified waitress. He was tall, broad shouldered, and intimidating as hell. Men like him were a common sight at the male dominated hospital—especially among the surgical staff. It brought her back to the days when she was berated as an intern for apparent lazy listening. After a thirty hour shift, she'd been too exhausted to double check the nurse's stocked supplies before an operation, and had the pleasant experience of having a sermon handed to her by the attending surgeon. Still, that hadn't been a public embarrassment like the girl near the kitchen. The chef jabbed his finger in the air about one inch from her flinching face. How humiliating. The waitress started to cry.

The poor girl couldn't have been more than twenty years old. She defended herself with words, and pointed to something on a plate in her hands, but the chef was having none of it. His tirade increased, along with his blood pressure as he shoved the plate back toward her body, spilling its contents all over her front.

A gasp shot out of Grace as she heard what he said, and it was horrendous. Too horrendous to repeat. But the worst thing was that nobody said a word. He was like that nasty television chef who didn't know how to back off. Half the restaurant this side of the stage were eyeing them, and no one did a god-damned thing.

"What a jerk!" Grace slammed her palm on the table in front of her, rattling the cutlery. She slid out of the seat and stood next to her table, arms folded, glaring at the chef.

She steeled herself to stomp over there and give the man a what for, imagining herself tall and invincible. Then she cleared her throat, smoothed her blouse and took a deep breath.

"I'll be right back," she said in a controlled voice to Lilo and then stormed to the kitchen. She skirted the serving area and walked right up to the couple. The waitress hastily tried to pick up the spilled mess from the floor while the chef glowered.

"Excuse me," Grace said, clenching her fists to stop them trembling.

The chef and waitress stopped and stared.

"Look," Grace added to the chef. "I appreciate you're having a bad day, because nobody deliberately sets out to treat another human being like garbage, but I don't know if you realize you're being rather hurtful."

"Who the fuck are you?" he clipped.

"Dr. Grace Go." She jutted out her chin.

"Well, Dr. Grace Go. I don't give a flying fuck if her poor little feelings are hurt. It's none of your business, so respectfully, *Go* fuck off."

Well. No need for cussing. Grace swallowed. This was harder than she thought. The man was much, much bigger this close, and his anger rolled off him in heat waves. She totally got how the waitress wanted to shrink back. But, it wasn't the first time someone made fun of her name, and it wasn't the first time a man tried to tell her what to do. Grace stood tall.

"I'm not talking about hurting her, although that isn't good either. I'm talking about the damage you're doing to yourself." She jabbed a finger in the air, just like he'd done to the waitress.

"What?"

"That anger isn't helping you. It's toxic. To you and everyone around you."

"Who the fuck do you think you are? This is my restaurant, I do what I want."

His restaurant? Grace paled. Oh yeah, wasn't Evan's

brother a chef here? Her eyes snagged on the Michelin star on his uniform. "I'm nobody, I guess, but—"

"Grace," came a low male voice.

She turned and found Evan and his very surly, unhappy older brother, Parker. The chef noticed too, and his face morphed from confusion to bottled fury. It was such a shame. He was extremely handsome, but the anger and hatred in his expression made him all twisted. The waitress fled.

Parker cocked an arrogant eyebrow. "If I'm not mistaken, brother, this is my restaurant, not yours, and I won't have you treating my staff like that."

But the chef ignored his remark and instead turned to Evan in accusation. "You know this… woman?"

What the hell did that pause mean? Did he have trouble distinguishing if she was female? Or was he insinuating she was a beast?

Evan stepped between Grace and the chef. "Yeah, and if you've got a bone to pick with her, you'll have to go through me."

"You know that can be arranged."

The tension in the air was palpable. Grace couldn't help thinking she'd started something she couldn't finish and perhaps the chef was right, it was none of her business. Now the whole restaurant stared, including Lilo from her booth, not ten feet away.

"Wyatt, don't make a scene," warned Parker. "Clock off and come over to the booth. The whole family's here. Let's talk."

The chef, Wyatt, darted a glance across the room to

where Parker indicated, then lifted his gaze to the ceiling and shook his head in disbelief. "Of course you're all here. You fucking railroaded me." He pulled his cap off to reveal black flattened hair, scrubbed it, and then stormed toward the kitchen. He came back a few seconds later with a ramekin, then went to the table where the rest of the family sat, mumbling: "Fucking pussies."

Evan exhaled sharply. Parker gave him a quizzical look.

"Don't be long," Parker said and left.

"You okay?" Evan's concerned eyes washed over her.

She expected some sort of chastisement, but not concern. "Yes, I'm fine. I'm sorry I put my nose where it didn't belong, but I couldn't let him talk to that woman like that."

"Somehow, I'm not surprised."

She blanched.

"I mean that in a good way, Grace."

A pang of worry speared through her when she thought about Wyatt who was clearly Wrath. The heartache he was about to receive. "He's not well. Go easy on him, Evan."

"He just bit your head off, and you're standing up for him."

"I know." She touched his arm gently. "He's been hurt. Try to remember that. You're about to turn his world upside down."

Grace thought for a moment that he was going to argue with her, but he glanced over at his family table, then tucked his hands in his jeans pockets and gave an abrupt nod. "Listen, I have to go. You'll wait for me, won't you?"

"Sure."

Then he left to join his family.

TWENTY-ONE

EVAN LAZARUS

When Evan returned, the hushed arguments were in full swing. The girls were in the middle of the u-shaped booth and on either side of them sat Griffin and Tony who were enthralled in Wyatt's explanation of what his ramekin full of brown fluff was. Parker stood blocking Wyatt's exit. Mary and Flint took up space next to Tony at the opposite exit of the booth. Thankfully, they were the last table at the end of the restaurant, and had a little privacy, otherwise the entire restaurant would be spectators to their current drama. Maybe he should have booked the private dining room.

Wyatt caught Evan's approach and made to leave.

"I'm not doing this," he growled.

Parker placed a firm hand on Wyatt's shoulder. An animalistic rumble came from the base of Parker's throat and he bared his teeth. "You're not going anywhere. It's high time you stopped acting like a complete fuckwit and dealt with this."

A hush fell over the table.

When Parker wanted to make his prideful opinion known, he did it in style, except this was the first time Evan heard that feral noise. The snarl had been utterly beast-like, and Parker prowled back and forth in front of the table, fists clenching, muscles rolling, veins in his forearms writhing. He looked like a giant demon, or fallen angel about to wreak havoc.

"Don't push me, Wyatt," Parker snapped. "This involves all of us."

"What the fuck do you care? You live in your Ivory Tower, far from the rest of us lowly peasants," Wyatt spat. "In fact, none of you are really here. Apart from the little fuck-up there, none of you give a shit anymore. You don't do anything to help the city. You say you do, but I know you're too proud to actually get out there."

Evan was taken aback; Wyatt had actually noticed he'd been trying to make things right. For a moment, Evan was transported back to elementary school when he fought with another kid in the school yard. He couldn't remember what it was about, but this other kid had thrown the first punch.

Evan knew he was special, and that his family was in hiding. His parents and siblings had drilled it into him, *You're stronger than the other kids, so stay out of trouble otherwise you'll get noticed. The Hildegard Sisterhood will find you and take you away from us.*

Evan was blamed for the fight. He'd only pushed the kid off him, but had caused bruising. Wyatt turned up, somehow there to save him. He'd defended Evan and explained to the teacher what he saw. In the end, Evan still received detention, and it had devastated him. He hated getting in trouble and feared it would cause the end of the world as he knew it.

That night when they got home, Wyatt had asked Evan if he'd heard the biblical story of Lazarus. Some guy who rose from the dead, was all Evan had replied. Wyatt had laughed. He never remembered much apart from that either, but the point was, Lazarus came back. He didn't quit, and Evan shouldn't too.

Thinking on those memories now, Evan thought maybe Wyatt wasn't a lost cause. Maybe he was fighting a hard battle, just like the Post-it note said on Grace's fridge.

"You asshole." Liza tried to reach past Tony and made a grab for Wyatt. "Don't you dare tell me I do nothing."

Liza was a cop. A damned good one, too. Tony tried to intervene, but it was Griff on the other side of Liza who pulled her back, much to her annoyance.

"Could we just focus on the reason we called this meeting? Sara," Griffin said.

"There's nothing to talk about," Wyatt snapped, and then scooped out a bit of chocolate from the ramekin.

"The fuck there isn't," Parker said, voice still laced with a lethal rumble. When Parker cussed, you knew he was at his limit. Pride usually kept the crass in check. "You know Evan had an exhibition where she was the sole focus. What you didn't know was that she turned up. Alive." Parker took a few moments for that to sink into Wyatt. When Wyatt turned ashen, Parker glared at the rest of his siblings. "And if the rest of you had come to support your brother, you would have known that too. In fact, if you were all there, perhaps someone else apart from Evan and his doctor would have seen Sara, and we wouldn't be stuck in this no-man's-land."

"*Mijo*," Mary said to Wyatt, voice soft and eyes full of pain for her son. "I think it's time to entertain the idea that Evan was right all these years."

"Bullshit," Wyatt dropped his spoon to the table. "This is some sort of sick joke, isn't it? You would have seen a vision."

"I failed." Mary slumped.

Flint draped his arm protectively around his wife.

"You failed?" Wyatt's eyebrows rose incredulously. "You fucking failed?"

"Wyatt," Flint warned. "You're hurting, so I'm going to let that disrespect slide. But you need to stop being hotheaded about this. We're all here to support you. In fact, all of you need to cool your jets, and think about this objectively."

"Cool my jets?" Wyatt shook his head. "We're all knee-deep in our sins, don't tell us to cool our fucking jets. You have no idea what it feels like to have a sin whispering evil things in your ear morning, noon and night. It's a wonder none of us have sucked on the barrel of a gun to shut out the pain."

"Wyatt." Mary's curt tone cut through the air like a knife, and when she spoke like that, woe was the person who ignored her. They all muttered into an uncomfortable lull that impregnated the air with a buzzing expectancy.

Evan hated the pained words coming from Wyatt. He knew he had to tread carefully.

"She murdered someone, then attacked my girl," he said

quietly. "Then I physically fought with her to protect Grace. I know Sara's alive, Wyatt. I saw her face two inches from mine."

Anger simmered in Wyatt's bright eyes. "You don't have any proof."

Parker cleared his throat. "That's not true. We lifted her prints from something she touched last night."

"The footage from the camera across the road confirms it," Sloan added, surprising Evan. That was the first he'd heard about CCTV footage being found.

"The prints came back a positive match, Wyatt," Parker continued. "And unless her corpse is walking around, brother, I think it's time we face the music. She's alive."

As usual, Wyatt turned his wrath Evan's way. "You screwed up once. How do you know this isn't the same?"

He referred to the fact that Evan neglected to mention he sensed Sara's envy at the building before it was too late.

Liza glared at Wyatt. "You got no clue. You think he messed up? You did, by becoming a giant mother-fucking turd. If it wasn't for Evan, we'd never know the truth."

"Fuck you, Liza."

"I'm already fucked."

This shit is going sideways, Evan thought. The looks from the high-brow patrons were starting to stick. Which was okay, he'd anticipated that, and he even planned for the eventuality of Wyatt losing his temper and storming out. The patrons were well versed in his tantrums so would most likely chalk it up to his usual. But Evan wasn't ready for Grace to see this display of family defectiveness. He knew they were precariously close to ending it all, but he loved his family, he had to keep trying.

On instinct, he sought Grace out. As though hearing his silent plea, she looked up and their eyes met. Instantly, he felt calmer. But when Grace stood with her friend, and headed to the exit, a new version of panic engulfed him. He'd told her to wait for him. Where was she going? He shifted to leave, but Parker took hold of his wrist and displayed the Yin-Yang tattoo to Wyatt.

"What do you see there, brother?" Parker said.

"I'm not doing this," Wyatt growled, barely glancing at Evan's tattoo. "Get out of my way."

Parker shoved him back then pointed a look at Evan. "Show him."

"What, now? Here?" Evan blanched. It was too public. People watched. Plus Grace was leaving.

All the above made Evan riled. What if he let loose more than a shock slip?

Parker folded his arms and moved his mountain of a body to block as much view of the patrons as he could. "Yes, now."

"What the hell?" Wyatt's gaze filled with rage and Evan knew he was out of time. One more second, and that rage would spill into violence.

Evan generated power in his body, let it build and crackle down his arms until it hit his fingertips and dropped a shower of sparks to the floor. He lifted his palm to place on Wrath's chest, but Griffin cried out, "No. Stop."

Evan curled his fingers at the last minute.

"It's fine, Griff," Parker said. "I took the shock. I survived."

"Don't you see? His fingers are sparking. For that to happen, the voltage is much more than what you received, Parker," Griffin added.

"Voltage?" Wyatt's dark brows pinched as he stared at Evan's crackling fist.

"He's met his balanced mate," Mary said. "His *real* balance." The insinuation hung in the air. Sara hadn't been the one for Wyatt, otherwise he'd have developed a power, too. "It's just how Gloria described it would happen all those years ago. From the pheromones, to the awakening of a powerful ability."

Liza's grip slipped on her beer, and the glass bottle dropped to the table. She gaped a look toward the windows of the restaurant as though something had grabbed her attention. And then, as though sensing unnatural dominos fall, each of his siblings—even Wyatt—lifted a head, and eyes to the street-side windows of the restaurant.

"You all felt that?" Parker's fists clenched at his side.

Sloan and Tony both turned back to their meal.

"Nah," Sloan said.

"I think a night-cap would be good," Tony added.

"It's early afternoon, Tony," Sloan chided.

He shrugged.

"Felt what?" Evan asked. He'd not sensed anything other than the usual level of envy.

"Something is wrong," Griffin said, nostrils flaring, as though he smelled the sin of greed.

Liza scooped her black purse off the table and checked

inside where her police registered weapon sat next to her CCPD badge. "I'm going to check it out. That was a shit load of sin."

Tony shook his head. "I'm on set tomorrow. Can't turn up bruised."

"I can't find my battle gear," Sloan remarked.

More like she couldn't fit into it anymore.

In classic Wyatt style, he used the opportunity to storm off.

"You're all a bunch of sissy girls." Liza slid out of the booth.

"I'm coming," Parker said.

"Of course you would after that remark, you prideful bitch," Liza shot back at him.

Parker's eyebrow arched in warning and he folded his massive arms against his chest, as if to say, bring it. Oh she would. She could.

Evan turned to Griffin. Motherfucker checked his goddamned wrist tattoo.

"No," he said. "I've already done enough generous deeds today."

Then he felt it… a slow ebbing of envy cranking up with each passing minute. Shit. Something deadly was about to happen, and Grace was out there.

Liza turned to her eldest brother. "We don't have time to suit up."

Parker smoothed his collared shirt and wiped imaginary dust from his shoulder. "We'll be fine like this. How hard can it be?"

Oh course he'd fucking think that.

"Someone needs their combat gear on," Mary warned. "Someone needs to be able to go all out if necessary."

"It should be you," Parker said to Evan.

"No. I'm going now. Grace is out there." Evan pushed past Parker, but was halted by a hand to his chest.

"I'll keep her safe," Parker promised. "You're the only one who's got the powers, Evan. If we need them, and you go out there like this, then you're not anonymous, you'll be compromised. As will we all."

Evan's teeth ground as he contemplated. "You don't let a hair on her head get harmed." Fuck. Shit. Was he really trusting them to look after Grace until he got there? He turned to Mary. "There's still a spare suit in the basement, right?"

Mary nodded and shot a glare at Sloan and Tony. "All of you have suits down there."

Flint stood. "I'll come with you, Evan. Someone has to man the comms."

That last comment was also directed Sloan's way. Before her gaming hiatus, she had helped him with tactical support. It was good practice to have someone sitting at HQ in front of a computer, checking maps, police radio alerts, etc. As usual, Sloan ignored the dig. She wiped her nose with her sleeve and then waved the waiter over.

Evan couldn't believe it. In the face of what they now knew, half his family still sat idle at the table.

"You make me sick," Evan said to them. Harsh, but true. "You were given these amazing gifts—"

"That we didn't ask for!" Sloan added.

"—that people would kill for!" Evan finished. "Don't throw it away on regret."

"Evan is right." Mary stood to join Evan. "I thought I was doing you all a favor by letting you choose another path. I thought maybe Gloria had failed in her creation of you, but it was me who failed. You have a choice. Get up and live, or stay on the path to your own destruction."

Evan didn't stick around to hear more. He bolted for the exit with only one thought on his mind: *Grace*.

TWENTY-TWO

DR. GRACE GO

"Why don't you stay at my place tonight?" Grace asked Lilo as they walked down the footpath, away from Heaven. The busy streets bustled with people walking to and from the many food establishments in the Quadrant area. Probably on their way home from a lunch date, or on their way to an afternoon coffee date. All of which, Grace didn't usually do because she was too busy at the hospital. That's why they were treating themselves to a luxury lunch today, because it was a treat for them to get out of work. Just another reminder of her empty personal life. She nudged her friend. "I could use some help with my investigation. You know you're better at that sort of thing than me."

Evan had his hands full with his family, and Grace had a few days off work which gave her plenty of time to investigate the new information she'd received from the Medical Examiner and to process everything that had happened between her and Evan.

"You know I can't resist a good investigation, but I really

should get back and try to patch things up with Donnie. He's already wondering where I went." Lilo waved her phone in the air.

"I've got a new lead," Grace said in a singsong voice.

"Ooh, you temptress." Lilo laughed. "But I promised Donnie I'd cook him dinner at my place tonight. I need to get back to the office and write a few things up so I can leave early to start the prep."

Grace narrowed her eyes. At Lilo's place for dinner. That was the third time this week. As usual, Donnie didn't want to be seen in public with Lilo. It broke her heart to see her friend used.

"Sounds to me like he wants to know where you are twenty-four-seven and you're not even officially dating." Grace plucked a leaf from a nearby tree and turned it over in her hands. "I thought you wanted to break it off with him. Now's your perfect chance."

"Easier said than done, Grace."

"He doesn't see your worth. I do. He's using you."

"Relationship advice coming from you, Miss. Lonely Hearts?"

Grace flinched.

"Sorry," Lilo murmured. "I didn't mean anything by it."

Grace sighed. "But you're right. I don't have experience with relationships. I'm just worried about you. I think you deserve better."

Lilo stared at her feet and shrugged. "I don't mind cooking him dinner."

Ugh. Sometimes, hearing about difficult relationships made Grace grateful she wasn't in one. Too hard. What she and Evan had was... instinctual, no... convenient? Physical. Sexual. Definitely sexual. She liked sexual. Dear God, she liked it. The way his rock hard abs felt still gave Grace the shivers down to her little toes. It would be nice to revisit that body when they weren't hiding in a storeroom. She hadn't even had the chance to see to his needs. It had been all her. That thought brought a flush to her cheeks. She'd have to rectify that.

Maybe she was okay with a convenient sexual relationship. Humans had physical needs. Doctors had needs. He was busy. She was busy. He had responsibilities. She did too. Who's saying they had to devote every hour of the day to each other?

But then again, he was Envy. He was violent by nature, and just being around him made her want to give in to those old toxic temptations for revenge.

Grace checked her watch. Speaking of responsibilities, she'd spent too much time avoiding hers. Time to get home and gather her thoughts before visiting Taco's aunty's place and then heading out to the address she'd received from the Medical Examiner.

"Shall we split a cab?" Grace asked. Lilo's work wasn't too far from Grace's home.

"How about we walk?" Lilo replied. "I know I said I had to get back, but if it's on the way, we can discuss your project as we go."

Grace checked her watch again. A walk would add another twenty minutes to her schedule, but the clear and crisp afternoon air wasn't bad for the beginning of winter.

Evan's morning sunshine had stayed around to keep the cold away. The sky was clear and blue.

"You can tell me about your progress," Lilo added. "My offer still stands—I'm happy to pitch the story to my editor if the facts check out."

"Okay. It's a deal. Let's walk and talk." Grace linked her arms with her friend, ready to start their journey, but a loud bang echoed against the tall buildings, halting their progress.

Alarmed, Grace and Lilo looked at each other.

The commotion down the street grew. Traffic slowed near them. Horns beeped. People shouted. Something happened in front of the coffee shop, not too far away. Grace couldn't see over the heads of the people running. Someone screamed. A gunshot, the screech of tires... then a thunderous *bang*, and it started to rain.

Grace held out her hand as water dropped in her palm. She looked up, expecting clouds, but the sun still shone brightly, causing a rainbow to emerge in front of her.

"It's an accident," Lilo said, pointing.

Up ahead, water sprayed like a geyser into the air.

"Someone's hit the hydrant," Grace said, shaking herself from her fright. "They might be hurt."

She jogged ahead of Lilo, barging past the fleeing crowd, toward the commotion. When she arrived, she forced herself to calm and breathe steady as she assessed the situation. A car lay overturned on the street, tires spinning in the air. Another had crashed into it and smoke curled from the carnage. Metal creaked and cracked. Something hissed. She whipped her gaze up and down the street at the impending traffic jam. An ambulance would have trouble getting through.

There had been gunshots, she was sure of it. But from where? She had to make sure the area was safe before she went in. First rule of first aid—check the area for danger.

It was odd. There were no drivers in the vehicles. No bodies littering the road, but sidewalk tables and chairs were turned over. Skid marks blackened the road leading up to the collision. One of the cars must have lost control, hit the hydrant and the sidewalk before ending back in the middle of the road, and colliding with the second vehicle.

"Wow. Are you seeing this?" Lilo had her phone out, scanning the street, recording. "This is Lilo Likeke, from Cardinal Copy News. I'm in the Quadrant where there appears to be a road accident of some sort. A hydrant has been hit. Gunshots were heard. People are running, but we can't see signs of injured. We're not sure exactly what's happened…"

Lilo continued narrating while Grace gave the scene another once over, this time noticing something about one of the vehicles. It was a large van and painted in Cardinal City General Hospital colors.

"It's a hospital patient transport vehicle," she murmured. "There could be someone sick in the back."

She stepped onto the road, then was pulled back roughly.

"Stay back," came a gruff, male voice.

When Grace turned, she had to look up to Evan's enormous brother, Parker. He could probably lift Grace above his head with one arm and not break a sweat.

"Something's not right," he said, dark eyes staring intently at the accident.

Grace checked for Evan, but didn't see him.

His sister—the one Grace thought to be a Victoria's Secret model—advanced on the scene with her pistol aimed at the wreckage, very professional like. A police badge dangled from a chain around her neck. She looked kick-ass. Like something out of a Law and Order episode.

"CCPD," she shouted, eyes focused on the upturned car. "Put your weapons away and come out with your hands up."

No movement except the wheels still spinning.

This was beyond strange. Where they criminals? Was it a terrorist attack? It was as though they waited for something.

A faint cry for help came from inside the van.

A woman. Hurt.

Grace's heart kicked up a notch, and adrenaline shot through her system. Her body trembled, wanting to move, but forced to stay.

No gunman came out.

"Someone's hurt," Grace said, more to herself than anyone else. She had to go.

Enough of this.

She broke from Parker and stepped toward the road, hands up, shouting. "I'm a doctor. I'm unarmed."

The second her foot touched the asphalt, a shot fired, and the ground near her foot exploded, spraying debris into her face. Grace ducked, people screamed. A rough hand jerked her back, and she slammed into a wall of hard muscle.

"Evan will kill me if I let you get hurt," Parker growled. "Stay back. Let the professionals handle this."

The cop had her gun trained up at the roof of the buildings in the street, looking for the sniper.

"She's got no backup," Grace said. "Someone is injured in there."

"You'll do no good if you get yourself killed. Backup's on the way." Parker tugged Grace and Lilo from the road and stowed them behind the protection of a fallen coffee shop table, upturned like a shield. "Stay down."

Then he crept toward his sister, still surveying the rooftops opposite the street. He pulled his phone out and spoke into the receiver. Grace followed their gaze up and spied a shadow behind the sign on the bakery roof. A sniper. She held her breath. Another shadow moved behind him… crept… stalked… until it converged. Suddenly, the sniper wasn't sitting, aiming at them. Instead, he dangled from the rooftop by a cord tied around his wrists. Not dead, just hanging, kicking his legs.

Grace's stomach flipped and her gaze whipped back to the roof. The second shadow was gone. Had it been Evan?

The rear doors to the patient transport vehicle swung open, and two white-robed and white-masked people jumped out, landing with a splash into the wet street. A third robed man dragged a bloodied and barefoot woman, gun to her head. Her tattered clothing barely covered her skinny frame as she bucked under his grip, twisting and straining to get free. But she was too weak. Too small.

Grace gasped as the recollection hit her. Sound warbled. The smell of asphalt slammed up from her memories, and the dripping sound of the hydrant water echoed loudly. It was the same sort of warriors who fought the Deadly Seven on the day of the building explosion. Long white robes flowed around their bodies. Hoods covered their heads. White, Halloween styled plastic masks with slits for eyes, slits for the mouth, and that was all she could see of their faces. She'd bet behind the masks was the same stretched skin she'd seen inside the lobby of the building before it collapsed.

"Are you seeing what I'm seeing?" Lilo said as she held her camera-phone up to record the scene.

"The fuck?" A deep, gravely voice came from behind Grace, shocking them both into turning.

Wyatt stood frozen to the spot, eyes wide, face pale, jaw agape. He wasn't the only one. Next to him stood Evan's mother and sister with a similar expression of shock and awe. All of them focused on the wreckage, on the injured hostage. Grace turned back and realized why they were so surprised.

It wasn't just the plastic warriors, it was—

"Sara?" Wyatt stepped forward.

"Wyatt!" Sara screamed and struggled in her captor's grip. "Help me!"

Wyatt roared and pandemonium broke loose.

TWENTY-THREE

EVAN LAZARUS

In his combat gear, Evan watched with equal amounts of morbid fascination, confusion, and horror at the scene unfolding a level below him in the street.

Water sprayed everywhere, misting the air, but it was clear the perpetrators were the same carnival freaks from two years ago. Dressed in white like cult members, masked in plastic, almost like that dude from the slasher film. They had a woman hostage… fuck him sideways. Not just any woman. *Her*. Evan knew her brand of envy anywhere. He'd stake his life on it.

And when Wyatt roared, breaking rank from his family, his suspicions were confirmed.

Sara.

This can't be happening.

Sara wasn't a victim.

She was the perpetrator! The ring leader.

What the hell?

He wanted to get down there, to join the fight. But after

he'd neutralized the sniper threat, he stayed up top to assess the situation. It was a smart battle strategy. He had to calm down. Remember his training. Higher terrain gave the advantage of opportunity if you used it well.

"Invincibility is a matter of defense," he murmured to himself, channeling one of his teachers in Japan as he prowled along the second-story rooftop, surveying below. A bad feeling lifted the hairs on the back of his neck.

Evan scanned the crowd of bystanders brave enough to stay and watch from behind the upturned cafe street furniture. Umbrellas, tables, chairs.

Panic choked him when his gaze snagged on a familiar face.

Grace was next to Parker. Thank God for that prideful son-of-a-bitch, because as long as civilians were at risk, he would protect them.

Stay there, Doc, Evan prayed. *Stay safe.*

Mary raced up with Sloan not far behind, joining the crowd behind the barricade. Sloan had gotten off her ass, after all. *No Tony. No Griffin.* All in their civvies—none in battle gear, like Evan. They'd be no use to him, or Liza, unless they wanted to give away their secret identities.

To make matters worse, more of those masked carnival freaks came out of the van and intercepted Wyatt as he attempted to get to Sara. To rescue her, not take her down. Why couldn't he see reason? Why couldn't he trust Evan?

There had to be at least four more hostiles that had jumped out of the van.

Evan counted.

One, two, three... Seven in total.

Significant number.

His mind traveled back to the restaurant, to the moment they'd all sensed sin flare outside. For that to have happened, seven perps would have sinned—either committed a crime, or were about to—at the same time. Very unlikely. Lust, pride, sloth, greed... most of them at once.

It was like they wanted to draw them all out, just like that day two years ago. None of the freaks spoke. None made demands.

Shit.

This was a trap. It had to be. And Evan was the only one who could see it.

Sara cried out and Wyatt charged forward like a bull, plowing through the first obstacle on his way to Sara. The robed body in front of him went flying over Wyatt's shoulder, and another took his place. Sara made more noises like a damned good actress.

Screw this.

Evan held back once. He ignored his instincts two years ago and look where that got him. They were finally trusting him again, and...

Enough.

He checked his face scarf and hood were in place, then backed up on the rooftop, and took a running start toward the edge. He vaulted over—caught some wicked air, and somersaulted, boots landing hard, denting the car roof. In a fluid motion, he commando rolled down the windshield and skidded across the hood to splash land in front of Liza locked in battle with one of the freaks.

She rolled her eyes at his flashy entrance.

Evan poked his tongue out in an immature move, hidden by the fabric of his scarf. Then he dropped and kicked, knocking Liza's opponent's legs from under him.

The freak dropped like a sack of shit.

"Thanks, dickhead." Liza grinned then bent to cuff the attacker. "Go get the rest."

"My pleasure," Evan growled through his voice modifier and pulled out his twin Katanas, rotating them wide, one on each side of his body.

Game on, fuckers.

He attacked, moving like the lightning in his veins. No hesitation. No quarter. Striking swift and true.

The next five minutes were all instinct.

Block, parry, defend, shove, slice. The hydrant still sprayed water in the air, making it hard to see clearly, but they were no match for him, not when he projected the electricity building in his body beyond its fleshy confines. It pulsed at a frequency only he could hear. He sensed which direction they'd swing, which side they'd kick, which angle they'd punch. God, he felt alive.

Evan blocked, whirled and sliced, careful not to kill. Too many people around, too much judgment. Disarm, disable… heh, heh—he chuckled as he sliced—disrobe. One white robe fluttered to the soaking ground. The remaining cloak left on the man—yep, definitely a man—barely covered the nude and barefoot body.

Freaky white dude junk was not what he needed to see. It burned into his retinas.

Liza saved his eyes and tackled the half-nude assailant to the ground. She used his own tattered robe against him, securing his wrists behind his head.

Evan turned his attention to Sara and advanced. Wyatt was a twin beast to Evan, pounding and clawing his way to Sara, except they wanted different things. Evan wanted to reveal her lies. Wyatt wanted to protect her. Another two freaks went down as they raced. The fifth met a spinning plate launched from the sidewalk—*Mary*. Good aim.

That left the sixth. Liza's gun trained at his head, and—a warning shot rang out—not from Liza.

The freak holding Sara had a gun and shot into the sky. He shoved the tip of his pistol back at Sara's temple.

"No!" Wyatt called out, his face contorting with panic and fury. He slowed his approach, palm out in hesitant surrender. One wrong move and Sara would get her brains blown out, at least, that was what Wyatt thought.

"Wyatt!" Sara screamed and jerked against her assailant who pulled her back toward the hydrant where the rain was heaviest.

Rage built to an impossible pressure beneath Evan's skin.

Either way this didn't end well for Evan. Sara would die, Wyatt would blame him, somehow. Even if Sara lived, Wyatt would find a way to blame him. This wasn't happening. He wouldn't let her play the martyr.

A quick glance around the area to gather his thoughts. Evan made a connection. Water. Everywhere. Sara and the freaks were barefoot. Liza wore rubber-soled boots, so did Wyatt. Nobody else was at risk on the puddled street. Good enough for him. He sheathed his blades at his back and then slapped his hands on the water at his feet. Electricity like he'd never known before arced from his hands into the water. It hurt. A buzzing sound tingled his ears, lightning forked from his hands in a burst. Bitter ozone rankled the air.

A split second later, Sara and her captor convulsed. The gun dropped.

Ideally, Evan should have shut down his power, but he didn't. He kept his switch on and watched them fry. Smoke curled from the water at their feet. Dimly, he became aware of someone screaming his name. Not Evan. *Envy*.

Grace shouted for him to stop. The look in her eyes—fear, horror, regret—all directed at him. It was a shot to his heart. Despite everything Sara had done to Grace, she still tried to protect her.

Evan looked at Sara convulsing.

Then back at Grace.

He couldn't put that look in Grace's eyes. With great effort, he reined in his power and cut off the current, holding his palms in the air in surrender.

When it switched off, both Sara and her captor fell hard to the floor. Wyatt ran to his fake fiancée. He took her in his arms and called her name. When she didn't answer, Wyatt's hate-filled eyes met Evan's, and then he shouted, "We need a doctor!"

Grace scrambled from her hiding place and jogged over. "Give me some space."

All the muscles in Evan's shoulders tightened. He didn't want Grace near that liar. He growled, stepping forward.

"Cool it, sparky." Liza's hand stopped him. He jerked back and looked down, shocked. It wasn't her hand. It was the butt of her Glock.

"Don't make me use this on you," she said.

"She's a fucking liar. We have proof!"

"I mean it."

"You believe this shit?" Evan's world was falling apart. Nobody was coming to him. They went to her. To help *her*. What did she have that he didn't?

Police sirens wailed, getting closer.

"The cavalry's here," Liza said, checking over her shoulder. "Take the hint and piss-off before you regret it."

"Liza," he breathed. "Don't believe her lies."

Her look of resignation said it all. They were choosing Sara over Evan, at least for now. He cast a toxic glance at the body on the floor receiving care from Grace and hoped she stayed dead, but as the ambulance officers raced through the crowd, he knew he should be so lucky.

With a heavy stone sinking in his stomach, Evan slipped away.

Nobody even noticed.

TWENTY-FOUR

DR. GRACE GO

It was dark by the time Grace returned home. Dark, cold, and miserable because she was hungry and tired. The events constantly replayed in Grace's mind. It had been a confusing day. Not at all what she'd expected. Sara turning up, claiming amnesia?

Grace didn't think so.

But she'd learned her lesson once never to assume. A young, fit and healthy young woman had come in late to the ER one Saturday night claiming to have excruciating back pain and unable to walk. At first glance, someone that young shouldn't have had the kind of back problem requiring a hit of morphine. The instant reaction from the resident on duty was a junkie fishing for pain meds. Grace was too new to argue and followed her resident's lead. But after two days of the woman crying in pain, they'd finally caved and sent her off for a scan. It turned out she'd herniated her L-3 and L-4 disc, making it impossible for her to walk. Grace remembered telling her father that story when she saw him next and he said, *Never assume, Grace. It makes an ass out of you and me.* Then he'd laughed his guffaw laugh because English idioms always sounded hilarious to him.

It wasn't only Sara's strange confession that bothered Grace. It was what happened when Evan placed his hands in the puddle he shared with Sara and her captor. Seeing those bodies seize from the voltage running through them had been traumatic, and Grace was used to trauma. Both shock victims lost control of their bladders, they smelled like burned toast, and the man's jaw was almost fused shut. That dark look in Evan's eyes would forever be burned into her memory. It broke her heart. He'd promised to let Sara live, not just so Grace could garner a confession out of her, but because murder went against everything Grace stood for. *Do no harm.*

When she'd cried out for him to stop, she wasn't sure if he'd listen.

But he did.

He tore his gaze from his attack and met her eyes. The darkness lessened, and he lifted his hands in surrender, cutting off his power supply.

Everything after that was a blur. Wyatt had shouted for a doctor and Grace ran out. Sara was seizing, but after a quick assessment, she'd rallied. Grace had rolled her into the recovery position and ordered Wyatt to keep an eye on her breathing. The other one, the attacker with the gun, had gone into v-tach. She'd ripped off his mask to reveal a deformed male face and a cleft lip. Grace pumped his chest and breathed life into his lungs until paramedics arrived with the defibrillator, allowing her to successfully jump start his heart into an acceptable rhythm.

His body had bowed, his hands seized into claws, and the color returned to his cheeks. A rush of adrenaline surged over Grace from saving his life, but then he'd screamed at her. *No*, he'd cried. *I was supposed to die. Kill me. Let me die.*

Grace was so taken aback that she'd not seen his hand as it slashed out to strike her. He missed her face but snagged her hair, pulling out a chunk. The searing pain snapped her out of her daze, and she'd called for a sedative. After injecting the man, he'd relaxed enough to let the paramedics move him to the hospital under the careful watch of armed guards.

When the madness was over, she'd sat back on her heels and took stock.

Wyatt crouched next to Sara who breathed evenly on her side. All traces of the furious chef were gone. This was a man who'd been in love with the woman at his knees. The same woman who'd almost died for the second time. He'd fought tooth and nail to get to her side. Most of those attackers he'd bulldozed through were injured the worst. They still groaned and writhed on the ground as the paramedics attended to their injuries, enough to move them either into police custody, or to the hospital.

When Sara opened her eyes, at first they'd held confusion, then shock… then she darted her gaze around, taking in the aftermath. It was the strangest thing, but Grace swore the woman looked dismayed before shuttering down her expression completely and holding onto her old fiancée.

"Sara," Wyatt had croaked. "Where have you been for the past two years?"

"Two years?" she'd gasped. "I've been gone that long?"

Wyatt nodded, sheer anguish on his face as he waited for more. Grace knew in her heart that he didn't want the truth to be real, but love was blind. He'd see what he wanted to see. No matter the fact that the entire situation was odd. Sara knew Grace and Evan were trying to expose her. She'd taken an offensive tactic, surprising them all. Played her cards before Grace and Evan could visit the address they'd gleaned off the Medical Examiner.

Maybe Sara knew.

Maybe the ME had warned her, or the ones she worked for—whoever *they* were.

"I can't remember." Sara began to cry as though her very thoughts were too much to bear. Grace didn't believe her for a minute, but the rest of Wyatt's family had gathered around. Sara turned to Grace and stared. Then: "*You*. I remember you. In the building. I told you to run, and then… the explosion. Oh, God. The building came down on us."

Grace's eyes narrowed to slits. Just exactly what *was* Sara's game?

"You were there?" Wyatt pinned Grace with a hard stare.

"Yes," she gulped.

"Is this true? Did Sara tell you to run?"

As if that explained everything. So Sara asked Grace to run, so what? She was now innocent? "Yes, she did, but—"

"I'm taking her home." Wyatt cut her off. Grace wanted to add that there was more to it. Sara had called the white-robed warriors in that day. She'd blown on a damned whistle! Some weird, high-pitched whistle. Plus, Sara's face had changed. Couldn't they tell the way her skin pulled a little taut over the bone structure of her face? She'd either had a face lift, or it was something else. Grace wasn't making it up. Something shifty was going on in this city, and Grace had been crushed right into the middle of it.

Wyatt lifted Sara's small, fragile body and cradled her in his arms.

"We need a statement," Liza said to her brother, her expression stern and shrewd. "You can't just take her from the scene of a crime."

Wyatt replied that Liza could kiss his ass and get the statement at home. Then he left, taking Sara with him.

The rest of that afternoon passed in a whirlwind. Grace attended the wounded bystanders. Mothers, children, fathers, and grandparents. There were many. None were gravely injured, but the damage bill to the surrounding area would be astronomical. Lilo had foregone her dinner prep for Donnie and reported on the incident, asking Grace for an official statement before letting her talk to the police.

Grace had also personally checked on the welfare of every other attacker. It was interesting that none of them had the same stretched, plastic look to their skin that the skilled robed warriors did two years earlier. Another man had severe burn scars to half his body, and a third was actually missing a leg and used a prosthetic. Another could barely move from the pain of muscle atrophy commonly seen in Lou Gehrig's disease. All serious stuff. When she thought about it, none of the men had fought with extreme skill. They'd gone down easy. The motley crew was a ragtag group of injured, sick and weak... all wanting to die, as though this was their last hurrah before entering the after-life. All were furious at their capture, shouting and taunting for the police to just kill them.

These tumultuous thoughts tumbled through Grace's mind as she returned home later that evening. On the cab ride, she'd dialed Evan's phone several times, and no answer.

She'd saved lives today, but she didn't feel like it was a success. Not a win.

Evan was gone.

Grace walked into her apartment, bone weary and soul heavy. The first thing she did was go to her bedroom and open the window to the fire escape, letting the cool night air in. She hoped against all hope that Evan would turn up, just like he did last night, but somewhere deep down inside, a dark voice teased her. He wasn't coming back. She'd stopped him from fulfilling his misguided mission, and he'd had enough of her meddling in his plans.

He wanted to end Sara.

Images of the attack flashed in her mind. That look of danger and laser sharp focus in his eyes. He'd been so hateful as he sent his power into the water, watching with satisfaction as Sara and her attacker fried.

She threw her purse on her bed, growling. That wouldn't have solved anything! Sara would be dead. His brother would hate him. They'd never get to the bottom of the attack on the apartment complex that killed her parents and many more.

Grace didn't want Evan to lose his humanity.

She peeled her coat off, kicked her boots off, and paced the space beside her bed. When she walked back across the path she'd taken, she kicked her fallen clothes out of the way in aggravation.

What if he never came back? What if he did… but reverted to the person she found at the hospital earlier—bruises all over his body. The way he fought today confirmed her suspicions. He was magnificent. He could fight, and she meant, really *really* fight. There's no way he'd have put himself in the position to be hurt and pummeled, unless he wanted it.

Unless she was right, and he punished himself for wanting something he couldn't have—vengeance.

Her throat closed up. Was he out there now, punishing himself? Getting beat up?

He'd said she was his balance because she felt no envy, but it was more than that. Perhaps Grace could stop him from spiraling out of control, from falling prey to the sin that plucked at his sanity. He just had to trust her. She could do this, not just by being near him, but by supporting him emotionally, from being his conscience when he wasn't listening to his own. There had to be a reason the world brought the two of them together.

Wherever he was, he needed her.

And she would find him. Determination solidified as a plan formed in her mind. Underground fight rings were common in the Narrows area, the very tail of the Cardinal City bird that joined the mainland by a bridge. She knew about these slums and their fighting rings because some of her patients had told her. The CCGH clinic was the closest free medical facility, only a hop, skip and jump from the seedier side of town. Too many had come in battered and bruised—to the clinic, and to Emergency. They'd all pretended to be brave, to want to fight for something— money, control, power—but when it came down to it, they all feared to die. Death made everyone vulnerable. They'd all looked at her with that quiet desperation, too afraid to voice their need. Each and every time, she'd assured them, no matter their upbringing or life choices. *I won't leave you alone.*

Tears burned her eyes.

"Right," she said, psyching herself up. She could do this, despite the impossible odds. Go find a fight ring, find Evan, bring him back. "Coat. Boots."

She scrounged around under her bed where she'd kicked her boot. Oh blech. So much junk under there. She really needed to clean the space.

"Goddammit, where are you?"

She flailed around the floor, searching blindly. Her face squished on the side of her mattress as she reached further. Then her fingers wrapped around the leather toe of her boot and her tears sprung free.

She'd found it. She found the boot. The perfect pair to the other lonely boot sitting on the floor of her lonely room.

She slumped against her bed, knees bent.

Oh, God. She *was* alone, and he wasn't coming back. She didn't know if she had what it took to find him. Who was she kidding? She didn't know if she had what it took to *keep* him. He'd always be doing this, going off to fight. Maybe not the fight rings, but in the city battling crime every night. He was a soldier. Now that she'd had time to process this, and see it for herself, she realized she loved that about him. Out of all his siblings, he was the only one left fighting the good fight. But it was the same thing that drove her wild with worry.

But fighting for justice was not the same as getting beat up as punishment.

Her chest constricted, and she gulped in air, trying to calm her derailing thoughts.

The crash of a glass bottle breaking on her fire escape stole her attention, and she jumped to her feet, holding her boot as a weapon.

She hoped. She dared. But it might not be…

A shadow fell to the platform and stumbled. Cursed loudly. Grace prowled to the window, slowly and carefully squinting to see clearly. The shadow wasn't acting like Evan. It wasn't graceful and lithe. It was heavy, sluggish… drunk.

"Evan?" Grace asked, voice wavering, boot hovering.

The stranger turned to her and stepped into the spilled light from her window, ducking to see inside better.

A tall, hooded man. Glazed eyes stared at her over a green scarf covering his mouth and nose. It was him. Her heart stuttered. Her belly fluttered.

His lids lowered as he looked her over with lazy entitlement, resting on her lips then traveling lower to her breasts. Yep. Evan alright.

He pushed his large frame through the tiny window, caught on something and fell in a tumble to the floor. The smell of bourbon wafted into the air as he landed face first.

"Ow," he moaned into the carpet.

"Are you drunk?" she hissed.

"Just a little." He held his fingers in a pinch gesture, then rolled to his side and pulled his scarf down. He heaved in a deep breath. "God it feels good to breathe again. This mask sucks balls."

Grace couldn't miss his bloodied and bruised knuckles as he took his hand away.

"You're drunk, Evan." She waggled her boot at him.

"Don't worry. I dropped the bottle before I could finish it. Wait, are you going to attack me with a shoe?" He laughed and snorted. "Look out, she's got a shoe."

Grace glanced at her boot and lowered it awkwardly, slightly embarrassed. Then the reality of the situation hit her. She wasn't the one who should be embarrassed. He should!

"*You*—" She bit her lip, trying to think of all the names she wanted to call him. Asshole. Jerk. Insensitive little—she threw the boot. "I was worried about you!"

He rolled to avoid being hit, still laughing.

Didn't do much good. The boot landed on his head, knocking his hood back to reveal the rest of him. Brown scruffy hair. Facial hair the same. Eyes puffed into amused slits. He sat up and leaned against the wall underneath her window. No, one of his eyes was more puffy than the other —there was also swelling and discoloration on his cheekbone.

Grace gasped. "You've been fighting, haven't you? And I'm not talking about this evening, with Sara and those—"

"Those freaks?" he finished, venom on his tongue. "That psycho?"

"That liar, yes."

His gaze snapped to hers.

She held firm. Let him see. Let him take in the emotion on her face.

"You—" his words cut off and his face crumpled. He took a deep breath. "You're on my side—" He choked up, unable to finish.

"Oh, Evan." She crouched to his level and traced his scruffy jaw with her fingers. "Has it been so long since someone believed in you?"

Her words were a bullet to his composure. He closed his eyes and leaned into her hand, then covered it with his large, rough paw. It melted Grace's heart. He needed her. This big, lethal hero needed her. More than anyone else ever had. And despite everything, he'd come back to her.

"Come on." She tugged him up. Goodness gracious, he was heavy. And smelly. The leather outfit might be suitable for battle, but it didn't fare well with dirt and… whatever that sticky mess was at his elbow. "Let's get you cleaned up. Bathroom's this way."

She took him into the tiny room consisting of a shower and a basin. She turned the faucet on and then inspected his face, checking on the puffy eye.

He stared down at her through thick lashes, silent.

Grace put his hand under the flow of water and watched as his blood stained her white basin pink. His wound must have stung, but he didn't flinch. The leather creaked on his suit as he readjusted his posture, leaning into her from behind, giving his arm more slack. His back pressed up against hers like a hot brand. Glancing over her reflection to him, she noticed the hilts of his swords weren't sticking over his shoulders. He'd either lost them, or left them somewhere. She sighed and pulled his hand out of the water to hold his knuckles to the light, trying to ignore the hard press of his body, now against her side.

"Swollen. Split," she said, inspecting. "But it doesn't look contaminated. No need for stitches either."

"Doc," his voice croaked. "You're my sun."

Her throat closed up. She couldn't look him in the eye. If she did, she'd have no resolve.

"And you're drunk."

"You make me warm," he continued. "It's how I can do all this."

He was intoxicated. She wasn't. She had to be professional about this. "We should get some ice on your eye. You'll feel better."

"No, no. You don't understand." He swayed and held up his hands. They crackled and buzzed. "*This!*"

The sparks skipped over his fists. It sounded like an exposed live-wire in her bathroom. "Evan. Be careful."

"You're not listening." He frowned, then let go of his power until the sparks dissipated. "Grace, I can do this because of you."

"What do you mean?"

"My power manifested because I met you. You're my safety net. We've all got an ability inside us, but our creator didn't trust we'd be able to use it responsibly without someone to balance us."

The world stopped.

She was responsible for the incredible power pumping in his veins? For a moment, the pressure of living up to what he was suggesting overwhelmed her, but then Grace remembered it was an echo of her thoughts, only minutes ago.

She *wanted* to be his conscience when he wasn't listening to his own. She needed to care for him. It was who she was.

He cupped her face in between his still warm palms. The touch heated her cheeks and sparked a zip-line down her spine. Naked, raw emotion stared back at her, so close she could see the flecks of brown in his green eyes.

Well, he wasn't the only one allowed to feel. She did too, and she wasn't used to it. She'd locked her emotions away for too long, and now they were hard to process. She had to know, had to be sure she wasn't making things up before she gave her heart to him.

"You stopped," she blurted. "Why did you stop?"

"What?"

"You *had* Sara. You could have killed her. It was what you wanted, but you didn't do it. Why?"

He frowned, arms dropping. "You told me to stop."

Oh God, she was going to bawl now. "You did that for me?"

"Yes."

"Even though you knew what would happen afterward? That she'd probably use the situation against you—that it would be the final wedge driving your family apart… maybe for good?" Grace continued. She never wanted for that to happen.

"I wanted to kill her," he admitted darkly. "But then I looked at you, and you were disappointed. I knew if I kept going, kept releasing my power, you'd always look at me that way and I couldn't do it. I never want to see you look at me like that again."

He turned away. His hair was mussed up, still in need of a decent hair cut, but she loved the way it curled over his ears and flicked out at the temples... as though it had a personality of its own. Her fingers itched to run through it. She also loved the way he smiled, wide perfect lips kicking to the side in a secret smirk that crinkled his cheek, just like it did now, as though he knew something she didn't. She loved how that smile turned wickedly smug after he'd had his way with her in the supply closet at the hospital. The memory brought a flush to her cheeks.

She wanted to ask, "How do you want me to look at you?" But she didn't. She chickened out. Instead, she pulled a fresh towel out from the cabinet beneath the basin.

"Here. You should get out of that smelly outfit and then have a shower. I'll go find something you might fit. I still have a box of my father's old clothes around somewhere."

Then she shut the door as she left the room and leaned against it for good measure while she tried to steady her racing heart. When the sound of the shower turning on filtered through, she pushed off the wood and went searching for that box of her father's belongings she'd kept instead of giving to Goodwill.

TWENTY-FIVE

EVAN LAZARUS

The scalding hot water of the shower knocked some sense and sobriety into Evan. Turning up drunk was a stupid thing to do. He should have come straight to Grace's and waited for her. She must think he had a few screws loose in the old noggin.

He washed his hair, scrubbed his body, and then did it again before turning the faucet to freezing cold—truly sobering up—and stepping out of her shower. Wrapping the towel around his waist, he searched for Grace. He didn't have to look far. The apartment was tiny. He found her in the kitchen, standing in front of the bench staring blankly at an open cardboard box. In the sink next to her was the smoothie she mentioned in the morning. It was half washed down the drain, but he still caught the hint of something acrid, something not fruity. A kernel of doubt grew. Maybe it was an attempt by Sara, and when it didn't work, she went for Plan B—manipulating his family again.

Evan tore his gaze away from the sink and back to the

box Grace clutched. The sides had been marked in red letters. *Dad*.

"I'm sorry," she said, voice flat, unable to look back at him. She reached in the box to touch something. "I don't think anything's going to fit."

Evan stood behind her, drinking her in. Tall, slim but curved enough to make him want to run his hands down her body and trace her dips and hills. Long brown hair draped over her burgundy cap sleeved blouse. The chunky white slashes randomly crossed over her arms made him wonder what sort of debris had gotten to her in the explosion. Evan didn't think he'd ever stop feeling guilt when he looked at her scars.

He leaned over her shoulder to peer inside the box. Water dripped from his hair onto the cardboard, staining it dark.

There were more than clothes in the box. Photo frames. Trinkets. He reached around her to lift the item she clutched, but she wouldn't let go.

She gasped as his body pressed against the length of her spine.

Carefully, he pried her fingers away and revealed the item, an open wallet with a photograph of Grace as a little girl.

Evan put it down gently, and then placed a palm on each of her hands, now clutching the box with white knuckles.

"I'm sorry, Grace," he murmured. "I'm sorry you lost your parents."

"It's not your fault."

Except, maybe it was. Because of his inexperience with his sin, he'd ignored the deadly levels of envy in Sara. He knew she was in the building before it collapsed. If he had followed his instincts, her parents might still be alive.

She might be the best thing that happened to him, but maybe he was trouble for her. He had no words.

This beautiful, smart, kind woman was sad, and he didn't know what to do. He wanted to hug her. Instead, he traced a path up her arms with his fingers, lightly scraping her sensitive, scarred skin with his rough touch. She shivered and leaned back into him.

"I haven't gone through all of their things, yet," Grace whispered. "Can you believe it? It's been two years and their house is still sitting there, empty and full."

"When you're ready, Doc, I can do it with you. Just say the word."

"Thank you."

She picked out something else. A framed certificate of her acceptance to the surgical board. She sighed. "My parents were so proud of me being a surgeon."

"But, you don't want to do it anymore?" he asked.

"It's not that I don't want to do it. I'm… I guess I'm afraid. My anxiety attacks could hit while I'm operating. I can't have that, especially if it's on someone's heart."

"Grace, you're amazing. I've seen you take control of a disaster and come out on top. I watched you from a distance as you worked on all those injured people today. You've got this. But, whatever you decide, you don't have to do it alone." He kissed the top of her head. Hell, she smelled divine. How was that possible after the day she'd had?

Her feminine scent drove him wild. Heat engulfed his body in a wave and his vision blurred, mouth turning to cotton. He wanted her. Bad. There was nothing between them but the jeans over her curved ass and the towel wrapped around his hips, getting tighter and tighter by the second. But while lust raged inside him, he forced his hands to stay gentle, to keep their path light until he encircled her front and embraced her gently. Hugs were the best. Hugs fixed everything. He wasn't going to push his irrational desires onto her. Not when she needed something else from him.

Then she turned around and gaped. "You're… wet."

Heat filled eyes roamed over his body, and Christ, he enjoyed seeing that. The way her gaze snagged on his abs, the way her lashes flared wide and how her pink tongue flicked out to wet her bottom lip. Within seconds, her hands gingerly followed the path her eyes took. Tracing. Exploring. Cool fingers ran down his chest, bumping over his taut muscles, sending searing hot shivers wracking through him.

His eyes fluttered closed.

"Yes. Touch me, Grace." The words came out a rasp.

Damn him. Damn him to hell, but he *did* want to influence her. He wanted her to smell the pheromones pouring from him in waves. He wanted her intoxicated by him, to never stop touching him. Lower. Lower, he thought.

Her touch disappeared.

His eyes snapped open. "Don't stop."

"Where?" she asked breathlessly. "Where do you want me to touch you?"

Before he could stop himself, he drew her hand to his lips. "Here," he said, and he pulled her fingers into his mouth, over his tongue. Her breath hitched, chest lifting, eyes clouding. He licked around her finger and sucked it in, then slipped it out and kept reverently tasting her skin. "And here." Past her knuckles, wrist, over her scars, inside her sensitive elbow—she moaned—up her smoother bicep, over her sleeve, to the dip where her shoulder met her neck. Perfection.

He nuzzled in deep and groaned. This. This is what he needed.

"I thought I was meant to touch you," she panted into his hair, fingers threading through his damp strands.

"Do you want me to stop?"

"God, no."

He smiled against her neck.

"But… I do… want to touch you. Tell me how you like it. Where?"

His cock twitched, speaking for him. Fuck. He involuntarily pushed against her belly.

She grinned and then rolled her bottom lip under her teeth, biting down with angst. She glanced down and confidently unwrapped his towel, eyeing him suggestively. "There?"

"You never finished your examination," he rasped, and she chuckled, then touched his stomach. He hissed. "Lower."

"I might need a closer look." Her fingers trailed. Stopped. And then she said something that made his heart freeze: "What do you want me to touch it with?"

Her wicked gaze broke him and he couldn't breathe, couldn't form a word because she lowered her body, still holding his fiery gaze, until she kneeled before him. She slid her hands enticingly down his bare hips, his thighs, and when her hot, slick mouth closed over the tip of his erection, he almost thrust in bliss. He bent forward and gripped the bench, straining to remain in control. It creaked under his forceful grip. It wasn't just the sizzle of electricity zipping down his cock, tingling his groin, and shooting up his spine. It was the power building inside him, crackling down his arms, sizzling at his fingertips. He had to keep it together. Had to—*oh fuck*—her tongue twirled in a move that sent his mind into madness.

He'd go early at this rate. Either burn the bench to tinder, or release in her sweet mouth.

"Mm?" She hummed, thinking he was trying to speak. He was. He failed. She hummed again, and it sent more pleasure skipping through him. Jesus, he would die right there. Her hands moved to his ass and flexed, pulling his hips to her lips and then relaxing as she slipped away. Then back again. And again. Her mouth was pure heaven. Everything he dreamed of. Hot, tight. Wet.

In a fit of urgency, he pushed the cardboard box out of the way and lifted her onto the bench, facing him, dazed. Still fully clothed. She didn't seem to care, just wanted her hands back on him, pulling him closer by his shaft. This woman, and that look in her eyes was carnal and full of deep desire for him.

God, he was in love with her. "Doc, you're overdressed."

She grazed his lips with hers, taunting him, challenging him. "Then undress me. Tear my clothes off."

The words shocked him into action. He ripped her blouse down the middle. Buttons popped and clattered to the floor.

When that was gone, he slipped her bra strap down, and reverently kissed her shoulder. He kept pulling the damned elastic thing off until her breasts sprang free. Creamy white and perfectly shaped with rosy nipples. Hell, yeah. He bent, sucked a puckered bud into his mouth and reveled in her groans of pleasure. When he let go, she was panting and dizzy with need, eyes glazed with passion.

"More," she demanded, fingers spearing through his hair and arching her chest into his face.

He kissed her ferociously while simultaneously trying to rid her of the rest of her cursed clothing. Arms, hands and mouth, trying to touch her everywhere at once. He unbuttoned her jeans, pulled her off the bench just long enough to slide the fuckers down, then lifted her back up. Her naked ass slapped on the counter top and she squealed.

Must be cold.

"Sorry," he muttered.

"S'okay." She drew his lips to hers, desperation giving her eyes a feral glint.

Fuck he knew his girl would go wild. Her messy bedroom was just the beginning, and he couldn't wait to explore every last messy iota of her life. Their next untamed kiss broke all their barriers. She opened her legs, and he pushed inside, groaning in the most desperate way. The shock of her tight sheath sent a euphoric haze over his vision. But... *shit*. Panic. He pulled out so fast it almost hurt. Stopped his heart.

"I don't have a condom," he cursed.

"Oh. Um. Okay, lemme think. It's okay. I'm clean and I get the contraceptive injection. Wasn't that long ago." She lifted her legs to lock around his hips, nudging him back to her core, already trusting him. "Don't stop."

"I'm clean." She didn't ask, but he said it anyway. "Get tested all the time. A few months ago…"

Her lips slammed into his, silencing him. She pulled at his hair, tugging sharply, giving every fiber in his body a jolt, and he deepened the kiss, all rough and full of passion. He wanted her now.

Now.

Shit. He shouldn't be like this, all macho demands and needs, but he couldn't help himself. It was like his heart wanted to climb inside hers. He should take his time with her. Give her something to remember, something to scream about. In a good way. There would be only one first time together. He wanted it to be the best. Pleasure her first. Let her come, then—she took his shaft in her hands, squeezed, and pulled his tip against her slick core, rolling it around, rubbing her desire. Seeing his woman using him to take control of her pleasure was the sexiest damned thing he'd ever seen.

"Why are you waiting?" she moaned, eyes rolling back in bliss.

"Damn it, Doc." He replaced his cock with his thumb, circling and toying with her until she whimpered something under her breath.

"What?" he asked.

She moaned again.

"What do you need?" he demanded. "Tell me. Like this?"

"Yes," she cried.

"And this?"

"Oh, God, please stop talking. Just… do…"

"What do you want?" Should he go down there? He would. He'd do anything she wanted him to.

"You. Inside. Now."

He thrust inside her to the hilt. The shock of it had them both clutching each other with sweet, shuddering desperation. It was heaven. A slick, tight, wet heaven. Always, with her. It would always be like this. No envy niggling at him. Just her consuming him. He gripped her hips, and slid out, then in again. "Like this?"

"Yes, Evan. You. Just you the way you are."

He grinned.

She giggled. "But, faster."

As much as she wanted, he gave it to her. Anything she asked for. She got. Faster, slow… faster again, until the sheen of sweat on his body blended with hers. Until her cheeks glowed with a radiant light, until she gasped, tensed and went liquid around him all at once. And then he joined her in his release, finally letting go, collapsing around her.

When it was done, when he came to his senses, he realized he'd fallen on top of her in a heap. To accommodate his weight, she'd laid back, head barely held aloft by the bench top. To apologize, he kissed down her body, starting from her neck to her belly, withdrawing from her as he went.

He was pleased to see he hadn't lost control of his power. No scorch marks on the bench, just a thoroughly sated woman. He smirked and gathered her into his arms to carry back to the bathroom. He loved that he'd made her like that, all heavy and dazed. It made every male instinct extremely satisfied. Now he wanted to care for her. "Let's get cleaned up, then to bed. I want to sleep with you in my arms, Doc."

"Sounds perfect." She smiled languidly and rested her head against his chest, stroking his pec with her hand. "We should probably go visit that address we got. You know, from the ME."

He paused in the doorway to the bathroom. "Don't you ever stop? Relax every once in a while and just do nothing?"

She looked up at him guiltily. "I don't sleep so well. I fill my time with… things to do."

"One day, I'm going to take you on vacation. Somewhere nice, like The Menagerie."

"Mm. I like the sound of an island getaway."

"I'll hire one of those big houses by the beach, and we'd do nothing all day but make love to the sounds of the ocean, and then maybe even in the ocean. Then out again."

She giggled. "That would be nice."

"I suppose we could get a bit to eat now and then."

Another giggle.

"And I wouldn't let you think about work for a second."

She frowned. "We really should go and check that address out."

He had a feeling he knew where that habit of hers came from. Her state of anxiety when she looked in her father's box was a pretty good clue. She hadn't dealt with her parents' death, instead she kept herself so damned busy she didn't need to. Keeping busy to avoid your problems was fine, for short periods, but it never worked in the long run. It was going to blow up in her face, and then she'd end up doing something stupid like Evan did when he let those cocksuckers beat him to an inch of his life. But, she was also right about investigating the address of the lab they'd discovered. Damn her.

"Not until the early hours of the morning," he conceded. "That's the best time for covert recon."

"What will we do until then?"

He flashed her a grin. "Don't worry, Doc. I plan to wear you out so much, you'll sleep until next week if you could."

And after he helped clean her up, he took her back to her bed and made good on his promise.

TWENTY-SIX

DR. GRACE GO

Grace woke groggily on her stomach. It was still dark, and warm, and Evan kissed down her naked back with soft, reverent lips.

"Mm." She wiggled in her sheets and was rewarded with his hand curving over her butt, stroking and teasing. When he lowered, his arousal pressed into her rear, reminding her of the previous night in the kitchen, and the things that made her heart race and toes curl. She pushed back, challenging.

"Doc," he groaned, strained. His voice rumbled down her back like soft thunder.

It did things to her insides, making her hot. She was so happy right now, so sated and content. He'd done the impossible, made her want to sleep in and stay in bed all day.

He brushed her hair from her back and kissed her neck, below her ear, eliciting shivers from his hot breath. "It's two-thirty," he murmured. "If we want to go…"

Her eyes popped open. "Oh, dear God. You're right."

He slid off her reluctantly, and the cool air seeped in.

Grace rolled to her side to look at Evan's silhouette lying next to her in the soft moonlight. The black lines of his tattoos were dark shapes down half his masculine body. The other half was smooth, clean skin. The space around his heart was also bare and ink free—as though he saved that special spot for a special someone.

She noticed a piece of paper and a pen next to him. "Were you drawing?"

"I usually do when I wake." His touch to the paper was almost melancholy. "I don't need to sleep as much as the normal person, and… the dreams," he elaborated.

She was almost afraid to ask. "What is it?"

With a shyness she hadn't expected in him, he held up the paper. It was a portrait of the two of them sleeping. It wasn't like the stark lines of his exhibition paintings, but crafted out of soft strokes and smooth shades. The care he'd taken around her face.

"Last night?" she ventured.

He shook his head. "It was a dream. I don't think it was last night… look at the pattern on the sheets."

"I don't have chevron sheets."

"I do."

His words hung in the air and her lips stretched into a smile.

The want must have shone from her eyes because his gaze turned fiery, and he kissed her, fast and furious. She vaguely remembered hearing the paper crumple under his body. As with last night, and every time she touched him, her fingers were drawn to him with a magnetic force. Her nails dragged around his chest, hard pecs, ribbed stomach... suddenly remembering the bruising that covered him only a few days ago, she pulled away.

It reminded her of where he disappeared last night and a spear of worry hit her.

"You left yesterday, after the battle. Where did you go?"

He rolled onto his back and lifted his hands behind his head to stare at the dark ceiling.

She lifted on her elbow.

"You were right," he said, frowning with concentration. "I went to find the men I fought the other night. In the Crows Nest at the docks."

The Docks! Not the Narrows. Grace filed the nugget of information away, for future reference. Just in case she had to chase him down because, let's face it, they were more than just together now. She knew it, deep inside her bones. She'd always find him if he needed her.

"I'd been going there for a few weeks to fight in my Envy gear. I kept my *fukumen* mask on, so no one could see my face, but they all loved to watch me hurt." He swiped his hand across the air in front of him dramatically and put on a showman's voice: "*Ladies and gentlemen. Envy, once a great and powerful member of the Deadly Seven, now reduced to rubble just like the building he helped destroy.*"

He sighed and dropped his hand. "I just wanted to feel in control of something, even if it was my own punishment."

Grace shimmied closer and cupped his face. How could she convince him it wasn't his fault? It was Sara. All Sara.

He glanced at her. "That morning I met you, I was

supposed to throw the fight the night before, but I couldn't do it. I saw how the crowd cheered for my opponent and I wanted it so bad, it was all I could think of. I hurt him. I lost control, and I won the fight. Still don't know if he survived but the owners of the fight ring took me out back and taught me a lesson, then dumped me in that alley. I could have taken them, but by that stage, I felt so bad that I'd lost control, I let them beat me."

"Oh, Evan." She wanted to kiss his pain away, but she stayed still and let him finish.

"Yesterday, I was so… hurt. You looked at me like I was some kind of monster, and Sara got her way again. I'd just helped neutralize the threat, and all you wanted to do was help *them*. I was so angry, Doc. So jealous. I needed to take it out on someone. The fight ring owners made sense. They'd beat me in the alley and left me for dead, so I wanted to do it to them. I started to. Got one punch in, but then couldn't finish. The dude hit me in the eye, and I left." He faced her. "It's all my fault. I brought this shit on myself. You were right. Taking another life isn't the answer."

"Stop." Grace kissed him gently on the lips, tears springing to her eyes. "You stopped. You didn't go through with it, and you came back here. Even though you thought I felt that way, which I don't, by the way. I could never think you are a monster." Grace's heart hammered in her chest. She had to know. Here goes nothing. "Why *did* you come back?" *To me.*

"Because I made a promise to you. I said I would keep you safe."

Her tears overflowed, and he saw. A frown etched

between his brow and he pulled her on top of him, snuggling into her neck, wrapping his arms around her. "Grace, I'll always come back to you."

It was exactly what she needed to hear. Seeing the box of her father's belongings last night had jolted something out of her that she hadn't felt in years: a yearning to belong, to be cherished. Their lips met and the kiss they shared was slow, passionate and filled with the love blossoming between them.

Evan broke away first. "I don't suppose I can persuade you to stay here, out of harm's way?"

"Nope," she said. "It's most likely a medical laboratory of some kind. I need to see what's there. I have to see this through. I owe that to the people who lost their lives in the building collapse. I want to get them compensation."

"Thought so. Okay." He rolled over the bed, changing their positions. "We're finishing this when we get back."

The thought brought a cheeky grin to her face. "Definitely."

Grace dressed in her jeans and the darkest hoodie she owned, a navy blue sports thing she hadn't worn in months. Evan had to put his leather pants back on, which he wasn't happy about. The smell had eased a little, and she'd sprayed it with air freshener. He'd had a black long-sleeved shirt on under the hooded jacket, so put that back on.

"I can't bring myself to put this jacket on," he said, frowning at the soiled lump of leather dangling from his hand. "There's got to be a better way to dress for battle. Laundering leather is a nightmare."

Grace shoved her boots on and stomped to fit them snuggly. "Surely you and your clever family can come up with something."

Hope filled his eyes for a fleeting moment. "They were working on something techie recently, but that stalled."

"Evan," Grace said, determination setting her jaw. "We're going to expose Sara and get your family back together."

He met her eyes and stared intensely. "I'm in love with you, Grace."

Before she could say anything, he rushed over and took hold of her arms.

"Don't say anything," he said. "I know we've just met, and I'm not expecting you to feel the same… yet."

"Evan," she said softly. "I care for you, I do…" she left the *but*, hanging.

But she wasn't ready. Not quite there.

He wasn't fazed. He smiled knowingly, no doubt thinking of the picture he'd drawn of them in his sheets. "Come on. Let's go."

TWENTY-SEVEN

EVAN LAZARUS

Evan took Grace on a detour to his loft apartment. He needed to get out of the leathers and into something suitable for stealth reconnaissance. Having some weapons and a car would also be good. He'd stashed his Katanas on a rooftop somewhere before heading to the docks, so had to re-supply. Definitely worth the delay.

When they arrived by cab, he decided to leave Grace downstairs in the tattoo studio. Despite complaining that morning, Josie had left the place neat and tidy. Being in her second year of employment, she was used to his random disappearances by now.

"Might be quicker if you stay here," he said and showed her a seat behind the reception area. "I'll be right back."

Taking the stairs out the back two steps at a time, he then jogged to his door, unlocked it and went inside. Like Grace's place, his was a mess. Worse. Clothes littered his bed, art supplies covered the side table and small kitchenette bench. Charcoal sketches were taped to all four walls.

Behind the taped artwork, graffiti plastered the walls. It smelled like adhesive fixative—a substance he used to stop the charcoal smudging—and residual spray paint. He gave the cluttered space a hard stare, feeling nostalgic for his old apartment at Lazarus House. That had multiple rooms: an art studio, a living space, fully equipped kitchen, luxury en-suite with a Jacuzzi. It also had a housekeeper that visited a few times a week and kept the place from turning into a dump. He wasn't averse to cleaning, he just didn't have time.

Right. Clothes. *Shit*. Mary had his alternate Envy leathers, and the one he'd worn last night was disgusting. Sweats and a hoodie it was, then. He dressed in record time, and strapped a knife to his ankle, slipped a pistol into the back of his waistband and put on a black baseball cap.

"And I thought my place was small," Grace said from the doorway, glancing around.

Evan jolted. He'd never get used to her holding no envy. She could sneak up on him at any time. "I thought you were waiting downstairs."

She shrugged. "I don't like waiting on my own."

That woman. Didn't do a thing he asked, and it drove him mad and wild for her at the same time. He just hoped she had the sense to follow his lead if they got into trouble. He glanced around nervously.

"So," Grace started, "why are you here and not in the same home as the rest of your family?"

He kicked a few stray items under his bed to clear some room. "I got into a fight with Wyatt a few years ago. We had separate apartments, but after the way he spoke to me after the bombing, I didn't want to breathe the same air as him, let alone live in the same building."

She silently moved around his bed, inspecting the sketches on the wall. "Because you told him about Sara and her envy, and they didn't believe you?"

"It was more than that. I'm the youngest. I'd just come off our seven-year training program. Hadn't seen most of them for years."

"Wait." Grace held up her palm, amazed. "Seven years? How old were you?"

"I started when I was fifteen."

"You've really had no choice in your life, have you?"

"Mary always said that after we completed our training, we could choose whatever path we wanted, and encouraged college. The training wasn't just physical, it was mental and tactical. She wanted us to be fully equipped to handle whatever came our way. I looked up to all of them because they'd already been fighting for the city while I was the last to come home. I should have said something about Sara earlier, just didn't think they'd believe me. As it was, after I told them, most of them didn't anyway."

"I'm sorry, I can imagine how that felt."

"Like I'd never be good enough for them. Always the green one, the less experienced. And now… I'm the first to unlock my powers. I'm the first to find my balance"—his eyes locked on Grace—"all because of you."

She smiled shyly and dipped her head. "I may be the one who triggered it Evan, but you're the one saving the world."

Something like pride glimmered in his eyes and he kissed her briefly on the lips, then sighed. He picked up a

ANTLM

duffel bag and stuffed it with more weapons and surveillance gear. "You'd think that would be enough to earn some respect, but I don't think I'll ever be good enough for them."

"That's not true. You're gifted Evan, and I'm not just talking about the electricity thing. Which, speaking of, I'd love to investigate more. It's fascinating to think how—" She cut herself off by biting her lip. "Sorry. Doctor speak. But the gift I'm talking about is your art." Grace gestured at the sketches on the wall.

It was enough to make Evan laugh. "The pretty pictures? They're a wasted talent. Parker's built an empire around his big brain. Griff's got a mind like Pythagoras. Wyatt is a renowned chef. Liza's the youngest female detective on her squad. Even Sloan has mad tech skills. She can hack into any computer system in the country. And, do I really need to mention Tony?" No son-of-a-bitch should look good in tights, but when his latest action film came out, jeez, Evan was so green. He had an ass like Alcatraz.

"Well, I think they're beautiful." Grace traced her fingers over another sketch on the wall, then paused. "Hold up. I think… I think this is me."

"Probably not. I drew that before I met you."

"I'm certain of it. That boy in the cap is Taco. He sells papers on the street corner. I'm the woman he's handing the paper to."

Evan frowned, squinting at the picture. "Taco?"

"Yeah, I know. It's an unusual name."

"No, I think you're right. I recognize that kid. He's the one who found me dressed as Envy in the alley after I got dumped. He was standing under a rusty fire escape ladder, throwing a baseball into the air and catching it, but the ball hit the ladder and it fell. I pushed him out of the way, and that's how I hurt my shoulder."

"That's why you had the stab wound? Because you saved a kid?"

"Maybe. Why are you smiling? Do I get a reward?"

She grinned and stalked toward him. The kiss she gave him was all heat, and promise of what's coming later. He couldn't wait.

"I have the day off work," she said. "I can reward you later for as long as you want."

"Now, that's the kind of rest and relaxation I'm talking about."

"Yeah, I—" she cut herself off. "Wait. Evan. The sketches on the wall."

"I know. I put them there."

She swatted him. "I mean, they're like the ones at the gallery, and this morning." She blushed, probably because she was thinking of being in his bed one day. He liked that. "It's not a wasted talent. It's prophetic. Can you, I don't know, sketch something now and find out what Sara's plan is?"

"I forgot about the gallery. That one where Sara was standing before the painting, and then it actually happened. Now this—you're saying the one with you and Taco is real?"

"One hundred percent."

"That's too many to be a coincidence. I've never tried to force a sketch. I usually dream and then sketch the scene when I wake otherwise I think about it all day. Drives me nuts."

"Oh." She slumped. "Then I guess, we need you to have another dream somehow."

"In the meantime, we need to go. It's almost four."

"You're right. We need to go."

Evan took Grace to the garage where his car waited. It was a newish black Mustang GT Coupe. Perfect for stealth night missions. Sexy matte paint, dark-as-fuck tint, bullet-proof windows. Everything he dreamed of in a partner, and then some. But that was before he met Grace.

He hopped in the driver side, stowed his duffel bag in the rear, and then reached across to pop the passenger door open. "My lady, your chariot awaits."

She snorted and slid into the front seat, clicked her seat-belt on and turned to face him, waiting for further instructions.

"What now, Evan?"

"Right." He faced the front. "I'll put the coordinates in the nav, then we're off."

"AIMI, it's Evan," he said. "Engine on."

The engine roared to life. Blue lights lit up the dash, and a female voice came through the speaker. "Good morning, Evan. It's early for a drive. Where would you like to go?"

"Oh my God," Grace murmured. "Your car is Kit from Nightrider."

"Not even close," Evan said. "It's AIMI. Our Artificial Intelligence Management Interface. It's just something some of the fam created. It won't make me coffee or anything. That's the next model."

Grace gaped.

"Just kidding. AIMI, this is Grace. Say hi, Grace."

"Hi," Grace said.

"Good morning, Grace."

"AIMI, I want you to authorize Grace as a user for this car."

"Not a problem. Please can you repeat this sentence after me, Grace? I need it for voice activation identification."

"Oh. Okay. Sure."

"My voice is my password."

That sounded ominous.

"It's fine. It's just for AIMI," Evan assured.

Grace repeated the sentence and then had to do it again another three times. AIMI logged her as a user. Evan told AIMI the address, drove out of the garage, and down the road. According to the nav, the destination was about ten minutes away.

"So," Grace said after a minute or two. "You still talk to some of your family then, if they made you this car?"

He shrugged. If you could call it talking. "Flint, yes. Mary, too. It's really Wyatt who I don't get along with, and that's understandable. But I haven't given up on him. Not yet. Sara's been lying to him the entire time he's known her. I can't imagine how it would feel if the woman I loved wasn't who I thought she was."

Grace placed her palm on his forearm in a comforting move. "He's lucky to have a brother like you."

Evan's heart stopped, and he turned to Grace. Her genuine expression led him to believe her words were the honest to God truth. He couldn't love her any less in that moment, and he couldn't despise Sara more. He turned back to the windshield, watching the road.

He mulled over Sara's motives.

"Sara felt deadly levels of envy," Evan said, tapping the wheel with a thumb. "Both before the bombing, and yesterday. I know she's envious—deadly envious—but of what? If we can identify her reason, then we have a better chance at getting to the root of her vendetta against us."

"That's a good question. I never thought to get to the root of her envy."

"You know how I told you I spent time living in different countries learning the art of war? One place was in Japan and at a compound managed by a Zen Buddhist Master. We learned to stay calm and vigilant in the face of death, and to take control of our mind in extreme situations. I never really did catch onto the whole detaching from material possession thing though. That's something Griff excels in. You should see his apartment. Anything that doesn't serve a purpose is out." Evan smiled. That guy was a hardcore control freak, but he was someone to look up to. If Evan only had half the control he did, then he'd be doing great.

"You really miss them, don't you?" Grace said softly. "How close you used to be, I mean."

A pang hurt in his chest. "Yeah. I do."

She squeezed his forearm. "So you were telling me about your Zen Master?"

"Oh yeah. We learned about mediation and observation to help us master our sin-sensing capabilities. One training exercise was to guess who stood behind a wall based on our sixth sense. I had to spend the day paying attention to other people in the compound and listening to how their individual envy levels fluctuated. People have minute differences in sin. It's like a fingerprint. I can tell who is standing nearby without looking at them. I can also work out what's causing their envy by the way it fluctuates near a certain person or object. The point is, Sara's envy doesn't fluctuate. She feels the same amount of envy around all of us."

"Even your parents?"

He'd never thought to include Flint and Mary in his observations.

"You might be right," he said. "I think she felt the most amount of sin around me and my siblings."

"Are there any identifying factors specific to you and your brothers and sisters?"

"Like, hair or eye color?"

"No, differences between your siblings as a whole compared to your parents. Like, the sin-sensing for one. Or maybe she's jealous of your entire family unit?" Grace knew she missed having a family, maybe Sara was the same.

"We've also been genetically enhanced, and our parents aren't. Don't know about the family thing, I never thought she liked me at all but maybe it was just me she wanted out."

"Do you think Sara wants special powers?"

"No. Mary's psychic. So if that were the case, Sara would feel envious around Mary too. Mary's also a better warrior than us. She used to be an assassin of the highest order which means it can't be our fighting skills. So if it's none of those, then what is it?"

"Anything specific about your DNA makeup that Mary

and Flint don't have? Apart from the sin-sensing part. I find it hard to believe someone would actually want that skill if it makes you feel so uncomfortable."

"Advanced healing and regeneration."

"Regeneration? As in, regrow a limb? Wow. Now I *really* want to run some tests on you."

Evan shirked back, unable to hide the distaste on his face.

Grace's eyes widened. "Oh, I'd never do it to share your data with a covert government organization or anything like that. It would just be for me. And maybe to help you make sense of it all. Plus, I'm a cutter. Well. I was. I like getting inside to see how things work. It's weird, I know. You can tell me to shut up any time."

He shook his head. "Yeah, I really don't like the idea of you cutting me open."

"Say no more. Okay, maybe just one more thing. You said your birth mother was the one who knew the most about it, but she's not around? And she spliced your DNA with other animals to give you skills like regeneration? I'd love to help you and your family somehow. But it's up to you, I won't pressure you, and I won't blab."

Evan relaxed a little. He'd always been concerned with letting anyone know his secrets, but with the Doc, he was learning to trust. This was the first time he realized she had his fate in her hands. She could sell his hospital scans and any other data to the highest bidder if she wanted. The work his mother did on them had never been replicated thanks to her destroying all her research in the fire that claimed her life, and the laptop they had of hers was incomplete, so any scientific information coming to light today would be valuable.

"None of us have tested the regeneration theory, but it was hypothesized. It's why Mary broke us out of the lab when we were little. The boss wanted to test the theory out."

"Oh my God. That's horrible." She shook her head, eyes wide. "You were children."

"Yeah. But this is why I fight now, so someone with a twisted God complex never gets in a position of power again. I mean, thinking you can control someone's health is... *holy mother of shit*. That's it! The Medical Examiner said Sara's body had some sort of heart disease, right? Now she's fine. Someone's worked on her, genetically."

"But she died. The records, and the ME said he saw her body cremated... but, now that you mention it. Some things aren't adding up. She looks different. Her skin is smoother, she has bloodshot eyes. After the incident yesterday, I examined all the attackers. Each of them was either sick or deformed. Maybe someone is promising these people a new life if they commit crimes for them, or maybe they're the byproducts of testing gone wrong."

Evan turned a corner, pulling the car into a dark street in the industrial part of town. "I think you're right. It's the best explanation we've got. We're still missing a piece of the puzzle, though. Something to connect a dead, sick body to a live healthy one. Maybe we'll find it here."

"You have arrived at your destination," AIMI said.

"AIMI, activate stealth mode."

The engine noise lowered to a whisper, and the headlights shut off. The front windshield lit up green with night vision capabilities, allowing Evan to see clearly where he drove. The external shell of the car would have darkened to an almost invisible, hard to see shade at this time of night. They were like a shadow.

"Wow. Does everyone in your family have a car like this?"

"Something like it. That must be the place."

They pulled up in front of a large warehouse protected by high chain-link fencing with barbed wire across the top. Evan coasted the Mustang past the front driveway, taking note of the sign. *Global Organization for Disease Control.* Guards and cameras at the gate didn't notice the dark shadow creeping silently along the road, but he kept driving.

"High security for a lab this time of night," he murmured.

"And busy." Grace pointed to a truck coming toward them down the road and turning into the GODC driveway, now behind them. "I guess it could be one of those twenty-four-hour places."

"Doesn't smell right." Half a mile down the road, Evan parked in a vacant, dark lot belonging to a closed tire shop. "Wait here," he said and reached into the back seat to retrieve his duffel bag.

"Wait here?" she squeaked.

"I'm just taking a quick look. Won't be long."

"Absolutely not. We already spoke about this. You need me. It's a lab—I'm a doctor. I might understand things in there that you don't. I'm not waiting."

"Grace, I appreciate you wanting to help, but I didn't realize it was so heavily guarded. This is one of those times where one person is better than two. I know about espionage. I can defend myself. I don't want to be worried about your safety. I'll capture what I find on camera and bring it back."

"Espionage sounds so serious."

"It is."

"But the girls that stay behind in horror flicks get slashed."

"The car will keep you safe. Wait, you watch slasher films?"

"A long time ago. I think maybe that's where my fascination for blood and the human anatomy started."

Evan couldn't help himself and laughed.

"What? Don't laugh. This is a serious moment. Anyway, I haven't had time to watch movies since I became a doctor."

"Yeah, we're going to fix that. Watching movies is a great way to blow off steam. You need more of that."

She gave him a coy smile. "Well, that's what I have you for, isn't it?"

Her smile hit him in the heart, and all humor fled. "Doc, please stay."

She closed her eyes and wrung her hands. "Okay. Fine. But if you're not back in twenty, I don't care how heavily guarded it is, I'm coming after you."

TWENTY-EIGHT

DR. GRACE GO

Grace sat in the car for five minutes and then started to panic. The concern wasn't for Evan's welfare, but her own. Before long, the small space inside the car without him closed in, she imagined water dripping from somewhere, and she knew that if she didn't get out soon, she'd have an anxiety attack. So she cracked open the car door to let the air in. Once the door opened, she thought she may as well stand outside, and then once she stood outside, rubbing her arms, she thought... a walk down to the gate would keep her warm.

What's the harm in taking a look-see?

She could assess how heavily guarded it was. Before she knew it, she'd pulled her hoodie over her head and tightened the drawstrings around her face. That should hide her features enough in case she got caught on camera. She jogged up the street, careful to stick to the cover of bushes and trees, until she stood where the neighboring building finished, and the fenced GODC complex began. Taking stock, she cast her gaze around the dark landscape and let the brisk night air and pine scent soak into her. The chain-link fence went on for about ten yards until it hit the main driveway and gate. The soft glow of yellow light came from the interior of a security booth set to monitor traffic in and out of the complex. The guard inside watched something on his phone, she could tell from the small blue glow flashing across his face.

So how did Evan get in?

She didn't have far to look. Nearby, a hole had been cut in the fence, the metal links rolled back, and Evan's duffel bag lay beside it. She snuck up, crouched and rifled inside for something to use as a weapon. Bolt cutters, a tripod and some sort of surveillance device. He must have taken everything else with him.

A glance at her watch told her it had already been fifteen minutes, but not twenty yet.

Did she dare?

The path to the laboratory warehouse was clear. A ladder ran up two levels to the flat roof. She'd bet that's the way Evan went. The hospital had rooftop access from a stairwell, maybe this place had something similar. A quick check to the guard in the booth, and down the driveway confirmed the way was clear. She crept through the fence, nearly cut herself on the metal, and darted across the grassed open space to the ladder. With heart pounding fast, she climbed quickly and breached the top with her lungs bursting from the suspense. Did anyone see her?

She ducked low and peeked over the rim of the roof. All she could hear was a distant owl, her own deep breaths and the soft wind whispering in her strained ears. No. No one saw her.

She jogged across the roof to the stairwell door propped open by a brick. Surely that was where Evan went. Who else would leave the emergency door propped open?

Taking it as a sign, she entered the dark stairwell and tiptoed down, surprised she had the wits to pull out her phone and activate the video recorder. Maybe she was getting the hang of this espionage thing after all. She wanted to notify Evan she was there, but worried it would vibrate his phone and give his location away, so she kept to herself. She was seriously buzzed with adrenaline, and couldn't stop thinking that someone could catch her at any moment. Upon reaching the ground level, she exited into a lit hallway lined with closed doors. Any of those could lead somewhere incriminating, or none could. She had to remind herself, this escapade could be a bust. There might be nothing incriminating within these walls.

Grace edged along the corridor and took a peek inside the window of the first door. Offices. Empty desks cast in dull light. She kept going to the next. A lab. Definitely a lab. She recognized equipment used for testing biological samples. Microscopes, incubators, and petri dishes. Not unusual for a lab that might research disease. A glowing light deeper into the room hinted at more.

She had to get closer. There didn't seem to be anyone inside. The lights were on half power, casting a soft ambiance. Hopefully the scientists had gone home. With her fingers on the door knob, she took a deep breath, twisted, and pushed until the door popped open. Air rushed out as though it had been equalized by a filtration device, and she'd broken the seal. Whoops. Oh well, if she'd just entered a bio-hazard area, it was already too late for her. But no alarms went off, so she continued through and closed it softly behind her.

A hand covered her mouth, and she almost screamed, but then a male voice hissed: "What the hell are you doing here?"

Relief flooded her veins, and she turned to accept the force of Evan's demanding, wild eyes. Okay, maybe he wasn't so relieved. He looked down right pissed as he removed his hand from her face.

"It's been twenty minutes?" she ventured with a shrug.

"No, it hasn't." His jaw worked, and he adjusted his ball cap. "I was just about to come back. Goddamn it, Grace, you should have waited."

Uh-oh. No Doc this time. Just Grace.

"Okay, well, now I'm here. What did you find?" She kept her voice low, taking his lead. "What's in those tanks down there?"

They cast their gazes down the length of the large room. Along the side walls were small aquariums filled with animals. Snakes, rats, insects… and those were just the live ones. Dead animals and animal parts floated in specimen jars. Gross. Grace shivered and crinkled her nose. The smell reminded her of the mausoleum at the hospital.

A sealed, plastic room sat to another side where she guessed a separate sterile environment was needed. Perhaps that's where the contaminants were. What really caught Grace's attention were the enormous cylindrical tanks shrouded in more dull blue UV lights toward the rear end of the room.

"I think you were right." Evan's mouth set in a grim line. "About the genetic engineering. It's too much of a coincidence. This lab is more than a center for disease control."

Her intuition twisted. "What's in those far tanks, Evan?"

"You'd better come and see."

Grace shuffled after Evan, trying to keep quiet like him, but the sticky floor made tiny squeaking sounds under her sneakers. With every passing step, queasiness rolled in her gut like the ocean tide. Any minute, an alarm could go off and they'd be toast. By the time she stood in front of a tall cylinder, she'd lost all coherent thought as her brain tried to make rational sense out of what she found. Floating in glowing, cloudy water were naked human bodies with tubes down their throats and stuck to their bellies—like umbilical cords. She stared at them with morbid fascination. It was as though they slept. Their chests moved up and down, like a baby breathing amniotic fluid.

"They look like embryos but fully grown," she said, pulling her hood off to see better.

Evan nodded, then frowned at her and pulled her hood back to shroud her face. "Keep that up. It's protecting your identity."

"Sorry. Thanks."

Evan gestured down. "Look at the labels."

At the bottom of each tank was a white label. On each label, a human name. Peter McKinley, Silis Davidson, Astrid Samson. She read on, and on.

"There's more." Evan waved beyond the first row of

tanks. "Some of them are young, some are older. Children and adults, all at different stages in their life cycle. None beyond their twenties."

"Oh my God." She was going to be sick. Children. Rows and rows of tanks filled the warehouse. She couldn't see where it ended. Grace crept in the shadows, reading the labels. "They've got dates on them. These with fully grown bodies have a date of almost two years ago. And these smaller ones aren't that long ago... do you think they're growing people? Is that even possible?"

"My father used to work in the tech department of the lab that created us. He had a friend in bio-engineering who could regrow a limb from stem cells so, yeah, I think it's possible."

A hissing sound came from somewhere as more air equalized. It was the jolt Grace needed to remind herself of their time limit. She took a picture of a tank, then focused on the labels and took another shot. "Lilo would kill to get her hands on these photos."

"Lilo?"

"My friend. She was with me at Heaven, but you didn't really get a chance to meet her. She's a journalist at the Cardinal Copy."

Evan's eyes narrowed. "We can't leak this yet. Not until we figure out what Sara's got to do with it all."

He was right. Evan walked next to Grace as they inspected more tanks, walking deeper and deeper into the eerie warehouse. The lights weren't all on here. Some tanks were used and discarded.

"Evan." Grace paused at an empty cylinder. The hairs on the back of her neck rose.

"What is it?" He came up behind her. "It's empty."

"Look at the label."

There, on the bottom of the first empty tank of an entire empty row, was the name *Sara Madden,* and the date listed was the day after the bombing, just over two years ago.

"Fuck," Evan said.

"If these… people are growing in here, and it takes two years… and, oh my God."

"What? Doc, what?"

"Evan. The Sara who turned up to your exhibition, the day after the two-year anniversary of the bombing, wasn't the original Sara. It was the one grown in this tank." Grace took a photo. The flash illuminated the empty cylinder.

"Fu-*uck.*"

"You keep saying that."

He pulled the peak down on his cap and looked down at his boots, thinking. "A clone. Sara is a goddamned clone. With the same memories as the one before." Evan's eyes lit up. "And more. She knew how to fight. The old Sara didn't."

He rushed over to the lab and moved stacks of papers around on a desk with a computer. "I saw something here before… where is it. There. Look." He held up a piece of paper for Grace to read. "Muscle memory. They've got schematic mark-up for a muscle memory program from martial arts experts."

"This is insane!" Grace's mind boggled.

Evan's posture stiffened, and he turned to face the exit.

He morphed from energized, to deadly, like a beast in the wild about to pounce on prey.

"Grace," he said softly. "I want you to listen very carefully and do everything I say."

He pulled his phone from his pocket and handed it to her. "Take this. It has photographic evidence of this place on it."

"Okay," she said. "Why are you giving it to me?"

Stupid. So stupid. The minute the words were out of her mouth, she knew. Alarm spiked in her body and, for the first time since a building collapsed around her, she felt helpless. She wasn't talking about the walls closing in, and not enough air, helpless. This was heart pounding, mouth drying, anxiety.

He didn't think he would make it out of there alive.

"It's safer with you," he said. "I'll be right behind you, but you'll need to get yourself out. "

Grace blinked rapidly, trying desperately to get her surgeon's brain to kick into action. She could handle this. If she ever wanted to get back to the operating theater, she had to learn to master her mind as well as the scalpel. Back in the day, if she felt anxiety before a procedure, she would take stock of her tools, and check items off a mental list. She could do that now. What did she need for an escape? C'mon, Grace. Snap out of it. Think. But she couldn't. She stared at the phone in Evan's hands, held halfway to her.

He put the phone in her pocket and then took her face between his hands. "People are coming, you understand? I sense them."

She nodded.

"When they get here, I'm going to disarm them. We'll run back the way we came and get out of here. If that doesn't happen—"

"No. No, it will happen, we'll get out of here."

He shook her gently to get her to refocus, but she couldn't see because of the tears blurring her vision.

"Grace. If this place is like the one that created us, Mary had to infiltrate it for two years before she was able to get us out alive. We lost the lives of two people in that escape—two very important people to us."

"Oh, God, Evan. Not helping."

"The point is, this place had ex-military security guards at the front. If the alarm gets triggered, listen to me, if that happens, then I'm going to create a distraction, and you need to get out of here on your own. Take the car back to Lazarus House. AIMI will know how to get into HQ." He darted a glance at the door, then hurried on, over Grace's whimpered protests. "The important thing is you get out of here alive, and with the evidence."

"But—?"

"Grace. I'll be fine. I can do this stuff blindfolded. Literally. You trust me, don't you?"

"Yes, of course. More than anyone."

"Then get yourself out. Whatever happens, I want you to promise me you'll do that."

Despite her better judgment, she nodded.

Evan pressed his lips to hers in a frenzied, passionate move, then was gone.

"The important thing is we both get out of here. Alive. *Together*," Grace hissed at his retreating shadow.

He turned at the last moment and nodded. "We get out together." Then he positioned himself next to the front door and waited.

Just then, the lights switched fully on, shocking the lab into brightness. A group of scientists in white lab coats walked in, chattering amongst themselves. Just like he'd surprised her when she'd entered, Evan darted out from behind the front door like a wraith. He pulled the closest scientist into a stranglehold, silently cutting off her airway until she slumped to the ground. The other three scientists, two men and a woman, realized their friend wasn't talking. All three pivoted.

Evan darted an almost imperceptible glance at Grace, then meaningfully down at the woman at his feet. He wanted Grace to know something about the woman.

But she looked pretty average. Grace checked out the other scientists. One woman had long gray streaked hair, and a proud face with a long nose. The second man was of Indian descent and in his fifties. The third and final man was white, young and had short brown hair.

Oh God, so what? What was it about them he wanted her to know?

The young male scientist launched himself at the big red alarm trigger on the wall. Evan drove his fist into his stomach, winding him. While he was occupied, the older scientist triggered the alarm and sirens blared through the building. Evan made short work of detaining the remaining scientists and shouted at Grace: "Put her coat on. Get out of here. I'll be right behind you."

Right. That's what he was doing when he looked at her

weird. Grace ran to the woman he'd dropped first and tugged her out of her white lab coat. It was harder to move her limbs than it appeared, but she managed to get it off and onto herself. Before Evan could relieve the coat from one of the men, a pair of scary security guards entered. Muscles bulged from their black tactical uniform. Their jaws were locked tight, prepared for action. They moved fluidly, half crouched, ready to shoot.

Immediately, they saw Evan as the threat. Assault rifles trained toward him. They hadn't seen Grace standing behind the door with the other woman. Evan bolted to the rear of the room—*He's going the wrong way!*—and picked up a metal stool. This was his distraction. He was going to break the tanks.

Grace's hand covered her mouth.

"Miss, are you okay?" said another guard to her as he stepped inside the lab.

She gulped. He thought she was the scientist. Grace nodded, eyes wide.

"I'm going to need you to evacuate. Follow fire drill procedures." He roughly shoved Grace out the door, launching her down the corridor, past another two soldiers running toward her.

That made five. Evan didn't have his swords. What did he have to protect himself? Would the electricity be enough? But he'd said to go. No matter what, he'd be fine.

He'd be fine.

He faced off with those robed attackers effortlessly. He'd be fine. The best thing for him would be for her to get to safety so he wouldn't worry.

She forced her legs to move until she jogged and her arms pumped. Her heart slammed against her ribcage. Then she *ran*. The last thing she heard was the sound of glass breaking, then guns firing, as her palm slammed the emergency stairwell door open and she bolted up the steps. With her lungs on fire, she burst through the rooftop exit and into the cold night. Two minutes later, she got down the ladder and through the fence to the car. She slipped into the driver's side, thinking if—when—he got out, they'd need a fast getaway. She could drive.

"AIMI, it's Grace."

"Good morning Grace. It's early for a drive."

"Start the engine in stealth mode."

"Yes, Grace."

The engine purred to life and idled.

"Where would you like to go, Grace?" AIMI asked.

"To the Lazarus House HQ."

"Would you like me to drive, or will you?"

Grace blinked. The car could drive itself? "I'll drive. Just wait. Not yet. Evan's not here."

"Very well. The destination has been programed into the navigation system. Estimated time of arrival will be ten minutes from departure."

"Great. Thank you."

She slapped her forehead. What the hell was she doing, thanking a car?

Five minutes later, and Grace was having a mild angina. Her chest screamed. She couldn't breathe. Where was he? She tapped her hands on the steering wheel and checked in the rear view. No sign of Evan. That was okay. That was fine.

She trusted him. She did. It took time to destroy a lab and overcome five heavily armed, expert ex-military security soldiers. She moved the car, so it faced the road, ready to drive out on a moments notice. Still no Evan. She dropped her head to the steering wheel, unable to let her mind travel to the worst possible scenario.

Then the door whipped open. Evan jumped in with an incorrigible grin and smelling like chemicals.

"I blew it up," he said, wild-eyed. Then he slammed his palm on the dash. "Drive, AIMI. Get us out of here."

Grace stifled a scream as the car whipped forward on its own.

TWENTY-NINE

DR. GRACE GO

Grace clutched the steering wheel as the car whizzed down the road, driving on its own. Next to her, Evan checked his mirrors. When a loud ping came from the trunk of the car, Grace jolted and bit her tongue.

"What was that?" she asked Evan.

AIMI answered. "It appears we're being shot at."

"Shot at!" Grace's frantic gaze darted to every mirror she could find, trying to find the source of their attack. She looked over her shoulder. Left. Right. There: Two motorcycles drove up behind them, their lights shining brightly in her eyes.

"It's all good, Doc. Keep calm. I got this." Evan unclipped his seatbelt and drew a .44 Magnum from his waistband. He hit the button to lower the passenger window. Before he could lean out and fire, the side mirror was shot off.

"Evan!" Grace shouted.

His lips pressed together. "Fuckers want a piece of me?"

He waited, fiery eyes tracking the path of the two riders coming up behind them. Dark black helmets over their heads. Black tactical uniform like the ones on the soldiers in the lab. Rifles slung over their shoulders. They split. One neared on Grace's side, one on Evan's.

Evan found himself with a rifle in the face.

In a lightning fast move, he tugged the gun, throwing the rider off balance. He refused to let go and the bike slammed into the side of the car, rocking it.

"It appears a foreign object has collided with our right passenger side fender." AIMI's voice came over the speaker. "Scanning for damage now."

"Don't worry about the damage, AIMI, worry about the hostiles."

"Scanning for hostiles. One on the right. One on the left. Would you like me to use evasive tactics to avoid another collision?"

"Yes," Evan grunted, still in a tug-of-war with the rider. Evan punched the helmet of the rider. His head whipped back, but he stubbornly stayed attached to the rifle, Evan, and the car. A crackling sound began as Evan's power lit up his hands.

The car swerved sharply to the right. Evan kept his tight, powered up grip, but the rider just wouldn't let up. Were his gloves rubber? They swerved again, and Grace's palm slapped the window to hold her balance.

A loud pop on her hand stole her attention. The rider on her side shot at her! A spider crack in the glass splintered outward. It was inches from her face. The rider's dark helmet visor turned to watch the road, then came back to her. She wasn't sure if he could see her, the tint was black, and they were in stealth mode. Whatever that entailed. But the rider pointed his rifle back at the window, ready for another shot.

"AIMI," Grace said, voice tight. "Evasive tactics needed on the left driver side. Left side. *Left side!*"

The car weaved back to the left, but the rider swerved to avoid the hit.

"Enough!" Evan shouted. He chopped to his side and jammed his attacker's rifle between the window frame and his arm. With his free hand, he pointed his own gun at the rider—right in the middle of the visor.

"Evan!" Grace couldn't help it. "Don't kill him."

He growled, roared, then lowered his weapon and shot the rider in the leg, sending him on a spiral, careening down the road.

The gunfire at Grace's window picked up. Bullets pelted the surface at Grace's head. Thankfully the bulletproof glass held. Evan shifted half his body out his window until he perched on the sill, aiming over the roof to the driver side.

A quick *bang* from Evan's gun, and the rider lost control of his bike, veering to the side to crash into a power pole in front of a gas station. Evan slipped back into the car in a fluid movement.

When he shut the window, she blurted, "Is he dead?"

"He'll live." Evan stowed the weapon in the glove compartment. "AIMI, drive around and make sure we're not being followed, then get us to HQ."

Grace's teeth hurt from clenching her jaw. Her limbs shook with the letdown of adrenaline. Her hands were claws. She held them in front of her face. Every muscle, every tendon, tensed with the buildup of lactic acid. She warned patients about this all the time. Too much adrenaline, nowhere for it to go. Now she… oh God, she cramped.

"Breathe, Doc, just breathe."

Grace exhaled through her mouth and inhaled through her nose. Evan repeated soothing sounds and directions. She focused on his voice and her breathing. In. Out. Calm. Don't think about the car driving itself. Don't think about the glass at her side being the only thing between her head and the barrage of bullets. Don't think about how that rider's body flopped around as he went down, skidding along the road.

The car coasted through the streets of Cardinal City coming alight with the first rays of dawn, but Grace's mind still traveled in a dark place.

This was Evan's life. The danger, the potential for death. If she let this—whatever it was between them—happen, then she would face fear her entire life. Not knowing if he'd come home, alive or injured or at all. Then she'd be alone again. No one to hold her at night, no one to soothe her when she was in pain. She wasn't sure if she could do it.

Evan reached over. "Hey," he said as he stroked her cheek. "It's okay, Doc. I won't let anything happen to you."

"It's not only me I'm worried about. You could have died!"

He snorted. "What, those riders? That was fun, that's what that was."

"How can you joke about this? And what about the other five? I had no idea if you were alive or dead when I ran from the lab to the car. I thought maybe I'd done the wrong thing and almost went back to find you, but—" her throat closed up.

The car slowed as it reached a corner, and Evan's strong arms pulled Grace into his lap, as though she weighed nothing. He adjusted her to straddle him, face-to-face. His warm hands engulfed her cheeks, thumbs rubbing gently on her chin. Green, calm eyes held her gaze. "Grace. I had them. You did what I asked. You got yourself to the car and safe. That's all I needed. You did good. You did good, baby."

"Five soldiers, Evan."

"A walk in the park."

"Did you kill them?" She covered her eyes, not wanting to see the truth in his.

He pulled her hands down. "At least two were alive to come after me."

"What?"

"Kidding. They all were alive. Just subdued. *The supreme art of war is to subdue the enemy without fighting*. I don't always follow that rule, but I'm trying."

She slumped against him, head falling to his shoulder as his arms encircled her, hugging her close. That steady pressure reassured her. His warmth reassured her.

They stayed like that for another few silent minutes as the car drove smoothly down the road. She'd lost track of where they were. City buildings whizzed by.

Evan's fingers traced patterns down her back in a soothing motion. It reminded her of a game she played with her mother when she was little. They'd take turns drawing a picture with their finger on each other's back and had to guess what it was. Grace would always draw a stick figure face, or a boat on the water. Her mother, a bouquet of roses or particular kinds of plants Grace had no hope of guessing. The memory made her smile, and she melted into Evan and pressed her ear to his chest, reveling in his strong, steady heartbeat.

After a few moments, he spoke. His voice rumbled through his chest, warbling the sound. "We got her, Doc. We got the evidence."

"We have the evidence tying her to the lab, but nothing yet tying her to the bombing."

"It's a start. It might be enough to get her to confess."

Grace wasn't so sure, but she felt better about it all. A few days ago, there was no hope. Now, anything was possible. Plus, Evan actually mentioned getting Sara to confess instead of killing her.

Evan's intrepid fingers trailed around her back, slipping up to her neck, and into her hair. It felt so good, so blissful that a moan escaped her lips. He tensed underneath her, muscles turning stiff. Another part of him hardened and pressed between her legs, right at her sensitive spot and she couldn't help but roll into him.

"Grace," he choked out, voice rough. He tugged her back by the hair and exposed her face to him.

Their eyes clashed. Darkness, need, passion. He was there. He came back to her. She lowered her lips until she tasted his. Licked along the bottom. Felt his labored breath against hers. Then a slow, long, fiery kiss that had them melting into each other. This. Yes, this. She could wait for him if she came back to this every time. She never wanted to give him up.

Grace broke from the kiss, pulling back. "Are you coming back to my place after we take the evidence to your family?"

His hands slid down her back and cupped her rear. He eyed her appreciatively. "Wild horses wouldn't keep me away."

A warm swell in her chest. She wanted to spend the morning, the afternoon, the night… the next night with him. Every night until she was back on the roster at the hospital.

"Evan," she said as the car slowed down and turned another corner, gently driving over a bump. "I think I'm falling—"

"We have arrived at your destination," AIMI said, cutting Grace off.

She glanced around. They were in a darkened garage lot filled with black vehicles of all sorts. Another Mustang. A few motorcycles. More sports cars. A Prius. An Escalade. She was ashamed to say she had no idea how they got there, or where *there* was. Headquarters, Evan had said.

"Grace. What were you going to say?" he asked, eyes hopeful.

Voices carried into the surrounding area. Lights switched on, illuminating an underground garage housing many vehicles. They weren't alone. Someone walked up to the car.

"Oh, no," Grace whispered and shuffled off him, but he wouldn't let her move.

"Grace." His brow furrowed in concentration. "Tell me."

"I—" She blushed.

The passenger door opened, revealing one of Evan's brothers. It was the one with the glasses and the shirt buttoned up to the collar. He frowned disapprovingly at Evan and Grace. "That's not a safe way to travel in a car."

"Shut it, Griff," Evan growled.

Another head poked out behind Griffin. The older brother with long hair: Parker. He lifted an indignant eyebrow. "We're woken out of our beds at six am by an alert from AIMI, and this is what we find?"

"AIMI alerted you?" Evan asked.

"She's programmed to notify us anytime the fleet is under attack." The big guy looked at Grace and stared.

She waved shyly. "Hi."

He didn't reply, just shifted his glare to Evan. "You have some explaining to do. Get inside to the common apartment. Everyone's waiting for you."

Evan helped Grace get out of the car and took her by the hand.

Parker glanced over his shoulder and frowned. "She's not coming."

Evan stopped. His shoulders lifted, tense. "She goes where I go."

"I don't mind leaving," Grace started, but Evan silenced her with his eyes.

"She knows more about this than you, Parks. She's coming."

If looks could wither, Grace would be a puddle on the floor from the one Parker shot her.

But Griffin stepped in to save the day. "There's no point sending her home now. She's in this too deep."

Parker shook his head and walked out of the garage,

disappearing into a doorway at the end. Griffin followed him.

Evan turned to Grace. "It's all good. You're with me."

"I meant it. If it's going to cause problems, I can go."

"Doc. You're not leaving my sight until we sort this out. You got the phone?"

She nodded.

"Good. Let's do this."

THIRTY

EVAN LAZARUS

With Grace's hand in his, Evan trailed after his brothers through the underground passageway in the Lazarus Building. He knew it would be a lot for Grace to take in, but they didn't have time to stop and talk about it. The guided tour would have to come later.

They passed the workout room, the tech lab where Flint usually tinkered, the science lab, and med-room where they repaired as many of their injuries in house as possible. Each of them had learned to be an in-field medic as part of their training, but if surgery was required—well, they'd never required it, so they'd never found out. Evan's trip to the hospital had been a mistake and the first of its kind for the family. He'd been lucky Mary turned up to take his battle gear home. If anyone had discovered it, his identity would be uncovered, then it was prison—or worse—for him and the entire family.

Parker made it to the elevator first and splayed his palm on the security scanner at the panel of the elevator. Evan noted he wore his favorite maroon pajamas. Pin-striped with satin piping, morning scruff on his chin, Hefner meets hipster style. Aw hell, were those loafers on his feet? Gucci, or something equally heinous. All he needed was a pipe and a playboy bunny on his arm. His long hair had been tied at the nape, but flyaway strands floated around his head. Must have been in bed when he got the call to meet. On the other hand, Griffin was dressed and presented for the day already. His routine had him up at five every morning for meditation and a workout before work. Blue tie and button-down shirt that could have been painted on his trim torso. Slick hair styled with a side part. He worked in the finance department at Parker's business, preferring the company of numbers and statistics than people.

Stepping into the elevator, Evan pulled Grace to his side. She fit right under his arm. Perfection. She slipped her arm around his waist and he couldn't be happier. Fuck anyone who tried to keep them apart. Ain't gonna happen.

The elevator stopped at the floor where the common apartment was, where Sloan usually played her games. They found the rest of the family sitting in the lounge room, all sprawled on the massive u-shaped sectional facing a massive flat screen television—complete with a grumpy faced Sloan, still in her sloppy sleep shirt. Even Tony had been dragged from wherever he slept these days, or didn't sleep going by the wired look in his eyes. Probably still up from whatever party he was at last night. Liza was dressed for work at the precinct, long pants, white shirt, brown leather jacket. Mary and Flint sat next to each other, hand in hand. Griff and Parks slotted themselves in at the edge of the sofa. There, standing behind the sofa and in front of an enormous pot plant, was Wyatt. Black scruffy hair, black shirt, and two-fifty pounds of hard muscle and wrath. He clenched his jaw at the arrival of Evan and Grace and then folded his arms as he tracked them across the room.

No use delaying, Evan strode to the front, between the flat screen on the wall and the sectional. "Where's Sara?" he asked.

Wyatt's brow lifted. Probably thinking of all the ways he was going to hurt Evan sideways until Sunday. Screw him.

"Resting," Wyatt said. "What are we doing here, Evan?"

Evan narrowed his eyes at the challenge. Every atom in his body wanted to rip his brother a new one, but Grace gave his hand a squeeze, calming him instantly. *Focus*, he told himself. He pulled out his phone and asked Grace to do the same.

He looked at Grace, then at his family. "I haven't officially introduced Grace to all of you. Doctor Grace Go, this is… is the Deadly Seven. My family."

A few scowls and daggers were shot Evan's way at his blatant referral to their secret.

"What, are we telling everyone now?" Wyatt snapped. "Should I put an ad in the classifieds?"

"You shared it with Sara," Evan replied. "At least Grace is my—" he cut himself off with a blush and looked at Grace. Mate. He was about to say soulmate. Saying it aloud made it all so real and would burst the bubble of what private time they'd spent together, but she was already the love of his life. He knew it deep down inside. Fuck conventions.

Grace shuffled her feet. "Maybe I should go."

"No," Mary said. "You stay."

"Grace is my balance," Evan finished. "She's the center of my universe, so she stays. Okay," he continued. "So the sloppy one on the couch, that's Sloan."

Evan dodged an empty soda can that came flying from Sloan's hand.

"—and next to her is Parker Lazarus, whom you've briefly met. He's the city's prideful golden boy—"

Parker rolled his eyes but nodded to Grace.

"—and then there's Griffin. He's… well he's Griff." The only one not knee-deep in his sin of Greed. Griffin slid his black framed specs up the bridge of his nose and stared at Grace. Evan pointed at Tony. "I think you met our designated Hollywood rat, Tony, at the exhibition. If he wasn't already glutting himself on the free booze, you may have had a chance to talk to him. Liza there—"

Liza cut him off with a hand raised in the air and a frown. She stepped toward Grace and held out her hand. "I'm a detective at the CCPD."

"Hi," Grace murmured and shook Liza's hand.

"And our parents, Mary and Flint."

They both waved.

"And of course, the big brute glaring in the back is Wyatt."

Grace gave a small, shy finger wave.

Wyatt ignored her, then pinned Evan with his stare. "What the fuck is going on?"

"You all need to see this." He turned on the big television and synced his phone. Within minutes, a slideshow of photographic evidence rotated on screen. "We found a lab that goes by the name of the GODC. As you can see, it's not really a Center for Disease Control, but something else entirely. Privately owned and secretly fronted for illegal genetic experimentations. Sound familiar?"

Evan flicked through some photos of random office papers, then a panoramic shot of the lab, close ups of specimen tanks—Mary gasped. Flint stiffened. Both edged forward in their seats to get a better look.

"And why did you need to drag us out of bed for this?" Wyatt grumbled.

"Because," Grace stood forward. "Samples from Sara's corpse were sent to this lab two years ago."

"And remind me why you're here?"

"Watch your tone," Evan snapped at Wyatt. "She's a doctor, remember? Or is your head so far up your ass you forgot?"

"Don't you fu—"

"*Mijos!*" Mary snapped, shooting to her feet, hands fisting at her side.

Silence blanketed the room. Mary walked toward the screen, a frown deepening in her brow. She pushed dark strands from her eyes as she investigated the pictures on the screen. "Tell us more."

Evan flicked the photographs until they showed the macabre human cloning tanks. "As you can see. It's not your typical research lab. They're growing people."

"Son-of-a-gun," Flint murmured.

Evan kept flicking until he got to the end of his collection of photographs, then pulled up Grace's shots and skipped to the end. The last photograph taken. The empty tank, and Sara's name. "Look at the name."

A chorus of gasps broke out around the room.

"What the fuck is this shit?" Wyatt started, but Liza stood and said: "Pipe down, Wyatt. Let's get more information before we go wild." Then she turned to Evan and Grace. "What exactly are you saying?"

Grace placed her palm on Evan's arm in a way that said, I got this. She took a deep breath and faced his family. It wouldn't have been easy. All eight of them, staring her down. Evan couldn't be more proud of his woman in that moment. Balls of steel.

Grace slid her sleeves up to display her scarred forearms.

"Two years ago, I was in a building when a bomb went off and collapsed around me. You may remember it. You all fought the white robed attackers out front." They all shifted nervously in their seats. Some scowled. Some darted their gazes to their family. Grace continued. "You may also remember, there was a point before the collapse that the robed men suddenly stopped fighting, and retreated to the apartment lobby."

Heads nodded.

"I was in the lobby taking a phone call while my parents were upstairs. Then Sara walked in and stood next to me to watch the fight through the window. I thought she was a spectator, an innocent bystander, like me. But she pulled out a whistle and blew it as she walked deeper into the lobby. Two-seconds later, the attackers entered the building and followed her." Grace's voice trembled, and she took a deep breath to gather herself.

Evan knew the memory hurt. He stepped up to her and touched her shoulder. It gave Grace the courage to continue.

"Sara turned to me and told me to run. Then she pressed the trigger on a remote detonator, and the rest is history."

"Bullshit." Wyatt's voice boomed. "That's not the story she told me."

"What?" Evan couldn't believe it. "What story did she tell you? Because, unless I'm mistaken, bro, she missed out the part where she actually died, and was recreated as a fucking clone in a tank." He pointed at the screen, evidence obvious.

"Clones? I mean, come on Evan, it's a little far-fetched," Liza said with a derisive raise of an eyebrow.

"More far-fetched than creating humans with the DNA of different animals? Humans with extra organs?" Mary added.

No one responded to that logic.

Tony groaned and wiped his face. "Screw this. I need to get to set."

Sloan parroted his groan and curled into a pillow. "Screw this. I want to go back to sleep."

Tony pushed Sloan.

"You're both a pair of juveniles. Wake up, Sloan. Fuck your movie, Tony," Evan said then turned to them all, meeting each of them in the eye. "I told you she was in the building after the bomb went off. I told you about her envy levels. No one believed me. I sketched her picture every morning because I saw her alive, not because I was envious of your relationship. No one believed me. I'm your brother, Wyatt. It's time to start believin' bro."

Liza snorted. "The eighties called. They want their ballad back, bro."

Was she serious? Why couldn't his family take this shit seriously. Evan felt like he was in the twilight zone. These women and men before him were meant to be the best humanity had to offer—better. He stormed over to the couch and pulled the pillow from underneath Sloan. He threw it at Liza. "You call yourselves heroes? We were all perfectly designed to save humanity from itself. You all can't even save yourselves." He pointed at the exit. "There's a company out there making deals with sick and deformed people, manipulating them into crossing the line and committing unspeakable crimes, all so they can bring them back to life as puppets. Does that sound right to you? Does that sound fair?"

"Hold up," Parker said. "What do you mean by sick people? What has that got to do with anything?"

"Those people who attacked yesterday were all sick or deformed," Grace added. "Just like Sara was before she died."

Wyatt's eyes narrowed. "Sara wasn't deformed. Or sick."

Grace nodded. "The ME report said she had a rare form of heart disease. The kind that happens after exposure to certain poisons. Officially, the records say she didn't have an autopsy, but when the ME was pressed, he confessed she only had weeks before her heart would have given out."

"No. We would have known about that."

Sloan straightened on the sofa and lifted her pointer finger in the air. "Uh… if I may?"

All eyes focused on her.

She blushed and shrunk behind the cushion that had somehow landed back in her arms. "When I removed all traces of her identity from the hospital records, like you asked, I came across some medical history. She was sick. Exactly what the doc said."

"Why haven't you mentioned this before?" Wyatt growled.

Sloan shrugged. "Because none of you asked, and she was dead anyway."

"You couldn't be bothered, more like it," Wyatt snapped.

"*You're* the bothered," Sloan shot back.

"See what I mean?" Evan murmured to Grace. "They can't save themselves. This city is screwed."

"Evan," Grace whispered. "That was you a few days ago. Don't forget that."

She was right. There might still be hope. He took a deep breath and turned back to them. "What you all need to think about is, why is Sara involved? Why would she have been placed in this family? To spy? To gain evidence? And from this lab, why?"

Tony spoke: "You're right. You said she stole the glasses we drank from at the gallery. She's been collecting biological samples." He shot Wyatt a concerned look. "Maybe long before she died."

"Jeez. I hope you haven't boinked her yet, bro," Liza said to Wyatt and shivered.

He stomped to Liza and got in her face. "So you're going to give up on her, just like that? If, and that's a big *if*, this is true… she's a victim. I won't give up on her. We don't quit."

Then he turned to all of them. "We don't have any hard evidence she was to blame."

"What do you call Grace's testimony?" Evan fumed.

"Hearsay."

"And the lab? Sara's name on the tank?"

Wyatt shrugged. "Anyone could have written her name there. It doesn't mean jack."

Until this point, Mary and Flint had been silent. Flint stood, his tall body unfolding until he towered above most of them at six foot four. He wasn't a fighter, he wasn't a warrior, but he was smart as hell. And the family respected him. The room stood still as his imposing figure walked to his wife and they shared a meaningful look.

"I think they found us," he said to Mary.

"Who found us?" Liza asked. "Somebody better start talking sense soon, or my brain is going to fucking explode."

Mary ground her teeth. "When you were attacked at the gallery, Evan, I thought maybe it was the Sisterhood. I told you all about them years ago. They're the ones who trained me to be an assassin. To weasel my way into high powered corporations and governments, and to take them down from within. I was supposed to deliver you all to them, and I didn't. I thought maybe this was them coming to make me pay for my betrayal. It never crossed my mind that it might be the man behind the lab that created you. That he'd been creating another lab, picking up where he left off all those years ago. I thought that after it was destroyed, he'd given up. We never heard a peep from him, and he never turned up in my visions."

"Are you actually saying this could be true?" Parker

waved at the screen. "It could be someone trying to recreate what they did to us?"

Mary and Flint both gave a curt nod.

"The man in charge, Julius, had a single minded purpose to create a world where sin didn't exist anymore. He was convinced human beings were a cancer spreading among the planet. His daughter and wife had died in an accident blamed on corporate negligence." She eyed Sloan. "Sloth was the obvious cause. He believed he could stop that from happening again by creating super soldiers. The only thing was, he wanted to kill all sinners while your birth mother focused on prevention. Your creation was the negotiation—beings capable of both."

Grace's phone rang, and she looked at the screen then caught Evan's eyes. "I have to take this. It's a patient. Is there somewhere private I can go?"

He nodded and guided her to another room of the apartment near the entrance. The elevator door was just closing as though someone had been in the room. Being so close to Grace, he couldn't sense envy like usual. He stood there while Grace took the call, but she looked at him weird, covered the phone and said, "Evan. It's a medical thing." When he didn't leave, she lifted her brows. "I can't talk about patients in front of you."

Evan glanced back at the elevator. The light indicator was going up. He frowned. Their building was private and secure. No one else should be in this room, so who was it?

Sara. Had to be. She'd heard what they were talking about.

Oh, hell no.

He glanced back at the common room and heard the argument in full swing. He glanced back at Grace deep in conversation and then back at the elevator door. It was a no-brainer. He punched the up button on the elevator and waited. Time to sort this out once and for all.

THIRTY-ONE

SARA MADDEN

Sara had laid all night on the big bed that used to provide so much comfort to her. Once, it had been filled with warm arms, a steady heartbeat and tender moments—and some fiery passionate moments—but now, Wyatt slept on the couch in the living room, or rather, he *had* slept on the couch. She'd heard him sneak downstairs not that long ago while she pretended to sleep.

When he went downstairs, she'd inhaled in relief, choked on exhale and coughed, wincing at the pain in her chest. The fit lasted too long and when she brought her hand away from her mouth, blood covered her palm. Her body was failing.

They'd warned her of this. Said, most replicates hadn't lived past a few months outside the tank. They also said they'd taken care of the heart condition she had, but they lied. It was back.

They lied a lot.

Her condition came about from an accident at her old

workplace—a pharmaceutical company where she tested a compound they promised was safe for human contact. But surprise, surprise, it wasn't, and they covered their tracks enough that if she took them to court, she'd lose. She didn't want to die then, and she didn't now.

Her last hope was harvesting the DNA of the only Lazarus child who'd unlocked his full genetic potential. So far, she'd tried collecting bio-samples, driving him apart from his new love, going so far as attempting to poison her. She wanted him split from his family and loved ones, so that when they took him, nobody would miss him. The Syndicate couldn't afford to have the rest of the Deadly Seven after them. *Too costly,* the boss had said. Easier to divide and conquer.

It wasn't supposed to go the way it did. She'd counted on Wyatt losing his temper. Evan was supposed to do the same. They should have killed all the Faithful in the attack, including her. She was supposed to die for a second time so the family banished Evan, but… Evan hadn't killed. She'd been so sure he would, especially after the way he'd attacked her outside the art gallery.

It must be the doctor's influence.

An ache in her stomach surprised her so much that she looked down at herself. Envy. Still there. So much it hurt. She wasn't even sure if she felt love or desire anymore, but there was one emotion she could count on: envy. They had bodies crafted to perfection. They never got sick, never hurt for long. She wanted that.

And she was so tired.

After the attack, Wyatt had protected Sara with his life.

He'd brought her back to his apartment and treated her gently. She'd claimed amnesia, but otherwise to be in perfect health, and refused to go to the hospital. Her new biology was fixing any new injury she obtained, like the electric shock, but not the one she was born with. The one they said they'd eliminate before bringing her back. Combined with the short lifespan of the replicates, her time was limited.

She'd gotten away with evasive answers to Wyatt's questions, but he wouldn't accept that for long. She knew him. He had a dogged determination. Loyal to a fault. She'd loved him for it, once.

That memory was enough to have her up and showered and into some nice borrowed clothes from Wyatt's sister. The dress was a bit loose but Sara tied it at the waist. She put makeup on to give the illusion of health, and tip-toed downstairs to search for Wyatt. She found the family talking in the common room. All of them. The doctor was there. Evan was there. When she caught the topic of conversation, she hid behind the door.

At first, her unfurling dread almost had her running for the exit, but then Wyatt defended her. He'd said he'd stand by her, even if what they said was true. It was enough to make her hesitate. And when she'd heard Evan and his doctor coming her way, she'd raced back to the elevator, slipping inside at the last moment.

When she got to Wyatt's upper level apartment, she paced the length of floor in the kitchen. Wyatt had said he'd protect her, that he wouldn't abandon her. Maybe that was good. Maybe she didn't need the Syndicate. He'd find a way to heal her without them. The instant the thought unfurled from her mind, another shut it down. There was no way the rest of his family would let him, not after the things she'd done. She'd murdered too many people.

Sara picked up the phone handset Wyatt had left on the kitchen bench and dialed. Two rings later and *she* answered: "You should be dead."

"I'm sorry. Things didn't go as planned. I had to improvise. This is the first time I've been able to get away." Silence on the other end. Sara continued. "Envy has photographic evidence of the lab and replicate tanks."

She'd been ordered to call them by their sins, not their names. She guessed it was a way of distancing them, of making them less than human. Easier to experiment on.

"This is true," Falcon said. "We have them on camera breaking in. The face of Envy was not visible, however, for a brief moment, hers was."

"Will you prosecute? Do this the legal way?"

"We cannot prosecute for something illegal."

"Of course." She felt stupid, but it gave her an idea. "Send the footage to this number. I might be able to use it."

"Sending now. Your directive hasn't changed. We need the asset—" a shuffling came through down the line and then another voice came on. The boss. She pulled the handset from her ear lest his loud voice pierce her eardrum. If he was angry enough to lose his temper, it wasn't good. When the tirade died down, she brought the phone back.

"…this is the last time I'm going to let you get away with this. Incompetence will not be rewarded. We can end you at a moment's notice. Do you understand?"

"I understand." Sara considered telling them about the

blood in her lungs, but they might not have the confidence for her to finish the job, and no matter what happened to this body, another could be made if she finished her mission and proved herself valuable. If she failed, they wouldn't bring her back.

"Good. Now, we need Envy. His DNA is the Rosetta Stone that will unlock all the other genetic research. Without him, we cannot bring our replicates to full term. Their cells will continue to rapidly mutate until they expire prematurely, like you. Bring him to us, and you are saved. Do this, and you will be handsomely rewarded. You will never feel sickness again."

Sara's fist clenched around the phone. She wanted that, so bad. She wanted a life where she could vacation at the beach and go swimming without losing her breath. She wanted a life long enough to have a family. It was a stupid dream, but she still wanted it.

"What is your plan?" the boss continued.

"I will use the footage against him, and if that doesn't work, there's the poisoned smoothie."

"After it's done, when can we expect you?"

"Soon." Sara hung up the phone.

"I always knew you'd slip up," came a male voice from behind her.

Sara spun to find Evan Lazarus standing before closed elevator doors. If they were closed, he must have been there for a while. Long enough to have heard her conversation. If she could feel fear, she might have. The look in his eyes could cut her down.

THIRTY-TWO

EVAN LAZARUS

Evan couldn't believe he caught Sara red handed, on the phone to—he frowned. Just who the hell had she been talking to?

He steeled himself.

"Who were you talking to, Sara?"

She stood wide-eyed at the kitchen counter. Dressed to the nines, ready to impress with her light brown hair tumbling down her shoulders, bright lipstick, and in a dress she got from somewhere. Knowing Wyatt, he'd probably gone out to get her new or borrowed items when she rested. He'd been good like that before Sara had died. Wrath was a destructive sin, but he'd curbed it, and channeled it into constructive pastimes. Like being the quarterback on the high school football team, and running track, or becoming one of the world's best chefs. It had been months since Evan had had a proper conversation with Wyatt. All because of the vindictive, psychopath standing in front of Evan with her mouth agape, still holding the damned cell phone.

The phone pinged. Sara glanced down at it and smiled. Then she turned the force of that snide emotion Evan's way.

"You got me." She lifted her arms in mock surrender. She walked toward him, heels clicking on the floor. "Whatever will I do to get out of this one."

"So, you're admitting it?" he said cautiously, stepping back to avoid her in his space. Why? After all this time avoiding him, why now? Because he'd caught one side of a telephone conversation? Unlikely.

"Yes. I am."

"Admitting what?"

She sighed dramatically. "You want me to spell it out for you? Fine. I admit that I faked my death. That—"

"Uh-uh, psycho. Try that again. You didn't fake your death. You *did* die."

"Fine, whatever, semantics. I died. Happy? I died because I set off the bomb that collapsed that building."

"And killed all the innocents inside."

She fluttered her lids to half-mast, as though Evan tried her patience, but continued her approach. "Collateral damage."

"All so you could have what, a second chance at life? To cheat the illness inside you?"

Sara stopped. "It wasn't an illness, it was poison."

"I don't care what it was, you lied. That's all we need to know."

"You should care what it was, because the same poison was in the smoothie I left at Grace's door."

The pressure on Evan's heart increased. "She didn't drink it."

Sara laughed and then came up to him. She slid her palm up his chest. Bile rose in the back of his throat and he whacked her hand out of the way.

"Oh Evan. Just how exactly did you think I got sick in the first place? You think I was born with heart disease? No, sweety. All I did was touch the poison, and it permeated my skin and went into my bloodstream."

"What the fuck are you saying?"

"I was at the receiving end of corporate negligence. You know I worked for a pharmaceutical company before I died, what you didn't know is that they failed me. They promised a new product that was safe for human trials, and it wasn't. My heart disease was the result. Grace has been exposed to the same toxin. It's already making its way through her veins, pumping toward her heart."

Rage heated Evan's vision and everything went blurry. Electricity snapped and crackled in his veins. "I'm going to kill you for this. And then I'll dance on your grave."

"But then, Evan, baby, you won't get the antidote." She smiled sweetly at him. "I don't want to hurt you, Evan. Or your lady friend. In fact, I'm the only one looking out for you. They cured me. Do as I say, and they can cure her too."

"You're whacked in the head, aren't you?" But even as he said the words, he began to power down, and she noticed. She thought she was winning. Let her. He wasn't through with her yet.

"The rest of your family doesn't believe in you. To be honest, they care little for you and your 'boy who cried wolf' antics. You're not an over achiever like your siblings. I mean, you couldn't even have your debut exhibition without scandal. Don't you see? You're simply not good enough."

Evan swallowed. "That was before I uncovered your secret."

She lifted her brows. "And what secret is that?"

"That you're a mother-fucking clone. That you lie and cheat and kill. That you've been using my brother for whatever sick purpose you have in mind. Well, I got news for you. I'll make you give me the antidote. It ends here."

"Oh, I don't think so, Evan," Sara crooned.

Why was she so confident? Why wasn't she begging for his mercy?

Sara splayed her hand on his chest again and pressed. "You see, I don't think you'll turn me in at all. Not when you see what we have on your new lady love."

A stone cold fist squeezed Evan's heart. "Be careful what you say next, Sara."

"So, you remember when you broke into the GODC this morning?" Sara said sweetly, fluttering her eyes at him. "Well, your lady friend got caught on camera. It's a real nice shot. You wanna see?"

Rage built in Evan's veins. A trembling, searing emotion that threatened to break free and crush Sara's throat right then and there. The electricity, sparked by his rage, zipped through his bloodstream, bringing it to the boil. Evan breathed. In. Out. Let's try that again.

"Touch a hair on her head, and I'll make it my personal duty to end you. Then I'll end them, making sure you never see the light of day again."

"Oh, Evan." She patted his cheek. "Sweet, baby, Evan. You really don't get it, do you?"

He frowned.

"You could try to take this from my dead body, but I don't have the original footage, and I don't have the antidote for the poison. They do."

"Then I'll threaten to kill you unless they give it to me."

This made her break into a fit of laughter that made her breathless. When she wiped the tears from her eyes, she cradled his nape. "It's not about Grace. It's not about Wyatt anymore." She laughed. "It's not even about me or them. It's about you." Then she pulled his lips to hers and kissed him passionately, pushing him against the elevator doors.

Everything inside him froze in shock.

The elevator doors opened, and they tumbled backward into the car, landing heavily on the floor with Sara on top of him.

"Evan?"

Oh, no. Grace.

"I know how this looks, but—" Evan stared up at her from his spot on the floor.

"It's exactly how it looks, isn't it Evan, baby?" Sara wiggled on him.

"Get off," Evan growled, and pushed Sara off.

She tumbled back into the apartment, giggling. "Oh, Evanikins, don't be so coy. This is what you've wanted. It's what you've wanted all along. Wyatt knew it. Your family knew it, and now she does. Admit it. You want me. It's why you painted me so much. Well, now I want you."

"No." Evan stood. He turned to Grace. "It's not true. She's lying. You know she's lying."

"I—" Grace shook her head, tears glistening in her eyes as they darted between him—the lipstick stains on his lips—and the beast on the floor. "I don't know."

"Doc…" Evan held out his hand, anguish ripping his heart apart. *Please don't believe it. Please. You're the best thing that's happened to me.*

Sara stepped behind Evan and placed her hand on his bicep in a possessive gesture. "Evan. Tell her the truth. No need to string her along anymore. You're with me now. Let her go, let her be safe."

The veiled threat in Sara's voice wasn't unnoticed.

Grace's liquid gaze met Evan's, and he knew with all certainty that he had to let her go. Just for now. Just until he got rid of the evidence incriminating her. Until he got the antidote. Until he got to the bottom of what Sara wanted.

To keep Grace safe, Evan stepped back into the apartment.

Her utter devastation cut Evan in two.

"It's for your own good, Grace," he said, voice trembling.

She tried to keep it together, tried to hold herself with that confident, proud demeanor he loved so much, but the second she slammed the close button on the door, Evan saw her face crumple and tears fall.

The doors shut.

Power generated in his body, amping up to engulf him. Electricity crackled at his hands, over his chest, down his legs. He felt it in his eyes, metal in his mouth, fire in his veins. Evan whirled on Sara. "You better make this quick. Tell me the truth."

Sparks skipped over his skin, bringing bursts of light to the dim room. Sara stepped back, humor fled. "They want you, Evan. No one else."

"Why?"

"Your new power has unlocked the riddle they've been trying to solve for years."

"You want to replicate this?" He opened his hands like claws. The power skipped between his fingers. "You want my power?"

"*They* do."

"Why?"

Anger flared in her eyes. "Why? Why? Are you fucking kidding me? You were theirs in the first place. You were supposed to wipe the world of sin and give it a fresh start. Humans are destroying this planet. You were the remedy."

"We won't be a party to mass genocide."

"This world is broken, Evan. I'm living proof. It wasn't bad enough that I was sick through no fault of my own, but the Syndicate had to come along and prey on my weak, envious need to survive and live a life like yours."

"You always had a choice, Sara. You could have chosen a natural death. You didn't have to take everyone else with you."

"You can say that, you with your magic blood, but you've never had your life expectancy cut to ribbons because of someone else's mistake." The vehemence in her tone shifted her features into something ugly. "I hope they win. I hope they use you to create more like you. I hope all the sin in the world is wiped out, because until it is, weak people like me will always be played for fools. We will always be the ones who suffer. Now, are you coming with me, or do I have to make good on my threat? One click on this phone and your precious doctor and her crime goes to the police, to the news network, to everyone, and the antidote stays hidden forever."

Evan's teeth ground. He had no choice. For now, he'd have to go with her. He powered down.

"Good boy." She strode back into the kitchen and unsheathed one of Wyatt's sharp cooking knives. She deftly flipped it in her hands. One false move and it would have sliced her palm in two. The action was a display of her new prowess with the weapon. "This is for extra motivation. You renege on your promise, and I'll gut you. They'd prefer you to be alive, but to be honest, they can collect biological samples even when you're dead. Just look who you're talking to."

"Shut up," he said. "Let's make this clear. I'll go with you, but I want her unharmed. I want you to send the antidote here immediately."

"Ugh. Like I said, we don't care about her except to leverage you, so as long as you're a good little boy, she's already forgotten about. I'll make sure you get what's coming to you once you're delivered."

Evan glanced at the elevator longingly.

Sara hit the down button. "Don't even think about telling your family. Not that they'd believe you anyway, but this little charade is to protect them too. The Syndicate will keep you alive because they need you. They don't need the rest of your family. Got it?"

He nodded. For now.

"Good. Now, let's go to the garage and pick a car. We're getting out of here."

THIRTY-THREE

DR. GRACE GO

Grace was going to be sick. What she'd seen had assaulted her eyes in a way she'd never thought possible. How could he?

Silent tears dripped down her face.

Eyes don't lie. Eyes saw the truth, no matter what it is. That's what she liked about being a surgeon. You open up a person to see the internal organs with nothing else blocking you. No sonograms, no digital imaging techniques, no ultrasounds. Nothing between the problem and you. Truth.

How could she have been so blind?

The elevator door opened to a floor she didn't remember calling. Where was she? She stepped out and looked around. Plain, carpeted lobby. Flower arrangement to the side, two open archways leading out of the room, the smell of violets, raised voices still in the midst of a heated argument. She was back in the common apartment. The one she'd just left. It looked so foreign to her.

She pivoted and slammed her fists on the closed steel elevator doors, screaming in frustration. She just wanted to get out of there. How the hell did you get out of there!

Footsteps thudded closer.

"Grace?" came a voice she recognized. "Where's Evan?"

The one who'd berated her in the restaurant. The one who'd also been so damned blind. She turned to face Wyatt and the wrath inside her flared, making him flinch.

"What's happened?" he asked.

"We've both been so blind." She wiped the tears from her face. "So blind. I want to go home. How do I get out of here?"

He stepped into her personal space, gripping her shoulders. A vein bulged in his forehead. "What happened?"

"Get away from me. I want to go. I have a patient to see."

The rest of the peanut gallery thundered into the room.

"Wyatt," Evan's mother said. "Can't you see she's traumatized?"

He blanched and let go. "Something happened. She's not talking."

"Grace," Mary came closer. "I'll take you out and call a car. You can explain on the way."

"No. I need to know now!" Wyatt boomed. "I felt your wrath. I know something happened."

"They're gone!" Grace shouted. Happy now? "My phone call ended, and I went to find Evan. I saw him take the elevator up to the fourth floor."

"My level," Wyatt murmured.

"When I got there, I caught them kissing. She said they were meant to be together. That they always have."

Wyatt roared and punched the elevator beside Grace's head, making her yelp and cover her ears. The dent he left was scary deep.

"Wyatt!" Evan's father shouted. "Enough."

Wyatt had the sense to look apologetic, but Grace was done. The person who'd called her was Taco's aunty. He'd not gone to the clinic like she'd requested and his condition had worsened. They were desperate.

She was too. "Just tell me how to get out of this place. I have a patient that needs me."

Mary flattened her lips and swiped her hand over the down button on the elevator, activating her biometric key. "I'll see you out." When they both went inside the car, Mary held up her palm to Wyatt trying to enter. "Just me."

The dented doors scraped closed, separating them from the crowd of eyes boring holes into her.

"This isn't like Evan," Mary said softly. "I hope you realize that."

Grace bit her lip. "I don't know what to believe."

"Believe in your heart. Don't give up on him."

Except, he'd given up on her. He said he'd never leave her, that wild horses couldn't take him away.

The doors opened to a bright, glossy tiled lobby that led to the street. Floor to ceiling windows banked on both sides. One looked into the restaurant Heaven, the other into the darkened nightclub Hell. One was busy with hopeful patrons, eating breakfast and starting a new day. The other empty, dark and desolate. Grace swallowed and walked to the exit.

GRACE UNLOCKED the door to her apartment and stepped inside, closing the door behind her. She leaned against the solid surface. A sweeping gaze across the cold, empty living space didn't make her feel better. Her indoor plants were dying. The box of her father's clothes still sat on the kitchen bench. Even the smoothie hadn't been disposed of properly and had soured the room. Fresh tears burned the back of her eyes and she squeezed them shut.

None of that now. Taco needed her.

Grace took a deep breath and went to find her medical kit. She found the bag in the closet, next to a box of her mother's belongings and checked to see that she had enough supplies. She'd restocked recently at the clinic, including taking a dose of antibiotics. Excellent.

She tied her hair back and washed her face. After she saw Taco, she'd come home, tidy up and water her plants. Then she'd call Lilo to see how she was doing after missing dinner with Donnie. Then… well, she was sure she'd come up with things to do. Only a few days left of her forced leave then she'd be back at work.

Two-seconds later, Grace went out the door and strode up the hallway to the stairwell. Two levels later, and she stood at the front of apartment eighty-three, knocking.

The door opened and it was Juliet, Taco's aunt, clearly at her wits end. She wore a sweaty fast-food outlet uniform. Her long dark hair was tied at her nape. Only twenty-years-old herself, she hadn't quite been ready for the responsibility of parenting two recalcitrant young boys, but she did it. She had to. Working two jobs to make the rent and help put the boys through school was hard. It was people like her who had been affected by the bombing that made Grace want to get the insurance claim approved.

Stiff chance of that now.

"Hi Juliet," Grace said. "I'm sorry I was delayed. Where is he?"

"Thank God, Grace. He's been in and out of sleep. He's got a high temperature, and he won't eat. I'm really worried. He's all floppy. I had to leave work early, but they need me back." Her bottom lip trembled. "If I don't return, I might lose my job. I don't know what to do."

Okay. This sort of panic, Grace could deal with. She could do a medical drama with her eyes closed. "You've done an excellent job in calling me. Take me to him, and I'll take it from there."

Juliet's shoulders dropped in relief. "He's in here."

Together they entered the small living room, similar to Grace's. The boys usually slept on the fold-out sofa together, but with Taco sick, Mason had taken to his aunt's bed in the other room.

Taco laid on his side, curled into himself as though he were cold, but sweat caked his dark brown hair to his face. His usual healthy glowing olive skin was pallid and had a sheen to it. Grace set her bag down and set to work. Going on what she'd heard the other morning, she was almost a hundred percent sure he had a chest infection, but you could never be too careful. Pneumonia was a hop, skip and jump away. After some routine checks, she injected him with a dose of antibiotics.

"He'll need some chest x-rays tomorrow," Grace said to Juliet, who had hovered despite being late for work. "Take him to the clinic and I'll make sure he's seen. I won't be there, but it's important he goes."

"Tomorrow? I have work tomorrow." Juliet winced.

"You know what? I've got the day off. I'll take him in."

"Really?"

"Yes, not a problem. I need something to do. And you don't want to lose your job."

"Thank you, Grace. You're a life saver."

"No problem. I know how much you've been doing to help these boys. I think you're doing a marvelous job. Don't forget that. Parenting is hard. Even harder when they're not your kids. Don't be so tough on yourself. I'll sit with him for a few hours, make sure he's okay."

Juliet's eyes teared up. "Thank you."

"Go." Grace made a shooing motion with her hand. "I'll check on Mason in a minute, and order us some lunch."

"Thank you, thank you. There's cold chicken in the fridge." Juliet swept about the room and collected her belongings. "And left over Chinese on the bottom shelf."

"Got it." Grace smiled. It felt forced and fake after what she'd just been through with Evan, but she did it none-theless. Couldn't make Juliet think she was upset over staying with Taco.

When Juliet was gone, Grace set about checking on Mason. The little guy was still asleep. It was almost eight in the morning on a weekday. Was she supposed to send him to school? Grace had no idea of the time of month. Was it school holidays? She shrugged and ended up slipping onto the sofa next to Taco and turning the television on.

She was still flicking through the channels when Taco stirred an hour later.

"Hey," she said softly as he opened his eyes. "How you feeling?"

"Doc?" His brow furrowed, but it was Grace who flinched. That was the nickname Evan used for her.

"Yeah, it's me, buddy." She wiped a traitorous tear from her eye.

"Why are you here?"

"Your aunt was worried about you. You didn't go to the clinic like I asked."

He groaned and covered his eyes. "Line was too long."

"Well, you would have gotten in, eventually. And if you did, I wouldn't have to come here and inject some antibiotics into your butt."

"You said the what now?" Taco's hand dropped from his face to reveal wide-eyes.

Grace nodded. "You didn't even wake up."

"Um. Thanks, I guess?"

"You're welcome. Now, what would you like to eat?"

"Grace," Taco said with serious eyes. "I'm not so sick you need to cry over me." Then his eyes lit up as a thought hit. "Did something happen to Mr. Envy? Is he okay?"

She frowned. That's right. He'd met Evan. "Uh..."

He gave her shifty eyes. "Remember I tried to tell you at the paper stand that there was someone special waiting for you at the hospital? He saved me from getting stabbed by a broken fire escape ladder. He also saved me from getting bashed by this really bad man. Did you see him? What's he like? Did you ask him about the bombing? Did you see his face, too?"

"Um..." How could she burst this boy's hero bubble? She pinched the bridge between her nose. "Taco, I didn't see him."

Taco's eyes narrowed. "You're lying."

"Why's that?"

"Because he told me the purse I found in the trash belonged to you, and that he was returning it to you. Did he?"

"As a matter of fact, yes. Wait. When did you find my purse? Were you out late at night when your aunt was working again? Did this have to do with the bad man?"

"Ah-ha! I was right." Then he whined. "Come on. What's he like? Have you met the rest of them? Can I get an autograph?"

"Nothing gets by you, does it?" She ruffled his hair.

"Stop keeping secrets."

Grace sighed. "It's just that, he's not who I thought he was."

"What's that mean?"

She couldn't believe she was baring her soul to an eleven-year-old. "It means, Taco, that some people make you believe they're one thing, but they're really another."

"So, what is he? What happened? Did you find the bomber?"

Her throat closed up. "I thought I got her, but then... the two of them ran off together."

"Like, boyfriend and girlfriend?"

She nodded.

"Ew."

"The eyes don't lie, Taco."

"His eyes lied?"

Grace gaped. Only from the mouth of a child did she realize she'd been thinking about this all wrong. Her eyes may have seen one thing, but Evan's had told another story. "He... oh my dear lord. Taco, I think you're right."

Eyes were the windows to a soul, and Evan's had been tortured. He never looked at Sara once, but kept his gaze intensely locked on Grace the entire time. The look on his face had been one of desperation and pain, not of embarrassment over the kiss.

It's for your own good, Grace. He was trying to protect her.

Sara threatened Grace. *Let her go, let her be safe.*

For the first time in a while, thoughts of murder swam in Grace's mind. That bitch! She did what she did best —manipulate.

Evan was only trying to keep Grace safe, and what did she do? She left him.

She clutched her chest. She'd left him alone, just like she'd begged him to not to do to her.

Grace stood. "I have to find him."

"Go Grace!" Taco whooped with his fist in the air and jumped on the couch.

"Will you be okay?" Grace checked Taco's forehead. Fever had gone down.

"Yeah, we're cool."

Good. Excellent. As she madly went about the room, gathering her belongings, she thought, I have to go to his family, somehow get them to trust her, get them to go after him. He was going into the lion's den alone; handing himself over to the enemy. She couldn't allow that for so many reasons. Finally, she saw things clearly. She would find Evan, help him, believe in him. Then tell him she loved him.

THIRTY-FOUR

EVAN LAZARUS

Evan sat in the passenger side of his brother's Escalade, staring out the cracked window as they sped down the freeway leading out of Cardinal City. Morning rush hour was still in full swing and it was slow going. Big city towers gave way to crammed apartments and a crushing feeling in his chest that he should have felt better about doing what he did. So why was he so sick inside? It wasn't the envy pouring from Sara in grimy waves, although, that was hard enough to stomach. No. It was his stupid idea to protect Grace, even if that meant breaking her heart.

He checked Sara in the driver's seat. Since they left HQ, she'd forced him to deactivate the tracking chip in the car, and shut down AIMI so no communication could get out.

Sara was the Trojan horse sent to destroy his family from the inside, he knew that now, but he was helpless to stop her.

They'd detoured at a boarded townhouse where Sara got out and urged him inside. The room she'd squatted in was pure squalor. Cold, dank, and devoid of decor except a mattress on the floor, some empty packets of ramen, and a laptop.

Sara had taken a few moments to collect her laptop and call someone, outlining the progress of her successful mission. She had him—their apparent Holy Grail or Rosetta Stone, or whatever the hell they'd called him—in her custody and was ready to bring him in. From what Evan could gather, they were to meet her puppet master at an undisclosed location for handover. That's where they headed now.

Out of Cardinal City, away from his home, his family and… Grace.

A new wave of disgust flowed over him. He hated himself. He couldn't do anything right. He should have followed his instincts about the smoothie and had it tested, and he should have made Grace stay in the car when they broke into the GODC. If he had, none of this would have happened. But Grace wasn't the kind of woman to stand by idly and do nothing. He smiled. Never in his wildest dreams had he imagined how great it would feel to have a woman so smart and kind like her in his arms. And he blew it.

Maybe he should have killed Sara when he had the chance. Maybe he still could.

Sara coughed. It started as short, random bursts but grew to big, phlegmy chokes. When she pulled her hand from her mouth, it was splattered with blood. Not just the heart disease then? Maybe more.

"What happened to you, Sara? Where did it go wrong?"

She wiped her hand on her clothes, scowling. "How

come I get sick, and you don't? Who decides that you're worthy of living, and not me?"

"Call me stupid, but you're not exactly acting worthy."

"Says you."

"Says a lot of people."

"I don't care." She flattened her lips in a stubborn move and ignored him.

Evan shrugged. Guessed that conversation was over. Maybe not.

She loved Wyatt once. He knew that was real. It had to be.

"You plan on getting Wyatt back after this?" Evan said.

Her grip tightened. "Wyatt's not relevant anymore."

"I don't believe that. You loved him. I know it. It's why you're doing this. I know you worked at the pharmaceutical company while you were dating Wyatt, which means, if that's where you found out you were sick, it happened after your engagement to him and didn't want to leave him. When you discovered who we were, it was all too much. Instead of asking for help—" Evan choked on his own words.

Asking for help. Maybe that's what he should have done. Instead, he'd gone off on his own. His vendetta had started out as a mission to reveal Sara's dark secret, to discredit her and throw him into the light again. But it ended up being more than that. A mission to save his family. Maybe it wasn't too late. There had to be a way out of this.

He slowly pulled his phone out of his side pocket and held it hidden between his leg and the door. There was only one person he could trust to not hang up on him. Grace was the last person dialed, so he hit redial and waited, keeping the phone hidden. Time to ask for help.

"Where are you taking me?" he asked.

Sara laughed. "As if I'd tell you that. Besides, I don't know."

"You know I'm only coming with you to save Grace. Now that I'm doing what you asked, I want you to uphold your end of the bargain—release the CCTV footage and an antidote for the poisoned smoothie."

"Nice try. I said once you were delivered, we'd do that. Plus, I told you we don't care about her as long as you comply."

"And then what? How long do you want me? What will you do to me?"

She smirked. "Who the hell knows? My job is to deliver you to the Syndicate, and then my life is over. They take a sample of my DNA and create me all over again." She slid a look at him. "This time, with the help of your unlocked DNA."

"And without a heart," Evan said. "Don't think I haven't noticed this version of you is different. Will you lose a piece of yourself every time you come back?"

"Shut up."

"He's going to come after us. Even without the tracking chip in the car, he'll find a way. Wyatt never gives up. He never quits."

"We'll deal with him if he does. You're the asset, not him."

The car approached an exit off ramp, but kept driving. Evan checked for a sign and read it out loud, hoping his voice carried through the receiver, and hoping even more that Grace actually listened.

After two street signs, Sara turned to him. "Why are you reading the signs aloud?"

He shrugged.

She wasn't convinced. Her gaze darted down his arm to see his hand squished beside the seat and door.

"What's in your hand, Evan?"

Crap.

"I swear to God if you ruin this for me, I'll hunt you and your precious girlfriend and family down until there's no one left. Now I'm not going to ask again. What's in your hand?"

He lifted the phone.

She snatched it from him, rolled the window down and threw it outside.

Evan watched in the rear view as it burst into tiny pieces on the asphalt, dashing his hopes along with it. Something else caught his attention in the mirror: a black clad motorcyclist zipping in and out of traffic, coming up behind them.

THIRTY-FIVE

DR. GRACE GO

Grace was back across town and at the entrance to Lazarus House, banging on the solid door between Heaven and Hell.

"I know you can see me. Open up," she said to the camera pointed down at her. "I have new information. You need to let me in."

She still clutched her phone in her hand even though Evan had inexplicably hung up minutes ago. She'd been surprised when the phone rang and Evan's name had come up. With equal amounts of apprehension and excitement, she'd answered, only to hear the exchange going on in the background. Now, more than ever, she knew she had to fight for him. She had to get the rest of his family to join her, and if they didn't, well, then she'd go it alone. Evan's life was in danger.

She banged on the door again, shouting for them to let her in. People passing on the street gave her odd looks. To anyone else, the door was a simple gray rectangle in a recess, belonging to neither restaurant nor nightclub. In the reflection of Hell's dark window, her hair was wild, unkempt and her eyes bright and manic.

"Let me in, damn it!"

The door opened. It was Parker. "No need to make a scene."

"Oh, thank God. Evan called."

He stared.

"He hasn't run off with her," Grace said. "She's black-mailed him."

Parker darted a glance around the street. People were looking. After the recent attack nearby, locals were wary.

"Alright. Come in."

Grace clutched her bag and phone to her chest, and followed him to the elevator, and then back up to the common apartment. When she got there, she found the living area had been transformed into a ground zero crisis center. The screen on the wall had footage from cameras around the city.

Taking a moment to evaluate the scene, Grace absorbed Evan's family and their dynamic. The movie star was missing.

Evan's father and Sloan sat on the sectional, leaning over their laptops perched on the coffee tables. Her dark pig-tails draped over each shoulder and she was still in her sloppy sleep T-shirt. The detective sister spoke on her cell phone, pacing. The brother with the glasses was also on the phone. Evan's mother rushed over to Grace. Well, it was more like a prowl than a rush. Grace couldn't imagine the woman would ever let her emotions get the better of her. The only sign of her distress were the flyaway hairs in her otherwise slick braid. It was as though she'd been rubbing her head to rid herself from a headache. Mary still wore her black gym attire. Slick yoga pants, and black, long sleeved compression top.

"Grace, I'm glad you came back," Mary said and gripped Grace's arm.

Grace gave her a small smile and glanced around before hesitantly asking, "Where's Wyatt?"

"He's already gone after them," Parker growled, his deep voice a rumble of discontent.

"But the tracking chip has been deactivated," Grace said. "How will he find them?"

"How did you know the tracking chip was disabled?" Sloan said from her sofa seat.

"Evan called me."

All eyes swiveled toward Grace.

"I knew it!" Sloan slapped her palm on the coffee table her laptop rested on, shaking it. "There's no way AIMI would hide from me. I made her."

"Ahem." Parker arched a wicked eyebrow.

Sloan flushed. "I mean, we made her together?"

"That's better."

"Ahem," Flint added.

Both Sloan and Parker stared at him. "We *all* made her together?" Sloan amended.

"I made the best bits," Parker mumbled, then turned back to Grace. "So, he called you?"

"It was a pocket dial, but I think he intended it. He said Sara had footage of me from when we broke into the lab, and that she was going to send it to the police if Evan didn't go with her. Evan didn't want that to happen, so he went with her. Plus, there was this smoothie left on my doorstop the other day. I think it was poisoned and intended for me, but I didn't drink it. He knows that. I don't know why he let her use that as blackmail. I'm completely fine."

"Why would they want Evan?" Griffin came over.

"Because his DNA has been unlocked since he met me. I think it has something to do with their replicates not surviving long after they're born from the tanks, and you all have advanced regeneration. It's why Sara was so envious of you all. One thing we gleaned at the lab was mortality rates are high. Sara is sick again."

A silence descended on the room. Mary paced the length of the floor wringing her hands. "I hate this," she said. "I hate not knowing what to do."

Grace felt more meaning underlined the comment because of the look of pity her husband shot her. Flint stood and disappeared into another room. A few seconds later he was back and gently placed a throwing knife in his wife's palm. He enclosed his big palms around hers and looked into her eyes.

"You still have your hands, and your brain. You don't need visions to tell you what to do anymore. You've kept us all alive and hidden from danger all these years. Never forget that. Now it's up to the kids to do what you've trained them to do."

"But, the last time we let them go off on their own…"

Flint flicked a glance at his children. "They weren't ready to act as a family. But they're learning." He shot a glance to Grace. "And we have her now. Grace has proven there's hope. Don't worry, we'll get Evan back. Why don't you start by going over some history that might shed some new light on this."

Flint went back to his seat and scrutinized the laptop. Mary inhaled deeply. Tension made the air thick. Then she began to flip the knife in her hand, catching it by the hilt and then flipping it again.

She looked at her children and pointed with the knife. "Your birth mother Gloria knew so much about genetic engineering. She hid your full potential under a layer of genetic junk that would have taken a lifetime for any other scientist to unravel. It was a safeguard to stop your DNA from falling into the wrong hands. If they need Evan, then whoever runs this GODC lab must be linked to the lab that created you. It's got to be Julius. At the start of the project, he persuaded Gloria to work for him and promised her that you all would be a balm—warriors who would protect and prevent. But the truth became apparent the older you all got. He kept bringing in new military partners from across the world. He wanted to weaponize you and use you to destroy half the world. What better way to isolate and eradicate sin than to have near invincible and lethal soldiers who could sense it.

"This is a nightmare. Everything we tried to avoid all those years ago, is coming back to haunt us... worse. They could create an army of people like you. We have to stop them. We have to get Evan back before they collect the right samples."

"How are we going to find him? The tracker is off."

"He read out a few street signs as they were driving,"

Grace said, mouth going dry. "Then Sara caught on to what he was doing and the line went dead."

"What were the signs?" Flint asked.

Grace told him and they worked out a direction Sara had been heading.

"We need more," Parker said.

"Maybe there is more."

All eyes locked on Grace.

"His paintings and sketches," she said.

"Yes." Mary rushed to her. "Have you seen something?"

Grace nodded. "At his apartment there were mountains of sketches. He thought half of them were junk, but when I was there earlier, I saw something in one of them that he missed. It was of an event that really happened. He's got some sort of second sight. There has to be more there."

Parker nodded. "Right. Grace, come down to the basement and we'll take some samples of your blood. I know you feel fine, but better be safe than sorry about the poisoning. Mary, then you can go with Grace to Evan's apartment, see what you can find. Sloan and Flint, you stay here and run comms. The rest of us, get into battle gear."

"No, I'm not getting dressed," Liza said, gritting her teeth. "I'm going as a cop."

"Unacceptable. You can't be seen with us. It will compromise your identity."

"I'll just say I received an anonymous tip. Having a cop there will be convenient."

"That leaves only two of us in body armor," Parker growled.

"I don't need it," she replied.

"Is that what you'd tell your SWAT team before sending them in?"

Parker turned to Sloan. She lifted her palms. "Don't look at me. I won't even fit my armor."

"This family is a disgrace," Parker mumbled as he stormed out.

"Come on, Grace. Let's get you tested and then we will go to Evan's place," Mary said, and then they left.

THIRTY-SIX

EVAN LAZARUS

A dark rider approached the Escalade as Evan and Sara drove down the freeway.

Evan's heart rate picked up. A million thoughts raced through his mind. If it was Wyatt, what was he going to do?

Sara noticed the power crackling in Evan's hands. She glanced in her rearview then back at Evan. "I told you I'd make your life hell if you ruin this for me."

"I didn't do anything." But he would. If he couldn't get to whoever pulled her strings, he'd stop Sara himself. That small moment with Grace on the call had boosted his resolve. He was going to fight his way out of this and get back to her.

Sara dialed on her phone. A voice came through the speaker on the handset.

"Where are you?" It was a low voice, devoid of emotion. Just hearing the sound made Evan cringe.

"I'm being followed," Sara said. "We're almost at the rendezvous point."

"I can see your coordinates. How many are following?"

"So far, just one rider. Probably Wyatt."

"You're not far. I'll send backup. Protect the asset."

Evan took the phone out of Sara's hand. "Asset speaking here."

No answer.

"I want you to delete the CCTV footage you have of Grace at your lab otherwise I'm getting out of the car right now."

Still no answer.

"Are you there? Who is this?" Evan tried again.

"If you do not cooperate, your Grace won't live to see another day."

And then the line went dead.

Evan threw the phone on the floor.

Sara planted her foot on the accelerator, lurching the car forward. She beeped her horn to get vehicles out of the way, but this was Cardinal City. Nobody moved for anybody.

The sound of a bike engine revving got closer. And louder. And closer.

Until the walls of the Escalade vibrated from the motorbike's sound, and a dark shadow peered through Evan's window, blocking out the sun. He recognized the gun metal gray helmet. A black stripe crossed the top from opaque visor to nape, like the shadow of a Mohawk. Black was the color of wrath.

The bike nudged Evan's side of the car, jolting it. Evan frowned at Wyatt and shook his head. Don't do it, bro. But Wyatt slammed the car with his palm, then gestured for them to pull over.

Some cars beeped, some ignored them. Some changed lanes to get away. But there was nowhere to go. They were on a three lane stretch of the freeway, headed west and toward the bridge that took them to the airport on the mainland.

"Do something," Sara said to Evan. "Get rid of him."

Evan hesitated.

"Get rid of him. You heard the lady on the phone. If you don't cooperate, your girl is dead. And believe me, Falcon follows through with her promises."

He ground his teeth and wound down the window, but Wyatt knew him. Once upon a time, Wyatt was Evan's sparring partner. He taught Evan how to defend himself in elementary school, and he continued to mentor Evan as they grew. When Evan came back from his training years, Wyatt continued to spar with him. He knew how Evan fought. The bike dropped back and darted around the rear of the car to Sara's side.

Evan thought Wyatt might swerve into the car again, but he didn't. He punched the windshield, gloved fist cracking the glass at Sara's head. Evan's eyes widened. That was bullet proof glass he cracked. He was seriously pissed.

Sara blanched, and then steered the car into him, closing the gap between the Escalade and the barriers protecting the river—with Wyatt in between.

Evan couldn't let that happen. He couldn't put Wyatt in danger. He yanked on the steering wheel, and the car spun, tires screeched in a three-sixty tailspin that hit the barrier on Sara's side and stopped. The smell of burned rubber filtered into the car.

"You idiot!" Sara pulled the chef's knife she'd stashed. "Now things have to get messy."

She tried to open her door, but it hit the median. She was stuck inside.

Evan wasn't. He got out of the car intending to get between her and Wyatt, but his brother torpedoed him, knocking him to the ground. The wind vaporized in Evan's lungs and his eyes watered. Wyatt straddled him. His big body loomed over Evan, dark and ominous. He wore his battle gear, which meant extra padding beneath the leather, and extra weapons. Nothing could be seen beyond the black visor of the helmet except for Evan's own startled reflection and the stormy sky above the river.

A gloved fist met Evan's cheekbone, snapping his head sideways, blurring his vision. Pain splintered, but he was used to pain. He worked his jaw. Still functional.

That's all he allowed Wyatt to have, and then he generated power in his internal battery. The currents shifted in the air, electrifying. He sensed movement from Wyatt a split second after he made it. Evan darted his head to the side and narrowly avoided Wyatt's fist as it hit the asphalt beside him, spraying rock. Hell, that guy was strong.

A muffled growl came from behind the visor.

Wyatt removed his helmet and threw it across the lane. It bounced on the road, causing another car to swerve. Then the traffic continued to whiz by on the freeway. Nobody willing to stop. So they shouldn't.

Animosity poured off Wyatt in waves, just as tumultuous as the ones in the river, smashing against the barriers, spraying a fine mist over them. His face contorted. Tendons ticked in his jaw. Blue eyes reflected the storm about to break.

"Why?" he growled and threw another punch.

"It's not me." This time, Evan lifted his arms to block the blow. Shockwaves reverberated through him. He could take a beating. If it's what Wyatt needed, he could give him that. He didn't mean it, Evan knew. Wyatt just needed to let the devil out.

"Stop it!" Sara shouted from somewhere. "You're damaging the asset."

Her voice only kindled Wyatt's wrath. He came at Evan again, and again, growling with feral frustration as his fists pummeled into him.

Then, miraculously, the weight of Wyatt's body disappeared from Evan.

Hesitantly, Evan lowered his arms, but wished he hadn't.

Sara held Wyatt around the throat as she backed them into traffic across the freeway. Car horns beeped. Tires screeched. And then a glint of light sparked where her hand was, and Evan registered the knife.

Panic gripped his heart.

A cocktail of emotions swam across Wyatt's face. Confusion, anger, betrayal, hurt. But he did nothing, no evasive maneuver, no negotiating with the terrorist. His body was limp and compliant in her arms.

"What are you doing, Sara?" Wyatt asked, voice raw. "Just tell me the truth."

"I must protect the asset."

"The asset." Slowly, Wyatt's eyes tracked to Evan's and narrowed.

"Let him go, Sara," Evan said, holding his hand out, reaching for his brother. "Stay in the car!" he shouted to the nearby people starting to get out of their vehicles.

"*You* get back in the car," Sara warned Evan. "We have places to be."

"My deal doesn't include you hurting Wyatt."

"Screw Wyatt. You're the only person I need to bring back."

"Somebody better start explaining," Wyatt growled, eyes darting to the crowd.

"Hey, lady! We're driving here!" yelled an irate balding man with a mustache.

"Shut up! Or you're next." Sara kicked Wyatt in the back of his knees, collapsing him execution style.

"Sara," Wyatt warned. "What the hell are you doing?"

"Oh stop being so stupid, Wyatt." Sara leaned down so her lips hovered near his ear. "Love can't conquer all." She rapped his head. "It can't fix a diseased heart."

Wyatt's jaw clenched. "You could have told me. I would have helped you."

"You can't fix me!" she screamed. "Some things can't be saved with your fists."

Murder flickered in his eyes. "Of course we could help you. Why do you think they need Evan's blood for their big breakthrough? They don't have all the information. We do."

"No." Sara gaped in disbelief. "They're closer to the truth."

"Close?" Evan said cautiously. "I thought you already had the antidote. I thought you said they already fixed you?"

Her silence was punctuated by a beeping horn, and the

smell of exhaust fumes as more cars coalesced. She whipped her gaze over Evan's head to the lanes behind him. The sound of a siren in the distance grew louder as did the high-pitched roar of motorcycles. Back up was arriving, but whose?

Sara's eyes widened at Evan, and her face paled as she realized she'd been caught in a lie. There was no antidote. And if she lied about that, had she lied about the poisoned smoothie? The footage?

She pressed the knife into Wyatt's throat. A thin sliver of blood trickled. "I'm done talking."

"Don't!" Electricity crackled and sparked at Evan's fingertips. All it would take was to unleash in Sara's direction, but the jolt might make her spasm and cut Wyatt's throat. He'd probably electrocute Wyatt too. And people were watching.

Wyatt could twist out of the hold Sara had on him. He'd done that kind of thing before. It was a classic self-defense move, so why wasn't he defending himself? Hurt. Pain. Agony echoed back at Evan when he turned to his brother.

The sirens grew louder.

"I'm sorry Wyatt," Sara said. "But I want to live which means I have to protect the asset at all costs."

"I'm sorry about you getting sick, Sara."

"Sorry doesn't cure me, Wyatt."

"But we could have been happy with the time we had."

Sara hesitated, sobbed. The knife dug into his neck, then a shot was fired. The sound ricocheted off the water, and it was impossible to tell where it came from.

Red liquid dribbled out of Sara's mouth.

Then she sliced.

Another shot had her violently jerking and the knife cut deep into Wyatt's throat. Blood mingled on the road between them. Sara's wide eyes pleaded for mercy, her red-stained hand reached toward Wyatt, but it was as she'd said, some things can't be saved at all.

It all happened in a daze from there. Evan moved under-water. Wyatt's hands flew to his throat to staunch the blood spurting out. Red liquid went everywhere.

Evan ran to his brother, dropped to his knees and tried to staunch the spurting with his hands, but Wyatt crawled toward Sara, dragging himself through his blood.

"Stay put, brother," Evan growled.

Sara choked, chest convulsing, eyes never leaving her fiancée until their hands met in the middle.

"Oh shit," Evan said. "Don't die on me, brother."

Wyatt gurgled. His body spasmed.

"No," Evan begged as the warm wet life-force bled through gaps in their hands. "A Lazarus never quits, remember?"

Wyatt frowned at Evan, but in his eyes, a wealth of understanding flickered back at Evan.

"I'm not going to let you die, brother. I won't let that bitch have her way. Come on, bro. Shit. What do I do? What can I do?"

An angel's voice came from somewhere. "Keep applying pressure, hard. Here, let me take over," Grace landed beside Evan and replaced his hands with hers. "We need to get him to the hospital. I have to pack the wound. He needs surgery."

Wyatt's eyes widened, and he shook his head vehemently.

"I'm sorry, Wyatt, but it's not up to you," Grace said. "I can't do anything for you out here in the field."

Wyatt's bloody hand snapped out to latch onto Evan's wrist, and he pleaded with his eyes. *No hospital.*

"Shit." Adrenaline jackhammered Evan's heart.

His eyes darted around the scene. A bloody faced Sara was being helped up by two black uniformed soldiers, similar to the ones he fought at the GODC lab. Another two dark shadows dropped to the road between Evan and Sara. Pride and Greed. Liza was running up, in between halted traffic, gun pointed at Sara and her companions. The cavalry were here. But so were more hostiles. Guns. Rifles. Spectators. Like Sara had said, it was about to get messy.

Evan stood and looked down at his beautiful Grace as she held pressure to Wyatt's throat and spoke calmly and reassuringly to him.

"Grace," he choked. "It's only me they want. I'll hand myself over then you can take Wyatt to the hospital."

She turned her face up to him and frowned. "No. You are not doing that."

"But they have footage of you breaking into the lab with me." He swallowed hard. "And that smoothie was poisoned."

"They can't use the footage without incriminating themselves, and I feel fine. Parker took some blood samples. If there's anything wrong with me, we'll deal with it. But I'm not letting you go. I should never have believed her lies in the first place."

Evan straightened. Of course. The human cloning tanks were in the footage. How could he be so stupid. The rest was probably all lies. Anger flared inside him, heating his bones with fire and napalm, humiliation... chagrin. He glanced down at Wyatt. His advanced physiology had staunched most of his blood flow, but there was damage to his throat. Real gaping damage. They needed to get him to safety so he could be looked after. Evan spotted the chef's knife near Wyatt's head and he bent down to retrieve it. Completely metal, the knife would conduct the lightning already bursting from Evan's fingertips.

"Don't worry, brother. I'll make her pay," he said and narrowed his sights on Sara.

She stood with her two armed companions, weapons pointed back at them.

"No, Evan!" Grace exclaimed. "No more bloodshed."

He hesitated.

Long enough for another loud *crack* to split the air and leave an echo along the road. People screamed and ducked in their cars. What the hell? What had just happened? It took Evan a moment to understand, but Sara's two companions also fell to the ground, and he knew this was a cleaning operation. The Syndicate wanted all traces of their failed mission gone.

"It wasn't me!" Liza shouted, now pointing her weapon around the area, scanning for a second shooter.

The sense of being watched sent every hair on the back of his neck standing up. Someone else was here. Evan crouched, knife ready. He couldn't let anything happen to Wyatt and Grace. They were his priorities now.

Sara was still alive and crawling toward Evan. No, not toward him... but toward Wyatt. Down at his feet, Wyatt did the same. With one hand clasping his throat, the other tried to pull himself through the puddle of his own blood, toward the woman who betrayed him.

"Stop moving, Wyatt," Grace ordered, but his determined free hand clawed the road, trying to get to Sara.

Another shot and the asphalt exploded near Sara's head and she whimpered, gurgling. "I'm sorry, Wyatt. I'm so sorry."

Wyatt rasped something unintelligible and pleaded with his eyes at Evan then back at Sara.

"What do you want me to do?" Evan was at a loss. "Kill her?"

Wyatt shook his head.

"Shit. You want me to save her."

Wyatt nodded.

Aw fuck. Fuck no. But how could he deny his brother the chance of being with someone that made him feel the way Grace made Evan feel?

"Fuck!" Evan growled. "Grace. Let me take over. Please help Sara. Wyatt wants you too."

Grace looked distraught at letting Wyatt go, but she did it as soon as Evan's hands replaced hers. He tried not to think about the wrong feeling of torn flesh under his touch, and focused on Grace crouching low as she went to Sara, now only a few feet away. A long strip of dark red had stained the road behind her from where she'd dragged her wounded body.

"Sara," Grace said. "Move your hand. I need to see the bullet wound."

Red liquid came out of Sara's mouth, and then she stretched toward Wyatt with a bloody hand, exposing the glistening mess at her chest. "Wyatt. I didn't tell them."

Grace's face grew ashen as she turned and locked eyes with Evan. *She's done for.*

"Tell us what?" Evan asked.

"About the mating bond."

Wyatt couldn't speak but he understood her. If Sara had held back that vital piece of information, it was a point for Evan's side of the war. The Syndicate wouldn't know about Grace's importance to him, not the truth anyway. A tear sprung from Wyatt's eye and then he reached out for Sara. That right there was the hope Evan wanted to see back in the world, in his family, in his city. It was the kind of hope he recognized in Grace's eyes every time they met. It was why he loved her.

"Wyatt," Sara sobbed. "Please remember me."

"There!" Liza shouted from where she stood in front of the blocked traffic and pointed down the road on the empty freeway lanes ahead.

In the distance, and barely discernible to the naked eye, was a single solitary car with the front door opened wide. Evan squinted. Behind the shelter of the door, a woman with white, long hair whipping in the wind sighted them through her rifle.

Greed picked up Wyatt's fallen Ducati motorbike. Pride started running toward the woman. He unclipped his gun from his holster, aimed and fired.

Sparks flew from the door of the car, but the woman didn't move. She didn't even flinch.

For a moment, Evan thought she would shoot his brothers—one running on foot, the other speeding toward her on the bike—but then moved her rifle to where Grace was with Sara.

Time slowed.

Everything amplified.

Evan heard the sound of his own screaming, but no gun went off. There was no need. Sara was dead, and the white-haired woman calmly returned to the safety of her car, reversed, spun, and drove down the freeway, escaping.

Evan breathed again.

Liza pressed her finger to her ear, listening on the communication device that connected her to the rest of the team. Greed and Pride returned to them. All three ran to Wyatt.

"The ambulance won't get through this traffic," Pride said through the purple scarf covering his mouth. "But the Escalade can get out. Can we move him?" he asked Grace who'd now come back to them.

"Let me see, Evan." She lifted his hand gingerly. A fresh, sluggish pump of blood welled and Wyatt's eyes rolled back in his head. She clapped her hand back on it. "I don't think it's his carotid, otherwise he'd be dead, speedy healing or not. But he needs to be intubated. There could be vertebrae damage. He'll need an infusion. We need a neck brace and stretcher and—"

"We have no choice," Pride snapped. "Greed, Evan, help

me lift him into the back of the Escalade. Take him back to HQ."

"No, he needs a hospital," Grace insisted.

"Negative," Pride said.

"I'm the doctor," Grace shouted. "Not you."

"You're a surgeon, correct?"

"Yes. I mean, I was. I haven't operated in years, and no, I'm not a throat surgeon. Cardiothoracic is a completely different area of discipline. And we'd need an anesthetist, and so much more."

"Doesn't matter. We've got the resources at HQ. We can talk you through what you need to know."

Without waiting for Grace's approval, Pride and Greed lifted Wyatt between them. Grace had to rush along to keep her hand on his throat and shifted into the back seat with them. She ended up squashed on one side with Wyatt's head lying prone against the seat, head in her lap.

When Evan looked back to Sara, it was then he saw what Wyatt left behind—a bloody hand print on the asphalt, stretched out, reaching for the body of his ex-fiancée.

Evan slipped into the driver side and planted his foot on the accelerator.

"Evan!" Grace exclaimed as the car took off. "I can't do this."

"Yes you can. You're an excellent surgeon, you just need some faith in yourself. I know you can do it. How is he?" Evan glanced in the rear view. The top of Grace's head was visible as she looked down at Wyatt.

"He's stable. He shouldn't be, but he is." Grace's head lifted, and their eyes clashed in the mirror.

They stared at each other. Seconds ticked by. There was so much Evan wanted to say.

"You came back," he said. Despite the despicable thing he did.

"I did," she replied. "You can't get rid of me that easily, Evan."

A warmth flooded his heart as he fought to keep his gaze ahead.

He could feel her presence in the back seat as she sat there silent. All he heard was Wyatt's steady, raspy breath, and the sound of the car driving over bumps in the road.

"You said you would never leave me, Evan, and you did."

He sighed. "I know."

"Don't do it again."

Their eyes met in the rearview. "Never."

"Good." She went quiet and then murmured. "We really need to get him to the hospital. I'm not comfortable with this."

Perhaps Wyatt squeezed her hand, or something, Evan couldn't see, but Grace's next words were directed at the man lying with his head in her lap. "But, you realize that if I make a mistake, you could heal wrong. I could do more damage than good. You might never speak again."

Wyatt must have confirmed his wishes because she sighed. "Okay. If it's what you want, I'll do my best."

THIRTY-SEVEN

GRIFFIN LAZARUS

Upon returning from the field, Griffin had showered and dressed into something more appropriate. The leather battle gear irritated him. Too many zips, pockets and jangly bits, all of which had the tendency to distract him to tears. He'd asked Parker many times to make a suit more streamlined and custom-built to his body and specific needs, but with everything going on lately, it had been low priority.

Now it might not even be on the radar.

Griffin joined the rest of his family as they waited in the corridor outside the surgery in the basement headquarters of Lazarus House. Usually saved for minor stitches and scrapes, the surgery had a single recliner chair, surgical instruments and various medical equipment Parker had purchased.

This past week threw Griffin's carefully formulated equilibrium into chaos. So much that he struggled to keep up. It felt like his training all over again. He was the fourth in the family to enter the seven-year program, and he almost didn't come out of it alive. The noise, the unpredictability, and the violence messed with his brain. Not to mention the face-shouting from the Marine's worst drill sergeant. The unwanted physical contact. Never inappropriate, just... unexpected. The lessons had been hard to learn, but once they were in his brain, they stayed.

Now, he did everything in his power to control the narra-tive, even if that meant letting people suffer because he refused Greed's calling once in a while. Through trial and error, he'd calculated the ratio greed and generosity had on his equilibrium, and he had a list of events he could refer to if he needed to push his balance back to equal.

Painful, but necessary. And effective.

"How's he doing?" A hand clapped on Griffin's shoulder and he jolted. It was Tony. Just arrived and red faced. His short brown hair was a mess, and there were broken capil-laries at the edge of his nostrils. Who did Tony think he fooled? It was obvious he had a substance abuse problem.

Griffin shook his head and shirked away from his broth-er's touch.

"Sorry," Tony added with a quick glance where his hand had been on Griffin's shoulder.

"It's fine." Griffin grit his teeth then forced himself to relax and nodded at the viewing window to the surgery. "He's been in there for a few hours. Parker's instructing Grace about the procedure. She's not an ENT surgeon, but cardiothoracic. Inappropriate if you ask me, but Wyatt didn't want to go to the hospital, and neither did Parker. Apparently her lack of throat experience is a risk they're willing to factor. Evan is assisting and Parker donated the blood. Wyatt will live, but he might not speak again. That part is unclear."

"Shit." Tony wiped his nose.

Griffin frowned at him. "We called you. Where were you?"

"On set. Where else?"

"You're on set a lot."

"I'm an actor, Griff."

That wasn't what he meant, and Tony knew it. But, who was Griffin to judge? There were more important things to focus on. Like Wyatt. Like Sara. The people who shot her and her supposed rescuers. Killed them dead in the street, in full view of the gathered crowd filming on their camera phones. Griffin narrowed his eyes. He'd chased down the white haired woman, but she'd gotten away and now an unsettled feeling churned in his gut.

The lab results from Grace's poisoned smoothie had come in and the toxin was a standard type that only harmed when ingested, so she was safe. At least that part had gone well for them.

Movement through the surgical window had everyone in the corridor on edge.

Grace stitched up Wyatt's neck wound, hands confidently moving the needle and thread in and out of his flesh until finished. She put her tools down and turned to Evan, eyes smiling over the surgical face mask. He tugged the doctor's mask off and kissed her. In front of everyone.

Griffin's feet shifted as he watched, fascinated. They were in love.

When they were done, Parker grinned and patted her on

the back affectionately. Wyatt was still asleep, but he looked stable.

Griffin glanced back at Evan. There had been a marked difference in his brother's demeanor since getting involved with the doctor. He had more confidence, persistence and less anger. He smiled more. She had been a positive influence on him, that was clear, and it went against everything Griffin knew to be true about the world.

You couldn't get better without practice—it was a rule that had been drummed into them during combat training. Suffice to say, if the former was true, then you don't magically balance your inner turmoil by being in a relationship with someone. It wasn't logical.

A glance down at his itching wrist tattoo showed him it was dangerously on the light side from his expedition to rescue Evan from Sara. Too much light was just as bad as too much dark. An excess or absence of sin in his blood had a way of bringing emotions out that he couldn't control, and with their superior strength and abilities, that was dangerous.

He could see why their biological mother would lock the new abilities away until they found their balance. That much power in an unstable mind could be catastrophic, especially now Evan's cells were mutating and growing stronger.

Griffin watched from a distance while Evan, Grace and Parker came out of the surgery to speak with the family. Seeing the way they all touched and hugged each other, and not wanting any part of it, was how Griffin knew he'd never find someone like Evan did.

He was too different. Too separate. He wouldn't know the first thing about being in a relationship.

But that was okay. He didn't need anyone. He managed fine on his own.

Griffin thanked the doctor for her help and then left his family to commit an act of greed.

THIRTY-EIGHT

DR. GRACE GO

Grace juggled the items in her hand and knocked on the door to Evan's Lazarus House apartment. After the threat against their family was revealed, Evan agreed it was best to move back into the complex. His brother Tony had also moved back, begrudgingly. They were finally a family unit again, and it was all thanks to Evan and his persistence. That persistence had also worn down Grace when he'd asked her to move in with him. To be honest, it hadn't taken that long. When given the choice of staying in her lonely apartment with wilting plants, or waking up next to the man she loved, there was no contest.

It had been just under a week since she'd stitched up Wyatt's neck, and the memory still gave her the chills. Not because she'd been afraid, or because of what she'd seen, but because it was the first time she'd operated since her accident. For so many reason's she'd put off going back to surgery, but now all of them seemed silly. Her anxiety never reared its ugly head, and despite the scarring in her hands, her fine motor skills were fine. In fact, they were better than fine. They were great! *She* was great.

She knocked again. Where was he?

It was almost dinner time and Grace had gone straight from the hospital to her old apartment then immediately here. Her stomach grumbled in protest. The door opened and there stood Evan: bare sculpted torso with a towel wrapped tightly around his hips, just like it had that first time they'd made love. Water dripped from his hair to his naked chest, delineating all the hard angles and planes in a way that captured Grace's avid attention.

Um. What was she saying? Thinking. She hadn't been speaking. Oh my. His abs bunched as he held his breath as enraptured with her as she was with him.

"Hey, Doc." He grinned and took the small box in her arms. "Is that the last box from your place?"

She nodded dumbly.

"You should have told me you were going over. I would have come with you."

"It's okay. Was just a little box. Also, I wanted to pick up this." She pulled a small frame from inside the carton, wrapped in brown craft paper.

"What is it?"

"Oh, you'll just have to open it and see."

He glanced over her shoulder to the only other door in the corridor. It was closed and belonged to Sloan's apartment. A cheeky glint flashed in his eyes as he pulled Grace inside and shut the door behind them. He lowered his lips to her ear. "Maybe I'll open you up instead."

And then he kissed her. It started as a small, reverent

peck on the lips. A *Welcome home, honey* type of kiss. But after one taste, his gaze turned devilish, and he honed back in on her mouth, pushing inside with his tongue, and turning hot, hard and heavy. It had been a long day and Grace had missed him every minute. A moan escaped her lips, and she melted into him, so glad she came home to this every night.

"I missed you," he said, peppering kisses on her lips again.

"I was just thinking the same thing." She wrapped her arms around his neck, smiling as she caught him darting a glance to the side where her gift sat propped against the wall.

"So… what's this?" He eventually pulled away, curiosity having gotten the better of him. Two-seconds later and his big hands ripped the paper to reveal the glass picture frame within. He held it out in front of him, staring intently.

Grace bit her lip. "Do you like it?"

"It's you and me. Of course I love it. It's the sketch I did at your place the first time we—ah." He blushed as he took in the drawing of the close-up of two of them embracing, eyes closed, on a bed covered with chevron patterned sheets, and looking very postcoitally satisfied.

"I thought you could start a new gallery wall. Fill it with happy memories this time."

"It's perfect. I'll put it near the photo of you and your parents," he said.

Her hand covered her heart. "You put my picture up?"

"Your family is my family."

A warm feeling spread from her hand to the rest of her body. "I love you so much."

"I love you more." He gently put down the frame and leaned it against the wall. "That's why I got you something too. I'm surprised you haven't noticed it."

She lifted her brows.

He pointed at his heart.

"Oh," she gasped. "A new tattoo."

It said Grace.

"You know the saying 'Envy eats nothing but its own heart?' Well... not anymore. I have you to protect it."

"Oh, Evan." She teared up. "I don't know what to say."

His eyes locked onto hers. She knew what his look meant and his intention shot a jolt of desire up her spine. Her heart beat fast. Her breath shook.

She had to say something to break the silence. "So... I changed the sheets this morning. Did you notice?"

"I did," he smirked. "Chevron patterned." He darted a glance at the picture of them, then back to her. The fire in his eyes burned brighter with every step he took closer. He pointed to his room. "Bed. Now."

"But we have to go down to dinner with your family."

"Dinner can wait. I'll only take a couple of minutes."

She squealed as he launched toward her, herding her into the bedroom where they made sure the couple of minutes became more and the only reason they left the comfort of their chevron sheets was the phone call from his sister Liza telling them to get their ass into gear and get down to Heaven before the kitchen closed.

⑦

EVAN LAZARUS

EVAN MANAGED to tear himself away from precious alone time with his girl and dressed into something dinner appropriate: black jeans and T-shirt. With his tatts, he looked like a thug, but who cared. Not Grace. She loved it. Since she'd requested to put herself back on the surgical rotation, and he'd been out patrolling again, they'd had to snatch rare moments together. She had some hoops to jump through. Re-certification requirements. He fought crime and needed more training with his power. He'd much rather stay in bed with her, but this dinner was important and immediately after it, he was hitting the streets as Envy. More than electricity buzzed in his veins.

He was excited.

No longer a slave to the sin clawing his gut, he felt rejuvenated and ready.

But first, dinner.

After Sara's attack on Wyatt, every Lazarus had agreed to a weekly family meal. Wyatt had isolated himself in his room and this was the first night he'd agreed to join them.

It was the first night they'd all be there, including Grace.

By the time they got downstairs to Heaven, they were told the family waited for them inside the private dining room. Usually reserved for celebrities and private business functions, the room was protected from prying ears by three sound-proofed mirrored walls, plus another wall had a flat screen television for presentation purposes. All mirrors, including the window facing the street, were two way—

meaning everyone inside the room could see out, but not the other way around. The giant table in the middle of the room sat under crystal raindrop chandeliers above.

A dedicated waiter stood in front of the open door to the dining room and handed Evan and Grace a menu to peruse before they went in.

While Grace scanned the menu, Evan couldn't help but draw his attention to the ruckus inside the room. He craned his neck to glimpse his family through the open door. Mary and Flint sat close together. She fit in snuggly under his arm wrapped around her shoulder. Both had relaxed, happy expressions on their faces as they took in the conversation between their children. Did he say conversation? He meant bickering and trash-talking. Parker and Griffin argued about something. Or rather, Parker goaded Griffin. He loved to tease him about his rigid lifestyle full of rules. Sloan and Liza laid into Tony about his growing superstar status and how some bimbo had asked him to sign her breasts. When it had happened, and the woman had tried to get into their dining room, Liza had casually placed her cop badge and gun on the table. Sloan and Liza were worse than an overprotective father towards a daughter when she started dating. That's why Evan had been surprised at how welcoming they'd been with Grace.

He shouldn't be. Who wouldn't welcome someone so genuine and beautiful as Grace? He glanced at her. She was nervous. Their impromptu make-out session in the elevator down from his apartment had displaced a few strands of her ponytail and left her lips swollen. He slipped the wayward strands behind her ears and she shot him a worried look.

"I'm suddenly not hungry," she murmured.

"Relax," he said and tugged her by the hand toward the table. "They love you. Just like me. C'mon. We'll say hi first, then order."

Mary was the first to see them. She and Flint stood.

"Grace!" Mary came forward and took Grace by the hands. "Come sit next to me, I want to learn about your first day back in the operating theater. Evan said it's a process, but I want to hear more."

"No, she can sit here," Parker said from across the table. "I have questions about the new suit I'm working on. I'd love to hear from a doctor about the biometric components and the stress on the heart—"

"Hey dickwad," Liza interrupted. "She has a name, and she's right there. You can ask her yourself instead of talking over her head. Hi *Grace*." She shot Grace a big smile then frowned at her brother.

The bickering continued when Sloan joined in about women's rights and respect. Then Griffin put his two cents in about the subject and Tony raised his hand for another drink. With a shy smile, Grace sat down in the vacant chair next to Mary.

But someone was missing. Evan cast a glance around the room, and over to the open kitchen, expecting Wyatt to be there. He wasn't.

"Where's Wyatt?" he asked, turning back to them.

Silence descended and knowing glances were cast around the table.

"What?" Evan said. "What's happened?"

"Sit down, Evan." Parker waved to the vacant seat between him and Grace.

"Not until you tell me what's going on."

Parker's jaw worked, and something dangerous flickered in his eyes. Evan knew his brother hated having his authority challenged, but he didn't care. He wanted to know.

"Evan, sit and I'll tell you." Without standing, Parker pulled out the seat next to him.

Evan sat down.

"Thank you," Parker said, took a deep breath, and then added: "He's gone."

"What do you mean, gone?"

"He left this afternoon. Has some things to work out, I guess." Parker retrieved a white envelope from his inside jacket pocket. "This is for you."

The bottom dropped out of Evan's stomach. "What the fuck?"

"Don't freak out," Parker said. "Just read it."

EVAN.

I've rewritten this letter about a million times and no matter what I write, the words aren't enough. The simple fact of the matter is: You were right. I was wrong.

I used to be proud of being someone you looked up to but, somehow, I let my sin get the better of me. Instead of protecting you, I raged against you. I forced you to shoulder the weight of a hero

alone—worse, I made you doubt yourself. For that, and for every-
thing after, I am sorry.

Please don't come looking for me. I won't be found until I've
learned to be the brother you all deserve, and the hero this city needs.

Wyatt.

EVAN SCREWED up the paper in his fist. "Are you fucking kidding me? Someone's got a trace on him, right?"

Sloan snorted. "I'm not stupid, bras. Of course I do."

"So let's go and pick him up."

"Evan," Mary said firmly. "We have to let him do this."

"Are you serious? He's our brother."

Tony took a swig of beer then met Evan's eyes. "We have to respect his wishes."

"Tony, if I respected his wishes, Sara would still have her claws in this family." His words made sense, and everyone knew it.

"If you keep pushing him, he'll fall balls deep into his sin," Tony replied. "Trust me."

"But—"

"Evan." Mary cut him off. "He needs to do this alone. It's what he wants. For now, we've got more pressing things to talk about. Like the Syndicate. They almost had you, Evan, and that could have had catastrophic consequences."

Another round of discontent rippled across the table. A knock came at the door and they all quieted as the waiter arrived to take the last remaining orders.

When the waiter left, Parker was the first to speak. "I don't think anyone can refute the fact that we can no longer afford the luxury of ignoring our calling. The fact that you've all agreed to move back to Lazarus House speaks to that, but we need to have a frank talk about the future of our unit."

Evan draped his arm over Grace's back lengthwise, gripping her far shoulder, wishing he could bring her closer. He needed to touch her. To know she was real. Somehow sensing his apprehension, she placed a hand over his and squeezed.

"We can't be half-assed heroes," Parker continued. "We need to make a full commitment." He met each and every set of eyes around the table. "Missions come first. We've all seen how useful Evan's new abilities are. It's best if our first priority is getting our own. Our enemy is smart, ruthless and is willing to shoot dead their own to avoid secrets getting out. That means they're planning something big. So, step up your search for your soulmate. Grace and Evan have proven it's more than a pipe dream. It's a reality."

"Who died and made you boss?" Tony sneered.

"You want to do it?"

Tony dropped his gaze and stared into his drink.

"Didn't think so. Anyone else got beef?"

No one, not even Liza said a thing. Throughout their existence, Parker had always been their natural leader. Mary and Flint mentored them, but when it came to what they did best—fight crime—Parker was the one in charge. Having him declared the official leader was a natural progression.

"Good. Starting tomorrow at five, we'll train daily before you head off to your day jobs."

Protests rose around the room but Parker lifted his palm. "No excuses. Find a way. If you can't make it, come and see me and we will work out an alternative. I want you all back in black before the week's out."

Suddenly, a loud electrical guitar riffed through the speakers.

"What the fuck?" Evan joined the rest of his family looking up to the ceiling as AC/DC's *Back in Black* came on, loud and devastatingly clear.

Sloan broke into fits of laughter until tears ran from her eyes. "I installed AIMI on the speakers, y'all."

A smile edged Evan's mouth. "You knew Parker would say that, didn't you?"

She sigh-laughed and wiped her eyes. "Yep. He's so predictable. Asked AIMI to play it as soon as she heard the words."

"Great." Parker shook his head, but even he couldn't hide his smile. "You're all buffoons. Now, let's enjoy dinner and celebrate Grace's official return to surgery."

To Grace's happy embarrassment, the Lazarus family cheered and whooped her good news, clapping loudly.

For the next hour the family discussed logistics of following Parker's orders. Liza had to transfer to another department. Tony had to meet with his agent, and so on. Mary and Flint would resume training and strategic support via comms. Griffin was quiet but attentive. There was a lot to do, but Evan knew they would get there. The vibe in the air was hopeful.

As they were all leaving for the night, Parker pulled Grace and Evan aside.

"There's something I've been meaning to speak to you about," he said.

"Uh-oh. What did you do now?" Liza punched Evan on the shoulder as she exited with Sloan.

Instantly, Evan lashed out and zapped her on the arm. She yelped and rubbed it, scowling at him over her shoulder as she walked, but then grinning as she turned the corner.

Grace hid a smile with her hand and Parker's brow lifted.

"What?" Evan said. "She started it."

"How do you put up with him?" Parker said to Grace.

She lowered her hand from her mouth to say, "With pleasure."

"Great. You're as bad as each other. Okay, well I pulled you aside to give you this." Parker handed another white envelope to Grace.

She opened it, eyes widening as she read. "Is this for real?"

Evan peeked over her shoulder to read. It was a letter from her insurance company approving the claim for compensation to all the home owners of the apartment building that Sara destroyed.

"Parks?" Evan said.

Parker cleared his throat. "I know you missed the deadline to prove Sara was the bomber, and I know that was our fault. If we had listened to Evan from the beginning, this would never have happened. We can't bring back your parents, Grace, but hopefully this can bring closure for everyone involved."

Grace's eyes blurred and Evan pulled her in to kiss her on top of the head.

"Thank you, Parker," she said, still clutching the letter at her chest. "How did you get them to approve the claim?"

"I can be very persuasive."

"You bought the company didn't you?" Evan said wryly.

He ignored Evan's question. "Like I said, Grace. It's the least I could do, especially after you worked on Wyatt." Parker held his palm out stiffly. "It is me that should be thanking you for everything you've done for this family, Evan included."

Grace sniffed again and stared at Parker's outstretched hand, bottom lip trembling.

"He wants you to shake it," Evan whispered.

But Grace launched at Parker and hugged him. Stunned at first, Parker's arms were stiff at his side, then he glanced at Evan questioningly.

Evan shrugged, grinning back. Grace was a hugger, he guessed. When she pulled away, Evan went in for his own handshake with Parker.

Parker gripped it sturdily, then said goodbye, leaving the two of them alone.

"Can you believe it?" Grace's glistening eyes shot to him as she waved the envelope then launched into his arms.

"Yeah, Doc, I can believe it." He kissed her on the lips and hugged her tight.

It wasn't too long ago that he'd been lying in a Dumpster, agonizing over his family's inability to rescue him. Now Parker had bought an entire company to say thank you to his girl. Whatever happened next in their battle against the Syndicate, Evan knew they'd do it together, with Grace by his side keeping him sane. Wyatt would be back at some point, he was certain. And if he wasn't, Evan would find him because that's what they did. They never quit.

THE END.

Thank you for reading *Envy*. I hope you enjoyed Evan's and Grace's journey. Next up is *Greed*.

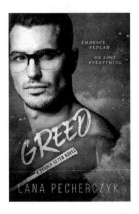

★★★★★Finalist for the 2020 RWA Prism Award for best Science Fiction Romance.★★★★★

Griffin Lazarus' restraint is notorious within his heroic family. His mastery over the sin of greed is second to none. What they don't know, is a shameful secret drives his discipline and one slip could mean fatal consequences for anyone close to him. When he's forced to work with a beautiful, feisty reporter poking around his personal life, his control swiftly unravels. Everything about her throws his beliefs into chaos. She's arousing, loud and infuriating, and craving her could be his undoing—or his redemption.

Lilo Likeke, an altruistic reporter for the Cardinal Copy, is hunting the story of a lifetime. *Who are the Deadly Seven?* If she can nail her unicorn story, she'll finally prove her apple falls far from her corrupt family tree. But when her mobster father is kidnapped, and she's drawn into his web of chaos, she soon learns you can't outrun your past, but you can choose your family. Trusting the man behind the mask might kill her story, but it also might save her heart.

GET THE BOOK NOW

JOIN LANA'S VIPS

Subscribe to Lana's newsletter and receive a free box set, first dibs on giveaways, special printable freebies and more. You won't want to miss out.

subscribe.lanapecherczyk.com

On Facebook? Join Lana's Angels Reader Group https://www.facebook.com/groups/lanasangels

CHARACTERS & GLOSSARY

The Deadly Seven

(Appearance in order of age from youngest to eldest)

ENVY: Evan Lazarus
SLOTH: Sloan Lazarus
GLUTTONY: Tony Lazarus
GREED: Griffin Lazarus
LUST: Liza Lazarus
WRATH: Wyatt Lazarus
PRIDE: Parker Lazarus

Mary Lazarus: Adoptive Mother of the Deadly Seven and ex assassin for the Hildegard Sisterhood
Flint Lazarus: Adoptive Father of the Deadly Seven

⑦

Other Characters:

Dr. Grace Go: Surgeon at Cardinal City General Hospital
Lilo Likeke: Investigative reporter at the Cardinal Copy
Josie: Deadly Ink Tattoo shop attendant & artist
Raseem: Doctor at Cardinal City General Hospital
Jeff Granger: CCGH Chief of Staff
Taco: 11-year-old boy, friend of Grace
Mason: 8-year-old boy, friend of Grace
Juliet: Taco and Mason's aunt
Azaria: Evan's art dealer & agent

The Syndicate

The Syndicate is a secret organization who believe the only way to save the world from its own harmful self is to eradicate all sinners, even if that means destroying half the world.

THE BOSS: Julius Allcott
SARA MADDEN: Ex-girlfriend of Wyatt Lazarus
FALCON: Enforcer for the Syndicate

The Hildegard Sisterhood

The Hildegard Sisterhood are nuns with a history reaching back to medieval times when the original Sister Hildegard struggled against a male dominated clergy. Now the world know her as the founder of scientific history in Germany, but back then, her opinions were disregarded until she claimed to have visions from God himself. Belittling herself as a woman in order to be heard was only the beginning of the humiliation the woman faced.

So she started her own abbey filled with women. That same abbey exists today and is a place where women are celebrated and their education encouraged—minus the male influence. Records at the Sisterhood archives reveal they had a hand in the rise of many women over history from *Joan of Arc* to *Indira Gandhi*. From *Catherine the Great* to *Margaret Thatcher*.

Under the surface of the auspicious abbey lays the secret mission that no woman will ever suffer the same struggle as Hildegard and they condition a select few "Sinners" to enforce this mission. These Sinners are trained as assassins for the cause: Sinners like Mary Lazarus. A necessary evil.

In the prequel novella, *Sinner*, Mary Lazarus escaped the Sisterhood who wanted to use the children for their own gain, much like the Syndicate who created them. To this day, she is still on the run.

ALSO BY LANA PECHERCZYK

The Deadly Seven

(Paranormal/Sci-Fi Romance)

The Deadly Seven Box Set Books 1-3

Sinner

Envy

Greed

Wrath

Sloth

Gluttony

Lust

Pride

Despair

Fae Guardians

(Fantasy/Paranormal Romance)

Season of the Wolf Trilogy

The Longing of Lone Wolves

The Solace of Sharp Claws

Of Kisses & Wishes Novella (free for subscribers)

The Dreams of Broken Kings

Season of the Vampire Trilogy

The Secrets in Shadow and Blood

A Labyrinth of Fangs and Thorns

A Symphony of Savage Hearts

Game of Gods

(Romantic Urban Fantasy)

Soul Thing

The Devil Inside

Playing God

Game Over

Game of Gods Box Set

ABOUT THE AUTHOR

OMG! How do you say my name?

Lana (straight forward enough - Lah-nah) **Pecherczyk** (this is where it gets tricky - Pe-her-chick).

I've been called Lana Price-Check, Lana Pera-Chick-ywack, Lana Pressed-Chicken, Lana Pech...*that girl!* You name it, they said it. So if it's so hard to spell, why on earth would I use this name instead of an easy pen name?

To put it simply, it belonged to my mother. And she was my dream champion.

For most of my life, I've been good at one thing – art. The world around me saw my work, and said I should do more of it, so I did.

But, when at the age of eight, I said I wanted to write stories, and even though we were poor, my mother came home with a blank notebook and a pencil saying I should follow my dreams, no matter where they take me for they will make me happy. I wasn't very good at it, but it didn't matter because I had her support and I liked it.

She died when I was thirteen, and left her four daughters orphaned. Suddenly, I had lost my dream champion, I was split from my youngest two sisters and had no one to talk to about the challenge of life.

So, I wrote in secret. I poured my heart out daily to a diary and sometimes imagined that she would listen. At the end of the day, even if she couldn't hear, writing kept that dream alive.

Eventually, after having my own children (two fire-crackers in the guise of little boys) and ignoring my inner voice for too long, I decided to lead by example. How could I teach my children to follow their dreams if I wasn't? I became my own dream champion and the rest is history, here I am.

When I'm not writing the next great action-packed romantic novel, or wrangling the rug rats, or rescuing GI Joe from the jaws of my Kelpie, I fight evil by moonlight, win love by daylight and never run from a real fight.

I live in Australia, but I'm up for a chat anytime online. Come and find me.

subscribe.lanapecherczyk.com
lp@lanapecherczyk.com

facebook.com/lanapecherczykauthor
instagram.com/lana_p_author
amazon.com/-/e/B00V2TP0HG
bookbub.com/profile/lana-pecherczyk
tiktok.com/@lanapauthor
goodreads.com/lana_p_author

Made in United States
Orlando, FL
01 September 2022